LOVE'S LABOR LOST
The Man Who Was Shakespeare

A Novel

Bob,
Good company in
a beautiful setting
Bruce

Bruce Hutchison

WillamHill Press

ISBN: 13: 978-1477451519

10: 147745151X

Facebook: Who Was Shakespeare
Web: whowasshakespeare.NET
BruceHutch@aol.com

Cover credit:
© Diana Faillace Von Behren
diana@buzzardseyeview.com

"I no longer believe that William Shakespeare, the actor from Stratford, was the author of the works that have been ascribed to him."

   Sigmund Freud

"I have never thought that the man of Stratford-on-Avon wrote the plays of Shakespeare.

   Lewis F. Powell, Jr., Justice of the United States Supreme Court

"So far as anybody actually knows and can prove, Shakespeare of Stratford-on-Avon never wrote a play in his life."

   Mark Twain

"I am 'sort of' haunted by the conviction that the divine William is the biggest and most successful fraud ever practiced on a patient world."

   Henry James

~~ Dedication ~~

This book is dedicated with love and gratitude to my wife, Nancy, her support and encouragement provided the inspiration to complete this book. And to our granddaughters, Candace Smith, and Noa and Lila Hutnik – all young, bright and eager for knowledge and truth -- may they learn about the true author of the Shakespeare plays when they begin to study the works of the greatest writer who ever lived.

~~ Acknowledgements ~~

I want to thank Diana Faillace Von Behren for her advice and for her excellent professional cover design. I also want to extend my thanks to John Max Von Behren for his help in translations to the Italian language. And my appreciation goes to my early readers for the gift of their time, encouragement and suggestions: Ceci Noble, John Weiss, Dan Allosso, author of An Infidel Body-Snatcher, and Mark Anderson, author of Shakespeare By Another Name

While *Loves Labor Lost* is a novel that follows the times and turbulence in the lives of Queen Elizabeth I and Edward de Vere, it is not an exacting biography of either, nor is it intended to be.

TABLE OF CONTENTS

PREFACE

The Winds of Conspiracy

"Affection is a coal that must be cool'd --
Else, suffer'd, it will set the heart on fire."
Venus and Adonis, Stanza 65

England
The Road to Windsor Castle
Mid winter, 1623

One might assume the winter snows would have cooled the hot winds of conspiracy. Not so this frozen winter day. As the heavy snow of February blinded galloping horses whose hooves cracked the ice along the road to Windsor Castle, royal hands warmed before the castle's huge hearth as thoughts of deception stoked its flames. "But at what price the realm?" James I, the King of England, thought as he drew his palms back from the heat, although he well knew the price, or at least suspected it.

Susan Herbert, her steeds plowing through a frozen mist that flared their nostrils, had no problem with secrecy or the price of deception. Beyond her husband, the Earl of Montgomery, she had confided in no one, certainly not in matters of this gravity, and especially not in the affairs of court. Had it not been the court's duplicity that had brought England to this regrettable day?

Susan herself was not above deceit and deception, or beyond ruse piled upon innuendo to cloak the truth buried beneath. She had learned from the master -- her father. When times required action, nay, when they demanded action -- "Act," she whispered to herself as her coach struck a frozen stump, lifted her delicate body from the seat, and slammed it back down.

Susan's hands trembled in her lap. As the coach settled again, she clutched her knees to hold them still and steady her nerves. The meeting ahead of her would be the most important of her life. It would determine a life or a death. She leveled her shoulders, leaned forward, poked a gloved finger through the curtain, and peeked outside. She was running late. Axle-high snowdrifts slowed her passage over Chads Forge and for several leagues along the road to Birnum, but the sight of Windsor's soaring towers reassured her that they were nearly there.

The sight of Windsor pulled her thoughts back to Hedingham Castle, to a girl of seven laying belly-down before the hearth, staring eye-level through the gate of a miniature village her father had constructed, much like the village of Colne at the foot of Hedingham Castle, the ancestral home of the de Vere family and the place where her father had been raised and where she spent much time as a child. She still had visions of the miniature knights and painted toy soldiers marching under tiny thatched overhangs, shuffled along by the push of her thumb. She recalled picking up the figure of a charwoman or a blacksmith between her small fingers, turning them to face each other and then speaking on their behalf, lowering her voice or raising it to suit the character. And she remembered her father playing a part, squealing in falsetto to exaggerate a maiden, then lowering his voice to mock an arrogant prince or bishop, and then falling out of character, laughing and rolling on the floor pounding his fists at his own embellishments. Pretense, Susan thought as she drew her attention back to the meeting before her. The essence of deceit posing as reality.

Phillip, Susan's husband, had participated in the plot and provided its financing. Yet, this final step, that which would conceal the truth forever, had been left to Susan, at age thirty-six -- a short-statured, thin-boned woman. And why not a woman? Had not the last monarch been a woman? Had she not sat longer and stronger on the throne than any monarch before her? Had she not launched the flotilla that defeated the Spanish Armada? Had she not spread and cultivated the seeds that spawned the most prolific increase in English literature the world had ever known, and had not that very proliferation set the stage for Susan's father, the creator of a body of work so explosive in its implication that its obliteration was now royal command?

Susan's horses balked at Windsor's drawbridge, impatiently digging in their hooves as melting snow trickled down their haunches, their power barely restrained by the thinnest of harnesses. As soon as the drawbridge thumped down and clanked into place, the steeds bolted forward without encouragement from the whip, rattling over oak planks and thundering beneath a brick archway before rumbling across cobblestone into a walled courtyard. As the horseman heaved the reins back, the coachman leveraged his rawhide brake against the spin of the wheels, skidding the coach to a stop.

Susan, donning leather britches, unusual even for her, tucked her rabbit-fur collar close around her neck, flung the coach door open, and hopped into ankle-deep snow before the coach's springs had fully settled. She glanced over her shoulder and nodded toward the chest strapped to the coach's boot. The coachman hopped down and elbowed snow from the chest's ribs, unbuckled its straps, and lugged it forward, trailing Susan up steps worn smooth by four centuries of royal visits before passing through double doors and into the massive hall of St. George. The coachman, his body still trembling from the wind and their haste, plunked his burden down at Susan's feet, knocking off chunks of ice that melted on the stone floor, then departed without further instruction, the slam of the doors behind him echoing down the long hall in search of a crack or a crevice in which to hide, and finding none, dissipating in the thick weave of tapestries that draped from the vaulted ceiling.

When all lay quiet, a tiny portal set within a larger door creaked open and a man with a baldhead poked through. His eyes swept down the hall and fixed on Susan before he opened the crack wide enough to enter. "His Highness inquires if you are alone in your presence, Madam," he asked, more breathe than voice.

Susan stiffened her spine to strengthen her resolve. "Quite alone," she said.

The man stooped and unsnapped a lower latch, then straightened and opened a second latch higher up, and one at a time, unfolded two sides of an enormous hinged door, releasing heat that swooped into the entrance hall and flushed Susan's face, still chilled from the cold. The immense silhouette of a man stood between Susan and a crackling inferno that consumed the wall behind him. Satan himself, Susan thought.

"You brought them?" the man's voice boomed, although in the shadowed darkness she barely saw his lips move.
She spread her palm toward the trunk at her feet.
"*All* of them?"

"As agreed."

"And the copies?"

"Here as well." She slid a parchment out from inside her coat and held it forward. "The inventory," she said.

"Leave it."

She pivoted and laid the document on the round of the trunk, the melting ice immediately staining it. "And the burial?" she asked, turning to face the man again.

"Reburial," he corrected her, then paused, his voice softer. He stepped toward her, growing taller and wider as he approached. "He would have conceded this a necessary sacrifice," he reassured her. "You are simply doing what is necessary in his stead."

"You'll destroy them then? You'll commit them to flames?" Susan asked as a log crackled and split in the fire, although Susan held a risky proposal in the back of her mind -- a deceitful, even treacherous alternative -- yet one that might fulfill her secret hope and still keep England from a renewed upheaval that could split the realm down its religious seams.

~~ YOUTH ~~

"Natural rebellion done in the blade of youth
When oil and fire, too strong for reason's force,
O'erbears it and burns on."

All's Well That Ends Well, V. 3

CHAPTER 1

Fire in the Night

"O, who can hold fire in his hand?"
Richard II, I, 3

Fifty-two Years Earlier
The 17th of August, in the Year of Our Lord 1558
Hedingham Castle near the village of Colne

The chapel bells clanged furiously. John de Vere, the Sixteenth Earl of Oxford, sprung up in bed, his heart thumping, sweat bleeding down his chest. Night bells bespoke one thing. *Fire!* At a bang on his door, he catapulted up and dashed across the cold stone floor.

"Your Lordship!" a high-pitched voice shouted through the cracks. "The theater! 'Tis a'fire!"

The Earl wrenched the door open and burst into the hall, racing behind a shorter, red-haired man who scampered ahead like a limp rabbit, hopping and stretching his right foot forward, then angling his left to catch up. By the time they darted across the great hall and flew into the west courtyard, flames had already spread from beam to beam across the roof of the old stables the Earl had converted into an outdoor stage for his theatrical productions.

The Earl, his eyes ablaze in the reflected fire, clutched the wooden rake thrust into his hand and joined the fray as a score of shadowed men dashed in and out of the flames, beating them back with brooms and horse-hair blankets whilst woman and boys sloshed buckets hand-to-hand from the central well.

By the first glint of sunlight, the inferno had banked to embers as scorched-faced men lay scattered on the ground, the bravest of them, when the fire began, having rushed in to pinch it back until falling timbers drove them out.

Slumped against the warm wall of the keep, the lingering smoke coating his throat and burning his nostrils, the Earl half-lifted his eyes as an aproned maid offered him water, his cracked lips able to absorb only a few drops. His face blistered, his legs spattered in mud, he rolled his eyes toward his manservant hunched over beside him. "Plunkin," the Earl whispered in a hoarse voice.

"Sire?" Plunkin answered without raising his chin, as if too exhausted to lift it from his chest.

"How did it begin, Plunkin?"

"I…" Plunkin hesitated. "I know not, Sire."

"Plunkin?"

"I shan't say for certain."

"You shan't, but you could."

"I might have seen a shadow."

"Whose might it be?"

"A slender shadow."

"Slender?… Slender as…?"

"I can only guess, Sire."

The Earl fixed his stare.

"I believe… I can only surmise," Plunkin said, avoiding his master's gaze. "It may have been… It may have been your own, young Edward."

****

"What are we to do with the likes of him?" an exasperated Lady Margaret cried. A tall, hollow-cheeked woman who habitually peered down upon her husband, Lady Margaret rose on her toes to further her height advantage when she wished to hammer a point into her husband's skull and twist it there until he admitted fault and acknowledged her position. As to the matter of their son, Edward, the Earl had abandoned all defense as he cowered on a bench while his wife paced over him, halting and lengthening her neck every time she turned, her fingers poking forth and flicking about like an angry hawk whose nest was being invaded. Lady Margaret would have her way. The price weighed too heavy if she did not.

"He needs...," the Earl began, unsure what to say, yet realizing a response was required. The problem was, he reluctantly agreed with his wife. The boy habitually yanked a dog's tail simply to see if it wagged the animal's body. He oft disappeared in the forest for hours, frightening the household for his safety and then denying it with one of his fanciful tales. He would plead he was pursued by one of his imaginary characters -- a warlock, or an evil fairy-queen, or his favorite, a three-horned, web-footed, green goblin he called Hornthrust, a devilish beast the boy claimed hounded him into the woods, begetting trouble there, then laying blame at Edward's feet knowing he would not be believed. Edward frustrated his father, although John well knew that whatever correction he imposed to discipline his son would not be enough to please his wife. She was rarely pleased when wheels spun smoothly and not at all with the least squeak. "I'm certain he had his reason," the Earl offered limply.

Lady Margaret threw her hands above her head and clawed the air, exaggerating emotion like the actors John employed. "Reason?" Lady Margaret mocked John's voice. "For burning down the theater in yet another of his outrageous make-believes? 'Tis precisely what leads him astray in the first place."

The Earl agreed with that as well, though he chose silence, his admissions often self-incriminating and calling forth another blade to further stab him. "The pebble rolls not far from the stone," Lady Margaret liked to say.

Lady Margaret rose on her toes and glared down at the shiniest spot atop her husband's balding head. "You haven't spoken to him, have you?"

"I've been weighing my words. I shall speak with him directly."

She spit breath through her tightened lips, as she frequently did to dismiss her husband or anyone else with whom she disagreed.

Edward bore a pain in his mother's side from the moment of his birth, although that hardly explained her distaste for others, her husband atop the list. She had screamed her son into this world and then blamed John for planting the seed that spawned him. Edward, or so the chambermaids reported, poked his head from his mother's womb and refused to continue, holding there as if to change his mind and crawl back in. Worse, when he did grudgingly exit, he seemed to grin, taunting his mother, knowing the poor woman had suffered through a twelve-hour labor. Thus enraged, when Margaret lurched to grab the babe's throat, the chambermaids caught his slippery afterbirth and pulled him away to save his life. To stab injury deeper, the infant developed colic, his wail echoing through Hedingham's halls, rousing servants and parents alike throughout the night.

At Margaret's insistence, Juliana -- a chambermaid suckling her own newborn -- took Edward to her quarters to allow Milady to rest and regain her strength. Unable to sleep himself, the Earl sneaked down to the servant's quarters to hold his son, reciting poetry to lull him to sleep.

"You've been with Juliana, have you not?" Margaret asked the next morning.

"Not with her. I could not sleep. I heard him cry."

"You've always found Juliana fair."

"The maid?... I take no notice of Juliana."

"You say her name with such relish. It sweetly rolls from your tongue."

"She's a pleasant sort, nothing more."

"Oh?... And I am not?"

"Of course you are, my dear."

"Don't lie to me. I know what they say."

"Pay no mind to them."

"So you agree, then... You and your son are of the same ilk."

"Our son."

"You are the one who required an heir. If I had not watched him creep from my womb, I should not be certain he was mine. He is more suited to Julianna's kind. Of her kind."

"Margaret, that's absurd."

"Or that other bitch."

The Earl knew Margaret would soon wind her way to this. She always did. She was referring neither to Juliana nor to his first wife, now deceased. She meant Mistress Dorothy, the woman in between, the woman the Earl might have married and perhaps should have, he thought as a grin escaped his lips. He did marry a bitch. She simply wasn't Mistress Dorothy.

"What's that smirk of?" Margaret asked. "You find this amusing?"

"Not at all," he lied, flattening his expression. The subject of Mistress Dorothy would never be settled, nor would the proper education of Edward, although of that, the Earl was less concerned. The boy read voraciously, spoke three languages at the age of eight, and had well taken up the sword. He rode and hunted, if not as the best, fair better than the least. All came readily. Too readily. He studied naught, absorbing knowledge as easily as he parried the sword. What the boy knew not, he spoke of so convincingly as to tangle truth with cleverness.

Edward bored easily and feared nothing, the theatre fire merely his latest indiscretion, although John conceded it more destructive than his usual pranks. Should the boy set his itchy feet upon firmer ground, perhaps he could manage the Earldom one day. There would be no other children, Lady Margaret having refused the Earl to her bed after Edward's birth. Edward, their only son, would be the next Earl, yet discipline would be required to rein in his rebellious nature, harness his fantasies, and redirect his attention to the road ahead and away from the birds and butterflies in the fields, half of which flew only in his head.

"And now the fire," Margaret said, raising her voice and seizing the opportunity to dig her claws in deeper. "It's time we considered sending him off."

"We can't abandon a boy of eight," the Earl protested, shaking his head without glancing up.

"Perhaps north," Margaret said. "To your cousin Manfred. When we sent him those unruly hounds, he made the better of them."

"He needs to remain with us. To experience running the estates."

"The estates?" Margaret tightened her jaw. "They run themselves. There is naught for you to do, let alone your lazy son."

"Margaret," John pleaded. "I don't…"

"England has changed," she interrupted, her hands inching close enough to reach down and strangle him. "Our insipid former king, that knave Henry, brought us to this. We became one nation under Henry. The warring castles that once fought each other now meet in Parliament to shake their fists and adjourn to trade jokes over grog. Warriors? There is not a knightly man among them. The barons and earls are no longer fighters. You are all farmers. There is nothing left to defend, nothing to pass onto your ne'er-do-well son but a worthless title and lands that bring naught but worry and expense." When Margaret paused, John felt the heat of her gaze permeate down his spine. He had heard this all before, though not quite this vehemently. He knew his best defense against her siege was silence. "And what will your worthless son do? Have you thought of that? There is nothing for him to do, save burn down the next theater you build out of your own frivolity."

****

"Why did you set the fire, son?"

"I did not, father."

"Plunkin saw you."

"I didn't set it, father. It caught on fire."

"What were you doing out there?"

"Playing a part."

The Earl's chest sunk in frustration.

"A play came to me whilst in bed," Edward said, eying his father cautiously. "I was playing the part on stage, marking off the actors."

"In the middle of the night?"

"I could not sleep. I went to the theatre to act upon it. I needed a torch for the light."

"Son…" The Earl hesitated. "Your mother and I have reached a decision. That is to say, 'tis I who've decided."

CHAPTER 2

The Queen and Her Entourage

"She had all the royal makings of a queen"
Henry VIII, IV, 1

Four Years Later
The 17th of July, in the Year of Our Lord 1562
On the Road to Hedingham Castle

Self-satisfied, Elizabeth Tudor, age twenty-eight, and on the throne a mere three years, eased back in the cushioned comfort of her coach in a rare moment of solitude. Her sparrow-like figure, already burdened under the weight of her crown, thankfully mirrored that of her mother, Anne Boleyn, and not the meaty beef of her father, Henry. Her auburn hair, the color of a robin's breast, topped high cheeks and a wide mouth that required no reddening with the morning makeup her ladies-in-waiting applied.

She oft found herself smiling and studying herself in her looking glass whilst her chambermaids emptied her basin and spread her frocks. She knew her maids and courtiers whispered that she was comely enough though a tad too vain. Perhaps they were right on both counts. Elizabeth considered her beauty a gift from God to be used for His glory and put to whatever advantage she might apply it for the betterment of England.

Her annual summer procession had slogged on a laborious eight leagues a day to reach the castle of John de Vere, the Sixteenth Earl of Oxford, in repayment for his support in her struggle to secure England firmly in the Protestant faith. Her Catholic enemies lay in wait on the Continent and likewise threatened her crown from within her own realm, although John, the Lord of Hedingham, raised Catholic himself, was not among them.

Her coach unexpectedly skidded and bounced, throwing her shoulder against the door. She had her mother's delicate body, yet in every other way, she was her father's daughter. She had not anticipated ruling, but had no doubt how to lead -- trust few, seek wise counsel, and extend her hand for a kiss of her ring whist clutching an ax in the other should flattering words belie treasonous thoughts.

When a wisp of dust seeped through a crack in the curtain, she reached forward and tacked the edge down, and then settled back into a cushion formed to fit her body. She had been a precocious child, blossoming and ripening into a young woman early on. Having a curious nature, she was eager to learn. She spoke French, and Spanish, and a rough guttural Dutch that the ambassador tolerated with a painful grimace. She wrote lengthy letters, scribed fair poetry, and dabbled at plays. As a girl, she skulked Whitehall's corridors cloaked as a boy, squatting in dark corners to absorb the dramas her father produced at court -- the performances considered unsuitable for tender female ears. Many parodied the court for the court's own amusement and were considered too scandalous for public presentation. Only highly censored, court-approved plays -- especially those that flattered the King or promoted her father's anti-Catholic views were allowed for public viewing. Ironic, she thought. She had studied theater, poetry, and foreign languages but naught of diplomacy and politics -- the very skills she now required as queen.

She slid a silk handkerchief from her sleeve and patted her long, arched nose. Bloody Mary, Elizabeth's older half-sister and predecessor, had temporarily wrenched the realm back to Catholicism during her brief reign and burned scores of rebellious Protestant bishops at the stake, nearly inciting civil war. Against the wishes of the wealthy earls and landowners, Elizabeth had brought the realm back to Protestant Anglicanism, the religion of her father, yet that had not settled the conflict. On whichever side she leaned, the other side despised. She knew that the issue of religion would require many generations before the people forgot what once *was,* knowing only, for them, what *is.*

Her carriage abruptly skidded to a stop, interrupting her thoughts. Before she could see to the cause, a fist rapped on her door. "Your majesty," she heard Cecil Burghley bellow.

"It pleases me," she called, adjusting her skirt before opening the door to a man as gray as a cloaked ghost.

"An axle hath broke on one of the forward carts. We shall be delayed."

When Elizabeth nodded, Burghley, her Chief Minister and closest advisor, bowed and quickly snapped the door shut. A pepper-bearded, ill-humored man, Burghley was nonetheless a brilliant tactician, a steadfast protector, and suspicious of everything and everyone. One of the few men Elizabeth could totally trust, Burghley had served her father, and beyond that, had intervened to save her life. When her sister Mary threw her in the Tower, threatening to behead her for not recanting her Protestant views, Burghley persuaded Mary to spare her younger sister if Elizabeth promised to hold England Catholic should she one day ascend to the throne. "In good conscience, I can not promise such," Elizabeth had told Burghley in her Tower cell.

"Madam," Burghley had advised. "If it *should* come to that, who would enforce it? *You* would be queen. A queen does as she wishes, including changing her mind." And now, as Burghley had anticipated, she was queen.

After reading quietly, she thought to summon one of her ladies-in-waiting to fetch tea and biscuits as refreshment, but before she could make her wishes known Burghley tapped her door again and indicated they were ready to proceed.

"What is the truth of the matter?" she inquired when Burghley's frown deepened more than usual.

"'Tis nothing of import, your Majesty."

"Tell me of it then."

"Just that we are coming close to Colchester. The sheriff informs me there may be thieves or worse. Those who..."

"Would have me drawn and quartered?"

"In the slowest of ways." Burghley was a rare bird who told her the truth while others feared her reaction and substituted flattery for fact. "I suggest we remove Your Majesty to a plain coach," Burghley advised.

Elizabeth knotted her brow. "These are my subjects, Chief Minister. They have my heart and the right to see me. We shall proceed as planned."

As Elizabeth leaned back and her progress started again, she looked forward to reaching Hedingham where she could rest among friends away from the intrigue and backstabbing at Whitehall. She daren't venture any farther north, where support for a return to Catholicism waxed strong, and where her royal coach might easily sink in a Northumberland mud hole and disappear. "Barbarians! Highway robbers!" the Northumberlands would claim. "And such a young Queen. What a pity."

John de Vere, whose modest castle lay just to the south of danger's edge, would organize a hunt and they would feast and watch a play or two, her host as fond of drama as the Queen. John, the Sixteenth Earl of Oxford and Lord of Hedingham, had withdrawn from London during Mary's brief reign, then staunchly supported Elizabeth's reinstatement of her father's Protestant reforms.

She grinned in spite of herself, thinking of Edward, John's twelve-year-old son and future Seventeenth Earl, of whom she had heard a mixed account -- Chief Minister Burghley having informed her that the young Earl was gifted but stubborn, with little of his father's discipline, and perhaps, in some ways, of the same wild nature as Elizabeth herself at twelve. They hadn't fully tamed her and never would. She suspected that she and young Edward had much in common and would enjoy each other's company.

CHAPTER 3

The Play's the Thing

> "All the world's a stage,
> And all of us mere players."
> *As You Like It, II, 7*

"And now, for Your Majesty's pleasure," the Lord of the Manor, John de Vere, the Sixteenth Earl of Oxford announced, waving a thick hand toward the front of his great hall. "A company of players."

John had set the stage at the head of his lower chamber, having decided on an interior theater after the fire destroyed his outdoor stage four years earlier. The result pleased him. He had raised a platform knee-high, painted its ribs a pale blue, trimmed the sides in olive-green with orchid stripes, and framed the sides with a thick crimson curtain. Above his proscenium, he hung his Bolebec crest -- a lion shaking a broken spear -- bequeathed to the Second Earl of Oxford in 1220 after supporting Henry III's ascension to the throne. The Oxford crest and its credo, Vero Nihil Verius, Nothing Truer Than Truth, had passed through the generations down to John, and would eventually fall to Edward, his only son.

"As to our principle performance," John announced to his guests seated at the head table and the three score others straddling benches set up along both walls, all feasting on partridge and venison and nibbling from overflowing trays of cheeses, fruits, and meat-stuffed breads. "I proudly present a one-act play penned and performed by... Well..." he grinned down at the Queen seated to his right. "I shall let the author introduce his work."

Two yeomen scurried along the walls and doused hanging torchlights as a third yeoman lit the candles that encircled the stage. When all had quieted, a boy of twelve entered stage right -- gray tattered rags draped across his slender shoulders, his face painted with ash, his costume's wings spread wide as he floated to the center of the stage.

Lady Margaret, seated to John's left, sharp elbowed her husband, but settled back when she noticed the Queen bend toward John and chuckle.

"What do we know of this?" the Queen whispered to her host.

"He wished to write something for Your Majesty's visit. He knows your love of plays."

"I do believe there is no end to your young earl's talent," the Queen said, easing back again.

"I pre'thee hark!" the boy-ghost commanded. "Bend thy ear hither. For I shall speak you true that danger is afoot. For I, young innocent Egar am falsely accused of what, in light of day, is blameless. I seek earthly intercession to set the record straight and restore my fair honor."

The ghost swung his hand stage left and drew his index finger to his lips. "I believe good ears and heart do come upon us," he whispered in an exaggerated stage voice and withdrew to the shadows as a short, red-haired man played by John de Vere's manservant, Plunkin, dressed in a fool's bellcap, entered stage left jingling his presence with a tilt of his head.

"Me thinks I heard the voice of young Egar," the fool said, stooping cautiously and glancing about. "Now dead upon this earth these past two days."

The ghost drifted in from the darkness and startled the fool, who covered his eyes and peeked between his fingers. "Egar?" the fool asked, cocking his head toward the ghost.

"You doubt 'tis I, Gyplunkin?"

"How can it be, M'Lord? Thou be dead."

"The gates of heaven and of hell are closed before me till justice doth prove me right and matters of this earth are settled."

"Upon what matters doth thou speak?"

"Those you yourself have understood and witnessed, and have delivered ill report."

"I know not of these."

"The fire, Gyplunkin. The theater. Which set itself aflame upon its own accord, merely at my presence."

"Unsavory," John de Vere whispered to the Queen. "He uses matters of his life and mine to weave his tale."

"Undoubtedly to make his point and win your favor... You have not seen this yet?"

"He would not show it to me."

Voices crackled though an open door at stage right.

"My Lord upon whom disfavor lies," the ghost said to Gyplunkin, "my false accuser comes accompanied by our Holy Savior. Gyplunkin, you must seize this good fortune to have Our Savior intercede on my behalf and set my poor soul free."

"But M'Lord..."

The ghost covered his face with his arm and withdrew as a male actor played by one of Lady Margaret's servants sauntered forth dressed in a woman's wide skirt and a curled orange wig topped with a queen's crown. A shorter man -- an undercook costumed in a puffed white shirt -- pranced shoulder-to-shoulder with the odd looking character.

John de Vere could not believe what he saw. He leaped to his feet and banged his fist on the table. "This must stop!" he bellowed. It was one thing for his son to parody his father as ghost, quite another to mock a guest, let alone this guest, the Queen!

"John," a quiet voice spoke. "Sit thyself down. Let the play continue. The lad has wit and mirth, and much talent for a boy of twelve."

"He has gall," John said, flopping back in his chair.

"Spirit," Elizabeth corrected him.

"Unbridled."

"As much has been said of me," Elizabeth grinned. "And I do recall stories of you as a lad. Or am I confusing you with another of my subjects?"

John swallowed a grin to keep from conceding her point while Elizabeth barely held her own mirth until their laughter burst forth together. As Cecil Burghley glared from farther down the table and Lady Margaret angled her shoulder to avoid watching, John gathered himself and rose. "Let the play proceed," he said. "Let the players play."

The actors, having halted their presentation in deference to the performance at the head table, bowed to their Queen and spoke their lines, the fool Gyplunkin pleading the ghost's case for forgiveness and the reinstatement of his master's favor. The Savior Queen commanding the performer in John's clothing to abandon resentment and reinstate Egar's ghost to privilege.

"A worthy moral," Elizabeth whispered. "Theaters burn. Accidents befall the innocent."

"I've forgiven him that long ago," John said, turning his head and shielding his mouth to keep his wife from overhearing.

"Have you told him thus?" Elizabeth asked. "I know how you love him. I suspect he loves you as much."

As the players took their bows, all eyes focused on the Queen as she slowly rose from her chair, her silk gown sparkling in the flickering light as the yeomen passed along the walls and relit the torches. The Queen hesitated, then raised both hands and clapped a rhythmic beat that gathered momentum as others in the hall, reassured that their Queen was not offended by the parody, stood and filled the room with applause and laughter, raising their goblets and jostling them above their heads as servants scurried along the rows, refilling them.

The author of the play, the future Seventeenth Earl, bowed deeply, and then raised his eyes just enough to reveal an impish grin as he peeked first at his father, then at his Queen, and then swept his palm across the stage, acknowledging his players.

CHAPTER 4

The Queen's Hunt

"Nature teaches beasts to know their friends."
Coriolanus, II, I

The Queen's mare, Abbey, reared back at the sight and stench of the mud-caked boar as the Queen, adept at the hunt, rose in the saddle as Abbey arched her back to meet her. The Queen had selected and trained Abbey for speed and agility, not for gentleness or ease of command. Still early in her reign, Elizabeth was already used to handling far more obstinate souls than Abbey. Like her mistress, Abbey had both a sternness and skittishness about her, exhibiting both sides in equal measure.

Abbey always performed as required -- be it chasing rabbit, fox, or boar -- and yet, when stabled, she could as easily romp playfully or raise her temper unexpectedly and kick through her stall. The Queen was aware that the stable lads compared Abbey's disposition with her own. She did not resent that. She favored it. Like much of what was said of her, a drop of truth swirled in a caldron of exaggeration.

Abbey spread her hind legs and held her stance, anxiously awaiting the nudge of her master's heels on her haunches to indicate the hunt had begun. Elizabeth glanced to her left and reined Abbey in when she saw her host slump in his saddle, clutching his chest. "John," she called. "What is it? Are you all right?"

John de Vere clutched his chest and rose slowly upon hearing the Elizabeth's voice. "'Tis nothing, Madam," he choked. "Catching my breath, that is all."

"I'm concerned for you," the Queen said.

"'Tis most kind of you," he said, straightening his spine. "But Your Majesty has enough to occupy her mind. Truly, I'm fine… But if…"

"John?"

"If something should happen to me. Something untoward. "

The Queen glared at him.

"Nothing shall," he reassured her. "Just, if it should, look after my son if that would please Your Majesty. Lady Margaret would not…"

The queen lifted a gloved hand. "Do not concern yourself with that. You shall be fine. I know of it. But, ease your mind. After all you've done on my behalf…"

"Thank you, Madam. And now, Sir Giles has organized the hunt and the horses are anxious to go."

John turned and glanced to his son, then tightened his reins and nodded to one of the swine herders. The herder acknowledged the gesture and untied the final knot from the boar's neck and slapped the sweating animal hard on its hindquarters as a second lad swung open the gate, sending the squealing swine across open field toward a line of ash trees two hundred meters distant. The Queen restrained Abbey until the prey had a fair start, then released her grip, dug in her heals, and sent Abbey gripping dirt and pounding thunder.

The frightened boar scampered wildly left, then right, then left again in a zigzagged dash for its life as it tore through thistle and brier, twisting and angling in odd and unpredictable directions, screeching in terror as it desperately tried to outrun its pursuers. When it wiggled under a hedge and burrowed beneath, the horses catapulted over, tracking the frightened animal's scent as it squirmed along a shallow trench and hopped out onto the flat again with death nipping at its heels. It scampered across the meadow, darted into a thin trace of wood, and then sprung out again, its stubby legs churning as fast as a waterwheel, yet still ill-matched against the thick-muscled haunches of horses trained for the chase.

A stone wall loomed ahead. The Queen knew from her many hunts that a boar rarely ran along the length of a barrier. It would sense a trap, but neither would it yield. It would leap the barrier if it could, and if it could not, it would turn to the hunters and kill or be killed.

Abbey reached the wall first, shaking her head as she reared back on her hindquarters, her loins taught, her eyes seared wide as she awaited the other riders to angle in from both sides to block the boar's escape, each mount holding back to protect its greatest vulnerability -- its shins. Abbey's nostrils flared as she sucked in air and dripped sweat around her saddle. Elizabeth knew better than to edge Abbey too close in fear she might bolt.

A sudden movement drew Elizabeth's eyes to her right as another horse reared up ahead of Abbey. "Hold back, Lad!" the Queen heard John cry as young Edward urged his frightened mount forward. Against the horse's will, Edward centered his reins and squeezed his shins hard against the steed's belly, attempting to reassure the terrified animal of its safety.

John de Vere's horse hesitated to edge closer, then slammed into Abbey's flank as the panicked boar drew its shoulders in, bared its teeth, and released a guttural growl, prepared to lunge and rip into horseflesh.

When Abbey raised her right fore-hoof, the boar sprung. As it lunged, Edward slipped from his saddle, fell onto the boar's spiny-haired hindquarters and grabbed the beast's ears as the animal spun, twisted, and shook, attempting to swing its head around and sink its fangs into the unwanted rider.

Two lancers rushed in, thrusting at air as they awaited an opportunity to pierce the boar without stabbing Edward's legs or belly. When the young earl wrenched the animal's head left, one of the lancers drove his weapon into the boar's rump, spurting blood, the smell and sight of which drove the horses to a frenzy.

The second lancer waited for the squealing animal to whirl back around, and then poked its eyes with the blunt end of his lance, momentarily blinding the boar as John de Vere, off his mount and on the ground, grabbed his son's feet as they swung by, leaned back, and yanked until the boy let loose his prize.

The boar's desperate moans mingled with the horse's high-pitched neighs as lancers repeatedly jabbed, cut and withdrew, and then charged in again, shedding blood in a frantic melee before the skirmish suddenly ended. The boar, after fighting valiantly to preserve its life, suddenly succumbed. The horses, the hunters, and the lancers, having prevailed in a contest of six against one, stood exhausted in silent respect as the near dead swine rolled to its back, its tiny feet spasming in aftershock as it awaited death to release it from its anguish.

John de Vere dropped to his knees and hovered over his son still sprawled on the ground. "Edward!" John cried as the boy opened one eye and squinted into the sun. "Did I get him, father?" he asked.

CHAPTER 5

Death and Banishment

"Youth is full of pleasance, age is full of care."
The Passionate Pilgrim, Stanza 12

Within six months of the hunt with the Queen, John de Vere died in his sleep, though not peacefully. His chest crushed and bleeding internally, his life seeped away in excruciating pain after being fatally injured in another hunt on the estate of his neighbor, Sir Giles, when Giles lost control of his horse and the animal tumbled and fell upon John, who had not yet mounted.

Plunkin, John's lifelong manservant, upon kneeling at John's deathbed, watched his master's cheeks slowly drain of color and found his master's skin as cold as Hedingham's castle walls. His eyes dilated, his fingernails curled on his chest where bloodlines appeared as though he had tried to tear himself open and reconnect his broken bones.

"How *could* he die?" Edward asked Plunkin as the heavy smell of funeral musk permeated the Hedingham crypt where effigies of the last two earls, the fourteenth and fifteenth, lay prone on stone blocks, their spirits awaiting Edward's father. The burden of the de Vere heritage -- the title, the castles, the estates -- traced back to 1066 when Aubrey de Vere supported William the Conqueror in his conquest of England. Yet Edward little cared for heritage. He cared for his father, whom Edward knew loved him despite Edward's apathy toward the affairs of the estates. "I myself find their upkeep arduous," John had once confessed, reading his son's mind, "It simply must be done. 'Tis our duty to carry on that which has been passed to us." Yet Edward knew, even then, that he had no interest in carrying on a laborious drudgery, the very prospect of which weighed heavy on his mind.

"*Why* did he die, Plunkin?" Edward asked his father's manservant, who stood next to him in the family crypt.

"They say 'twas a hunting accident at Sir Giles' estate."

"They *say?*"

"'Twas thus reported, 'Sire.' While you were away at school."

"Do not call me 'Sire.' I detest that."

"Unbeknownst to you," Plunkin said, "these have been dour times. Your father kept it from you. Since your departure, the revenue has not been substantial. As the future master of the estates, you must…"

Edward turned and glared down at the much shorter Plunkin, a loyal manservant who rose only to Edward's chin, although Plunkin was a man near twenty years beyond Edward's twelve. "It was *she,* was it not, Plunkin? Be of truth."

Plunkin lowered his head whilst keeping his eyes fixed on Edward. "Twas not, I swear thee true. He was ill and weak before the accident. He kept that from you."

"She sent me off to school, then killed him. She and Giles."

"I swear she did not. 'Twas an accident."

"You know of that first hand?"

"'Twas reported thus."

"By who? By Giles? By one of Giles' men? By my mother?"

"I know naught of such matters, Sire."

"Leave me with him then."

Plunkin bowed and shuffled back, stirring dust that scattered in the dim yellow light as he left the crypt.

With Edward's feelings a mixture of anger and uncertainly, he lifted his eyes to face the stone sarcophagus that contained his father's remains. "Why have you left me?" he muttered, his words echoing around the walls.

Beyond Edward's love for his father, he knew naught if he was capable of love. At the internment services for family and friends, he had bit his tongue to squelch his tears and keep his witch of a mother from pitying him. Now, standing alone before his father's body, he sunk his teeth deep into his lower lip, broke the skin, and shed blood to punish himself for not being the son his father desired and deserved.

Feeling suddenly weak and dizzy, he stepped forward and gripped the edge of the coffin's lid. Mad at his father for abandoning him, livid at himself for all the trouble he had caused, and furious at his mother for her distant and unloving ways, he bent at the knees, and with great anguish ground the lid back. He laid his lips on the narrow opening and whispered into the cold darkness, "I'm sorry for everything father. I love you."

"Pity me not," a voice sighed from somewhere behind him.

He sprung up and turned. "Plunkin!"

A shadow swayed in the dim light.

"Father?... Is it you come back to speak to me?" he asked. But when he spread his arms and stepped toward the apparition, his hands swept through emptiness.

CHAPTER 6

A Cruel Departure

"Let me not think on it.
Frailty, thy name is woman!"
Hamlet, I, 2

"I requested your presence before your departure," Lady Margaret announced, rocking on her toes in the same great hall in which Edward had once performed for the Queen. It was now *Edward* who sat at the bench beneath his pacing mother, as his father often had.

"Naturally, changes are forthwith," Margaret said.

"I expect so," Edward answered, hoping to get this over with and leave Hedingham for good. It offered him naught but painful memory.

"Your father's untimely departure has left us all in a lurch. Your care and wardship has now passed to Cecil Burghley."

Edward sprung to his feet. "Wardship?... I have no need of wardship."

"Sit down."

He glared at her.

"*I* am master of Hedingham now," Lady Margaret stated firmly. "Sit!"

Edward shuffled back until his calves brushed the bench, then plunked down.

"I shall have my hands full managing these bothersome estates. I cannot properly see to a boy. You shall receive a small allowance. The bulk of what is due you, thanks to your father, shall pass to Burghley for your wardship expense. I shall make do with whatever I can ring from the properties until you come of age and they pass to you."

"Forfeit me my allowance now and I shall live on my own."

"I think not."

"I shall take an apartment in London."

Lady Margaret spit an exasperated breath through clenched teeth. "'Twas not my idea, although I approve. It was the Queen's and your father's. It seems they connived behind my back. Think of it this way, with Burghley, you will be close to the Queen and under her privilege. That should suit you. The foolhardy woman is as frivolous and undisciplined. She feasts and romps and shows her plays, putting off what is most serious -- a return to the proper church. Perhaps that is why she favored this arrangement. She sees herself in you. Her Chief Minister is at least a sober man of order. He holds her to a tight tether. Perhaps he can do the same with you. 'Tis precisely what you both require."

Edward stood slowly. "I shall stay at Hedingham and run the estates myself, as father would have wanted."

Margaret's eyes narrowed. "You're right. He would have wanted that. Fortunately, he saw you as I do. Playful, bright, foolhardy, and ultimately ineffectual. No. I shall manage the estates. In that way there will be something left to manage when they eventually come to you. In the meantime, I shall have help."

A door open behind Lady Margaret and a bearded man floated in like a character in one of Edward's plays, although this man, their neighbor, was real.

"Sir Giles," Lady Margaret grinned, surveying the man head to toe, "has lost his own poor, dear wife to the plague. Being of like in our situation, we intend to marry."

"Marry!" Edward jumped up. "'Twas this villain who killed my father! 'Twas his horse that crushed him to death!"

Lady Margaret quickly grabbed Sir Giles arm as he started to lunge for Edward. "No. Stop. Listen Edward, it was an unfortunate mishap. That's why we need each other. We are both alone now."

Edward stood quietly stunned, his hands at his sides. Lady Margaret said nothing further while Sir Giles grinned. The couple, side-by-side, hand-in-hand, glared across at Edward, allowing no room between them.

"Father," Edward whispered.

Silence answered.

~~ THE QUEEN ~~

"She shall be loved and feared."

Henry VIII, 5

CHAPTER 7

The Powers That Be

"Which is justice, which is thief?"
King Lear, V, 6

The Queen's Chief Minister, Cecil Burghley, had built Burghley House at the epicenter of power, strategically located midway between the Crown at Whitehall, and the City of London, England's rapidly expanding commercial and financial center to the east.

Political and pecuniary vigilance, at which the Chief Minister was equally adept, required a sharp eye both directions. If either power center developed a structural problem that might weaken its foundation, the Chief Minister would be the first to see it develop from his portal high atop Burghley House's central tower. From that vantage point, and with information obtained from well-placed spies, he felt reasonably assured that he could predict and manage events from whichever direction they occurred.

The Queen, for her part, had squirmed uncomfortably on the throne at Whitehall for four years, although she never showed her discomfort in public. The illegitimate daughter, in the Pope's view, of Henry VIII and Anne Boleyn, the union and subsequent execution of Anne split England into a religious divide. The Catholics, both at home and abroad, believed Elizabeth's claim to the throne was illegitimate. The Protestants backed the new Queen who supported her father's Anglican beliefs. Philip of Spain, the self-appointed defender of the Catholic faith on behalf of the Pope, with his army and an Armada to back him, salivated at the thought of a Spanish invasion to restore England to the true and proper faith. North of Spain, and within striking distance across the channel, Catholic King of France would sooner claim England for himself rather than allow his Spanish rival to command a power base across the narrow divide.

Elizabeth, cowering on her tiny island, had little resources to protect herself against her enemies, her father having drained the island's coffers with his indulgences in elaborately constructed estates and castles, six wives and costly French wars. Upon taking the throne, Elizabeth was in desperate need of funds for armaments to defend herself. Within her realm, the Catholic and Protestant factions squeezed the crown from both sides. The long established Catholic gentry thought Elizabeth had drifted too far from the tenets of the old church, whereas the newly christened Protestants -- primarily merchants and those who worked the lands -- believed she had done little to rid England of the vestiges of its Catholic faith. Elizabeth's least tilt in either direction raised the ire of one camp and sharpened the swords of the other.

If Elizabeth, this young, fledgling Queen was to prevail, Burghley, her chief counsel and henchman, realized she would need to employ all the cunning she could muster, and even if she played her limited assets well, her continued rule would necessitate a certain calculated brutality and a loyal minister to carry it out in her behalf.

John de Vere, the Sixteenth Earl of Oxford, had at least been wise enough to support his Queen despite his Catholic leanings. Whether that inclination rubbed off on his twelve-year-old stripling, young Edward de Vere, remained to be determined.

"Call him forth," Burghley said, eyeing a servant who bowed, turned, and departed.

Cecil Burghley -- the Queen's Master of Wards, among his other duties -- stood stiffly in the center of the wide entrance hall, his hands clasped behind his back and his chin jutting forth as a thin-elbowed Edward de Vere entered, crossed the room, and looked about as if he were master of Burghley House. Burghley -- a tall man with ever shifting beetle-like eyes -- frowned, sizing up his latest charge as Anne, his youngest daughter, age seven, stuck her head between high banister rails and looked down at the newest member of their household with John Lyly, another of Burghley wards, peering over her shoulders.

Master of Wards was not Burghley's favorite task, though it was one of his more lucrative. Had he been born of peerage -- an earl or baron -- as had the boy before him, the fortunes of birth would have smoothed his path to power. Instead, he was forced to employ willfulness, manipulation, and cunning -- some would say *ruthless* cunning -- to cut, claw, and maneuver his way to the third most powerful position in the realm, now bowing only to the Queen. Born a commoner, Burghley had fought his way to whatever privilege he had achieved, yet he never rested easy, knowing that a loose grip on his position tempted those clambering behind him to plunge their knives in his back and employ that leverage as a fulcrum to boost themselves higher.

Nonetheless, despite Burghley's position as the Queen's counselor and Chief Minister, he was barely able to command enough personal resources to finance his enormous household expenses and set enough aside to begin construction of a new estate with gardens, grounds and deer park on the thousand hectare parcel he had recently purchased near the peaceful country village of Stamford, eighty leagues north of London.

The Chief Minister could not cajole Parliament to raise taxes on his behalf, as the Queen might, nor could he, being of poor lineage, draw on an inheritance as could his wealthy wards who could hardly complain of the small percentage he took as income to manage their fortunes and provide them the surroundings and education suited to their stations.

"Welcome to Burghley House," the Chief Minister said, glaring at his latest chargling. *"Burghley* House," he repeated. "Remember that name. Like the roses you may have noticed in the garden on your way in," he nodded toward the door, "that require attention and pruning to keep them from growing wild, so you too... Step forward." He waited for the boy to close the distance between them. "Good. I am certain we shall acquaint ourselves pleasantly so long as you tend a few simple rules. Is this understood thus far?"

"Thus far."

"Doth arrogance slip from your tongue?"

"Compliance."

"Very well. I shall take you for your tongue and not for your demeanor. As to your primary tutor, you shall be pleased at this, I have employed Arthur Golding, your uncle."

Edward grinned.

"Do not be so gleeful. He is translating Ovid's *Metamorphoses* from the Latin, a monumental task your uncle says, with many stories within it. If you show promise at Latin, I should not be surprised if he used you to help with his rendering... Now, as to the rules at Burghley house. I understand, according to your mother, your father was quite lenient."

"I have no mother."

"According to your mother, you have a willful nature, some of which may be to the good once properly harnessed. I shall set the rules to start, not that I expect that you will remember them. First and foremost, I shall advise you as to the nature of character. I suspect a rather lengthy undertaking ahead given your upbringing heretofore. Second, you shall be judged by both your words and your acts and are thus advised to hold your tongue and not twist it to your own ends. Which, I understand, by warrant, is difficult for you."

The boy stuck this tongue out, pinched it, and then flipped it back and choked a grin.

"Your tongue robs your stomach," Burghley said, nodding and jabbing his finger. "You shall have no dinner this night... Thirdly, I expect you to be friendly and familiar, yet not overly so. Friendliness throws an opponent off. Yet, by no means be garish. Is this familiar to you?"

Edward nodded.

"Do not dull thy wit with vulgar friends. Follow the church, not the arts, which I am told in your case, requires a change of direction. Was it not you who burned your father's theater down?... Beyond that," Burghley said without waiting for an answer, "respect your elders. Is all this within your grasp?"

Edward curtsied.

"Straighten up and do not foul me. I keep a strict account and I hold your ledger minus from the start. I shall not let the next infraction pass this easily.... Now, as to manners, give others thy ear, not thy wisdom, such as it may be. Do not dull your mind with entertainment. Is this clear?"

"I..."

Burghley touched a finger to his lips. "Thy *ear,*" he whispered. *"Not* thy tongue... Take the measure of a man, yet reserve thy opinion as thy purse. I shall tend that myself, as required. Neither a borrower nor a lender be. And this above all..." Burghley hesitated.

"To thine own self be true," Edward finished Burghley's list.

"How do you know this?"

"Your reputation precedes you. You say it to all your boys."

"Life's proper principles *are* the same for all... And, to thy queen be true."

"If she be true to me," Edward muttered.

Anne, Burghley's daughter, giggled, drawing her father's eye to her and Lyly on the staircase.

"All three of you to your rooms," Burghley said, his booming voice filling the hall before turning back to his new charge. "We shall soon see how far you ride on impudence."

CHAPTER 8

Fast Friends

"The bright day is done."
Antony and Cleopatra, V, 2

"May I show him to his room, father?"

"If you must," Burghley sighed to his daughter. "But be quick of it... And you... Lyly," he pointed to another of his wards. "Get you to your own quarters without supper for listening to words intended private."

Anne Cecil – short-armed, narrow-waisted, her braided hair the color and texture of straw as it bounced behind her -- led Edward up a staircase, then down a long hall lined with framed maps, and through a narrow arched passageway that he could touch on both sides with arms extended. "I have seen your trunks," Anne said. "Father says you are a clothes hog."

"Hogs don't dress."

"Father says you have more clothes than I, a girl."

"Then *you* should have more."

"Father says I should favor simplicity in dress and manner."

"Then I shall acquaint you with the other side of both."

"Would that not be of cost? Father bears thrift of great importance."

"I am an earl," Edward said, glancing down a hall that widened with doors along both sides. "Yet his house is bigger than most that I possess."

"Theobalds, father's county estate, is even bigger. And father is planning yet a third. He says he has earned it."

"Stole it," Edward said.

Anne spun around. "That is rude of you."

"Does he not take his money from mine?"

"You are not his only ward. He serves the Queen and does so at her behest... Did you not know? Father says it is she who would have you here."

"I met her once. I hardly know her."

"Father says she took to you. That she made a promise to your father."

"To what end? To care for me? I can care for myself."

"Father says 'tis always best to accept what cannot be altered." She stopped and nodded toward an open door to the left. "This shall be your quarters."

He followed her into a small, brightly lit room that faced the sun in the morning, with a thinly padded four-poster bed at the center against the left wall consuming half the space, a desk opposite the bed, and a round-topped chest nestled to the bed's right.

Anne grinned.

"What amuses you?"

"All your trunks. There is not enough room... Be on time for dinner," she gigged.

"You forget. I have none."

"He will feed you if you say you're sorry."

"Then I shan't eat."

"Pretend. Father says you act in plays."

He glared down at her.

"He says you wrote a play to mock the Queen."

"Not to mock her. Merely to show her the lighter side."

"Father was not pleased."

"I believe Her Majesty was."

"Well, if you change your mind as to supper, be on time. Father won't wait. He will starve you to teach you a lesson."

As soon as Anne left, Edward snapped the door shut and hopped on the bed without removing his boots. He was certain there was a no-boots-on-the-bed rule and wished to break it immediately. He lay there till after dark, occupied by characters and thoughts, spurred on by the events of the day. He rose, lit a candle, and looked about in search of paper and a quill. Surely his wardmaster would have placed writing implements somewhere, lessons being so prominent to his purpose. When he found what he sought, he shoved a chair up to the desk and grinned, amused at the lines that occurred to him, writing them down quickly before he lost them.

After some time, he wasn't sure how long, he was startled by a rap on the door.

"'Tis me. John... John Lyle."

The door squeaked ajar and a lad of broad shoulders and a broader smile eased inside and closed the door behind him. "Speak softly," he whispered when he turned. "Burghley's spies are everywhere. I'm to be in my own room to study after dark."

"Let them report us," Edward volunteered. "I shall say I came to your room and fetched you."

"'Twould still be both of us kettle-boiled in the morning for disobedience," Lyly said. "Here." He crossed the room and held out his hand. "I brought you this." He laid a broken chunk of bread on Edward's desk. "We can't plan our punishment, but we *can* plan to eat. It simply takes a bit of thievery."

"I think we shall get on well, the two of us," Edward smiled as he bit off a mouthful.

"I heard an earl was to be among us. What is it you think, so far?"

"I hate it," he said, setting the bread next to his papers.

"As do I... I was hoping you'd be a little younger. More of my age. But 'tis a mere two years difference and you will have to do, the newest of his herd."

"Herd?"

"Burghley rounds us up upon the death of our fathers until we reach eighteen, the age of accountability. He manages our monies and gets paid by the head. The more heads in his herd, the more he takes for himself."

"As the Queen's minister, why does he require funds?"

"Her Majesty has little monies of her own. She has castles. Her father, King Henry, left her naught. If she were not Queen, she would be a pauper. She could not afford her own keep. She sets a date for Parliament when her purse draws empty and they debate her budget request as though she were a common beggar. Burghley, to fill his coffers, runs his school for us lost and wayward wealthy. We have such a burden to bear that he guides us into manhood by lightening our load along with our purses... What is that you're writing?" Lyly asked, jutting his chin toward the papers on Edward's desk.

"Our wardmaster's rules."

"You needn't bother. He will frequently remind you."

"I am putting them down as a character in a play might speak them. As a parody that requires no embellishment."

"A play?... You are a playwright?"

"I try my hand. Perhaps one day I shall find the right part to suit these words. Our wardmaster takes himself most seriously. He is already a caricature of a character."

"Read it to me. I write myself. I shall bore you with mine to get even."

Edward shrugged, slid the candle closer, and read.

> This I advise you.
> See to your character.
> Give thy thoughts no tongue,
> Nor any unproportioned thought to act.
> Be thou familiar, but by no means vulgar.
> Do not dull thy palm with entertainment.
> Beware of entrance into quarrel.
> Take each man's censure, but reserve thy judgment.
> Cost thy habit only as thy purse can buy.
> Be not expressed in fancy, rich nor gaudy.
> Neither a borrower nor a lender be.
> Borrowing dulls the edge of husbandry.
> And this above all, to thine own self be true,
> And it must follow, as the night to day,
> Thou canst not then be fool to any man.

"Be it comedy or tragedy?" Lyly asked.

"As with life, joy and misery run together, so an audience may laugh until they cry. If I get our wardmaster's words right, they will take the measure of the man."

Lyly sat on the edge of Edward's bed where they talked and laughed until Lyly yawned and stretched and then left for his quarters for fear of being discovered.

CHAPTER 9

The Words to Move a Quill

"Salad days,
When I was green in judgment."
Antony and Cleopatra, I, 5

Edward slept uneasily his first night in his new surroundings, dreaming of ghosts who whispered words he could not understand, intermixed with visions of wild boars nipping at his heels. When a bright sun opened his eyes, he was at first uncertain where he was. Had he awakened from a dream or fallen into one? He sat up and glanced around the room toward the desk and papers. His list of Burghley's rules. This was no dream. This would be his new life.

He rose, slipped his arms through the same shirt he wore the day before and crossed to the window to observe long morning shadows stretching across a well-tended rose garden, the stalks of one plant bent across a wooden gate as if trying to pry it open to escape Burghley's clutches. The training of roses little surprised Edward. The Chief Minister undoubtedly had rules for them as well. Murder or misfortune had taken Edward's father and now tied him down under Burghley's care for reasons only God knew.

Even with his newfound friend, John Lyly, Edward's days at Burghley House soon grew long, dull and tedious as weeks of boredom turned to months that seemed to stretch ahead toward an ever-receding horizon.

Edward took his studies from several tutors. To Burghley's credit, he employed the most learned in their fields. At least in this account, his wardmaster spared no expense. He and the other wards moved among their tutors by the hour. "If I know where you are to be, an eye can be kept upon you," Burghley announced. Thankfully, free time was allowed for playing chess with Lyly and even for chasing Anne in her childish version of hide-and-seek, Anne, being a girl and younger, requiring the older players to provide more clues as to which of the massive rooms they intended to secret themselves.

Twice-daily prayer on the stone-floor of the chapel quickly wore sores on Edward's knees that soon hardened to calluses. "I am happy to see the first fruits of God's good work," Burghley said when Edward showed him the result. "The Lord uses pain to draw attention to a matter before he advises."

One afternoon after chapel, Burghley asked, "Did you pray for guidance or absolution," as though these were the only two acceptable requests.

"Absolution," Edward lied, thinking his wardmaster would wish to provide the guidance himself, although he might, on occasion, allow the Lord's absolution. If Edward had answered truthfully, he would have said, "The Lord and I are bored with each other. I spend my time shifting from one knee to the other, making up stories to keep from nodding off." He *would* have said that, but he had already learned, after much experience, that he preferred his supper to an honest last word.

At other times, when he could not resist a last word, he found it best to say it *after* supper. Punishment on a full stomach allowed an extra hour alone in his room where he could put his grumblings, his thoughts and his ideas to paper, though he was always careful to omit names when his writing applied to those around him, allowing for at least a superficial denial should his wardmaster rummage though his notes.

"I am keeping a journal myself," Lyly said when Edward showed him his. "The most awful things occur to me. Do you think that a sin?" Lyly asked. "I think them anyway. Is it sinful to write what you think?"

CHAPTER 10

Lessons

"Thou speakest wiser than thou art aware."
As You Like It, II, 4

A whack on the back of Edward's head jolted him up from his desk. "You've been dozing," Burghley growled, his words rolling off his tongue as though sweetly relished their taste. When Edward turned and glanced up, Burghley stood above him, tapping the knob of his cane with his index finger. Edward's wardmaster regularly checked to verify adherence to his prescribed routine, quiet time being allocated for study, not for sleep. "Idleness breeds laziness and frivolity," he admonished.

"Good. Then when do we frivol?" Edward asked as he straightened in his chair and rubbed sleep from his eyes.

"Without the straight line of discipline," Burghley said, "life stumbles through the mire. I have made a few changes in your routine. Here they be." He thrust a list forward.

To Edward, who preferred following his own lead, both Burghley's old and new regimens tied him to the rack as if in Whitehall's torture chamber, stretching him in the rack's direction instead of his own.

7:00 - 7:30	Dancing
7:30 - 8:00	Breakfast
8:00 - 9:00	French
10:00 - 11:00	Writing and Drawing
11:00 - 1:00	Meal, Rest, and Study
1:00 - 2:00	Geography and History
2:00 - 3:00	Ancient Latin and Modern Italian
3:00 - 4:00	Exercises with the Pen

4:00 - 5:00	Common Prayer
5:00 - 7:00	Rest and Supper
7:00 - Morn	Study - To Bed

Locked into Burghley's new schedule, Edward nonetheless, with noted exceptions, progressed well. Although providing Burghley a good report in language, Edward's French tutor added, regarding his student's willfulness, "I do believe this impudent young man would pull his stockings on backward and wiggle his toes simply to see if he could poked a hole in them."

Required general reading was interspersed on weekends with riding, the hunting of rabbits and deer, swordsmanship, jousting, hawking, and horticulture. One of Edward's riding tutors informed the Chief Minister, "The lad out rides the many of us. And yet," he felt obliged to add, "he should pray forgiveness on Sundays. When he hunts, he chases an invisible creature and oft lets the true meat escape." Even as a year passed in the hunt, the other students were unsure what to make of him. At thirteen now, he oft outwitted them or twisted his words to make them think he had.

Confined to his room for reading the Latin *Quintus Ennius* during his French lesson, he peered out his window across to his wardmaster's prized rose garden. The Strand -- the well-trod road fronting Burghley House -- saw only an occasional traveler this evening, with more sails and water taxies on the Thames beyond than carriages or riders on the road.

Upriver, away from the sea, Edward angled his view east in that direction, toward Westminster's spires high behind the chimneystacks of Whitehall's administrative buildings that snuggled as close around the royal quarters as bricks and mortar allowed. Edward could easily recite Whitehall's four hundred year past along with its more recent history that skulked through its courtyards and passages, and down its dark, narrow alleyways. The view out his window brought to mind Henry IV and his nemesis, the First Earl of Northumberland, who contested Henry's legitimacy much as the northern earls now questioned Elizabeth's. And then another Henry came to mind, Henry VI this time, driven out of Normandy after first being crowned king of France and of England. And yet another Henry, Henry VIII, Elizabeth's father, who chased six woman through the corridors and up and down Whitehall's stairwells until he grew too old and fat to catch his final wife, Catherine Parr, who cradled his three-hundred-pound body in his huge royal bed and nursed him like a baby.

When Edward turned his head and looked in the opposite direction, west toward the sea, the Tower's spires stretched toward the heavens with its Tudor flag, the very same tower that William the Conqueror constructed to protect London from foreign invaders, and where, ironically, he himself took refuge after Londoners considered *him* the invader.

The Tower had since been put to bloodier uses. After commanding Anne Boleyn's head be separated from her body with a single blow of the ax, Henry VIII ordered her head buried in a wooden crate at the center of the crosswalk in the west Tower yard to be trod upon throughout eternity. The Queen's half-sister Mary, in her brief reign as Henry's eldest daughter, imprisoned Elizabeth high in the west Tower to peer down upon her mother's buried head and contemplate her own fate should she refuse to convert to Catholicism.

Edward, raised Catholic, did not consider his own religious doubts worth the severing of his head, as the Queen apparently once had. At close to fourteen and not yet ready to face his maker, he had trouble enough unraveling the mysteries of this life. The workings of the next, especially after his father's untimely death, he would leave to God although Burghley's tutors seemed to weave the Lord's admonitions into whatever subject they taught. Still, Edward delighted in probing his proctors with questions they oft tiptoed around and could never straightly answer.

"If good is solemn and evil makes merry, doth the Lord spin no enjoyment? If the Bible forbids idols and icons, what then is the cross? Why does God's law forbid us the very desires he has given us? If the theater draws out God-given emotion by pretending upon the real, what then *is* real? Is it what we see before us or how we feel within us?"

His French tutor, often irritated at his most willful student, nonetheless jotted a complimentary note to Arthur Golding, Edward's primary tutor, who read the final line to Edward. "I see that my work with Lord Oxford shall not be much longer required."

Arthur Golding challenged his brightest scholar with his own prized and lengthy project, the first English translation of Ovid's ancient *Metamorphoses*, its many plots and complicated Latin wording capturing Edward's imagination and providing him with the background to spin a tale of his own he entitled *Venus and Adonis*. Yet Edward understood his uncle's intent -- simply to have an apprentice help him with his lengthy translation.

In early May, in the Year of Our Lord 1564, Golding wrote to Burghley, smiling as he read his report to Edward before sending it:

> "Be it known to others, and I have had experience thereof myself, how earnest a desire hath naturally grafted Edward to read, peruse and communicate, and knowledgeable as well in histories of ancient times and recent, and also of the present state of affairs, and that not without a certain pregnancy of wit and understanding to become thereby the equal to any predecessor whereof great forwardness give assured hope and expectation.
>
> Your humble servant,
> Arthur Golding

"Just because you are brighter than most," Golding said, glaring down at a section of *Metamorphoses* he himself had translated, Edward having crossed out and corrected his tutor's work, "you are no less expected to exercise precision and exactness in executions."

"I have been."

"Really? We shall see." He grabbed the text from Edward's desk. "What is this cross-out?"

"'Vilia miretur vulgus, mihi flauus Apollo.'" Edward said, reciting his correction from memory. "You translated wrong, Uncle. 'Tis 'vulgis.' It is singular. Not 'vulgus.'" Edward glanced up. "Do you see it?"

"An oversight. That's quite enough for today."

CHAPTER 11

A Commoner

"I have no spur
To prick the sides of my intent,
But only vaulting ambition,
Which o'erleaps itself."
Macbeth I, 7

Restive thoughts surged through Cecil Burghley's mind as he paced the halls of his mansion, as he was wont to do each evening. Stoop-shouldered, his hands tightly clasped behind his back to keep them from flying about and cutting the air -- concerns, resentments, and opportunities raced through his mind and collided with one another. His spies had advised him that untold riches were to be had in the new Americas for those explorers and adventurers willing to risk life, limb, and fortune in their pursuit. But Burghley preferred a steadier course that avoided risk, while raising the tide of his fortune and, most importantly, his stature.

Fortune was easy, its inevitably a matter of planning, maneuvering and, when needed, an ample measure of ruthlessness and scheming. To acquire the power and prestige that a commoner like himself did not come by easily required generations of carefully constructed, layer-upon-layer scaffolding, build upon accomplishments for which Burghley had to thank his father and grandfather.

David Burghley, his grandfather, has risen in favor at Henry's court to reach the rank of High Sheriff of Northamptonshire. Richard, Burghley's father, built upon that achievement and became a frequent courtier at Henry's court which soon awarded him the duties and privileges of Royal Page, then Groom of the Robes, and finally, High Sheriff of Rutland, a position from which, to Burghley's delight, his father confiscated a considerable share of treasure when Henry ordered the Catholic monasteries closed and pillaged.

Thus Burghley realized early on that power could be accrued and built upon. Under Queen Mary's short reign, he was, with luck and much politicking, appointed chief administrator and caretaker to Hampton Court, where Princess Elizabeth resided. Their relationship, at first formal and distant, had slowly grown to the point where they came to know and trust each other as the young girl matured to a young woman. It was there-upon, as much from caring as opportunity, that Burghley had interceded on Elizabeth's behalf when her older half-sister, Queen Mary, contemplated beheading the young princess for refusing to recant their father's Protestant views.

Following the sudden death of Mary, it seemed entirely natural, then, that the newly crowned Queen Elizabeth I appoint Burghley, her trusted counselor and friend, as the new Queen's Chief Minister, High Treasurer, and Head of Privy Counsel, all high offices falling suddenly and unexpectedly under Burghley's tight-fisted control.

Religious and political enemies lurked everywhere, the two camps fused together by Henry's abandonment of the Catholic church, and Burghley soon stood in the midst of the heat and heart of that swirl. He well understood that a bloodletting would be required to purge the land of domestic and foreign Catholic supporters who would have the queen's own neck in hopes of returning the kingdom to its former religion.

In order to keep his newly found powers from slipping from his grasp and the kingdom from falling into the hands of England's enemies and conspirators, the new Chief Minister appointed Francis Walsingham -- reputed for his guard-dog ruthlessness and determination -- to hunt down, and quietly dispose of anyone suspected of conspiring against the Elizabeth or the realm.

Yet, t'was neither religion nor the assurance of heavenly absolution that found a home in Burghley's heart. His religious views altered as politics required, although he found it prudent to pin the new Protestant cross upon his cloak to signify what he stood for and whom he opposed.

In the midst of danger and chaos lay opportunity, and Burghley steadfastly determined to not merely strengthen and fortify what had been passed to him, but to add in a single stroke to that wealth and opportunity that which had hitherto never been contemplated by his ancestors.

The accumulation of power and personal wealth struck no upper boundary. There was always the possibly of further increase. The prestige and privilege that accrued from a royal bloodline, on the contrary, hit an impenetrable barrier for a commoner, even a commoner of Burghley's exalted status. Wealth accumulated upon itself. Royal status was conveyed through bloodline alone. One was either born with it surging through one's veins, or one was not, and Burghley was painfully aware that he was not.

It occurred to him -- pacing in a straight, even line, one foot placed carefully in front of the other -- that there might be a means to quietly slip through that barrier; not for himself, but for his progeny, should he find a way to maneuver his bloodline in a royal direction. After all, Anne Boleyn, Elizabeth's own mother, had been a commoner who, through marriage, produced the current Queen. And therein lay the path to be followed.

He stopped pacing, unclasped his hands, and climbed the stairs to the upper quarters of his wards. Whenever opportunity emerged, by virtue of his family's tradition, Burghley was of mind to clutch it by the throat, squeeze it tight and make it his. The current opportunity had fortuitously been sent to him, but it was the sort of prospect that would require more patience and negotiation than strangulation.

His most recent ward, Edward de Vere, the future 17th Earl of Oxford, was indeed disobedient, unruly and willful, and yet, he was of royal descent dating back to William of Orange when a distant relative of Edward's married William's sister and was granted the Oxford earldom. Burghley's own two sons could be handed wealth and power, but neither he nor they possessed a drop of royal blood. And neither did his only daughter, Anne. None-the-less, Anne would be of marriageable age one day, and should she marry royalty, would be capable of extending the Burghley line with a royal grandchild.

And so, Cecil Burghley, as he entered the darkened hallway where his ward's rooms were located, paused quietly before Edward's door and began scheming with his latest ward in mind.

CHAPTER 12

A Man's Worth

"A living dead man."
Comedy of Error, V, 1

Sundays after church, in what Burghley considered a "generous concession," Edward's wardmaster allowed his charges a walk in the afternoon -- their "weekly escape" Edward and Lyly called it. They fabricated their destination, never quite sure where they were headed, oft telling Burghley they wished to visit Westminster Abbey to bask in God's glory. Edward didn't think Burghley believed them, although he didn't challenge it, perhaps wishing a day to himself without two of his most troublesome charglings.

They frequently wandered east toward the Tower, then swung north along what remained of the original Roman wall, then left the city through Aldgate and struck out across an open field. At other times, they meandered upriver to wander through Whitehall's labyrinth of streets and winding alleys, past the cottages, stables, and shops that served the royal presence and relied upon the crown for their sustenance.

"Have you heard?" Lyly said one Sunday as soon as they escaped Burghley House and tentatively headed toward St. Paul's.

"Heard?"

"The spectacle. 'Tis a spiking."

They took a shortcut south, cutting through Colwich Alley and dashing across Watkins Green toward Fleet Street, and from there, slipped down on a low-tide riverbank and stepped around puddles to avoid soaking their boots or slipping on the rocks.

When they reached the base of the Thames crossing, they grappled a dangling rope line and heaved up on its pilings, and from there, onto the bridge, where they hurried down the span packed on both sides with all manner of shops that included, among others, a blacksmith, a haberdashers, vegetable sellers, a central green garden with a chapel, and carts filled with all the other necessities that a small bridge-town required to sustain the inhabitants of the three-tiered apartments stacked above the shops, their bay windows poking out over the water for at better view of the flow rushing beneath.

As they neared the south end of the bridge, Edward spotted a small crowd, their heads raised, two or three among them pointing skyward. As they neared, Edward squinted in horror at a man's severed head secured high upon a spike, his mouth open, fresh blood dripping down the stake.

"Looks a bit like your cousin William," Edward overheard an aproned woman nervously giggle to the man standing next to her. "On one of his better days."

"Who is he?" Edward asked the woman.

"The recently departed?" The woman looked at Edward and then glanced up the pole. "That be a father."

"What be his offence?"

"For being Father Beaumont. For saying mass."

Edward stared at the woman whom he thought, by her dress and apron, to be a merchant's wife. "Would the *Queen* know of this?" he asked.

She shrugged.

"I suspect not the details," her husband lowered his head and answered. "Her Majesty pontificates." He glanced up the pole. "Others administrate in her behalf."

Suddenly sick, Edward staggered to the rail, leaned across and vomited in the river, remaining there until he emptied his stomach three times. His head spinning, he turned and slid onto the deck. When Lyly carried over a pint and put it to Edward's lips, he shoved it away with his hand. " 'Twould hold no better," he said.

Lyly slid down and joined Edward. After a while, most of those who had gathered about the spike had tired and left. The two remaining, one a tall red-bearded man with a waist-length cape, the other, shorter and clean shaven, both wobbly on their feet, stared up at the pole as they spoke. "You first, then," the taller said.

"Nay, you," the other elbowed.

The taller man extracted a fistful of farthings from his purse. "Me first, then," he said. "The first to get two in a row, takes all the other has."

"Agreed," the second man nodded, matching the heft of his own purse with that of his friend.

One at a time, they took turns pitching coins toward the head's open mouth, laughing when they struck an eye or an ear and their coin plunked back, then jabbing each other and slapping their knees when one flipped in. After a goodly number of throws by each, the taller man collected his winnings and staggered off. The second, shorter man, waited until his friend passed beyond the tollgate and then, paying scant attention to Edward and Lyly, slid the lid off a nearby barrel, dipped both hands inside and extracted a handful of rotting fish heads. One after the other, he tossed the fish up the pole, aiming for the chin or the forehead, trying to dislodge coins stuck on the tongue or caught in the front of the mouth.

"Money to the end," Lyly said. "What be a man's worth?"

"Not much for a head alone," Edward said.

CHAPTER 13

Sergeant-at-Arms

"I have no other but a woman's reason."
Two Gentlemen of Verona, I, 2

"Rook to Castle. Checkmate," Edward said, a smirk curling his lips.

"They warned me that you were clever at this game," Elizabeth said. "That you well surpass Burghley's other wards. But you be not so clever at politics. You defeat your Queen in the first round, and then smile as if to make the larger of it."

"'Tis just a game," Edward said, still grinning.

"Nothing at court is *just* a game. Which, already, even at your young age, I suspect you know... Set your pieces. We shall play another."

The Queen laid out her white whilst Edward set his black, and then the Queen moved a pawn two spaces forward whilst Edward jumped a pawn to mount his attack.

"You father played, did he not?" the Queen said, studying the board.

"He taught me."

"Knowing John, he did not well tolerate losing to his son."

"Nor to anyone. He liked the win, but not an easy game. He tutored me to play my best."

"Tis a game of territory," the Queen said, resting her thumb on her chin. "The Queen, by all accounts, is the potent piece," she added. "And yet, if the King be taken, the game is won."

"'Tis unfair to the Queen," Edward agreed. "Yet even more to earls. There *are* none. We have rooks." He tapped a rook. "We have a king, a queen, and bishops. Church and State. Yet no earls."

Elizabeth slid a pawn forward to block Edward's pawn. "And yet the King would lose without his queen, or likely so," she said. "She holds the power yet not the position."

"'Tis true of *this* game," Edward said, his eyes fixed on the board. "Yet, at court, sometimes the roles are not so strict. If a piece be missing, another takes its place."

"Such as Queen for King?" she asked, raising an eyebrow and looking across at Edward. "If so, only with reluctance. Your game *and* your thoughts exceed your age."

"I am not so certain of that. Father called courtly politics a deadly game that sharpened wits *and* axes."

"Treachery is part of it, that be true," she said, toppling her King with her index finger, then resetting it.

Enjoying a game with the Queen from time to time helped Edward pass his days at Burghley House. The Queen, when she was of mind, called him to Whitehall at her whim or leisure, often irritating Burghley by disrupting his ward's routine.

"I am told you still write plays," Elizabeth said one afternoon as they sat in her outer chamber overlooking the Queen's park as a pale sunlight streamed through the curtains.

"Still?"

"You wrote one for me. Do you recall? It upset your father."

"More so my mother, I do believe."

"When not burdened with matters of State, I write a bit myself, though I prefer poetry. My Chief Minister frowns upon it. He sees no purpose to it."

"Perhaps he is right."

"I think not, and neither do you or you would not waste your own time."

"It fills my hours. My mother, that dear witch, was fond of telling my father that nothing remained for earls to occupy themselves. Would Your Majesty wish to hear what I wrote of the woman?"

"Of your mother? You have the words with you?"

"In my heart. 'Tis thus…

Suspend thy purpose, if thou didst intend
To make this creature fruitful.

Into her womb convey sterility.
Dry up in her organs of increase
And from her derogate body never spring
A babe to honor her. If she must teem,
Create her child of her spleen
That it may live to torment her.
Let it stamp wrinkles in her brow of youth,
With tears fret channels in her cheeks,
Turn all her mother's pains and benefits
From laughter and contempt, that she may know
How sharper than a serpent's tooth
To have a thankless child."

"You speak so cruelly of her. And of yourself."

"To write truth is to write as one knows it. You know my mother."

"A scathing description, yet honest. I knew your father better. I knew what *he* thought of her. Perhaps you would hear something I wrote, though I have not committed it to memory."

"Such would be my delight."

She stood and crossed the room to a three-tiered desk, opened a middle drawer and withdrew a sheath of papers. She sifted through several, replaced most and carried one back. "I have changed this several times," she said, examining it as she sat.

"Change with purpose," he said. "'Tis key to a good write, I think."

"I shall read, then. But you must promise to tell your Queen what you think."

"I shall."

"I believe you will. Most would not. They fear my displeasure." She cleared her throat and began.

The doubt of future foes exiles my present joy,
And wit me warns to shun such snares as threaten
    mine annoy.

For falsehood now doth flow, and subjects' faith
    doth ebb and flow,
Which should not be, if reason ruled or wisdom
    weaved the web.
But clouds of joys untried do cloak aspiring
    minds,
Which turn to rain of late repent by changing
    course of winds.
No foreign weight shall anchor in this port.
Our realm brooks not seditious sects,
My sword through rest shall still their edge
    employ
To roll their tops that seek to change what future
    shall joy.

She glanced up. "Well?" She waited.

"It hath a punch of honesty. There be truth within it... Yet it lacks..."

"Lacks?... Lacks what?"

"Subtlety."

"Subtlety!" she tightened her lips and spit the word. "The truth requires not subtlety. Deception doth require it."

Edward shrugged. "That as well."

She glared at him. "I do not frighten you, do I?"

"Should you?"

"I am your queen."

"And a comely one."

"Who, at my age, could easily be your mother."

"For that, by my calculations, you would have brought me forth at age fourteen, thirteen when conceived. I think not. I have one too many mothers already."

"What else have you writ? Recite another."

"What does my Queen wish to hear?"

"Something soothing. Not of swords or mothers."

Edward thought a second. "This then. A poem of courtly love, of love forlorn. I have written it as a courtly lady addressing her secret lover. They cannot speak in public for fear of discovery. Thus they must act as strangers, though she assures him that her feelings are still genuine. I have made it thus...

> Though I be strange, sweet friend, be thou not
> so.
> Do not annoy thyself with sullen will.
> My heart hath vowed, although my tongue say
> no,
> To rest thine own, in friendly liking still.
>
> So let me seem, though I be coy,
> To cloak my sad conceits with smiling cheer.
> Let not my gestures show wherein I joy,
> Nor by my looks my love appear.
>
> So where I like, I must not vow my love,
> Where I desire, must I feign debate.
> One hath my hand, another hath my glove,
> But he my heart whom most I seem to hate.
>
> Thus farewell, love: I will continue strange.
> Thou shalt not hear by word or writing aught.
> Let it suffice, my vow shall never change.
> As to the unsaid rest, I leave it to thy loving
> thought."

"Quite sad," the Queen said. "How do you recall a poem of such length?

"I have written and changed it so much, it is committed to memory."

"I oft fear I shall never find such love as you describe."

"I fear the same," Edward admitted.

The Queen laughed. "You are but a boy. Yet still, you write of love."

"I write the words as I believe them, though I have not yet felt the truth of them."

"I fear I shant myself."

"But you are queen."

"A queen who instills more fear than affection. Those who would woo me, fear me, and do not try, or else woo me to their purpose, that being far from love."

"Then they be unworthy of you."

She eyed him. "You are much like your father. Except, of course, far less disciplined and, I think, more playful. Perhaps they are the same, the playfulness being the free part of thinking, the one feeding the other."

CHAPTER 14

Burghley's Roses

"Our remedies in ourselves oft do lie."
All's Well That Ends Well, I, 1

"Shall we play a trick on the old man?" Edward said. "To humble our wardmaster?"

Lyly beamed.

"We shall pluck his suspicious nature and make light of what he prizes most, his precious roses. He has just planted new yellow ones this day. 'Tis a perfect time to play a trick and make a switch."

They waited until late afternoon, when they knew their wardmaster took to his study and barred the door to bend over his accounts. Edward pilfered two shovels, two trowels and buckets, and a hoe from the garden house while Lyly stood guard outside, the servants and gardeners predictably resting whist their master occupied himself.

Lyly made his way to the rear garden gate, wedged the latch open and trudged across the trimmed-grass field to the edge of the woods whilst Edward, ducking low along a shoulder-high hedge, carted his own bucket and tools around the backside of the garden house. When he straightened and peeked around the corner, he heard a finch chirp -- a good sign that no one was about.

He peered across his wardmaster's rows of roses, toward two freshly planted bushes in the center. He drew a breath, crouched low, and crept forward, eying the manor house for any indication of movement. When he reached his target rose, he dug around the newly tilled soil then stooped and scooped earth away from the base with a trowel, further loosening the soil before working the trowel down and underneath the bush. As Lyly squatted in the next row, they gripped the base from both sides, avoiding the thorns as best they could, then giggled, wiggled, and carefully lifted the new plant from its hold.

"Quickly," Lyly said, glancing nervously over his shoulder. "He'll see us."

They traded their uprooted rose for the three-pronged, knee-high weed that Lyly had carried from the woods, wedged it into the hole, scooped back loose soil, and tramped it flat around the roots with the toe of their boots. While Edward plunked their confiscated rose into Lyly's bucket, Lyly brushed away the darker dirt that had scattered on the path.

Trusting Burghley's habit of inspecting his garden after balancing his books, they quickly gathered their tools, then hurried back down the row and along the wall of the garden house. At the very moment Edward turned and looked behind him, the garden gate opened and Burghley plodded though, the burden of money bending his spine and lowering his eyes.

The Chief Minister turned a sharp left and entered the garden along the fence before proceeding down an end row, then stopped and glanced up abruptly as if he sensed something wrong but knew not what. He flicked his eyes about, then gasped and stretched his long legs across two rows, letting his robe fly like the wings of a hawk and ripping its hem on a thorn as he flew toward the three-pronged weed in his prized center section. He stood over it, his hands on his hips, scowled down, and then bellowed a roar as he whirled around and marched back toward the house.

"I must hurry to beat him," Edward whispered to Lyly. "Don't tarry at your task."

Edward dashed around the far side of the manor house, through the servant's entrance and up a narrow service stairway, pausing at the top to peer through a slot in the wall that overlooked the garden. Lyly, stooped in the middle row, patted down roots, having switched plants and reset the rose.

When Edward reached his room, he snapped the door shut just as foot steps clambered down the hall. He scrambled to his desk, opened *Metamorphoses,* and tried to steady his breath.

"Master Oxford!" Burghley's voice rattled wood.

"Who is it?"

"A word, if you please."

As soon as Edward let his wardmaster in, he grabbed Edward's ear, hauled him into the hall, and dragged him down the staircase and out the back. When Burghley finally turned him loose, Edward cupped his ear and tried to shove the pain back inside his skull.

"Young Sir!" the Chief Minister began, straightening an index finger toward his garden. "What is *that?*"

"A garden," Edward said, still holding his ear.

"In the garden."

"Roses, Sir."

"In the *middle* of the garden."

"More roses."

Burghley reached for Edward's ear again but missed when Edward drew back. "Follow me," the wardmaster said.

Edward trailed, stretching his legs to keep pace. When he chanced a glance back toward the manor house, he saw Lyly's hands dance from a second floor window. Not minding his step, he tripped and plowed into Burghley's back, then caught his balance and stumbled forward.

After reaching the center row, the Chief Minister stiffened and glared at the surprise return of his yellow rose planted in its usual spot. "Is *this* one of the jokes you are so famous for?" he asked, straining to maintain control of his voice.

"Would I play a joke on my wardmaster?" Edward said, trying to keep his laughter from bursting.

"That itself is a joke." Burghley eyes narrowed. "You twist your words to hide the truth, yet truth be what it is. Since you favor weeds so much, you shall pull them this afternoon and all the morrow. As to your friend, John Lyly, you enjoy each other's company so much, you will be privileged to enjoy it further whilst the gardeners take a holiday from their task."

CHAPTER 15

Gray's Inn

"They stumble that run fast."
Romeo and Juliet, II, 3

In September of his seventeenth year, Edward sat at his desk at Gray's Inn -- London's premier law school -- staring at the Bible in front of him, the lines out of focus as his thoughts traipsed through the ancient hills of southern France. His proctors monitored eyes, not fantasies. After flowering under Golding's tutoring, followed by a year at Cambridge and a Master's Degree at Oxford, Burghley enrolled Edward at Gray's, Henry III having established the Inn to set the foundation for his new judicial system a brisk walk from his new high court -- just far enough to fill the lungs and clear the mind of an advocate or a judge without losing the temper of a case. By the time of Edward's arrival, Gray's had long sponsored a student theater to teach its budding lawyers how to speak with an actor's confidence in preparation for their day in court.

The Inn's student quarters provided few comforts, no more or less than Edward was used to at Burghley House -- a small chamber containing a bed barely wide enough to turn once without toppling out, a goose-feather pillow, a bookshelf attached to the wall across from the bed, a desk set by a recently leaded window, and a single chest with hardly enough space to contain Edward's everyday cloths, not considering his evening wraps, which he agreed were more than most, given Gray's discouragement of ruffs and satins as frivolous flaunting. "One can only hope the Inn imparts the value of the simple life," Burghley had told Edward the morning he shuffled him off.

The worst of the Inn's constrictions, however, was his room left little space to pace when his racing thoughts could not be contained and forced him into the hall to walk and jell a line before rushing back to capture it on paper. With no looking-glass in the room, or anywhere else at Gray's, Edward could not view the costumes for the plays he had already begun to write for Gray's stage.

"An early rise and plain food holds the mind to piety and to the law," Robert Childs, Gray's headmaster, announced to the first assemblage of incoming students.

Edward did not subscribe to Child's austerity, although he agreed with Child's notion that the Inn's simple breakfast of roasted pine nuts and boiled porridge steamed a student's eyes open at five-thirty in the morning, an ungodly hour for waking or for eating, let alone prayer before breakfast.

Lyly, still trapped at Burghley House, oft came by when he could escape Burghley's clutches to pass biscuits through Gray's fence at the ten o'clock study break, looking out for Edward just as he had the first day they met. "How be it *this* week?" Lyly often asked when they were allowed to meet face to face, discussing the very regiment that Lyly would soon follow himself upon his entrance to the Inn.

"Eat while you can," Edward advised.

A breach of Gray's rules fined a student's meager allowance and provided grit for legal argument at student court, although rank and privilege more often carried the day over wit and persuasion. "A fine argument," a judge would agree, and then pronounce, *"Guilty."*

Hair too long or curled below the neck cost a pence. Smuggled food cost two -- *three* if a student continued chewing after a hand grasped the nape of his neck. Spitting on the grounds forfeited two pence. The fine for "general uproar," a catchall category, rested on the senior judge's discretion, with fair warning as to the rules having been posted on a plaque at the front of the dining hall.

SHOUTING, SPITTING, SINGING, LETTING WIND,
LAUGHING
OR OTHERWISE CREATING UNDUE DISTURBANCE
SHALL BE PUNISHED FORTHWITH

Burghley's absence as Edward's wardmaster was the single pleasant element that set Gray's Inn apart from Burghley House. Yet, even with that slight advantage, Edward was still obliged to spend holidays with his wardmaster at Burghley House. Like most prisoners the particular jail didn't matter -- Edward's thoughts frequently turned to escape and the means to carry it out.

With escape and freedom in mind, Edward arranged to meet Lyly outside Gray's gate on Sunday, a day assigned for reverent contemplation of God's infinite judgment and wisdom. The older students guarded the halls after noon meal, skulking the corridors and peeking into rooms when they failed to find an undergraduate in chapel or hunched over his Bible in study hall.

Edward calculated, if he and Lyly hurried and held their timing close, they could attend a two o'clock performance at the newly enclosed Red Lion Inn's stage where Richard Burbage, the Red Lion's owner garnered good coin and patronage by presenting plays that an audience found more witty and entertaining than the tired madrigals and religious offerings that the Puritans deemed appropriate in London. The Red Lion's current offering -- *The Temper of the Moon* -- was based upon one of *Metamorphoses'* classic tales that Edward helped his uncle translate.

"We shall see if it misses the mark of Ovid's original." Lyly said.

Sitting at the desk in his room and hearing nothing in the hall, Edward stood and eased his door ajar to peek into the hallway. He found the other students' doors closed, save one, the guardian's, the only senior on the underclassman floor. He closed the door quietly, skulked back to his desk and continued writing a poem where he had left off, making good use of his time, as he often did, by writing for himself. He read the lines he had previously written.

The laboring man that tills the fertile soil,
And reaps the harvest fruit, hath not indeed
The gain, but pain and if for all his toil
He gets the straw, the lord will have the seed.

The manchet fine falls short unto his share.
On coarsest cheat his hungry stomach feeds.
The landlord doth possess the finest fare.
He pulls flowers, the man the weeds.

The mason poor that builds the lordly halls,
Dwells not inside them,
They are for the high degree.
His cottage is compact in paper walls,
Not of brick or stone, as others be.

The idle drone who labors not at all,
Sucks up the honey from the bee.
Who worketh most, their share doth fall the least,
Were due deserve, the just reward decreased.

Edward's fellow classmates at Gray's Inn praised his poetry, yet oft dismissed its sentiment, thinking it too romantic and lacking practical understanding, as those studying the law are want to believe. His case law tutor, after reading Edward's poem on the rights of the indigent and the poor position of labor, explained to Edward that if there were no Lords for *whom* to labor there would be no labor for Edward to romanticize.

Edward's first attempt at a Gray's Inn play -- *As It Was Liked* -- although he hadn't fully settled on the title -- raised good spirits as comedies often do.

Still hearing no footsteps in the hall, the student guard apparently having not yet made his rounds, Edward straightened and stretched. Where *was* the room check? Perhaps Edward's proctor had relinquished his duties to sneak out himself. Finally, upon hearing a sudden creak in the hall, Edward sat back in his chair, lowered his eyes, and stared down at the Bible open in front of him. When his door inched opened, Edward turned his head and nodded, then glanced down again, awaiting the door to close and footsteps to fade.

When he was sure it was safe, he stood and shoved his desk far enough away from the window to squeeze around and angle behind. He unhooked the latch, then leaned out and glanced in both directions. With no one in sight, he hoisted himself through the opening, slithered out onto the overhang and eased to the edge and dropped off, grappled to his feet and hugged the wall. If luck ran with him, he would be back in time for supper. If it soured, he would accept his punishment as the price of a day's entertainment.

CHAPTER 16

Across the River

"If this were played upon a stage,
I could condemn it as improbable fiction."
Twelfth Night, III, 4

Edward bent low and crept beneath a row of shoulder high evergreens that ran along the edge of Gray's inner courtyard where he waited for the student in the gatehouse to close his eyes and droop his head as he always did given the tedium of the job. At the guard's first nod, Edward crouched and sneaked past, then straightened and scurried around the corner.

"Yo!"

Edward jumped as Lyly slipped from an alcove.

"Where have you been?" Lyly asked. "I thought they caught you."

"The room check ran late."

They hurried down the Strand toward the river, a safe passage in daylight, the city far more dangerous at night with thieves and ner'-do-wells skulking about and seeking any advantage the dark night allowed. London's enterprise and exuberance had exploded under the Queen's rule, its population swelling from two-hundred-thousand a mere fifty years prior, to twice that number during Her Majesty's reign. All manner of shops, taverns, inns, and dens of commerce and iniquity, squatted shoulder-to-shoulder, with homes and dwellings nudging each other for every nook and cranny, the shopkeepers, the homeowners, and even the squatters, complaining of the noise and the stench, yet relishing the excitement, the prosperity, and the convenience that burgeoning trade and profitmaking spurred. The Queen's enemies quietly protested that she had little to do with the increase, that London's growing port was set to expand and overflow with trade and commerce before Elizabeth stepped upon the throne. Nevertheless, the captain at the helm when the tide comes in was rightly credited with steering the ship to harbor.

Progress, as measured by the volume of sewage draining downhill toward Fleet Street, caused many a man and maiden to throw up their breakfast upon leaving their quarters, the sun-heated cobblestones mixing and baking the human contribution with fresh plunked horse-dung and urine along with the contents of morning slop pots dumped from second floor windows. Experienced morning strollers quickly developed a two-step shuffle that shunted them out of harm's way at the first clatter of a shutter above their heads. Nonetheless, in Edward's view, the price of holding ones nose and occasionally stepping aside was well worth the city's new liveliness and vitality. Thankfully, when he and Lyly angled down Barley's Row, the welcomed odor of fresh-caught pickerel led their noses toward the Thames three blocks before they arrived.

"A ride across?" a rower with a pirate's skull-and-cross-bones tattooed on his bicep hollered up from the middle seat of his boat as soon as Edward and Lyly reached the docks.

"We're off to the Red Lion" Edward called as he and Lyly climbed aboard, Lyly finding it harder to set his balance as the choppy waves of an incoming tide mixed with the river's flow to jostle their boat side to side.

"The Red Lion it be," the rower said as he glanced over his shoulder and used his oar to push off the ramp.

Their rower held his course in the shifting current by alternately rowing with one oar and then the other. "Would you lads have a yen to strut your feathers with a lady?" he asked, winking and glancing toward the shore when his boat found a steady channel. "I can fetch you a good price in the offing."

"And what be your commission?" Edward asked.

"For old or young?"

"Young, if we go," Lyly chimed in.

"You get more with old. You get experience."

"And clap and wrinkles."

"That be true. You get more for your purse."

Edward had ventured across the river before, though not for the ladies. He hoped to induce their charms without recompense and had not yet tasted the whores. It seemed, thus far, the ladies chased him without his having to pay, although he often wondered if they favored him for himself or for his title as Edward de Vere, the Seventeenth Earl of Oxford.

When he had prior crossed the Thames with Lyly and one or two of Gray's Inn upperclassman, the classmen favored the cock fights and bear bating, Those blood-spattering sports alternately fascinated and disgusted Edward, who switched between shielding his vision to staring wide-eyed as six sharp-fanged dogs trained for slaughter ripped a bear apart, charging the tethered animal and then backing beyond its reach to regain their courage before lunging again as the frightened bear stood on his hind legs and clawed the air in a frantic effort to knock a dog aside to save its life as one dog after the other emitted a high-pitched bark and charged in again as the crowd cheered, jeered, and jostled their hands in the air to place bets on how many dogs the bear would kill before succumbing itself.

How could humans inflict such cruelty on a lesser animal, Edward wondered when he first saw it. And yet, was not evil a natural part of being human, if not to engage, at least to observe from a safe distance? And did not that instinctive horror prompt ammunition for good drama? Was not evil, in a classic tragedy, oft the heart of the plot?

"One of these days." Edward said to Lyly, holding tight to his bench, "they shall drive *all* the plays from London, even the few allowed at the guild halls. If that be the case, Southwark should be a good spot to place them."

Once under the Tower Bridge, they set ashore downriver from Southwark, paid their fare, and waved down a horse-drawn carriage to covey them the final quarter league to the Red Lion Inn, but as Edward turned and stepped down from the carriage, a man with knife in hand lunged behind him.

CHAPTER 17

The Red Lion

"The poet's eye in a fine frenzy rolling."
Midsummer Night's Dream, V, 1

As Edward spun away from the knife, Lyly grabbed Edward's waistcoat and yanked him back. "Stand back from this," Lyly said. "'Tis not meant for you. Tis Knyvet he's after."

As Lyly and Edward stepped back, a long-armed man with a blade lunged at Knyvet, who sidestepping at the last second, allowed the man's momentum to sweep past him, whereupon he booted this attacker in the seat of the pants, sending him stumbling forward to catch his footing.

"Amazing grace," Edward said.

"A swordsman's dexterity," Lyly agreed. "He teaches fencing. He would mince that thief if a sword were in his hand."

Knyvet crouched and waved his fingers, daring the man to venture forth and try again. "You wish to cut my purse from me, my friend?" Knyvet grinned. "Come and try again. If you can take it, it be yours." The thief raised both hands in surrender and backed into the gathering crowd, then whirled and scurried away.

"Don't ever fight him," Lyly whispered to Edward "He's as good with his sword as his fists, and worse still with his temper."

Edward and Lyly walked up the back steps and found a rail bench directly across from Knyvet who nestled close to a woman whose tight bodice barely contained her ample bosom as she leaned toward him and whispered in his ear.

"Not his wife," Lyly said. "An acquaintance, no doubt. A city friend."

"He hath rather good taste."

"You should feast your eyes upon his niece, Nan Vavasor. A ravishing woman. More *your* age," Lyly smirked.

"And thus your meaning?"

"And thus I know your taste. They say she has a certain…."

"A certain…?"

"Spirit."

"Is that what they call it?"

"Whatever they call it, she has it."

A player appeared on stage from around a screen. He ambled to the center and awaited the audience to settle, then lifted a chalice in his right hand and a chunk of bread in his left, as if offering a feast instead of a performance.

"Ammunition," Lyly whispered. "If we throw a jibe or an apple, he is well armed to toss something back."

"We play a farce," the tall, lanky actor said, grinning at his words, two or three in the audience already snickering at the performance. "We tell a tale of brave Pyramus and sweet Thisbe. In our review, we add a dog, and clowns, and jugglers."

The audience jeered.

"Yet tragedy remains within our story," the actor said. "Poor Pyramus. In the depth of internal suffering, stabs himself. Then a wolf, played by our lively dog Penelope, eats Thisbe for lunch." He glanced toward the curtain. "Our DOG!… For LUNCH!"

Two hands held a white terrier out from behind the screen and dropped it onstage. The frightened dog glanced behind him, and then turned and scurried to middle stage, dragging a yellow rope-tail tied to his own.

"They gain attention," Edward whispered. "Yet lose their story."

"I believe they care not," Lyly said.

"Pyramus does stab himself," Edward said. "That part is true in Ovid's version. Yet in the story as Ovid tells it, a lioness mauled Thisbe, not a wolf."

"Clearly not Penelope then." Lyly grinned. "No dogs at all in *Metamorphoses.*"

"You have eaten Thisbe," the actor said, resting his fists on his hipbones and staring down at the dog.

Penelope cocked her head and glared up.

"I see by your teeth that you plan to eat me as well."

The actor reached inside a pouch and extracted a bit of meat wrapped in a cloth. "Do not devour me!" he called.

When the actor held the meat up and shook it, the dog hopped on its hind legs and barked. The audience roared. As the actor shuffled off and the dog followed, a paper-moon dangling from a fishing line swung out from behind the screen as a round-faced actor, his head and arms poking through three holes in a crate costume, waddled on stage. "I am a wall," he said, tapping the crate with his knuckles. "The moon shineth over me." He pointed to the moon hovering off-center on the stage.

"The moon shineth *over* him!" someone from the audience shouted. *"Over* him!"

When an arm reached forth to reposition the moon, the screen that backed the stage tilted forward and toppled, exposing two boys who glared at each other, then reset their screen and crawled around behind it.

"I *am* the wall," the actor repeated, tapping his chest-crate again.

A boy too tall to play the part of a woman stumbled onstage playing Thisbe, his pigtailed wig lopsided, his lips fattened with red paint. "I speak to my lover who resides behind this wall," he squealed in an exaggerated falsetto as several in the audience whistled and smacked their lips.

From behind the partition, a prompter called out every fifth or sixth line.

"We hear you! We hear you!" someone in the audience shouted.

The wall leaned forward, nearing toppling. "Oh!...... Oh!...... Oh!....," the wall kept repeating.

A half-eaten pear hurled toward the stage. The actor playing Thisbe caught it in his left hand, squeezed it, and flung it back as Penelope bolted and growled then leapt into the audience. Those in the front rows raised their elbows to protect their faces as several in the middle rows fell back.

Richard Burbage, the Red Lion's owner, rushed onstage, waiving his hands. "We have fireworks!" he yelled as a flare shot out from a side corridor, missed the center court and whirled toward Knyvet, who raised a stool and deflected the projectile while his consort covered her head and ducked below the railing.

"Knyvet is the better part of the show," Lyly laughed. "Burbage should compensate him."

Edward nodded agreement. "They bastardize Ovid's story, yet enliven it, though it would be far better played if written and acted well."

A few in the audience remained in the courtyard as the actors hopped off stage and dispersed inside the inn.

"How *would* you write what we just saw?" Lyly asked. "Would you make it comedy or a tragedy as Ovid intended?"

"It could be played as both," Edward said. "By holding true to the serious side, yet adding a comedy within to lighten the mood before it darkened again."

"I like that," Lyly said. "And thus draw laughter as your aim." He thought a moment. "Yet, there would be no point in writing a play. You could clearly not present it there." He notched his head back toward the Red Lion. "No earls could write for this or any other pubic stage."

"No earls," Edward said. "At least not as ourselves. Yet, if I wrote it, I could play it for the Queen. She enjoys plays and would love a farce. I have her ear."

"As I hear it, you have more than that," Lyly said.

"And you hear…?"

"You have her affection. I hear she is fond of you."

"I sense she is."

Edward reached Gray's Inn well after St. Peter's bell had struck the end of the dinner hour. He hid outside the gate to catch his breath and waited for the guard to nod to sleep. When the guard's head drooped, Edward grinned and slipped past, then screeched, "Yeehhhhhhhh!" as a finger and thumb grabbed his ear and twisted.

CHAPTER 18

The Muse

"When I hear sweet music."
Merchant of Venice, V, 1

Edward spent a fortnight shuffling plates, platters, tankards, and silver-rimmed bowls from the fire-heated cook-yard down sixteen rows of tables that patiently awaited Gray's Inn dining room door to fling open to a hoard of famished students ready to devour everything edible, then leave their devastation for Edward and two undercooks to clear and reset for the next disaster.

Yet, Edward did not mind. While his body hustled betwixt the hall and yard, his imagination spun on Caesar, Helen of Troy, Brut Arthur and a dozen other mythical characters and ancient histories, including the Red Lion's inane rendition of one of Ovid's stories performed as *The Temper of the Moon*. At least the Red Lion's *Moon* was a departure from the usual morality plays. Still, it remained distant from the art a play might be, including Edward's early effort that he had written and acted for the Queen on her visit to Hedingham. Why not please Her Majesty again, Edward thought, as he and Lyly had discussed? *The Temper of the Moon*, inept under Burbage, clearly held the elements of drama. He could certainly create a better rendition than the Red Lion's inane and unintended farce.

As Edward waved his scrubstone in the air, he mouthed lines and speeches as they occurred to him. He thought to pen a play of myth, mirth, and confusion, loosely following Ovid's tale yet adding to it. He would write of a marriage planned by day, uncertain in its love at night. He would set a wedding at a duke's castle, yet both betrothed would be uncertain of their love, neither having chosen their partner.

"They dream of who they truly love," Edward mumbled as he scrubbed. "Who they *might* love would speak to them in dreams at night, whist doubts and recriminations would consume their thoughts by day.

Whaaaaappp!

A spoon whacked the back of Edward's skull. "Yaiiippp!" He whirled around and dropped a pot as the kitchen master scowled down at him.

"You have struck an earl," Edward said as he straightened and rubbed the back of his head.

"At Gray's, my friend, you be a student, and a cook's helper as punishment. Scrub harder and hold your mutterings to yourself."

His two-week kitchen stint was passing quickly. Exhausted at night, characters, plots, and lines still twisted in his dreams, then accompanied him to the cook yard in the mornings, where he half-wrote the play in his head as he scoured, washed and set table. Two acts had fully formed by the time Gray's headmaster restored him to full privileges.

"I hope you've learned your lesson," the headmaster said.

He had -- watch his time more closely when next he escaped.

With Saturdays and Sundays allowed as time off for midlevel students, Edward spent the next three weekends hunched over a desk in a corner of one of Burghley's upper rooms with quill in hand. Lyly, excited about Edward's project, rushed up the stairs to join his friend whenever he could escape, napping sporadically while Edward wrote or stood to pace to act a part with gestures. "I shall enliven the tale with fairies and animals," he told Lyly.

Lyly, half awake, rolled his eyes and moaned.

"Let's see... I shall name them... Ordinary names for the court characters. But for our dream sequence, names to suit a dream, that our audience would take as fanciful, as dreams are want to be."

He straddled his chair, lifted his quill, and wrote.

"Toppsy Tervey... No... From bottom to top... *Bottom*... I shall call one character Bottom and make him an ass, so Bottom is well suited to the part."

As names revealed themselves, he listed and read them aloud for sound. "Theseus, then," he said to himself, not much caring if Lyly was listening or not. "Theseus being the legendary King of Athens, I shall leave him as he stands in Ovid's *Metamorphoses.* Theseus shall be our Duke's name then, which should please the Queen who will see herself in him... Then Hippolyta, betrothed to Theseus... Now, as to the players, we have Bottom, our ass. I shall play him as a donkey, a real ass... Lyly, what do you think?"

Lyly glanced up. "You speak to me?"

"Who else is in the room?"

"Several. I do not see them, yet I hear them jabber."

"You are of little help."

"I inspire you by being the poorer writer."

"Slower, not poorer... *Snug!*" Edward said.

"What?"

"Snug and Bottom. I shall add Snug, which would make the four Flute, Snout, Snug, and Bottom."

"'Tis a mouthful"

"These be the characters in our dream sequence. Their names do speak their flavor. The audiences shall stretch a smile, if not a laugh, by their names alone."

Lyly yawned as Edward jotted.

"As to the fairies, there is room for playfulness here as well." He penned several possibilities, scratching out two and leaving four -- Cobweb, Peasblossom, Moth, Mustardseed -- thinking to add others as needed.

With his rough characters in place and Ovid's myth as plot, the rest quickly filled to scenes.

Act I, Scene I. Theseus' palace, Athens
Enter Theseus, Hippolyta, and attendants.

Theseus: Now, fair Hippolyta, our nuptial hour
Draws apace, four happy days bring
Another moon. But, methinks, how slow

The old moon wanes! She lingers my desires
Like to a step-dame or a dowager,
Long withering out a younger man's revenue.

Hippolyta: Four days will quickly steep themselves
in night,
Four nights quickly dream this time away.

That be our story's beginning. Its setting and its time. Now a second scene, still Act I. Lysander and Hermia will be the characters on stage, the two whose love will switch, as love can do, then later reunite. A play can do what life cannot -- contrive a clear ending, and a happy one at that.

Enter Lysander.

Lysander: Ay for aught that I could ever read,
Could ever hear by tale or history,
The course of true love never did run
smooth,
But either it was different in blood,
In war, death, or sickness did lay it to a
siege,
Making momentary as a sound,
Swift as shadow, short as any dream,
Brief as lightning in the collied night,
That, in a spleen, unfolds both heaven and
on earth,
And ere a man hath power to say,
'Behold!'
The jaws of darkness do devour it.
So quickly bright things come to be
confusion.

"You have a sour view of love *and* life," Lyly muttered, sitting up and leaning back against the wall.

"'Tis struggle makes the story."

"You have your characters, your opening lines. But who shall play them?"

"I have in mind the Blackfriar Boys. They have acted for the Queen before and would relish the opportunity again. Yet we still need a bit of magic to bring a sparkle to our story."

"Isn't *all* love magic? A trick? A ruse? A slight of heart and other body parts?"

"We shall have the fairies apply their magic to make the lovers switch, as the gods accomplished in Ovid." Edward glanced toward the window. "We need a chief fairy to do the deed... I have it... *Puck* from our mythical Robin Goodfellow, our ancient legendary Hobgoblin. And why *not* Puck? Our audience would know him from their tales as children. They would understand our fabled Puck as clearly mischievous and magical. I shall have him use his powers to confuse the lovers when they wake, so they fall in love with who at first they see, be it man, woman, or animal."

"Tis a lot to play with there."

"Then switch them back to clear thinking so we have our happy ending and thus our comedy. I shall have a character to introduce and set the story before our play begins."

Edward thought a second, then wrote.

> Actor (yet unnamed): Our play is the most lamentable comedy and most cruel death of Pyramus and Thisbe. Yet, 'tis just a play to be enjoyed.

"You expect they'll believe the magic?" Lyly asked.

"We'll suspend belief, as in dreams, for the truth that lies within. If we present at court, even poorly, they shan't have pears or apples to throw at us. They'll employ silence and stares to fling their daggers at our players' hearts."

"A play, once writ, after absorbing the sweat and ink that gave it life, breathed or died on its own," Edward wrote after Lyly left, then shoved his pages aside, dropped his head to his desk and slept.

CHAPTER 19

The Queen's Pleasure

"The wheel has come full circle."
King Lear, V, 3

While studying at Grays Inn, not far from Burghley House, Edward spent weekends and summers at his ward masters home. On a bright Saturday morning, after a breakfast of porkshank and poached quail eggs, Edward invited his wardmaster for a walk in Burghley's garden, hoping that a full stomach and the aroma of the Chief Minister's prized roses might sweeten his normally sour disposition.

"I have set a play to words," Edward said, striding next to Burghley along a row of budding roses.

"In Latin, I should hope. From Golding's tutoring."

"In my own words. In the Queen's English."

Burghley turned and stiffened his backbone. "The Queen's English could be put to better use."

"I wish Her Majesty to see it."

"I think not… You never admitted switching this," the Chief Minister said, standing over the center rose bush and pointing down.

"I received my penalty without complaint. Is that not admission?… I wish to please her. To put her to amusement."

"She has fools enough for that." Burghley bent over a rose and gently brushed a speck of dirt from a pedal. "Why seek my permission?" he said as he stood. "You see her often. I am certain you have your own means of persuasion."

"I wish to surprise her. Not as to the play, as to its author. She will see the author when it's writ and I introduce it. "

"She already wastes too much time in frivolous pursuits."

"My play urges marriage."

Burghley raised himself to his full height. Edward knew his wardmaster would relish anything that might urge the Queen to marriage and bring her to issue.

"'Tis a comedy to show the fickleness of love," Edward told him. "That marriage rests on higher purpose." He twisted truth, although it wouldn't matter. Burghley rarely attended plays and would squelch them all if he could.

"Do not put this to favor, yet if an opportunity arises, I shall broach the subject."

The subject thus broached and accepted, the opportunity to perform flowered on Monday, the 14th of May in the Year of Our Lord 1568, the day of the spring festival. Edward had rightly sensed the Queen could not resist a play, especially one urged by her Chief Minister. His reasons alone would intrigue her.

Edward recruited the Blackfriar Boys, a traveling theater group that had performed for selected audiences at the guildhalls and the court, and were rightly eager to present for the Queen again. The players learned their parts with delight and laughed at all of Edward's Snug and Bottom jokes -- a good omen.

With the stage set in the chamber outside Whitehall's west dining hall, Edward hid behind a folding screen as the Queen arrived, followed by her entourage, all those present bowing to the Her Majesty and awaiting her to sit. When the audience settled, Edward drew a breath, opened the side curtain, and crossed to the center. "Majesty," he bowed. "Our boys present a play of fortune and misfortune. Of love that flies on fickle wings, then flits off again at whim. But I shall let the tale unwind as the players play it."

Edward adjusted their collars and costumes and shuffled his players out on cue, occasionally peeking at the audience and, in the Act V, seeing the audience in tears through the wedding scene. The boys acted well, Bottom wearing his donkey ears as if unaware that he had grown them, the Wall playing the Wall without embellishment, which made him out the bigger fool. The innuendo amused the Queen. The play's bawdiness brought her to laughter. The boys had drawn their audience into the story and wrung emotion from them.

In the final scene, Puck, alone onstage, surveyed the room and spoke his final lines. "Whilst these visions did appear," he said, and then paused in good dramatic fashion. "Yet seen in this weak and idle theme, no more yielding than a dream that any one might have. 'Tis ended as a wakeful dream. As I, your servant Puck, shall leave you to you bed and to your own dreams."

Puck's charm and stage demeanor had worked its magic as he turned and slowly sauntered off, lifting the Queen and the audience from their seats, ready to follow, only to realize they *were* spectators, that Puck's dream *had* drawn them in. When the Queen applauded, all hands followed as the actors returned to the stage and took their bows.

"Playwright," the Queen called.

Edward shuffled back out and bowed to his Queen, and then to his audience and his players, just as he had at Hedingham those many years ago.

"I shall have a word with the playwright," the Queen said, dismissing her entourage whilst Edward's players doffed their costumes and retired to the antechamber for biscuits and cider.

"If your father were here he would have banged his fist on this one," the Queen said.

"As he did at Hedingham?"

"John would have bristled and then winked. You've come a long way, though you still mock your Queen."

"Mock Your Majesty?... Me?"

"In a playful way with your grounds for marriage."

"If love be fickle, why should you, or anyone, marry for a fickle reason?"

"Marry for county, then?" she asked. "Should that be the cause for matrimony?"

"Whatever reason chosen seems to have its weakness."

"Why not marry for love, then?" she asked. "Is it not as good a reason as any?"

"Love is not always what it seems. Least of all to lovers. And what it once seemed doth change as lovers change and come to know each other."

"You are wise beyond your youth. Do *you* believe love is fickle?"

"Passion is."

"At seventeen years, you have experienced this?"

"Seventeen is the height of passion. I see love flick from flower to flower, landing where it will, then flitting off again when next it spots a blossom whose nectar fills the air."

"You *are* aware of my predicament," she said.

"Certain European royalty wish to marry you."

"They don't give a farthing for me. They wish to breed me. An ass would do so long as it be a male ass that they could harness to produce a male hier."

"Is there no one you love?"

"There is an ass or two scurrying about, though none I love or wish to marry. Beyond that, no real man could deal with a queen as wife. He would be the butt of jokes. Grist for one of your plays."

"None of mine, though it would make good comedy."

"There *is* Alençon, who sails from France to court me."

"I have heard he cares for you."

"Would Alençon, by coincidence, be the ass in your play? Your Bottom? And me the one who succumbs to an ass by magic?"

"Madam... I..."

"You are bright, with many talents. If I were younger, I might court you myself. Some say I do already, despite our ages."

"You are queen and a fine looking woman. They say you could possess any man you wish."

She raised her eyebrows. "They *say* that?"

"Well, perhaps not *all* they say."

She laughed. "You always were one to speak your mind... I've not laid eyes on Alençon. They say he resembles a frog."

"Some frogs are comely. Better than an ass."

The Queen leaned back and examined Edward head to toe. "Perhaps I *shall* marry you then. 'Twould be better than an ass or a frog."

"By at least a snort or a croak."

"It might solve my piglet problem, yet 'twould devastate my foreign policy. I shall entertain the frog. Diplomacy requires it... Keep to your writing. Are you working on others?"

"I am polishing an idea for a Prince of Denmark to deflect the tale from our court should others see it placed there."

"And *does* it find its place there?"

"If others see their shadows, let them determine if it fits their body."

"You are always one for edging on the shadow side. Plays not well considered are oft mistaken in their meaning."

"Or taken *without* mistake."

"And yet, in the right circumstance, they might yet serve a purpose beyond mere entertainment."

"To what end?"

"To serve England."

CHAPTER 20

Blood

"Green in judgment, cold in blood"
Antony and Cleopatra, I, 5

. Edward had seen Anne Burghley half naked on several occasions, stealing furtive glimpses whist passing by her room, her door oft left ajar. Her thin legs and small breasts more amused than aroused him. He enjoyed making sport of her boyish figure knowing she detested it. On one occasion, after dressing and preparing to leave for the city, he spied her naked as he passed her room, her head cocked, leaning back before her looking glass, examining her breasts.

"You look too much upon them," he called from the doorway.

She whirled around and covered herself with her arms.

"As a pot doth not boil if watched too close," he said, "too much eye doth stunt thy growth."

"You!" She grabbed a pillow with one hand and flung it at him, landing short.

"Ahh! A pillow joust." He raised his arms in mock protection.

Forgetting she was bare, she clinched her fists to charge him, then stopped and retreated to wrap a spread around her.

"The jouster withdraws to the bastions," he teased, lowering his shoulders and rushing her. He grabbed her by her tiny waist, lifted her kicking and swinging, and tossed her onto her bed, then jumped in behind, hissing like a snake as he lowered his head and crawled toward her.

"I shall tell father."

"Tell him what?... That I tickled you?... That I tickled you *here?*" He ran a fingernail down the arch of her right foot, bowing it in.

"Stop that!" she giggled.

"Or *here?*" When he ran a knuckle down the crook of her leg, she flattened her palms and pounded his chest. To stop her, he shifted atop her chest and pinned her down. *"Well,* little girl? What now?"

"I am *not* a little girl."

"You *are* little."

"What *am* I to you?

"A little sister."

She wiggled free, slithered back to the head of the bed and pulled a spread across her upper portion. "I do not wish to be *anyone's* little sister."

"Then I shall be your tickler."

She sprung up and swung at him, dropping the spread to reveal herself again. They wrestled until she drew the spread across again and they both flopped back in a fit of laugher, in the midst of which, a noise alerted Edward -- a cough or a wheeze. He sat up and brought a finger to his lips. Then he heard a sniffle as if someone tried to snuff a sneeze. "I do believe we have a rat among us," he said, eyeing a tapestry with an unnatural bulge poking forth hanging on the furthest wall. "I think your father sends a mole to spy upon us." He slid a knife he always carried with him from its sheath.

"Edward, be careful."

"I merely mean to frightened him. To take his measure and send him scurrying back to your father."

He slipped from Anne's bed and crept across the room, suddenly aware that the bulge might hold a weapon of its own. The bulge jerked. Anne screamed. Edward lunged. His knife slit the fabric and sunk into an unexpected softness. He withdrew his weapon, its point dripping blood. He must have wounded the culprit. "Bastard Burghley," he muttered.

Anne rushed over and clutched Edward's shoulder as the tapestry ripped from the wall, revealing a man that Edward knew, one of Burghley's cooks. The man gripped the fabric a long moment, and then buckled and slithered to the floor.

"Good Lord, Edward!" Anne yelled. You've killed him!"

"No. He is merely wounded."

"He *is* dead!" Anne cried. "Or else dying!" She stooped and pressed her palm on the man's chest, the pressure forcing out blood that stained the cook's shirt.

****

The Chief Minister, perhaps recognizing his complicity in sending a spy to tempt his own death, was more conciliatory than Edward deserved or had the right to expect. Beyond that, Burghley did not wish to compromise his daughter in testimony. When he convened the required inquiry, the six judges -- three of whom owed Burghley favor -- ruled the stabbing accidental, Burghley having implied in his written statement that the unfortunate cook caused his own demise by inadvertently falling onto Edward's knife.

Nonetheless, in the quiet of his room, Edward realized that his playfulness his "frivolity," as his mother often called it had killed a man. He had never felt guiltier, and thus far, had never had more reason.

CHAPTER 21

The Chase

"Show me the steep and thorny way to heaven."
Hamlet, I, 3

Sunlight streamed through tall aspens as Edward's horse stirred air though the stillness of the woods. A shadow darted across the trail ahead of him, followed by two others in quickly succession. He dug his stirrups in and galloped in their direction. As the trail widened, a glint of metal sparkled through thick brushes to his left. When he flicked his reins he thought he caught a glimpse of crimson and cream, the Tudor colors. He dug his horse in harder but soon lost his prey.

He held still and looked about, then cupped his ears, and slowly turned his head and listened. When nothing further stirred, he trotted up a small rise and dismounted, hoping for a better view, but heard neither birds, nor wind, nor any other sound. His quarry must have found a hole and burrowed inside. When he dismounted and turned to untie a flask from his saddle, a blade eased across his throat tight enough to slit his Adam's apple should he swallow.

"Your business?" a voice whispered.

"Out... for... a... ride," he gasped.

"A rider who follows a rabbit is either a fool or after the rabbit."

"Fool then," Edward said.

The heal of a boot caught the small of his back, spun him around and shoved him a safe distance away. Three armed men glared at him -- the one with the knife closest in, the other two, their swords drawn, far enough apart that rushing one would leave the other unscathed. Without further word, they escorted him down a hidden path and around a mound of grass where the Queen sat on a blanket, grinning up at him, her riding cap tied beneath her chin.

"Come. Join us," she said. "We are having a picnic. There is far more here than I could ever eat."

"Whatever pleases Your Majesty."

"Sit beside me then. *That* would please me. There are not many who would dare and even fewer I would invite."

When Edward glanced over his shoulder, his escorts had disappeared.

"They are not far off," she said, following his glance. "They take good care of me and hold my secrets with their life."

"And what secrets *be* they?"

"If I told, they would not be secret, would they?… Come… Sit. " She patted the blanket next to her. "The maids will serve us when I call."

He sat facing her and crossed his legs.

"Now," she said. "What of this chase with your Queen as prey? Do you still chase boars as you once did at Hedingham?"

"My Queen is hardly a boar. She is far more complicated."

"And more comely, I should hope."

"Very much more comely and clearly more difficult to catch."

"Such difficulty would not sway a skillful hunter."

"And if *you* were the hunter?" Edward asked. "How would you catch a queen?"

"That would take great cleverness, though I think could be done. I was taught to hunt at Hatfield, before they thought of me as queen." She looked down and straightened a fold in the blanket. "We had picnics by the lake then," she said, looking up again. "There were guards, of course, but no boys. Myself and my nursemaids and a few other girls only. Now that I am Queen, I suppose I can have a man at a picnic if I choose. A young man. Still, we have guards, though they be blind by pledge and loyalty. What harm could a young man be?"

"What harm could *any* man be? There are many who would picnic with you if they could."

"And stab me in the back while doing so."

"Or steal your heart. Every eligible prince worth his title desires your company and many would have your heart."

"I am married to England. She is a jealous husband and taskmaster."

"All those suitors. *Any* would be lucky."

"I'm getting too old."

"Your eyes, your hair the color of a golden sunset, your fair complexion, all belie your age."

"Would *you* have me then? If I were not your Queen? Simply as a woman?"

"I would have the woman *and* the Queen. I would not hold your station against you. But your taskmaster? *That* I would never be."

She laughed. "But today you shall be. Today 'tis *my* duty to serve."

When Elizabeth clapped twice, maids appeared from the woods carrying boards of minced meats, sliced apples, pears, breads, and cheeses on small wooden platters they arrayed in a semi-circle at the foot of the blanket, then bowed and departed. As soon as they left, the Queen lifted an apple slice in one hand and a sliver of cheese in the other. When Edward leaned forward and opened his mouth, she stuffed both in a once. "There," she said. "That is all you'll get from me."

He choked and chewed. "Far more than I deserve," he said when he was able.

"At least for now," she added.

****

As Edward and the Queen relaxed together and engaged in quiet conversation, the seething danger that had long brewed in the north overflowed the border. Mary Queen of Scots, Elizabeth's cousin, climbed down a rope ladder from her Holyrood Palace in Edinburgh, hooded and cloaked as an ordinary maiden, and slipped out of Scotland into England near the village of Glencastle in the darkness of night on the May 14th in the Year of Our Lord 1568.

The Queen of Scots had finally so infuriated her subjects that she was forced to flee. The Scots had reluctantly tolerated her marriage to Lord Darnley, a drunkard, although they found some sympathy for Darnley after the Queen's lover, the Earl of Bothwell, killed Darnley, strangling him in Holyrood Castle's courtyard after Darnley managed to escape an explosion Bothwell set for him inside the castle. To add injury to murder, the Queen immediately married her husband's murderer, thus further inciting her subjects. Yet, even in the midst of her unpopularity, Mary still managed to outflank Elizabeth in one crucial matter -- she had produced a healthy son and heir, James. The Scotts snatched James from Mary's grasp before she fled, whereupon they hoped for more stability and less intrigue with James as ruler and a regent in charge until he came of age.

The same mindless fear that drives a terrified mouse scurrying from one hungry cat to the next sent Mary straight into Elizabeth's clutches. English forces captured the Scottish queen cowering behind a stack of hay in the corner of a barn in Bithberton, a mere six leagues south of where she crossed the border. Elizabeth was hardly Mary's loving cousin. The two had never met and Burghley's spies had carried back ill report regarding Mary's disposition and seditious intent. The Scottish Queen should have expected little sympathy-- and perhaps did -- preferring confinement in England to imprisonment in her homeland.

Elizabeth, on Burghley's advice, placed Mary in custody at Sheffield Castle. Yet the question remained, did Mary's captivity in England hold and protect the very devil Elizabeth most feared -- a Scottish Queen who had vowed to wrench England back to Catholicism and place Elizabeth's crown on her own head? Now that Mary was in English hands, was she a step closer to the English throne barely wide enough for one? The forces that wished to seat a Catholic monarch now had a body they could scoop up and pluck down on the English throne, when and if, of course, that chair was empty.

CHAPTER 22

Playing at Death

"Heaven take my soul, and England my bones."
King John, IV, 3

The smell of roasted pig and the sweat of horses permeated an air already saturated with the scent of danger. Stallions neighed and stomped damp earth as maids and maidens giggled and stretched their necks for a better view of the men who tightened straps and adjusted armor in front of the jousting tents. Some knights would prance away unscathed this day, their breastplates unscratched, their purses full, while others would be carried off the field with their pride and metal dented, some with fractured arms or legs to match their broken spirits.

With knights and steeds upon the field instead of actors on the stage, the joust, for Edward, provided as much, or more, drama as any stage performance. Both stirred excitement and emotion, the tiltyard nonetheless, the more dangerous of the two.

Edward's mother was right, a knight's position as the defender of the castle had long passed with his father's generation, although Edward would never concede her as much. He had hardly spoken to the woman since her abrupt marriage to Sir Giles, on whose property Edward's father had died under mysterious circumstance.

The skills once required in defense of lands and castle had fallen to mere sport. Yet maids and maidens -- those delicate creatures no longer in needed of a knight's protection -- still enjoyed the manly combat the joust provided. They wallowed in anticipation, leaning forward or standing at the moment of the charge, their ears cocked toward the pounding of hooves, their eyes dilated at armor gleaming in the sun, awaiting the clash of metal and the grunts of men and the whining of horses. The pretense of death stirred their juices. They averted their glance at the first spill of blood, yet encouraged their favorites to battle with the perfumed handkerchiefs they laid upon extended lances.

On the day of Edward's run, a festive crowd of merchants and craftsmen poured out from the city at dawn, hoping to shake a few coins loose from those attending. The tradesmen were accompanied by an assorted mix of students from the inns escaping the drudgery of their studies to feast their eyes upon half-exposed bodices, seamen flowing up from the docks and out through Bishopsgate, ladies-of-the-night seeking daytime customers, and pickpockets grinning as they shook their hands to loosened their fingers in anticipation of a profitable afternoon. As the assemblage gathered and the joust approached, onlookers jostled each other for viewing room while nibbling sweetbreads, chestnuts, and roasted apples, and anxiously savored a chance to glimpse royalty even at a distance -- the Queen and her entourage entering up a private ramp at the rear of the viewing stand.

"Tis a lively crowd," Lyly said, peaking through Edward's tent flap as Edward prepared for his run.

"The sight of blood draws the best and the worst," Edward said, sitting on a stool as his squires suited him up, "the brave *and* the foolish."

"Which do you consider yourself?" Lyly asked, dropping the flap and entering.

"Brave if I win," Edward said, sucking in his stomach in to allow his steward to tighten the threaded waistband around his belly. "A fool if I end up on my arse."

After having stripped naked, Edward's skin had been oiled with goose grease, and then powdered with lavender and layered with a thin-clothed undergarment. A flexible garment of interlaced rings was laid upon that to keep his armor from scratching and pinching, and that overlaid with a breastplate and then, working down, a vambrance, tassets, cruisse, an upper and lower poelyn, double-hinged knee-wings and metal foot stirrups. The hinged metal gloves and helmet were held for last. Fully armored, Lyly and a steward squatted at Edward's sides and helped him to his feet.

"A tortoise out of water," Henry Howard stuck his head inside the tent and laughed as he entered. "But once on your horse, a different matter."

"If I can *get* on my horse."

"They will haul you up."

"Let them tie me in it then."

"Disallowed or they would... You've drawn Hatton as Red Knight," Howard said. "I think he bribed them. He wishes to knock you from your saddle."

"And off my high horse with the Queen watching. He desires to replace me in her favor."

"She has many favorites. She flits from petal to petal."

"What mean you by that?"

"Simply that she uses her charm for political increase, as a Queen should. You spend more than your share of time with her. Others are jealous."

Edward shrugged inside his armored suit.

"Be careful of Hatton. He is older and more experienced. One sharp blow, well placed and..."

"He may have experience, but a lance is heavy and age doth weaken him."

"See that you hold your own lance as high as your bravado. And look to the stands. I have brought a visitor to watch you win or lose."

"Oh."

"Nan Vavasor. Whom we have kept well hidden in the north till she has fully ripened. Why pick the fruit until its ready? I shall have her wave to you. If you still be on your feet when it is over, I will introduce you at the masque."

The trumpet's call-to-quarters stiffened Edward as Howard and Lyly balanced him outside the tent, where a horseman held the reins of an armored roan.

"Hatton charges straight and even," Howard warned. "Deflect with your shield should you miss with your lance."

Edward hauled one foot into a stirrup as Lyly and Howard boosted him into the saddle. At a second trumpet blast, the horseman led him to the edge of the arena. Once there, he awaited the final entrance call, then trotted to the starting gate and pulled his reins in. Edward, as White Knight, faced Hatton as Red, each flying their colors from their helmets.

The tiltmaster lifted a palm, glanced to the riders, and signaled to Hatton. With more tournament wins, Hatton galloped to the center of the stands, and wheeled his horse about to face the Queen, Burghley and Anne sitting to Her Majesty's right, and Robert Dudley, the Earl of Leicester, stiffly in place to her left.

Hatton lowered his lance toward the Queen. She acknowledged his gesture with a nod and placed a handkerchief upon his lance point, whereupon he raised his weapon and let the scarf slide down, then slipped it off and tucked it under his horse's sash.

"He butters her like cake," Edward's thought.

Edward nudged his mount forward. If the Queen curried favorites, he could as well, and well within her sight. He pranced to the center, whirled around toward the stands, dipped his weapon, then swung its point left to Anne Burghley who bobbed in her seat and scrambled for a scarf. As she nervously laid it on Edward's tip, a striking presence drew Edward's eyes toward a comely face and fetching body leaning forward in the stand next to Henry Howard just below and to the right of the Queen. Nan Vavasor, no doubt -- the maiden Howard had described with such tempting delight.

Before Edward could shake loose of her presence, his horse took charge and led them back to his start, where his squire handed him his helmet. He slid it on, flipped his visor down, and squinted though its horizontal slits, the sun instantly breaking a sweat across his forehead. Thus encased, he felt oddly safe, as though nothing, or no one, could penetrate to harm him. Much like England, he thought, falsely secure across the channel divide.

He struggled to restrain his mount from bolting as the tiltmaster elevated his hand, hesitated, and then chopped the air, drawing the crowd to a frenzy and sending Edward's mount galloping toward Hatton's lance as Edward raised himself high in his stirrups, leaned forward and blinked to clear his vision. He jammed his elbow against his lance-brace and tried to hold the weapon steady along the horizon as he squeezed his knees against his horse's ribs prepared to land a strike or take one. The roar of the crowd echoed inside his helmet, thunder rumbled past, both lances missed.

He pulled in his reins, flipped them about, and swung his horse around to face his opponent. His mount, weighed down by armor, panted heavily through flared nostrils as the tiltmaster raised his hand a second time. Edward steadied his lance. The crowd hushed. The tiltmaster sliced the air. Edward kicked. His horse lowered its head, tightened its hindquarters, and charged. Edward, his eyes blinded by sweat, aimed toward the sound of pounding hooves as he floated high in his saddle. Fire slammed his chest, reeling him back. He spun around and wobbled, then shoved his heels in to grab and take hold. His horse whirled left, twisting its head ahead of its body.

"Hang on!" a voice yelled. "You near felled him!"

"What!" Edward's voice echoed inside his chamber. Hands from someone on a ladder lifted his visor and poured wine down his gullet. "Aim lower!" When Edward chanced a glance toward the crowd, reds and yellows blurred in billowing streams across a blinding sky. His visor slammed down again. A slap startled his horse. The animal bolted and lurched forward.

Edward squeezed his ankles hard against his horse's belly. He sucked in air and dipped his lance. He raced ahead at a steady gallop then tightened his grip and squeezed his elbows. He waited. Hooves pounded. Metal clashed. A collision jolted his spine and whiplashed his neck. His horse shrieked, then whirled about and sprinted forward as Edward lifted his faceplate to a deafening roar. As his vision cleared, he glimpsed two of Hatton's squires lifting their fallen knight and wrapping their arms beneath his shoulders as they lugged him off the field.

"You've won!" Lyly cried. "You beat the bastard!"

Edward slumped in his saddle.

After a round of awards and ribbons, the Queen and her entourage adjourned to prepare for the evening's masque at Richmond Court, while Edward and those combatants still able to walk squatted in the river and let the water wash across their bodies as they scoured sweat from their faces and soaked their wounds before resting in their jousting tents, recalling victory won or lost.

When Edward awoke and sprang up, he was uncertain where he was. Then pain struck his lower ribs rushing his memory back. He *had* won. He had taken Hatton and had the bruises to prove it, although he had little memory of how he had accomplished that. Never mind. Victory to the victor, much of life a coincidence, like a word spoken at an opportune moment, or a lance jabbed or mis-jabbed, the point either hitting or missing its intended target.

Edward stood slowly and stretched the stiffness from his joints, then left his tent to dress and ready himself for the evening's festivities.

CHAPTER 23

Disguise and Overture

> "Love looks not with the eyes,
> But with the mind,
> And therefore is winged cupid
> Painted blind"
> *A Midsummer's Night Dream, I, 5*

The Queen's pearl earrings swayed and teased her neck as she laughed and watched her courtiers cavort behind the thinly veiled innocence of masks. Edward, the day's champion, lowered the half-faced mask of a white-beaked eagle, swallowed the pain in his ribs, and nodded to the Queen as he held a maiden's hand high as she twirled beneath his arm. Hatton, hidden behind a lion's mask, slumped on a stool in a corner, his elbows on his knees, his head resting in his palms.

Edward watched a lady-in-waiting whisper something in the Queen's ear, drawing her laughter. When the lutes began a line-dance, Elizabeth rose and stepped onto the floor, lifting her dress to ankle-length and snapping her fingers. As she spun and danced toward the end of the hall, she turned and extended a hand to Hatton, who bolted up at the Queen's gesture, and then rose to her invitation, whereupon they danced, both light on their feet as if the Queen's graciousness had eased his pain and raised his spirits. The other guests -- a hundred-fifty elves, imps, goblins, fairies, and assorted creatures - stared at the odd couple, averting their eyes when the Queen glanced in their direction.

"They move well together," Edward's partner remarked when the music stopped and Hatton bowed and kissed the Queen's hand.

"Only fair, I should say," Edward replied, and then sucked his belly in, leveled his shoulders and marched through the crowd that cleared a path before him. "Your eagle has come to roost," he said when he stood before Elizabeth. Without looking directly at him, she reached behind to a maid who handed her an ostrich mask. She covered her face and turned toward him.

"Your Majesty," Edward said.

"*Majesty?* I see no royalty here. Only birds and dancers. Have you come to fly or dance?"

"Whatever your Ladyship desires."

"Then dance with abandon. You are the day's victor. Let us see if you prance as well on your feet as you do on your horse."

At the Queen's nod, the lutes began a bassa and the couples on the floor twirled and shifted in unison, each reaching out to touch their partner's hand at arm's length, then backing off in a perpetual in-and-out motion, unwilling to fully join, yet reluctant to part, as the Eagle and the Ostrich eyed each other though their masks. When the lutes quickened the pace, the other dancers moved aside and opened the center as the two birds swirled and spun until the Ostrich clutched the Eagle's forearm to steady herself and they laughed and held each other to keep from falling.

"Her Majesty...," the Ostrich spread her fingers above her breasts to quiet her breathing. "My Queen," she began again. "She tells me... Just a moment... She tells me you do *many* things well... You dance. You write. You play a fair game of chess. Where else might your talents lay?"

"Where would you like them to lay?"

The Ostrich thought. "I shall have to ask my Queen of that," she said. "When next we meet."

When the Ostrich bowed to Edward and withdrew, Edward glanced about in search of Nan Vavasor, hoping to meet her as Howard had promised, yet saw her naught. As the pain in his ribs stabbed him again, he determined to abandon the masque for a good night's sleep when a page slipped up behind and handed him a wax-sealed envelope. As soon as the page departed, Edward broke the seal and read the note.

The Ostrich wishes to see the Eagle in her quarters to curl and lay upon her nest. An eagle should not refuse an Ostrich of rank.

CHAPTER 24

A Dangerous Offer

"The evil men do lives after them."
Julius Caesar, III, 2

"Nan?" Henry Howard asked when he and Edward next met, as Howard slid his right foot back and parried left, deflecting Edward's sword. "She took ill just after the joust and begged to leave. I'm sure the two of you shall have a chance meet in the future. At present, we have more important matters to discuss."

"Court politics, no doubt," Edward groaned, loosening his wrists to better balance his sword. "I have little interest in politics or intrigue."

"There is fire burning in the north," Howard said. "All of England could be swept up in its flames should they burn their way south."

"You stab a colorful phrase. I shall have to use that in one of my plays."

Howard lunged. "Nero fiddled while Rome burned."

"As to say *I* write when I should engage?" Edward sidestepped and asked.

"We need your effort, not your distraction."

Edward attacked, driving Howard back. "How is *that* for effort?"

Howard dropped his point and threw his free hand up. "You play at fencing as at all else. If you would accept the least responsibility, perhaps you could prevent an impending disaster. You are in a position to…" Howard stopped and shook his head. "Walk with me."

They left the fencing yard and ambled along a shoulderhigh hedge that separated Whitehall from the homes of ambassadors, diplomats, and courtiers that stretched down Mulberry Row and two roads beyond. "With danger swirling about," Howard said, "'tis time you took matters seriously and made your stand as I have."

Edward halted and glared at his uncle. "Not stands. *Schemes.*"

"Call them what you will. They are still most urgent."

They strolled again.

Edward respected his ten-year-older uncle. He admired Howard's flare, his style, and even his religious certainly. Yet, even while Edward's northern relatives held to their Catholic religion, Edward's father had supported the Protestant Crown. Howard and his friends would topple that delicate balance in hope of swinging the ensuing chaos to their favor.

"You are near of age now," Howard said. "And will soon come into your own."

"I *am* into my own."

"You are still under Burghley's thumb, as everyone knows."

"Under his watch. Not his thumb."

"Precisely my point. We need someone to keep a close eye on the Queen's Chief Minister. Someone who lives in his house, whom he would not suspect."

"Who is this 'we' of whom you continue to speak?"

"Your father's old friends. Myself and others."

"You wish me to spy on Burghley? With what in mind?"

"Opportunity. An opening."

"'Tis not Burghley you're after. 'Tis the Queen."

"We are not *after* anyone. We are *for* England."

"And the Queen is *not?*"

"She is not the best for England."

"I have little use for such matters."

"Edward. Understand me in this. You are an earl. You have duties. Responsibilities. Loyalties."

"To the Crown."

"Nay, to the nation."

"You speak of treason."

"I speak of justice. Mary Queen of Scots, a good Catholic, sits under house arrest in England where she knits and grows old. By rights, the crown should rest on her head."

"Yet it came to Elizabeth. And through no desire of her own."

"Elizabeth is a bastard child. Declared so by the Pope and by Henry himself before he changed religions and reinstated her. Her claim is not legitimate, yet there she sits."

"And you wish to *un*seat her?"

"The earls have always been Catholic. As was your father. As was England until Henry decided he knew better than God."

"No, not God. Better than the Pope."

"Better than God's ambassador, then... All we desire is a return to our religion, however that might come about."

"And would that not also mean power returned to the earls?" Edward asked.

"If that be God's will, yes. As it was *before* Henry, before he stole our religion and much of our land."

"I shall keep to my pastime, my writing. I should rather endure ink on my fingers than blood on my hands."

"Be forewarned. Whilst you wear down the point of your quill, others sharpen their blades. Take care you don't find one buried in your back."

CHAPTER 25

Sacrifice

"I am in blood stepped in so far,
Should I wade no more."
Macbeth, III, 4

Having established himself well in the joust, Edward renewed his request to prove his worth in battle.

"Then go chase the Scots," the Queen finally relented. "Then you shall see that real combat rests more on blood than glory."

In the Year of Our Lord 1570, Elizabeth finally granted Edward permission to fight the long rebellious Scottish clans. The clans had always been emboldened under the banner of Mary Queen of Scots, who did nothing to dissuade them from crossing over the border to attack and rampage before her captivity. They found no reason to discontinue their sorties after her arrest.

To counter that constant menace, Elizabeth encouraged those Englishmen with lands and means -- the barons and the earls who had once fought each other -- to maintain and sharpen their fighting skills against the Scots, yet required them to raise their own force and fight at their own expense. "Perhaps you shall discover the true cost of war," the Queen advised Edward before sending him off. "'T'will be a burden for even you to bear."

Edward gathered two-score men in the south and raised others as he marched north. By the time he reached Bamburgh, fifteen leagues south of the Scottish border, the dust of sixty mounts followed, Edward promising to pay them in coin or booty, yet knowing the Scots had little to confiscate beyond their pride. If it came to it, Edward would be obliged to sell another of his estates to pay his men.

He established his northern camp inside the thickly-pined Yeavering Forest, scattering his fighters among the trees, most of them chewing on salt beef and crusted bread, and trading stories and laughter to buoy their spirits and distract themselves from the impending battle. As Edward munched his own dry bread, a forward scout slipped back into camp after nightfall to report that a group of rebels -- seventy-five to a hundred in number lay just north of Etal, itching for a fight.

"We shall take them in the morrow," Edward informed his lieutenants, realizing that familiar territory favored the enemy, and the longer he waited, the more opportunity for surprise dwindled.

He spent the night hunched over a map, contemplating competing strengths and strategies. With the Scots close at hand, caution outweighed recklessness. No man slept the night and all were up before first light, tightening their tugs, strapping on leggings and boots, and sharpening swords and battleaxes. After a meal of cider and cold gruel, Edward led them through the dark along a narrow path that wound between tall willows and low-lying bogs until they reached the edge of the woods where they faced a lowgrass plain that rose to a steep hill a hundred fifty meters beyond the tree line. There, he divided his men, half to the center, a quarter to his right, the remainder back into the woods to his left.

Those in the center moved to the edge of the wood and held there as three of Edward's men lit scattered campfires along both sides to confuse the enemy as to their exact location and numbers, the fires still burning as a murky yellow dawn emerged to warm the morning chill. Looking first to his right and then to his left, Edward watched a man tightened his fists around his shield, while most stared straight ahead, aware that some among them would to sacrifice limb or life, or take it from another this day.

Edward thought of his father and wondered if he would approve of his son following the ancient ways of chivalry. As he adjusted his reins, a boy to his right, no more than thirteen or fourteen, gripped a pole topped with the flag of England. "Hold your banner firm," Edward instructed the lad who jolted his backbone straight and hoisted his staff aloft toward a hawk as it circled the field awaiting the day's carnage.

With the enemy still hidden beyond the rise, Edward looped his horse around to the front of the line and turned to face his troops. A few veteran fighters rode amongst them, the rest mostly scallywags and conscripts out for bounty, untried lads recruited from the countryside who joined for the camaraderie of men out for the kill, and those who joined simply on to escape the drudgery of spring planting, all hoping for victory cheers upon their return.

"Men of England," Edward looked along the line and began, his voice echoing through the trees. "God and good cause lay upon our side. Our queen expects we shall fight with strength, valor, and honor. Yet, beyond our cause, beyond the right or wrong of it, remember this. Those you fight today would whack the limbs from your body, boil your inners in your blood and have them for supper. Blood *will* flow this day. Slaughter will be had."

He paused to allow his image to fully absorb. As a writer, he knew the effect and impact of words. After a hushed silence, he began again. "On England's throne, the Scots say our queen falsely sits. They say she is God's enemy. I say to you this. God will show His enemy defeat. If you safeguard England well, your wives shall welcome you as conquerors and your children will acknowledge you as heroes and saviors of the crown. If I survive among you, the least of you will share his part in the glory. In the name of God, queen, and country, make the best of you this day."

He nudged his horse around again to face the empty field. He held his restive mount steady as the earth stood oddly quiet, only an occasional impatient hoof digging in the ground to break the silence. After a prolonged wait, a cloud of dust rose on the rise above and shimmered in the early morning sun. Then the points of lances poked up on the horizon, then the heads of horses shaking their manes, followed by a string of mounted riders flanked along the ridge. All stood stiff and still, as if freshly painted on a canvas sky, as if Edward could dismount, amble leisurely across the field, wander up the hill, run his fingers across the paint and find his fingertips wet with color. Then, suddenly, surprisingly, a helmeted commander burst through the center of the enemy line astride a ghost-white stallion. He galloped to the front of his ranks, raised his sword to arms length, and shook it as if he meant to puncture the clouds.

Edward thought he saw fire in their commanders' eyes, yet knew he could not at that distance. He wondered if fear squirmed in their leader's saddle as it did in his. The heavy breathing of the horse next to him drew Edward's attention to the man to his left who slapped leather against leather. That sound, mixed with the smell of horses' sweat, reminded Edward of the joust, with one crucial difference. Those men were out to win. These were out to kill.

For a long and uncomfortable wait, the line of mounts and riders rested on the crest as if uncertain whether to fall back or roll forward. Then the enemy's commander hoisted his sword three times in slow succession, then lowered and pointed it. When he kicked his stallion's shanks, the steed jolted and lunged, tilting a wave of men and mounts forward downhill.

"Hold," Edward called, his voice steadier and firmer than he felt. As hooves pounded and sped toward them, the horses along his own line stomped and whinnied in terror, their fear barely contained by the strained muscles of anxious riders.

Edward looked at the flag boy and ordered him to raise his banner only when the battle-horn sounded, and then looked straight ahead. He waited. He held. With the charge near upon them, he shouted, "Now!" The battle horn blew. The flag boy raised his staff. English horses flew from the woods behind him. The two lines slammed and tangled as swords clanged and whirled above heads, and mounts rose to their haunches. Ball-flails spun. Maul hammers spiraled. Clubs swung as battleaxes encountered flesh. Pikes pierced ribs and blood spurted as long-knives hacked arms and shoulders. A man's head, whacked from its body, tumbled to the ground, then bounced and rolled beneath bloody hooves like a melon kicked across a melon patch.

Obscenities permeated the field. A lad to Edward's left toppled from his horse and found himself trampled as the riders around him tried to keep from being thrown. Those still on their mounts twisted in their saddles, determined, if they were to die, to take others with them. When all seemed lost, Edward's reserves rushed in from both sides of the woods and pinched the chaos into closer quarters, ramming unwilling men and mounts against each other.

As Edward's vision burred, he thrashed at everything that moved as if cutting untamed wheat at harvest. He caught the whites of a man's eyes as he passed, the man's head flung back, his throat slashed, blood gushing. Time warped, then stopped and then held no meaning. Finally, mercifully, the melee dissipated more than ended. The remnants of those Scots still able, hobbled off the killing field, or were carried off by comrades or tired horses.

A few near-dead lay in the field on their backs, their arms spread like angel's wings, their eyes riding high in their sockets, staring at an empty sky in disbelief. The chokes and groans of the wounded and dying mixed with coughs and prayers as the stench of urine and feces peppered Edward's nostrils and burned his tongue. His own horse, dizzy and no longer able to stand, toppled and fell, throwing Edward to the ground, the animal, mortally wounded, laboring its final breaths.

Giddy and disoriented, Edward grappled to his knees and knelt among the carnage, searching for the glory but finding only annihilation -- a fighter's cause, whatever it was upon his arrival, soon decayed with his body, buried under endless summers and long frozen winters. With nothing settled, who had won? How many men were worth the life of a country?

An unexpected breeze drifted over the carnage, rumpling a dead man's hair as a whisper drew Edward's eyes to the boy who had raised the battle flag. Edward leaned across the boy's chest and touched his ear to the boy's lips. "Moootherrr," the boy groaned, then hacked blood into Edward's ear, shuddered and closed his eyes.

Edward yanked the flag from the boy's loosened grip and scrambled to his feet and rammed the pole into the hoof-softened earth as lightning streaked across the darkening sky and thunder rumbled in its wake. God had seen enough. A storm would sweep through this night and wash the field clean. Edward lowered his eyes, no longer able to look or contemplate his complicity.

CHAPTER 26

Death and Abandonment

"Murder most foul."
Hamlet, Act I, 5

Winter's frozen fingers seized London in a stranglehold beyond the great London Bridge. All commerce, the life-blood of London, had ceased. The tall masts of sailing ships tilted with the final tide and frozen in place at angles that crisscrossed and overlapped as if engaged in some mad sword fight until the Devil himself blew a cold breath up the Themes to temporality halt the carnage.

Nothing moved. The breeze stood still. Businessmen, who ordinarily strolled out from London Gate to take the air and contemplate a venture, remained hunched over their desks with their shutters clasped against the unrelenting chill. Hopeful lovers who chanced a flirtatious encounter along the walkway on warmer days cuddled their hopes and dreams beneath thick woolen blankets whist more practiced lovers toasted there feet and warmed each other before a crackling hearth.

Only the mad or the foolhardy ventured out this day. Thus, why had Edward chanced such an outing? Self-punishment? Guilt? Flagellation for sins committed, both known and imagined? How many had he killed in the meadows of Scotland in the season just past? How many times had he come within a hare's breath of his own death? How often did the Grim Reaper groan in aguish as he narrowly slipped his sword past Edward's neck? The bodies of the fallen that day were long buried, yet their ghostly apparitions shadowed and haunted him.

A patch of brown suddenly sprung up from the steps leading down to the riverbank then quickly darted back. A thief? What manner of thief would be so desperate, so depleted, so in need of sustenance that he would brave such bitter cold? Pickings were slim in the dead of winter and larcenous fingers oft froze as they stretched for a dangling purse.

Edward hunched his shoulders and patted the sheath beneath his cloak to ensure his blade was at the ready as he crept forward. At the last instant, hoping to advantage surprise, he leaped, then fell back and let his shoulder's droop.

A lad, an mere urchin, glared up at him, his pale eyes wide in fear, his backbone arched, his legs crouched, prepared to attack or withdraw, whichever proved the safer. There was something eerily familiar about this lad, something about the trepidation in his eyes that Edward instantly recognized, something that burned Edward's heart and soured his stomach.

He clenched his fists to fortify himself then drew a long breath as he reached in his purse and tossed the lad a farthing. The boy stooped to pick it up but quickly dropped it, his fingers too stiff from the cold to fully grasp the coin before he scurried away.

Feeling suddenly dizzy and straining to keep his balance, Edward turned and slowly retreated, knowing the lad would watch from a safe distance and return for his prize when the way was clear. In delirium, a ghostly voice came to Edward' as he staggered away from the river, headed toward higher ground. "Revenge this foul and most unnatural a deed," the voice shrieked.

What unnatural deed? Edward wondered. Yet he knew the deed and well knew the voice. 'Twas his father's voice. And the boy by the river? The lad reminded Edward of himself at that age -- that very same look of surprise and foreboding when his mother called him forth that fateful day at Hedingham to pronounce her marriage to the man who undoubtedly murdered his father.

"Murder most foul," the voice groaned.

Murder? Was it truly murder?

"'Twas abetted by my wife, your mother, that adulterous beast," the ghost of his dead father cried in anguish, perchance speaking from purgatory or from hell.

Adulterous indeed, as surely it was. 'Twas no wonder that,

even now, fully grown, Edward reviled and mistrusted, yet longed for an older women's love and affection. At the very cusp of his maturing, at the tender age of twelve, his own mother had abandoned him for her lover, who, as her accomplice, had undoubtedly murdered his father. If a mother's womb is thus sour and the milk of her breasts venomous and deadly, what evil might lie beneath the sweet scented lore of every woman?

Edward easily recalled how cruelly his sharp-tongued mother had treated him and his father. How she had cast her evil spell upon them both, which his father, even as an apparition, seemed powerless to shed.

He glanced up and shook his head to clear his mind as he squinted toward the bright sun that faded all signs of the ghost, its moans now replaced by a sudden whirl of wind beating up from the river urging him forward.

And yet, he thought, as he measured his steps, even if fowl deeds were thus as he perceived them, what to do to render past deeds right when the only plausible action seemed inaction? No sword possible now to pierce the heart of his father's killer, he being already dead. No rope now to ring the neck of his mother who lay out of reach already in her grave.

Perchance 'twas avoidance of guilt that led him to indulge in the finest furnishings, the best of clothes, and the most extravagant expenditures -- all with a false sense of purpose to conceal his need to finish something yet undone. Perchance 'twas also the reason he wrote. Comedy or tragedy, he forged imagined steps that left no marks and planted no footprints. As playwright, he conjured artificial tears and laughter that shed no real blood. Unlike life, that always reached an end but oft' no conclusion, his plays -- confused and uncertain in the midst of Act II -- set the stage for all's well that ended well in the final scene, or at least ended with a plausible coherence. Real life ended in as mudded in the end as muddled throughout, it's final scene untimed and untimely, its purpose lived by an idiot, signifying nothing, then heard from no more.

Whatever the true tale of Edward's own purpose, a full

honesty required a deeper probe of the well that spat his lines and fed his soul. Was his affection and love affair with the Queen -- herself an older woman -- a substitute for a mother's love he never felt or tasted? Would the long festering anger and mistrust of that witch block him from loving a woman -- *any* woman? T'was his hither-and-naught, love-hate affair with the Queen merely an underlying and shadowed attempt to alter what could not be altered?

The ghost had dissipated -- floating at a distance now, yet somewhere close at hand. The answers, whatever they be or not be, lay ahead of him, played out as lived.

CHAPTER 27

Rebellion

"What's done cannot be undone."
Macbeth, V, 1

There is no stopping an idea riding on an incoming tide. It sweeps over all in its wake. When the news flooded London's streets, Edward burst into Burghley's study. "Is it *true?*" he asked.

Burghley grinned without looking up. "What kept you? I thought you would have heard sooner."

"Is it true that Norfolk proposes marriage to the Queen of Scots?"

"He seeks such that arrangement. Ambition spurs him."

"But she is captive in England and Her Majesty would never approve. Norfolk requires her permission."

"Only if he wishes to remain in England. But suppose he were willing to forgo that?"

"To be a Scot?"

"A provisional Scot." The Chief Minister squared the papers on his desk and slowly rose from his bench. "Should the Queen of Scots be released or somehow freed," he said, looking Edward squarely in the eye.

"Freed?"

"If she were rescued or released from captivity, and they were married, and Mary somehow came to occupy the English throne... Well ... Norfolk would then be both Scottish *and* English, would he not? Any son born of them could well end up ruling both countries from a unified throne. 'Tis a natural joining, is it not? 'Tis all one island."

"The Queen would never release her cousin, and would be flatly against such a union."

"Nonetheless, the Catholics have been scheming, your uncle Henry Howard among them. They try to convince Her Majesty that such a match would be in her interest. They argue that Mary should marry Englishmen rather than a prince of France or Spain. That the son of such a union would reduce the pressure on Her Majesty to bear a prince herself."

"But Mary is Catholic, as is Norfolk. The throne of England is firmly taking root in the Protestant faith."

"They tell the Queen that wouldn't matter for the present. Yet secretly, the Catholics would quietly wait their opportunity while the Protestants would see no change, at least at present."

Edward knew the Chief Minister wasn't telling everything. He rarely did. "Such a marriage would satisfy *no* one," Edward said, testing Burghley's veracity. "Norfolk, perhaps. He would have his reward but the northern earls aren't interested in privilege for their children. Tomorrow being *in* the morrow, they prefer their lands and power restored now."

"The earls wrap their banner around Norfolk as the highest rank among them," Burghley said. "Though that be of little worth these days. They are a desperate lot, a dying breed. It matters not how they scheme. Today, money and power shifts from the lands and the castles to the explorers and the merchants. As the Queen's cousin, Norfolk has always considered himself a few rungs beneath the throne. He looks up and salivates. The northern earls have never accepted her father's Protestant reforms and despise her for reinstating them."

"'Tis a natural resentment," Edward said. "They hold to their ways. Which does not mean they would turn against their Queen."

"The north is far from London. They have always insisted on their own laws. They resent the Queen's rightful taxes and oft do not pay. 'Tis cheaper to bribe the Queen's tax collector whose throat they can wrap their fists around. I suggest you caution your uncle, Henry Howard of the dangers on the road that he and others trod."

"He listens naught to me."

"The question is, do *you* listen to him. The ax man hones his blade. Norfolk has been arrested."

"What!"

"So then, you have *not* heard all of it. He makes his bed in the Tower, the Queen to dispense of him at her pleasure."

Edward, shaken by the unexpected news, stumbled from Burghley House and wandered aimlessly along Kidwell Alley and across Marshall's Glen, weighting the matter with each step, finally concluding that he was overreacting -- that the Queen, under Burghley's practical guidance, would hold Norfolk in the Tower a fortnight, and then send him north to caution the others. After all, what had he done but propose a foolish marriage?

Edward meandered home and slept unencumbered. The calamity he had feared, and then dismissed, held back a fortnight. What had began as rumor and gossip, slowly attached meat to its bones. The northern earls, in their confusion and disarray after Norfolk's arrest, feared for their own safety and thought to seize the wolf by the throat. Were they to lose their cause and perish, they would sooner die in battle. The Queen's spies reported that the northern earls had grouped and galloped south, hoping to gather momentum and numbers along the way.

News and speculation spread, parceled out in taverns and inns and swiftly carried to London. The Earls of Westmoreland and Northumberland, in collusion with the Sheriff of York and three hundred followers, half on horse, half by afoot, had reportedly burst through the gates of Durham and broken into the Cathedral, smashing the Protestant communion table and tossing Henry's Anglican prayer books into the aisles and torching them. One witness reported that the rebels painted crosses on their foreheads, genuflected, and then held Catholic mass before proceeding south, drawing in Catholic sympathizers to swell their following as they rode. One man among them galloped south and waved a proclamation he swore the earls had tacked to a post in front of Durham's Pigskill Tavern.

JOIN US BRETHREN.
FOR THIS QUEEN HATH TAKEN UP LAWS
CONTRARY
TO THE HONOR OF GOD AND AGAINST THE
REALM.

In a war of proclamations, Elizabeth produced her own, sending runners out to post in inns and taverns, and onto trees as far north as they dared venture.

RELIGION BE NOT THE USURPERS
ENTERPRISE. THEY SEEK
TO GRAB ENGLAND'S YOKE AND HAND IT
OVER TO A FOREIGN REALM WHICH WILL
PICK OUR SPOILS CLEAN, BURN OUR HOMES
AND RAPE OUR MOTHERS AND DAUGHTERS.

The Queen's declaration frightened Edward. He feared not for himself or for the northern earls caught in the grip of their convictions. He feared for Elizabeth. He knew her strategy, her desperation, the risk she took. She would look to her subjects to support her, praying that even the reticent Catholics among them would not subjugate themselves to a Scot. Forced to choose, she clung to the hope that they would choose their own.

Having taken the city of York, should the northern earls advance and rescue the Queen of Scots from her Sheffield Castle confinement, they could proclaim her legitimate queen and give Mary's supporters further cause for rebellion.

Elizabeth confirmed Edward's fears on November 22nd in the Year of Our Lord 1569 when she dispatched the southern Earl of Shrewsbury to remove the Queen of Scots from Sheffield and convey her a heavier-fortified castle farther south. At the same stroke, the Queen mustered twelve thousand cavalry with the promise of confiscated northern properties upon victory, in hopes of weakening her enemy's hand in the north and their Catholic supporters in the south.

In the uncertain days that followed, Londoners boarded their shops, shuttered their windows, and hunkered in their root cellars, awaiting the approaching storm.

Information filtered in slowly. The earls of Cumberland and Derby reportedly hesitated in joining the other northern earls when their castles were reached, sniffing the air and observing the direction of the wind before they set their course. Ordinary villagers, instead of joining the Catholics amass as expected, closed their doors to await the outcome. The northern earl's hastily gathered army slowly peeled away and drifted back to their homes with the news that the Queen of Scots had been removed to the south and that an English force marched north to greet them. Those northern earls still in the field headed home, hastily galloped north to cross the Scottish border or scrambled for the Channel in search of boats to escape to France. Others, those who had feared to join either side, fortified their castles, and held their necks close to their shoulders.

The southern Earl of Shrewsbury, after successfully removing the Queen of Scots farther south, advised the Queen to pursue a swift reprisal against the northern earls and their followers to give future foes pause to reconsider. "Hang one in each village as example," Shrewsbury advised.

Upon weighting that advice, Burghley wrote a capture and execute order that the Queen scanned and signed.

> Those in open rebellion in the north to be hunted, arrested, and tried forthwith. Those judged guilty of treason are hence to be led from their place of confinement to a suitable gallows and there to be hanged until half dead, hence to be cut down and their bowels taken out of the belly and thrown to the fire. Their heads to be cut off and their bodies divided into four parts, the head and forequarters set up for display and disposed of at Our pleasure.

This given under our name from our palace at
Whitehall.

Elizabeth R

When a judge at York requested leniency for a man he said
was forced to join under threat of reprisal, the Queen wrote back,
"We are not in a sparing mood."

Burghley -- predictably, in Edward's view -- complained of
the added expense of the trials and the need for them. "The rebels
have forfeited their right to trial," he protested, calculating that the
fines for those killed or those who managed to avoid the noose added
a mere pittance to the Queen's coffers. That meager amount, added
to the expected annual gain of rent from the rebel's confiscated
properties, hardly dented the indebtedness the Queen had already
accumulated during her reign. "The whole venture adds nothing but a
drop to near empty barrel of indebtedness," he grumbled, dangling
his purse in front of Edward and anyone else who would listen. "She
raised an army to give chase, which saw no battle yet cost to feed
their mouths and horses. She could have sent ducks flying north at a
cheaper rate and with similar result."

By the end of an unusually cold and snowy February, the
executions, the reprisals, and the repercussions had passed, yet Mary
Queen of Scots remained alive and well in England, reading,
knitting, and quietly plotting her future course from her new
confines. A few of her supporters had been permanently silenced,
others temporarily hushed, yet many still hovered over their castle
fires, warming their hands and quietly plotting overthrow. The sparks
that set the rebellion ablaze had been doused, but only in part, for the
embers of rebellion still glowed beneath the surface.

CHAPTER 28

The Queen's Proposal

> "A young man married
> Is a man that's marred."
> *All's Well That Ends Well, II, 3*

"Minister Burghley has proposed a matter I should like you to seriously consider," the Queen informed Edward, an edge in her voice as though she knew the idea would not set well.

"The Chief Minister schemes as his livelihood," Edward said as they circled the lake at Richmond Palace.

"That is his usefulness," the Queen said, slowing her pace. "He out schemes my enemies."

"Does he consider me such?"

"He assumes everybody is an enemy. His *and* mine."

"And what does he propose for me?"

"That be the proper word." The Queen stopped and faced him. "He proposes marriage."

Edward tried to choke his laughter back but abandoned the effort. "And does he have a particular candidate in mind?"

"He would have you marry Anne."

"*Anne?*... His daughter, Anne?"

"Why not his daughter? Is that such a poor prospect?"

"I am not in love with Anne. We have been raised together since I came to Burghley House."

"Marriage within a household is not uncommon. You are not related."

"The Chief Minister who despises me? 'Twould make me his son-in-law?"

"He respects you."

"He respects my rank. He detests *me.*"

"It would be a good match for Anne, assuring her future."

"And assuring Burghley's lineage beyond a commoner. Perhaps that supports his cause."

"She is a budding girl. 'Tis a natural time for a father to…"

"Let her mature a year or two. Come into bloom."

"The girl adores you. I see it in her eyes."

"She is as a sister to me."

"A sister you have spied upon."

"She has spied on me."

"I hear you have spied upon each other. That you have seen her naked."

"Is there nothing of which Burghley doth not inform you?"

"He does his duty."

"He seeks your favor."

"Of course, he does. He is faithful in that as well."

"He simply wishes his daughter to marry an earl."

"There is nothing wrong in that."

"'Tis not enough reason for *me* to marry."

"Such a union would have advantages both ways."

"Passion not among them."

"You make too much of that. Anne is a fine girl. It matters not if Burghley benefits."

"She *is* a girl."

"With a woman's desire."

"A maid who parts her legs does not a woman make."

"As wife, Anne will open her heart to you… I advise you to marry."

"Do you order this?"

"Only if required. I ask it, for now."

"And your reason?"

"I have one, but you will not like it."

"'Tis your reason whether I like it or not."

"Relations are delicate with Spain. They hold their ships from attack in expectation of a marriage with me. Too many know that you and I have spent much time together. A good deal of it alone in my quarters. Gossip spreads. Speculation as to the nature of what we do and how we feel for each other. Your marriage to the daughter of England's Chief Minister would deflect idle tongues."

"Let them wag."

"If you *were* mine, I would not give you away."

"No one gives me away."

"Edward. I care for you deeply. You would profit by settling down."

"Tied down, your mean... You yourself..."

"Should what? Settle into matrimony? Yours is personal. Mine is a matter of state. You think I am fretful for me in this? I am concerned for you. Any offspring would still be yours. As Seventeenth Earl, is it not your duty to produce an Eighteenth?"

He cocked his head.

"I know what you're thinking. That it is my duty as Queen to produce an heir to the throne."

"Is it not?"

"We are not discussing my prospects. We are discussing yours."

"You *are* a woman, with a woman's desires"

"Queen, first."

"First, but not all."

"First and last. Unless you were in my position, you could not understand."

"Yet, still an abundant woman," he said, standing back and examining her fully.

"And you are insolent."

"I am bent to say what I see, if that be insolence."

"And young and foolish."

"My eyes do not deceive me."

"Other's already envy you."

"Perhaps they have reason."

"There are reasons to marry other than love."

"Such as?"

She looked out across the lake. "You see those swans swimming so peacefully?... They mate for life. Only death separates them. And yet, the lake is artificial. Created by man, like a state. 'Tis a manmade dam that holds the water back. A barricade that requires tending. Whomever I marry, be he Protestant or Catholic, French or Spanish, there will always be those who would have me marry someone else. By *not* marrying, the dam remains intact and all my suitors remain hopeful. The swans swim in relative peace."

"I shall *not* marry Anne Burghley."

"Your father listened to his Queen."

"You did not command him whom to marry."

"Perhaps I would have if I could."

Edward clinched his fists. "My mother was fond of telling me I gave her a troubled birth. She more than punished me for that."

"I *had* no mother that I knew. She was beheaded at my father's hand for birthing a useless female." She patted her stomach. "And if this womb does not come of issue... Well." She looked down and waved her finger toward Edward's crotch. "And if those loins of yours do not spring forth and land their flow in some damp, dark space, there will be no future earl of Oxford."

"Then I have the answer to suit us both," he grinned. "I shall marry you."

The Queen stepped back. "Is that such a painful thought?"

"Not at all''

"Of course, it is. I am far too old for you."

"You enjoy younger men and are well suited to them."

"For amusement. You speak of marriage."

"Anne is a child. You are wiser. Fully matured."

"Marry Anne."

"I have no wish to marry anyone. I wish to travel. I am at the age I should."

"We can take travel under consideration... If you were to wed, we could still enjoy each other's company. There are few I can speak to frankly, who do not flap their tongues to fit the occasion. And *no* one who writes as well as you. Since I shall never be as good, I shall always envy you and always learn."

"I wish to be more than the Queen's..."

"Tutor?"

"If I could travel I…"

"Think of marriage as a first step. Then we shall see."

****

The Queen, dressed for the wedding in a gown with a bejeweled bodice, stood at the side of Westminster's Lady Chapel and smiled as Anne and Edward spoke their nuptials under the eves of the Church of England, the very same church her father had established and christened.

"Lord, consecrate this union," the white-robed Anglican Bishop said as Anne and Edward knelt before him. "Bear and hold these Christian souls to join in holy wedlock for all to witness, sanctified by God and by the Queen in full faith and love. Let all foes that wouldst endanger this bond cease in their encumbrances. Love sought is good. Love given, all the better. As loving husband…" He nodded to Edward, "and as wife…" He turned to Anne, then raised his hand above their heads. "As these earthly vines entwine, let God's love grow in all His blessings."

After solemn prayer, the Bishop bid the couple rise, and then gestured to Edward to lift Anne's veil, take his bride by her hand, and accept her as wife. Edward closed his eyes and leaned forward. He quickly kissed Anne, and then opened his eyes to the Queen, who nodded her approval.

On the Wednesday of the second week of their marriage, Edward rushed from his study to read Anne a sonnet and seek her opinion. When he finished reading and glanced up, she had drifted off, her knitting sunk to her lap.

Two months after the wedding, with Edward and his new wife looking on, the Queen tapped Cecil Burghley's shoulders with the Sword of State, installing her Chief Minister, a commoner by birth, as a Lord of the Realm, henceforth to be addressed as Lord Burghley.

Seeing less of the Queen after his marriage and finding himself less interested in the intrigues and connivings of court,

Edward retreated to his study at his new apartments on the south side of Willow's Mews. With Anne occupied in her own rooms - knitting, sewing, or staring vaguely out the window -- while writing consumed Edward's time, interest, and energy. Much like a wild fire propelled by a perpetual breeze, he was often unable to douse or even slow the words that came to him long enough to apply them to paper. Plots, both ancient and modern, emerged unexpectedly, then twisted, spun, and changed and swept back again for him to reexamine, reshape, and rewrite.

Characters, half or fully formed, tiptoed across his mind's heated embers, while others floated above them, unscorched by the pathos and passions that swirled beneath. Still others stomped off in anger or confusion, or else rushed into the fray, muttering lines in Edward's head until he stained their words upon the page, often chiding him to write their speeches before they were fully developed, and then scolding him to scribe changes as they formed.

And yet, Edward was aware that spending too much time writing by himself, hiding incognito with his characters, paled his skin and soured his disposition. He had, on occasion, to remind himself to forgo words on paper in lieu of footprints on the ground, duller though they be by comparison. This day, he determined to set his pen aside to wrestle a tennis racket. He would trounce Lyly in a match. "Don't bother sitting," he said as soon as Lyly bounced through the door after Edward sent a servant to fetch him. "We shall have a game today," he added as he slipped on his jacket and they left Edward's apartments.

"How goes marriage?" Lyly asked after a silence.

Edward shrugged. "'Tis an earthy joining, I'm afraid. Neither made in heaven nor in hell. It lacks the blessing of one and the heat of the other."

"She will grow on you."

"Like mold. She complains I hide from her to write."

"And you deny it?"

"I say nothing. I have no defense. When I read to her, she falls asleep."

"You are not so easy to live with."

"How would you know?"

"No writer is."

"You're right… 'Tis not her fault I find her boring. I wish it were otherwise."

"Which? That you be the duller or she the sharper?"

"Either way would work, but we cannot switch our natures."

"And in bed?"

"She closes her eyes and waits for me to bring the act to her. Thus, when I bring it, with her eyes closed, she cannot see. She tightens her brow and waits for me to finish."

"And what do you make of it?"

"Nothing comes from nothing."

CHAPTER 29

Fireworks

"Friendship is constant in all things,
save the office and affairs of love."
Much Ado About Nothing, II, 1

The outbreak of the Northern Earl's rebellion during Norfolk's Tower confinement allowed time to uncover Norfolk's second plot to unseat Elizabeth. That discovery left no doubt about how to dissuade him from further treason. At sunrise on the 2nd of July in the Year of Our Lord 1572, a single swing of the ax separated the Duke of Norfolk's head from the rest of his body.

The day following Norfolk's beheading, still shaken by the execution and in fear of his uncle Henry Howard's involvement, Edward, as the realm's leading Earl, was barely able to hold his legs steady enough to carry the Queen's ceremonial sword at the opening of Parliament. At the first break in the morning session, Lord Burghley approached his son-in-law outside the chamber. "Her Majesty wishes you to organize the festivities and fireworks for display at Warwick Castle when she arrives there in her summer progress," the Chief Minister said, stoking his beard as though nothing untoward had happened, as though Norfolk's death was a mere drop of blood in a huge state bucket. "She thinks of you as theatrical," he added. "More theatrical than practical, I should say."

"I serve at the Queen's pleasure," Edward said, knowing Burghley wished to thank him for accepting, yet found himself incapable of forming those words.

"Yes, well then," Burghley stammered.

Burghley had not yet thanked Edward, nor would he, for earlier organizing Westminster's fireworks display to celebrate Burghley's installation into the Knights of the Garter, honoring the Lord Minister's long and faithful service.

"Where shall I procure the men and funds?" Edward asked.

"Many seek the Queen's favor and would pay to have it. I shall see to the finances. You see to the festivities."

The Queen, in her customary fashion, set about her summer progress at the end of May in the Year of Our Lord 1573, with Edward, as usual, among her entourage. Midway through, she ordered her procession halted and commanded her following to see to themselves whist she accompanied Edward to his estate at Havering-on-Thames, where they languished and sat for hours on the bluff overlooking the river, watching the skiffs and barges slowly drift downstream.

"We've spent many hours together, you and I," the Queen said. "You've grown since we first met."

"Older, not the wiser, I'm afraid."

"What's this I hear of you and Hatton?" she asked.

"Hear what?"

"That you envy him."

"Hatton?... I envy no one."

The Queen grinned and relaxed. "You are not my only friend, you know."

"Madam, I..."

"Yet you be my *favorite* friend."

Edward leaned on his elbows on the blanket spread beneath them. "Your favorite pawn on the royal chessboard?" he asked.

"Hardly a pawn. There is only one Oxford, a unique piece."

They laughed.

"Sometimes I wish I was a child again at Hatfield," she said. "Looking out at the lake behind that castle and sailing toy boats across those waters before they thought of me as Queen. The summers seemed to never end."

"That girl is still in you. And here you are now, watching boats drift by."

"Age creeps up on me. Time and events move quickly these days."

"For all of us." He looked at her. "Age does you well."

"Oh?... Then I *am* aged?"

"Not so much."

"Older than I wish to be. Old enough to be your mother."

"I never thought of you as such."

"Old enough to be your queen, then."

"Age has nothing to do with age. You *are* my queen. Yet, beyond your crown, far more than that."

"How shall I take your meaning?"

"Just as I say it. That you are a queen, a woman, *and* a girl. All of it… Right now… As here we sit."

"Just the two of us."

"Able to do as we please."

"Please, such as…?"

"Read poetry," he smirked.

"We've done that," she said, grinning like a maiden, as though forgetting that she was queen. "Now what shall we do?"

He reached out, hesitated, and then ran a fingertip down her shoulder. She stiffened but did not pull away.

"We are divided by age," she said. "By duty. By fate."

"Yet, neither by heart nor distance. Love knows no rank."

"You dare say that word to me?"

"I say as I feel."

"Love has many degrees of meaning."

"All the more reason to pluck the flower while the dew is still upon it."

"Then you say I'm ripe for plucking?"

"I say we all are, in our time, or we wither on the vine."

"Forlornly," she said. She lowered her eyes and sighed, then hesitated, reached across the gulf between them and touched his hand. "Let's pretend I am not your queen. That I am just a woman."

"'Tis a woman I see."

"And I shall forget that you are married."

"Wed only at your urging."

They remained a week at Havering, losing themselves in each other. They lounged and ran barefoot through knee-high grass, chased butterflies in the pasture behind the manor house, and spent long afternoons sitting and picnicking on the bluff above the river.

Elizabeth cooked. "Not so well," he told her.

"Then we shall play," she said, the evening she led him to her bedchamber. *"That* we both do well."

On their seventh day together, a courier arrived carrying what he professed to be an urgent message from Burghley.

> Your Majesty,
> Plans wait in anticipation of Your Majesty's presence. If it pleases, when shall we expect Your Majesty's return?
>
> Cecil Burghley,
> Your Faithful Servant
> Lord Minister and Treasurer

"Blunt, but to the point," she told Edward after reading it to him.

"Tell the Lord Minister I shall return shortly," she informed the courier. *"Too* shortly," she whispered when he departed. "I must go then," she said to Edward. "Duty beckons. And you must go as well. You are in charge of the fireworks."

"Not just yet," he said. "Come lay with me once more. We shall make our own fire."

The Queen rejoined her summer progress at Sussex Castle whilst Edward stayed another day at Havering, perched on the cliff above the river, watching the boats and barges float by and vaguely considering the possibility that he might indeed marry Elizabeth and find himself crowned a prince or even king. He well understood she would never allow such, that it misfit her politics. Still, barely skirting danger, as he oft did in his plays, he thought to sign his name with a crown and seven strokes above it, for Edward VII, as he would be in that position, simply to ponder its implication. He stood and ambled back to the manor, then wrote his signature as such and held it up to the light.

CHAPTER 30

A Fateful Child

"Tis childish wickedness to lament or fear."
Henry IV, V, 5

On the morning of the 14th of June in the Year of Our Lord 1574, the Queen, suddenly and unexpectedly -- as she had late in the prior summer -- broke off from her summer progress and returned with Edward to his Havering estate accompanied by her personal physician, two loyal maids, and a handful of long-trusted guards sworn under the threat of death to secrecy. She had squeezed her midriff in with bands and corsets for months. She had gout, which, for a while, she used to explain her swelling, yet of late there was no denying the protrusion growing from her belly. She would rest at Havering and have her child there.

Edward remained at her side, reading, reciting poetry, and seeing to her meals and then falling asleep next to her in bed. When her labor began, the physician shooed Edward from the chamber and ordered wet rags heated on the hearth and a stringent liniment prepared.

Edward paced the hall until well after dark as grim faces scurried in and out with foul smelling pots they refreshed and carried back between sporadic groans that grew more frequent and intense as the night wore on, and then a final cry released a scream, and then a moan, and then silence, and then the scampering of feet as the door flung open and the physician burst through.

"Is she alright?" Edward asked as the physician rushed out.

"She is weak."

"May I see her?'

"If you must," he said, glaring over his shoulder. "Be brief. She requires rest."

When Edward entered, she was propped up on a pillow, her face drained, yet smiling when she saw him.

"We have a son," she said. "Come see him."

A pink, naked infant suckled her breast.

"He enters hungry," she said. "He sucks what's left of me... What shall we call him?"

"Alexander, I should think," Edward said. "After Alexander the Great."

"I think Henry, after my father and grandfather. Which would make him Henry the IXth should he come to that."

"King Henry," Edward repeated, savoring the sound of it. "If that be the case, I shall have to write yet another King Henry into one of my plays. There are so many, they are hard to track."

She touched a finger to her lips. "Say none of this in the open. Our son's life rests on shaky ground. Events will take their course."

"Later events, perhaps," he said when the maids left the room, carrying the baby with them. "What are we to do *now?*"

"This was not unexpected," she assured him. "All has been considered. The less you know for now the better. When you hear of Southampton, you shall understand."

The Queen rested six more days and then, over her physician's protests, she had her maids prepare for their return to her progress. Burghley had been writing daily, inquiring of her health and saying that others were beginning to wonder if she was gravely ill, that this had been the second year in a row she had broken off her progress without explanation.

As soon as the Queen departed, Edward, being neither with his newborn son nor in the Queen's reassuring presence, felt the gravity of his situation and panicked. What if word of the birth leaked? Such news would be perilous, catastrophic even. The crowns of Spain and France would be delighted to learn she was able to have a child, while infuriated that she had one. Her value as a wife and bearer of an heir by European royalty would plummet. Without the promise of a marriage and a progeny as restraint, Spain would likely attack immediately. There were those who said Phillip was already preparing for invasion. France, fearing a Spanish enclave directly across the narrow Channel, would likely strike preemptively. The Queen's child, born in less than innocence, could quickly set England and half the Continent ablaze. Thus, Edward thought it prudent to avoid any fuse that might ignite that explosive situation. He determined to escape without the Queen's permission and observe from a safe distance as events unfolded.

He hurriedly packed four trunks and departed Havering for Dunwich on the coast, whereupon he hired a fisherman's skiff to transport him to Bruges, Belgium and from there, traveled inland to Flanders. Yet, despite his intended secrecy, one of the Chief Minister's spies must have followed and reported his whereabouts to Burghley. He had not yet been in Flanders a fortnight when a messenger arrived with the Queen's written command, ordering his return. Lyly immediately informed Edward when he reached London that Henry Wriothesley, the Second Earl of Southampton, had also fled England and that the Queen ordered him back at the same stroke of the pen.

After seeing to his trunks, he reported at once, as commanded, to the Queen in her private chambers at Bolingbroke, three-quarters through her progress.

"There was no need to run," she said.

"I feared repercussions. When you left, I felt uncertain."

"I could not tell you this before. Plans were not completed and might have put you in increased jeopardy."

"We put each *other* in jeopardy."

"Sit beside me," she said.

He drew up a bench and sat next to her.

"Henry Wriothesley," she said. "The Second Earl of Southampton."

"Wriothesley?... Lyly mentioned him... *You* mentioned him. What of him?"

"He has wavered in his loyalty to me, as have many. Burghley has the evidence. I have seen it."

"Lyly said he fled as well."

"He knew I wished to see him. I had him escorted back, and for good cause. I asked a favor of him, one that offered him little choice. By complying, he avoided the Tower or worse. By obeying, he gained an annual sustenance and kept his freedom and his life, along with his lands and estates."

"If he takes our boy," Edward said, understanding her intent.

"The boy gets a name. Henry, just as we thought."

"As *you* thought."

"Yes, Henry, named after my father and his grandfather, and now after his adoptive father, Henry Wriothesley, the Second Earl of Southampton. He shall be, when he comes of age, the Third Earl of Southampton."

"We simply gave him away?"

"That's not as harsh as it sounds. Wriothesley's wife, Mary Browne, is a kindly woman. I know her well. She has been a lady-in-waiting to me many years and lost her own infant son eleven months ago, shortly after the child's birth. Her *only* son. At her age, she will not have another."

"Thus Southampton would have no heir," Edward interrupted.

"And you, more than most, know the importance of that. We both do. The Southampton earldom would die unless..."

"A son and heir is born. Or seems to be."

"It solves a problem for all. The boy has a father and inherits a title. He shall be raised at court around his adoptive mother and myself. I will see to that by keeping Mary close to me. Southampton will claim him as his own son on threat of death. Any rumors of the child's origin can thus be dissuaded."

"As if nothing happened."

"Nothing *has*. There is no record. Loose tongues don't flap from severed heads. All know this. 'Tis that important."

~~ *ABROAD* ~~

"Travelers must be content."

As You Like It, II, 4

CHAPTER 31

The Continent

"Tis an ill cook that cannot lick his own fingers."
Romeo and Juliet, IV, 2

No reason remained for Elizabeth to hold Edward in England. The farther she distanced herself from him, the more rumors died, and the safer for all concerned. Thus, she granted Edward an eighteen-month travel license with an extension possible at her pleasure or at his request -- ample time for gossip and innuendo to wither on the gossip vine and blow away in the breeze.

Edward would miss neither Anne nor his marriage. She seemed more a child than she had at Burghley House -- early to bed, late to rise, always under foot, little to interest her, little to say. He hated matrimonial confinement or confinement of any sort. Lately, he had lost interest in bedding his wife and had not slept with her for months prior to his departure. An extended absence would relieve them both.

The Continent's prospects excited him -- its art, its architecture, its history, its sophistication that spilled onto London's docks in crates stuffed with French wines, furniture, Italian frocks, and Belgian stained glass that bent a rainbow light that soared the imagination.

Leaning over the starboard rail of his departing vessel, England at his back, the haze of the France on the horizon, Edward felt as if the chains of England had slipped from his ankles and he had sprouted wings to soar into cultures of which he had only read and dreamt.

Once in Paris, he procured apartments in the central La Taruant district directly across from the Seine, where he remained a month, bountifully entertained by the Marques de Forgues, Beauvoir Marquette, Pierre du Bougnenisse, and their courtiers, all of whom wished to ingratiate themselves with the English earl and partake of the lavish catered parties he offered.

With the help and guidance of Forgues, the group's self-appointed leader, Edward leased the Château Baluftière for two days and nights and employed the best Parisian chefs to set a banquet for one-hundred-fifty, although closer to two hundred attended, many accompanied by new found friends anxious to see the dandy-dressed English earl who well spoke their language and spent so freely in their shops. *Un comte anglais parade et nous amuse.* "An English earl parades and amuses us," Edward's groom overheard one of them say and thus reported to Edward.

On the evening of the feast, twenty white-vested boys and as many frill-aproned maids set the meal's first course along the Château's eight meter long, central table -- oyster shell dishes of raspberry conserve, silver serving bowls of rabbit broth still simmering as they arrived, and gosling fricassee thickened with whipped butter and goat's cream. As the line of servers replaced the bowls with pewter plates, other cooks' helpers shuffled from the kitchen with finger-crocks of steaming puff-pasties that Edward's chef called *la tremoulette,* their cracked browned tops running with streaks of sugary yellow mustard that puckered the lips and coated the tongue.

Fools and jugglers mercifully provided a brief digression from the meal, accompanied by flutes and mandolins that plucked and resonated through the main course of venison steaks bleeding on the plate, boned pork joints smelling of sage and hickory, along with bread-stuffed pigeons and poached pheasants that lined up bird-to-bird, head-to-tail down the center of the table, each fowl encircled by overlapping pounded pigs' tongues and tiny dishes of pâté au meaux that persuaded several portly guests to unsnap their garnards and expand their vests to accommodate the dessert of cream-flan, toasted walnuts, and tart orange mousse.

Edward's French guests smiled more politely and nodded more frequently in conversation than the English. The Parisians sliced smaller portions using polished knifes and dainty cutting implements while Londoners preferred ripping and tearing with their fingers then flicking away the unchewable or inedible, although both the French and the English drank and gossiped well into the night and then leaned on their servants as they staggered to their carriages, undoubtedly ill in the morning with headaches and bloated stomachs. As the French Attaché whispered to Lord Montague, the English Ambassador, who later passed it on to Edward, "Our benefactor knows how to host a party for the French. He pays *them* to prepare it."

Elizabeth would be pleased that Edward had well presented himself to her French cousins, and would soon hear of it through Burghley's far flung eyes and ears, his spies near always in attendance at foreign dinners, scoffing down gratis pheasant along with hearsay, rumor, innuendo, and whatever other juicy scuttlebutt floated around the table or crawled out from the kitchen. Information sailed well across the Channel, the worst news and ripest gossip fetching a sharper ear and a thicker purse than the dry but true.

Burghley's blood would boil with the news of Edward expenses, yet Edward knew the Lord Minister would relish a secret pride in an Englishman besting the French on their own ground, even though the exorbitant cost only added to Edward's chronic indebtedness. He had recently received a letter from the Lord Minister informing him that his creditors were seeking recompense for expenses overdue on his London apartments and two of his estates in Cornwall and Bilton-Upon-Avon. Why, he wondered, did not his lands and properties pay their own upkeep? He employed a manager. Why did he not manage the funds at least as well as he managed the sheep and the grounds? The castles, in particular, were more expense than their worth, their yearly cost outweighing any utility they provided. With these thoughts in mind, he wrote back to his father-in-law.

My Lord Minister,

Whereas I perceive by your Lordship's recent
letter how hard money is gotten, I wish to

inform you that my man writeth that he would
fair pay my creditors some part of what is
owed as such payment can be made. Let my
creditors bear with me and take their days
assured that I am left in a strange country,
unknowing yet what I may require of funds. If
I cannot yet pay them as I would, I shall pay
as I can, presently preferring my own
necessity to theirs. If, at the end of my travels,
I shall have something left of my provision,
added to any profits from my lands and
estates, whatever they may be, I shall bring
down my debts as I am able.

Edward Oxford

Nonetheless, and regardless of the expense, knowing he
would unlikely travel so extensively again, he could hardly depart
Paris without a bit of shopping that stuffed three newly acquired
trunks with the latest in wide-ribboned pantaloons, an array of
feathered caps, puffed shirts, ruffs, leather gloves, velvet doublets,
two full-length riding cloaks, eight silk-lined waistcoats with
matching shoulder wraps, a dozen wide-width garters, a box of
plumes and another each of handkerchiefs, scarves and trescuts, and
quite naturally, five pairs of boots -- three knee-high, two
ankle-length and one midcalf.

Yet Paris, like any appetizer, merely roused the appetite for
more beyond itself. Thus, on the morning of March 4th in the Year of
Our Lord 1575, at the age of twenty-five, Edward awoke before
sunrise, and anxious for further adventure, prepared to move on. He
gathered his servants, his newly filled trunks, and his scattered
belongings and left Paris, leading his entourage through an early
Spring snowstorm to leave behind memories of banquets and
fashions, along with French curiosity and covetousness masked as
friendship and hospitality. He had felt a lively French interest, yet no

kinship as he tucked his collar about his neck to hold the chill of France at bay.

After leaving the city, his carriage and carts trekked eastward through low-lying Alpine flats that slowly melded into rolling hills which themselves gradually rose until the air thinned and Edward determined to stop and rest, contemplate, and write.

He procured lodgings in the village of Tinbourgh in the Alsace, sleeping in the mornings until ten or half-past, and then lounging on a sun-warmed balcony, nibbling bread and cheese and sipping wine as he penned his thoughts of travel in the new journal he acquired in Paris. He intended his travel writing as an exercise in wordplay, to use his experiences to perfect his rhyme and rhythm. He experimented with sonnets, a form that seemed to fit his playfulness with words, yet forced him to peel away their excess to reveal the kernel of his intent and meaning.

In the late afternoon, before taking an early evening meal, with the sun cresting over the village roofs, he left the inn and wound his way up a steep trail toward a tiny, white-spired Alpine church buried deep in shadow beneath thick pines. He entered through a narrow central door, a musty dampness filling his lungs as he knelt on a cool stone floor and stared up at a faded portrait of Madonna and child. Looking at her gentle face, transfixed by the her steady gaze, he wondered if Christ, despite the influence of his Holy Mother's loving kindness, might take revenge upon England for Henry's dismissal of the Holy Roman Church. If the Pope had condoned Henry's divorce, there would be no question of Edward's loyalty, no need for an Englishman to choose between Catholic and Protestant. England would have remained Catholic as it had been since Constantine converted the Holy Roman Empire to Christianity. Nor would there be any need for Edward to be wary of the religious trap he knew awaited him. His uncle Henry Howard, having influence in Catholic circles on the Continent, would undoubtedly have informed his fellow conspirators in Europe of Edward's itinerary, his uncle still hoping to convert Edward to his cause.

After two days of rest and writing, and after taking time to write Burghley again requesting the Lord Minister sell a portion of another estate, Edward departed on the next leg of his journey on a Sunday afternoon after attending service at the Alpine chapel, staring up again at the Madonna who, in her silence, stirred questions in him with her eyes whilst keeping her lips sealed.

After leading his entourage through a mud soaked Bohemia and contemplating its rich history and lush beauty as he might apply them to a setting for a play, Edward slipped quietly through a valley that funneled him into Milan, hoping that Burghley's and Henry Howard's spy-hounds had lost his scent in the thin Alpine air.

His steward had gone ahead to procured adequate lodgings. Upon Edward's arrival, he climbed up a set of creaking stairs, crossed a wide, high-ceiling room and flung the shutters open to flood the space with sunlight and circulate the stale air. He kicked off his dirt-caked boots and instructed his servants to boil water and fill a tub in the rear courtyard to soak away the layered dust and ease his jarred bones. After bathing, dressing, and meandering down to ask of supper, he encountered a black-robed, double-chinned man with a long, goose-like neck floating up from a stiff white collar. "Welcome to Milan," the man stepped forward and said.

"And you are…?"

"God's humble servant. I am here on behalf of the Monsignor. I hope your journey has been pleasant."

"Reasonably so."

"The Monsignor will be pleased to hear that. He has asked me to extend his regards, and requests your presence at his residence at you convenience. Immediately, if possible. He is looking forward to meeting you."

"Yes, well, I…"

"I am prepared to transport you myself. I have a carriage waiting."

"I have not yet supped."

"Neither has the Monsignor. You will require a cloak. The nights are chilly in these valleys. I shall wait while you fetch one."

The trap had been set and was about to be sprung, Edward thought as he fetched his cloak and reluctantly left with the Monsignor's humble servant.

CHAPTER 32

The Monsignor

> "Words without thought,
> Never to heaven go.
> *Hamlet, III, 3*

"So," a red-robed Monsignor stepped forward and said soon after Edward opened his carriage door and stepped out. "You thought you would sneak around me?" Without waiting for an answer, the Monsignor stretched a grin, then turned and led Edward inside a flat-roofed villa and down an entrance hall lined with dark portraits of grim-faced cardinals, all long-jawed and scowling.

They entered a room of bound books that lined three walls, and just inside to the left, a gold-leafed, open-faced Bible stood on a raised lectern requiring all who passed to acknowledge, or at least confront, God's holy word.

"I was informed you were coming," the Monsignor said as he turned to face his guest.

"My shadow seems to proceed me," Edward said, suspecting that the Church employed as many spies as Burghley engaged for England.

"Please... Sit."

As the Monsignor stepped forward, Edward backed up and plucked down in a high-railed side-chair, its flytrap wings seemingly prepared to snap shut and lock him in should he try to leave.

"You've had a long journey," the Monsignor said as he sat on a wider, thickly cushioned seat across from his guest. "I wish to hear of it. I don't travel much."

"I should think..."

"But first, I must ask... There are rumors as to..."

"Rumors fill the air these days," Edward interjected. "One can hardly breath without considering the implications."

"Some implications cut closer to the heart of matters," the Monsignor said. "What is your true belief, if I may be so blunt."

"I believe in the Lord."

"Yes. Well, indeed so. As we all do. The question is, *which* Lord?"

"How many are there?"

"Only one that is true."

"Are we discussing the Lord or the Church?"

"They are one and the same. The rock that Peter built. Your father, he and his generation in England, were loyal to the church. I understand your father had a chapel."

"Bequeathed to him at Hedingham."

"And that he prayed there and is buried close by."

"Do you keep records on all the Lord's children?"

"A shepherd keeps a close eye. Lambs go astray. You're father was..." The Monsignor hesitated. "He remained out of the fray," the Monsignor continued, measuring his words, "when he might have joined and supported the proper side."

"He was not much for politics."

"He supported your queen, who is... Shall we say, in the kindest of ways, not a friend of the Church."

Feeling the wings of his chair about to wrap around and suffocate him if he misspoke, Edward held his tongue.

"I hear you yourself skirt the edge," the Monsignor said after a silence.

"What is it you want of me?"

"Despite your father's reticence, he kept his faith. There are those who prefer an England returned to the fold."

"Our Queen..."

The Monsignor raised his hand. "'Tis not entirely of her doing. The original sin, the fault, lies with her father. Still, she might repent and undo the damage. The Pope would gratefully accept her spiritual return. Her subjects could take their sacraments again, as many do in secret anyway, even at their peril."

"The Queen has said many times she means not to invade men's hearts. It is not their religious practice that leads to treason, it is their intent to overthrow her."

"Unfortunately, sheep follow their shepherd wherever a shepherd leads, be it on the straight and narrow or toward a precipice... What are your immediate plans, then, if I may ask?" the Monsignor said, his voice lightened as he changed he subject.

"To see Italy. To soak in as much as I can."

"If I understand correctly, you write?"

Edward stared at the Monsignor. "In small measure," he answered.

"Perhaps then, you will have some interest in our folk tales and our stories of ancient times."

Edward said nothing.

"Where will you be staying, may I ask?" the Monsignor inquired.

"I thought to make Verona my central quarters."

"I have heard you have already made inquiries."

"Is there *nothing* you don't hear?"

"I feel it my duty to make your visit as informative as possible. In accordance with that, there is someone in Verona I should like you to meet."

"I, ahh..."

"Friar Gugliamino. I have asked the good friar to call upon you, if you have no objections."

"Would it matter if I did?"

"I cannot force correctness upon you. I can only open the door and pray the Lord will bid you enter."

"Will we meet again?"

"I think not, but you may be hearing from me."

Edward had intended to stay in Milan at least a week, although after his uncomfortable visit with the Monsignor, he decided to depart as soon as possible and sent a man ahead to Verona to assure that accommodations had been arranged. When favorable news arrived, he packed and left quietly, asking the driver to flog the horses.

CHAPTER 33

Friar Elmo

"My conscience has a thousand tongues."
Richard III, V, 3

Friar Elmo Leonardo Gugliamino looked nothing quite so complicated as the sound of his name. "'Tis a mouthful, to be sure," Gugliamino admitted in perfect English. "But most call me Elmo, which seems to better suit," he grinned. "I like it better myself."

Friar Elmo stood big-eared, short, bald, and round -- like two melons atop one another, the top, his baldhead, shinier than the larger bottom sphere. Quite clever of the Monsignor, Edward thought. Instead of saddling him with a Catholic bulldog on him, he sent an overweight basset hound with a poetic name and an angelic face.

"The Monsignor tells me you have a interest in our folk tales," Elmo said, his lower melon bouncing to the beat of his words.

"The Monsignor seems to know quite a bit about me."

"He has his means."

"All in praise of the Lord, I presume?"

"But, of course... Then you know of our storytelling troubadours."

"We have them, like in England."

"I understand that yours play their lutes and tell their tales separately, the one following the other."

"They sometimes sing their tales."

"But do they sing in character?" the friar asked.

"I do not take your meaning."

"Then you have *not* heard. Ours play their stories entirely in song, each singer taking on a different part. We add costumes and settings. It is quite elaborate."

"I should like to see this."

"The Monsignor thought you might."

"Somehow, that does not surprise me."

"He is not as devious as he seems. He believes he *is* doing the Lord's work."

"And you? What do you believe?"

"That miracles abound… Antonio Duodo? *Duke* Duodo. A good Catholic soul. He presents what we call an 'opera' three weeks from now, a musical story set in parts. He is in rehearsal now. I could arrange an invitation, if you wish."

Edward had procured a three-story villa on Verona's Via Mazzini, two piazzas north of the Piazza Signori and two piazzas east of Via Duomo. After climbing three tiers of narrow stairs that turned a sharp right at every opportunity, a heavy door opened to a thick, curtain-draped barrier that, when elbowed aside, revealed a small sitting room containing a walnut cabinet with carved nymphs clinging to the upper portion of its curved legs, a matched pair of fluted armchairs with inlaid splats, and a floresque, marble topped side-table sitting farther along the same wall. At first glance, the furniture appeared more decorative and elaborate than any Edward knew in England, and more detailed, finely inlaid and sculpted than any he had seen in France.

Directly in front of him, straight across the room, stood a cabriole-legged, leather-topped desk with fold-down side-slats that looked as though, when opened, would cause the piece to sprout wings and fly away.

To the right of the desk, a double-door opened onto a tiny, wrought-iron balcony with views of the River Adige, and across the river, perched high on a hill, stood the pillared ruins an ancient Roman amphitheater, its layered semicircle rows as if awaiting a performance that very afternoon.

The balcony's overhang would provide shade in the morning, while the arching sun, its low afternoon rays sparkling off the flowing water, would brighten Edward's spirits for writing after the noon meal. The ancient ruins would stir his imagination and remind him that he was in the midst of a history that carried ancient stories he could well adapt for the present day.

As soon as he settled in and changed his clothes, he heaved the desk closer to the balcony to take advantage of the view. He sat and adjusted himself in the unfamiliar armchair, then opened a small, round-topped box and extracted his ink crock, a handful of flat-tipped quills, and a fist-full of paper. As he laid his implements out on the desk, he anticipated remaining at least a year or more in Verona and its environs -- long enough to take its measure and sufficient time to require the services of a vellum shop and quill maker.

In his first days in his new quarters, he acquired the habit of rising with the sun, splashing his face from a cold basin his groom set out, then dressing quickly, tucking his pouch containing his paper and quill-box beneath his arm and walking east at a pace brisk enough to stir his morning juices and awaken his muse. On his way, he often purchased a hard-crusted sweetbread from a side-alley bakery and, upon arriving at the same piazza each day, claimed the same bench on the shady-side of a winged-horse fountain that drew its water from an ancient Roman viaduct.

Edward laid his sweetbread to the right side of the stone bench and his quill and ink to the right of that. Like an owl that sits quietly on a limb looking about and observing without being observed, Edward quickly melded into the bench, calling no attention to himself while occasionally glancing up and taking note of the human condition. He saw the delight on a young girl's face as she skipped and danced across the piazza and seemed joyful for no other reason than joy itself, then an old man with a silver-knobbed cane hobbling on the edge of his life, leaning toward his own death and struggling to keep from falling, knowing, if he stooped, he might not rise again, and a young couple, twenty-five meters apart, making love with their eyes from a distance, while others crossing the piazza, drifted by one another like stars, lost in their separate dreams and dramas, unconcerned and unaware of any existence beyond themselves.

Edward jotted notes to use for possible characters as Veronans crossed the piazza, their performance as natural as nature, their acts well known, their names unnamed. He munched his sweetbread and scribbled thoughts and speeches as they occurred to him as voices -- tentative at first, then babbling and jabbering so furiously that his pen could barely keep up and he had to order them to slow down and speak in turn.

As days passed on the bench, a regular group of men and women ventured out each morning, some to purchase root vegetables or wood for their cook fires, others for the pure purpose of strolling, still others to stretch the sleep from their legs and take the measure of the day. As Edward watched, he occasionally mimicked gestures to take the feel of their speech. To Edward's foreign ear, Italian pressed far more vigor in its utterance than English, tickling their vowels with the lilt of an uplifted eyebrow, the trust of a palm, or a slightly raised shoulder to emphasize a subtlety or nuance. Where Londoners half-smiled and grunted, "Good morning," Veronans stretched a far wider grin and belted a hardy, *"Buongiorno!"* Whereas Englishmen sat politely and held their hands in their laps, Italians sizzled as if on a hot skillet, unable they couldn't hold their bodies still, their hands in constantly flying in odd directions.

When ideas stopped flowing -- usually two hours or sometimes three after he arrived to claim his bench -- he brushed sweetbread crumbs from the leggings he acquired in Paris, gathered his notes and implements, and retraced his steps around the fountain and across the piazza, taking care to avoid fresh pigeon droppings. He usually returned by an unfamiliar back alleyway, whereupon to observe the more vibrant life that oft hides behind the public facade three boys chasing each other with as many dogs barking at their heels, a chubby-legged woman hauling an overflowing laundry basket up from the river as her neighbors hung high multicolored laundry-flags across the gap from house to house for a stranger to pass beneath as a dozen eyes followed him until he passed safely out of sight.

The instant Edward climbed his stairs, the characters that had materialized in the piazza found their voices again and chirped like nervous sparrows, chatting and interrupting each other until he sat at his desk and stained their words to paper. "There," he often muttered, their silence finally acknowledging their satisfaction that he had captured their intent.

CHAPTER 34

The Cloisters

"O heaven, were men but constant, he be perfect."
Two Gentlemen of Verona, V, 4

Surprisingly, Friar Elmo left Edward alone for most of his first two weeks in Verona, climbing the stairs only twice to knock and inquire how Edward was getting on. On the Monday morning of the third week, Elmo hesitated when Edward opened the door, "Would you care to join me later at the cloisters?" Elmo asked. "If you have time, that is. I've something I wish to show you."

The cloisters -- a marble-striped, arched, Franciscan friary with crossed walkways separated by triangles of neatly trimmed, emerald-green grass, squatted low and flat along the east wall of the Zeno Maggiore Church, as far on the opposite side of Verona as Edward could walk without passing beneath a city gate. Upon arriving in early afternoon, he rapped the chapel clapper and awaited its echo to dissipate and the heavy door to slowly squeak open.

"Ahhh!... Benvenuto!" Elmo said, sucking his belly in enough to squeeze through the gap and join Edward outside. "I saw you from the tower." He glanced over his shoulder. "I rushed down. I don't run so fast these days." He thrust his stomach forward. "I eat too much. The sin of gluttony... Come. Walk with me in the gardens."

The friar led him along a neatly raked pebbled-path, through an arched doorway and into a small rectangular courtyard shaded by the church on its far side and by orange-tiled porticos around the other three.

"I come here for prayer," Elmo said. "Most of the brothers pray in the dark. I sit too much in the dark, so I like the sun... I hear you have cloisters in England."

"Most were shut down or doled out as booty to Henry's supporters, or if not that, converted to manor houses or left to fall in ruin. My father took me to one of the few that remain. Compared to this," Edward said as he glanced about, "'tis sad to recall those weed-filled squares that once bloomed gardens."

"If your Henry had produced a male heir in his first marriage, those gardens would still be in flower, would they not? Still things may yet change. God has great patience. He keeps his own timetable. Earthly kings receive no special treatment."

"Often worse, by my reading," Edward said. "Even when the Lord intervenes in a monarch's affairs, the results are often disastrous."

"There is much we don't understand."

"I fear far more than we do."

"That is why I like these gardens so much," Elmo said, glancing around. "God's creations speak for themselves. You don't have to wrestle with doubts."

"You *have* doubts?" Edward asked, surprised at the friar's frankness.

"I have singed my toes on hell's fire, if that's what you imply. I believe in God. Why not in his counterpart?"

"I do confess, I've felt my own backside warmed from time to time while skirting too close to those flames."

Elmo chucked. "I see why the Monsignor thought we might get on."

"Is this what you wished to show me?" Edward asked. "These gardens?"

"Yes… Well… That too. But not exactly." He glanced away, and then looked back. "Not for the Monsignor. For myself. He knows of it, of course… Well, now that you've brought it up, I suppose I should show you out of courtesy."

"Absolutely."

"Yes… Well, then… But not here. Too many eyes. It's not a religious matter. More one of guidance."

"I could use a little."

"Not yours. Mine. I seek *your* guidance."

"I would be the last person to…"

"You would be the *first.*"

Guilt struck Edward for suspecting this shy, gentle man, although, on second thought, the devil often employed the most innocent as his emissaries, and the Monsignor was himself a clever devil.

"We shall taste the grapes," Elmo said, his cheeks flushed. "Among my other duties, I tend the cellars. Would you care to aid me in my chore?" he grinned.

"Partake of the Lord's harvest? Refusal would be a sacrilege."

"The wine will keep our tongues from drying out."

Edward followed the friar across a stone terrace and beneath a heavilybeamed doorway. "Watch your head," Elmo said. "I forget. I usually come alone."

They angled along a curved, shoulder-wide hall and then spiraled down a narrow winding staircase, Elmo lighting a candle to lead their way, its reflection glowing off the rounds of kegs stacked floor-to-ceiling along both walls.

"These cellars," Elmo said as they stepped onto an earthen floor, "to me, they feel holier than the sanctuary. After all, our Lord rose from a tomb darker than this. It reminds me of his sacrifice." He sat his candle on a tiny wooden table, brushed off two stools, and scooted them side-to-side. "Don't breathe until the dust settles."

"It does exude a presence," Edward said, reminded of his father's tomb at Hedingham and the ghost who once whispered to him there.

Elmo lit two more candles, their flames steady in the still air. "I keep the inventory," he said, running his eyes down a row of barrels. "And in that capacity, I select the wines for Holy Communion. I feel obliged to test before offering one to the flock and sometimes you can't be sure on the first try."

"A solemn duty," Edward agreed as they sat. "Requiring a certain expertise."

"Years of patient practice. And, of course, a love of the job." Elmo lifted two goblets from a shelf, blew dust from their bottoms, and then filled a small portion of both. "I believe you'll favor this," he said, plunking Edward's goblet on the table and sliding it across. "I move down the line as I go."

Edward sipped and swished the result across his tongue.

"You know how to savor."

"England is a nation of brew and ale. Yet we receive frequent gifts from the French ambassador."

"Ahhh! The French! What do *they* know?... What do you think of it?"

Edward sipped again. "A bit tart," he said. "A smoky flavor."

"Quite right. Not our best." Elmo said. "We try another. Sometimes it takes several to discover the one that's just right." He tossed what remained of their goblets in a bucket, rinsed them in a water filled cask, and then half filled each from a keg that required a longer reach.

"A heavier fruit than the last," Edward said as he tasted. "Apricot or pear, I believe."

"Plum. Does it suit you?"

"Quite well."

"Then we shall see if the flavor holds to the bottom," Elmo said, retrieving Edward's goblet and filling it and his own in equal portion.

"Is this what you wished me to see...?" Edward asked, nodding toward the casks.

"Indeed, 'twould make a good show, but t'was not my intent." Elmo bent at the waist, slid a crate out from beneath his feet, opened the lid, and extracted a thin bound folio and a small stack of papers. "Since I spend so much time down here, I use this as my workplace and study. Our quarters are tiny. We lead a simple life. Not much is allowed, and certainly not this," he said, holding up what he extracted.

"Sedition?"

"Some would call it that... A play. A comedy."

Edward snickered. *"That* is funny." He glanced at the stack. "And these are all yours?"

"Most are. A few are yours."

"Mine?"

"The Monsignor came by them through one of his many sources. Not that he approves. Yet, he knows I write and overlooks it. Perhaps he thought that a natural connection between us."

"And which of my writings sprouted wings, flew all the way from England and landed in the Monsignor's lap?"

"This." Elmo extracted the folio and passed it across. *"A Hundreth Sundrie Flowers."*

"My name is not on that."

"Truly?... 'E. Ver' is stamped on several of the entries? Does not 'E. Ver' refer to Edward de Vere, a thin disguise?"

"A partial mask is not meant to cover the entire face," Edward said. "Those who truly wish to know can easily see beneath it."

"Why would one wish to hide even part of such a beautiful face?"

"'Tis not beauty that requires hiding. 'Tis politics that necessitates a false front."

"For me as well," Elmo said.

"How so?"

"My penance. The politics of the church. They accepted me into the priory on condition. They permit me to taste the wine and have my fill, as well you see." He tapped his goblet with a thumb. "We all bear at least one vice. Some, more than one. They tolerate my excessive taste for wine as long as I hold it within the cloister. But I am not allowed to lay with women. That was my downfall. Mixing the two. Too much drink and too much company. The priory offered me drink and shelter if I renounced the company."

"And how did wine and women point you to me?"

"Those were not the worst of my sins. It was the writing that topped my list of evils. Poetry *and* plays, no less. I forsook the church. The Monsignor sent his dogs to retrieve his stray. He herded me back to the fold. I have a child by a woman I did not know. I remember neither her name nor her face. Other parts, I do recall."

Good Lord, Edward thought. Did the Monsignor know of Edward's son by the Queen? How could he?

"Now I write in place of women," Elmo said. "Some of it rather poetically erotic. Do you think that an enticement or a distraction? The ink dries so quickly, yet the words remain to study and tempt. My wine, my poetry, my prayers fill my days. It's the nights ... Perhaps you would consent to read some of what I've written, though 'tis far below your caliber."

"I should be delighted."

Elmo shuffled though his papers and lifted out three from the middle and laid the others down. "Perhaps these then... Tell me. Do you think it possible to live without a woman once you've tasted one?" he asked as he handed them across. "I mean forever, unless they have them in heaven? I have friends among the brothers, but is that enough? Once you've tasted the devil's bawdiness, does the flavor ever leave? Or is it like the wine? Once tasted, you never forget. You never loose desire."

Edward had no answer and said so. "In that realm, I am writing ahead of my age and experience," he admitted. "I steal passion from Ovid, from the classics. I make up what I have not fully experienced."

Edward hoped he had only begun to savor the delights of women, having tasted the Queen's teasing excitement, her grace, the explosive exuberance of an experienced woman – all weighted against Anne, a mere girl who knew not what to give nor what she wanted, who shut her eyes and mouth to avoid the sight and taste of it.

As Edward left the cloisters and returned to his apartments, the river dampness soaking thought his vest, he wondered, *could* a man sustain himself on a male relationship alone, friar to friar, brother to brother, with no sex involved? He had not lain with Anne in months before he left. He contemplated what it might be like if he and Friar Elmo lived in Verona as male friends, as simply as that. The friar seemed amiable enough. Could writing substitute, at least in part, for a fuller sensual life? If he and Elmo were together -- not as English earl and friar, but as two gentlemen of Verona - could the unchecked passion of one for a woman wedge a split between them? Could such a woman separate them knowingly? Deliberately? Deceitfully?

Edward grinned at his thoughts, as he often did, surprised at the source of plots and characters.

CHAPTER 35

Villa Duodo

"An honest tale seeds best
Being pleasantly told."
Richard III, IV, 4

A week and a fortnight after they met, Edward accompanied Friar Elmo for an evening of song, fest, and merriment -- of opera at Villa Duodo in the rolling hills three leagues north of Monselice, a half-day's journey southeast of Verona. "Far enough in the county," Elmo said, "they can sing their lungs out and only the hills complain. They attempt to resurrect the classic Roman theater set to music. They call themselves *Il Camerata, The Club* in English, and try to outdo each other. They flaunt their excess and take delight in it. The Duke will be pleased to display his vanity to an English guest. He will insist we stay the night."

Duke Francisco Duodo set his stage much like Hedingham's, although Duodo set his feast in one room, his production in another, whilst at Hedingham, with fewer rooms, all stood in one. When the Dukes' thirty guests finished their meal, he rose and invited them into his viewing room where harps and mandolins soothed digestions and induced a mood of fantasy.

In a Whitehall performance for the Queen, all awaited the Queen's entry and then bowed before sitting. At Villa Duodo, all sat at once, paying little homage to their host.

The Duke, a tall, angular man with a sharply trimmed goatee, stepped onto the platform as waiters topped his guest's crystal glasses with sweetened Mozelle. "Welcome to the house of Duodo, my friends," the Duke began in Italian. Whatever Edward didn't understand -- although his Italian was becoming more fluent Elmo leaned across and translated. "We are in for a delight this glorious night," the Duke said. "In the spirit of the ideals that sparked the flowering of our Roman classics, sculpture, and architecture, we do our part to inspire a new generation of Italian renaissance. In this regard, I proudly present an opera in our renewed spirit of music, its story expressed entirely by song." He nodded toward Edward and switched to English." We try out our new operatic form, as our regular guests know. I have contributed costumes myself," he swung his arm toward a swan encrusted partition, "and have added a new screen for our singers to conceal themselves. We shall present three short pieces this evening. The first, *The Tragical History of Julius Caesar,* from our Roman past, that followed by a brief companion piece, *Mark Antony and Cleopatra,* a tale of love gone awry and sadly sunk into the sea." The Duke paused, as if relishing his metaphor. "After an intermission, our third and final piece..." He grinned. "Well... One of local history, and recent, but I shall hold that as a surprise."

As the Duke stepped down, Elmo whispered to Edward, "Our Italian history *was* once world history, was it not?"

"Poetic *and* military," Edward said. "Both stolen from Athens and Sparta."

"Borrowed and well elaborated upon."

"I concede as much," Edward said. "If I had found as much history at home, I might have stayed in England to write of it."

When a loose-jawed woman three seats down the row leaned forward, twisted her head and scowled, Edward and Elmo quieted themselves and leaned back quietly as flutes whistled a quick tempo and two tambourines thumped what sounded like a march of Roman legions. As the beat slowed and the music faded, an actor in a feathered helmet crept onstage, wide-eyed and furtive. He glanced about as though fearful an enemy approach, and then unexpectedly belted out his thoughts in song.

Other players entered in their turn and sang their parts -- a deep chested man playing Brutus whose baritone rattled the chandeliers, a clean-shaven lad who hit a note that tinkled the crystal, and a heavy-bottomed, ample-bosomed woman playing Brutus's wife, Portia, whose voice was at once guttural, and yet, in soliloquy, as her part called it forth, struck a softness as sweet and gentle as a flowing spring.

The grand impact of song, of words set to music, released both sorrow and laughter, thumped Edward's heart and flushed his cheeks. He found his emotions swept away in the magic of illusion, his hands trembling in the clutch of a soloist's aria until she floated offstage and turned him loose. He had never experienced a performance that intensely gripping and exhilarating. Why could this not be accomplished in a play with spoken words alone to carry the same impact of tone and emotion? What words would be required to seep beneath the thoughts and minds of an audience to penetrate their hearts?

The same seven actors altered robes and roles, flowing in and out or the performance as different. In *Caesar,* the actor who played the lead, attired in leather shoulder pads and an eagle-crested chest plate, strutted onto the platform, looking about and puffing forth his armor. In *Antony,* a dark-haired Cleopatra sauntered forth. Her voice, sweet yet strong, feathered the air. Antony, played by the same actor who played Caesar, plodded out, clenched his fists and bellowed a somber resonance of loss and heartache. The two together send a wave of excitement and erotic energy flowing through the hall.

Both works -- *The Tragical History of Julius Caesar* and *Mark Antony and Cleopatra* -- conveyed simple tales, mere outlines, yet each transformed Edward's notion of what a dramatic work could be. He found himself caring more for Caesar and Cleopatra than the events that entangled their plights. *That's* what plays should execute, he realized -- *character* as story with *plot* as structure. Players should struggle as much or more *within* themselves as between each other, their turmoil revealed in soliloquies as much as by the clash between them, although without music, that would require words well chosen.

Stirred by *Caesar,* exhausted after *Antony,* unexpectedly angered at the brutality of Brutus, Edward gulped sweet cider and chatted quietly at intermission, still struggling with his Italian, nodding when he didn't understand a word or a comment as he anxiously anticipated the final presentation.

"Una storia di amore," the Duke announced when his audience returned. "A story of love."

The tambourine tapped and then, after a hush, a crimson-gowned woman drifted onstage, spread her feet in a solid stance, and sang *Il Giulietta nell'amore, appuntare il suo Romeo*. Giulietta, in love, pined for her lover, Romeo. When the singer's voice softened, Romeo entered. The two lovers, their fingers entwined, their eyes locked, blended in a vocal unity that filled the room and teased tears from an audience who anticipated their future.

Romeo singing his longing beneath Giulietta's balcony, begging her to let him climb the vines and wrap her in his embrace. After being secretly married and then discovered by feuding parents, the lovers conspire to escape Verona and assume new identities in other lands. To accomplish that end and ensure she is not followed, Giulietta persuades a monk to mix a potion to mimic her death. When Romeo fails to receive the note she sends to convey her plans and discovers her still body in her family tomb, he believes her dead, and, in his despair, swallows his own poison and succumbs. When Giulietta awakens to find her lover dead, she holds a pillow to her face and suffocates, all the while, singing her lament.

As the deceased lovers lay quietly upon the stage, Duodo's audience sat spellbound and motionless, drained of emotion. After a long silence, the audience breathed a collective sigh and rose from their chairs, still quivering in disbelief as the actors playing Romeo and Giulietta slowly rose and took their bows.

After thanking his audience and his players, the Duke urged his guests to mingle and enjoy the remainder of the evening on the patio or in the gardens, although a few left, begging forgiveness for other engagements. "Most from jealousy," Elmo whispered to Edward. "He has outdone them all."

Duodo and ten others, Edward and Elmo among them, adjourned to a side room for wine and conversation. Seated in a circle, staring across from Edward, the Duke asked Edward's thoughts.

"I have none," Edward said. "I thought *not*. I felt."

"Then we succeeded in dramatizing our history and our local family tragedy. Our stories are quite true in their basics, the tale of our lovers played out neither long ago nor far from here. A family feud between the Montagues and Capulets. The Montagues supported the Pope, the Capulets threw their weight behind the provincial Duchy. Church versus state. The lovers caught in between."

"We have that split in England," Edward said. "In our case, the old church versus the new."

"So I hear," the Duke said. "I understand that you.... How shall I say it? *Lo so che hai coinvolto personalmente.* That you are personally involved."

Edward glared at Elmo, who mouthed one word. "Monsignor."

"I prefer to stay out of politics." Edward said. "As in your tragedy, no one profits in a family feud."

"Sì, when you are caught, you are squeezed whichever way you turn."

"So it seems."

"Our lovers squeezed to death. A bitter lesson for all."

"It makes good drama, yet better watched than lived."

"I understand that you are staying in Verona. Our Giulietta is buried there. I myself grew up in Verona. We Veronans hold tight to our history. Our separate nation states have always warred, yet our religion binds us. We are all Catholic."

"And Roman, I should think."

"Roman. Etruscan. Barbarian. We are a modern mix, although the ancient Romans conquered our lands and bound us as one for a long time. On Rome's fall, we split again. It was the Church that reunited us, along with much of the Continent. Your country included."

"Bonds break," Edward said.

"As our Romeo and Giulietta, the families in our tragedy. 'Tis from a novella written of our recent history by Luigi Da Porto, a Veronan himself. He titled it *Una Novellamente di Due Amanti Nobili*. We, of course, changed the title and adapted it to song."

"I should like to read the original."

"Da Porto's? I shall find it in my library and have Friar Elmo bring it to you."

Edward and Elmo departed Villa Duodo after staying the night, the lingering effect of the opera's tone and characters still ringing in Edward's ears as their carriage made its way down a hillside road that was inspired, according to Elmo, by Rome's Via Sacra and its twelve stations-of-the-cross, each chapel on the road constructed by a earlier Duke to remind us of God's glory each time we left and returned.

"I should like to stop at the lower chapel," Elmo said. "The crucifixion shows Jesus' death in its starkest form. That is the heart of it, is it not? Our Lord's death and resurrection. The promise of life hereafter."

"If we are forgiven," Edward reminded him.

They halted their carriage at the bottom of the hill, climbed out, and entered a circular, white-walled chamber, Edward waiting just inside the entrance while Elmo stepped forward and knelt beneath the crucified Christ. He prayed quietly, then genuflected, stood, and hurried out without looking up or speaking. Without understanding why, Edward stepped foreword and fell to his knees. He lifted his gaze to the tortured Christ nailed on the cross. The Lord's head hung in sorrow, blood dripping around his forehead, his lower right rib punctured and oozing.

Edward thought he should cry at the sight of such suffering, but no tears came. After staring in silence, he averted his eyes. He stood, turned his back on Christ's sacrifice, and walked out.

"You truly believe, then?" Edward finally asked as they departed and the villa disappeared behind them.

"Why take a chance? If God's word be true, then Jesus prepares our way. If not, belief in his promise at least fills *this* life."

"A cynical view."

"Practical, I should say. We all wrestle with doubts and the consequences of our actions. Heaven or hell, in this life or the next, we pay one way or the other."

CHAPTER 36

The Balcony

"She hath pursued conclusions
Infinite of easy ways to die."
Antony and Cleopatra, V, 2

During those infrequent times when scenes weren't swirling
in his head or characters stomping about speaking their minds or
arguing with him, Edward walked among the structures of the past.
He roamed Verona's streets and byways, oft times ambling beyond
the northern gate and along ancient country lanes leading toward the
villages, all the while observing and noting what he heard and saw.

The Italian Renaissance, with its renewal of art and literature
in the classical mode, excited, delighted, overwhelmed, and dazed
him. He had experienced nothing of its like it in England, which,
from a distance, now seemed shamefully backward with no classical
period to hark back to, let alone revive. Italian art decorated the
villas and apartments and painted frescos left little empty room on
city walls. Classic statues stood erect in every piazza, many with
fountains spreading their cascades around ancient feet or trickling
over knees or across foreheads. "Good Lord," Edward thought as he
passed beneath the fingered shadows of the Porta Lovia Gate. "If I
could only put all of this into the plays this city inspires and do it
justice!"

Travel had molded changes in him. He had grown. He would
not return the same man. He could not. That man had left him. Now
his only path was forward, and he knew not where that led except,
for now, home to bed for the evening.

The next morning Edward was awakened by Verona's
church bells, from its largest to it tiniest, they rang like a chorus of
barrel-chested hawks attacked by high-pitched chickadees every
Sunday morning, waking Verona's inhabitants with guilt for the

prior evening's frivolities, while basking them in the sounds of God's eternal love.

Edward stretched his legs out from under a thick quilt and climbed from bed just long enough to use the slop-pot, then crawled back in, retightened his curtains, and burrowed under until the cacophony ended. He rose a second time before God's glory rang the end of services and remained in his apartment, writing the remainder of the day, and awaiting a quieter Monday.

After writing throughout the following morning and early afternoon, he left his apartment and headed north, toward the first of two locations that Friar Elmo had pointed out on their return from Villa Duodo -- the first, Giulietta Capulet's crypt in a graveyard next to the Church of San Francesco al Corso.

"The same as in her death scene," Elmo had said. "At least in Da Porto's portrayal. Perhaps he even wrote his death scene there. He lived nearby." Farther along, in pinched-in quarters closer to Palazzo della Ragione, Elmo also pointed out Giulietta's former home, and then Romeo's old residence farther along on the Via Arche Scaligere. "That's where they say he lived," Elmo had said. "We have no idea where Romeo is buried."

As Edward passed through San Francesco al Corso's iron front gate, a chill came over him. He stuffed his hands beneath his coat and headed toward a cypress barrier that shielded the church and its cloisters from the road. A trimmed-hedged path guided him down a loose-stone walkway that paralleled a row of low-roofed cottages. Nun's quarters, he thought. After the path curved right, it wound toward a round-walled mound, its lower portion buried in the ground with stone steps leading to an open doorway.

As Edward stepped tentatively toward it, the burial vault exuded the ghostly familiarity, an aura of his father's tomb in Hedingham, as though his father's ghost had guided him here.

He drew a long breath and peered toward the chamber as three black robed women -- vultures with a final warning -- skulked across the path to his left, their heads cloaked, their faces hidden, only their scythes missing should they be grim reapers.

He eased down the first step, then down the next four and entered a domed chamber, the trunk of a gigantic tree visible through a single oval portal that spilled a dim yellow light across the floor. He waited for his eyes to adjust and then eased toward the flat raised monument, bending forward just enough to read block Latin letters chiseled across the breastplate. *"Tristifico laetabilis."* In English, *"Saddened joy."*

As he backed toward the wall and sat on a raised ledge, he was made aware of his own temporality. He realized, unlike Romeo or Giulietta, there would be no one to document or dramatize his story -- a comic-tragedy or whatever it be -- as da Porto had Giulietta's. Writers and playwrights freeze history's greatest winners and biggest looser in time for those in the future to thaw and read, while most end their lives with their names on tombstones, their stories, as fragile as their bones, soon faded and forgotten.

Was this the tomb of Da Porto's Giulietta, as Elmo said was commonly believed? And if it was, Edward thought as he stared across at the raised stone coffin, did Da Porto sit where Edward sat as he penned *Romeo and Giulietta's* death scene, perhaps squatting on the same bench, writing for hours, and then returning day after day, plying pen to paper until he had it right? Had the two lovers died here as Da Porto depicted in his death scene? Had he written of true reality, or had he blended fact with fantasy, as storytellers do, embellishing truth to suit his purpose?

Edward fished paper from his pouch, uncorked his ink, and sat them next to him. He envisioned a new crypt scene, a modification of Duodo's opera. When an image emerged, he glanced down and wrote "Juliet," the English variation of "Giulietta," then recorded lines as she seemed to speak them.

> Juliet: What if, when I lay within this tomb,
> I wake before the time that Romeo
> Come to redeem me? That is a fearful point!
> Shall I not be stiffened in this vault,
> This stifling air upon me

And here to die ere my Romeo comes?

Edward tapped his foot and waited, the thick damp air in the enclosure stifling his breathing. In the guise of his characters, he often felt their stirrings, and rejoiced or wallowed in their passion, joy and exuberance. The more he saw life though a character's eyes, heard their thoughts, or felt the tingling of anticipation in their fingertips, the more, in that moment, he became them, floating in their skins as he wandered through an ordinary day, only half aware of the duller life that swirled around him.

"No," he straightened his backbone and muttered. She would *not* have done it that way. Not suffocate as in Duodo's opera. Who could hold a pillow to their face and speak or sing, let alone hold that cover there long enough to die?

"I stabbed myself," he heard Juliet whisper. "Then dripped my blood across my lover's body... Can you see it?"

"I can," Edward mumbled, and as he wrote.

> Juliet: They wash his wounds with tears.
> Mine be spent for Romeo
> When theirs are dry.
> He made a highway to my bed,
> But I, a maid, die maiden widowed
> In my wedding bed
> Where death, not Romeo, did take my
> maidenhead.

Once primed, lines flowed, Juliet's apparition suddenly sitting on her coffin, leaning forward and spewing words for Edward to catch.

> Juliet: I never shall be satisfied with Romeo,
> Till I behold him once again.
> If I could find a man
> To bear a poison, I would temper it
> To sleep in quiet.

The rhythm misread in some of it, yet was set enough to later fix. He preferred to capture the essence of a speech or scene as it came, then labor over rhyme and nuance at his leisure. He jotted, crossed out, and jotted again, and then stood to stretch and walk outside. When he retuned, he listened as Juliet spoke again and then scribed her words until his fingers refused to bend without complaint. Juliet must have tired as well. When he looked up, she had withdrawn to her tomb.

By the time he left the crypt, night's shadows blanketed the graveyard as a steady breeze buoyed him through the gate and then dissipated in the city's maze of cobbled streets and alleyways. He hadn't eaten, yet wasn't hungry. He angled left at Via Viento, urged downhill until the passage split, and amazingly, without intent, he found himself standing beneath Giulietta's balcony, its shutters closed and darken.

He saw no apparition, yet heard Juliet's words stirring the air. "I thought I heard my Romeo... No. I have not. I want it thus, and thereupon imagine it."

A family clash had killed two lovers. The Montagues versus the Capulets. When words flowed again, Juliet spoke in a quiet but easily distinguishable voice.

> 'Tis but a name that is my enemy.
> Thou art thyself, though not a Montague.
> What is a Montague? 'Tis not hand, nor foot,
> Nor arm, nor face, nor any other part
> Belonging to a man. Be some other name!
> What's in a name? That which we call a rose
> By any other name would smell as sweet.

Edward thought he might have Elmo play a friar -- an intermediary, as the Monsignor employed Elmo to intervene in Edward's life. Juliet would enjoin the friar to provide a sleeping potion to feign her death and thus enable the lovers to escape.

Friar: (shows Juliet a vial)
    Take thou this vial, being then in bed,
    And this distilled liquor drink thou off,
    When presently through all thy veins shall run
    A cold and drowsy humor, for no pulse
    Shall keep his native progress, but surcease.
    No warmth, no breath shall testify thou livest.
    The roses in thy lips and cheeks shall fade
    To paly ashes, thy eyes' windows fall
    Like death when he shuts up the day of life.
    Each part, deprived of supple government,
    Shall, stiff and stark and cold, appear like death.
    And in this borrowed likeness of shrunk death
    Thou shalt continue two and forty hours,
    And then awake as from a pleasant sleep.
    Now, when the bridegroom in the morning comes
    To rouse thee from thy bed, there art thou dead.
    In the meantime, against thou shalt awake,
    Shall Romeo by my letters know our drift.

Juliet:
    Give me, give me! O, tell not me of fear!
    Farewell, dear Father.

Edward shivered. Like Duodo's audience, he sensed the tragedy ahead -- that Romeo would not receive the note and think his Juliet dead, and in his grief, take his own life.

Edward turned away from the balcony, sad for his characters and sad for himself. As he turned and walked uphill, the notion of love and its absence ran through his mind. What would induce a man or woman to die for love? He knew how to write it, yet knew it not from life. He plodded back to his apartment and slept a restless night, wrestling his blankets as characters and plots swam in his head, each struggling for the words to stand on solid ground.

CHAPTER 37

The Jew and the Sea Captain

"Let me be cruel. I will speak daggers."
Hamlet, III, 2

Rising early to leave Verona and explore Venice, Edward journeyed east along dusty roads, munching an apple or a fist-full of walnuts for sustenance and arriving at the edge of the Venice lagoon as the setting sun soared its fire across the water and emblazoning the city's domes and tiled roofs. Edward dismounted and looked across at a golden island whose beauty writers and artists, with their finest words or brushes, barely hinted at.

He boarded his horse at a mainland livery and stepped onto a barge with six others for the last shuttle of the day, those arriving later, by choice or circumstance, forced to accept quarters at a dockside inn.

After a smooth ride, the barge gently bumped a landing at the steps of St. Marks' Square, leaving behind a flock of squawking seagulls only to be accosted by a hoard of pigeons that apparently hadn't eaten in all day and saw Edward and his fellow travelers as their last chance for an evening meal.

Edward was well aware as he stepped onto the landing, of Venice's historic command of the Adriatic, its stilts dug early in the lagoon to form a floating barrier against Roman invaders from the south. While the Thames tickled London's feet, sporadically lapping at her skirts, the Adriatic engulfed Venice and forced her to sink, swim or tread water as curve-nosed gondolas navigated its twisting arteries like multicolored waterbugs ferrying freight and passengers to the steps of homes or warehouses whereupon half-sunken doors opened to holes in the wall that quickly swallowed vessel, passenger and cargo.

Edward had sent a man ahead to secure temporary quarters, desiring to spend substantial time in Venice while retaining his Verona apartment as his base. The double rental would displease Burghley, but at least with correspondence, Edward would not have to hear the Chief Minister bellow his displeasure.

He made his way along the north canal to Rio Garzotte in the Santa Croce district where he located the address that fit the key he had been given. He climbed the stairs and flopped across a canopied bed, dozed an hour, and woke well after dark. Famished, he left by a side entrance and found an open refectory two blocks south, in the direction of San Marco. He spotted a rare empty stool at a back table with several hefty men wearing seamen's caps hunched forward munching crusted chunks of dark bread, then washing it down with mugs of what looked like brown slime.

"We are a city of traders," an olive skinned sailor with wide nostrils and a thin mustache informed Edward after asking his nationality, the brown slime loosening his tongue to flap at will. "I am a Moroccan myself, a Moor. A Venetian now. I captain a ship with ample goods to haul. The Venetians accept me as a prince of my trade. I am of use to them, and they to me. I believe they would wed me to one of their daughters if I pointed to one. Or *say* they would, then stab me in my sleep the night before the wedding... With the color of *this* skin?" he grinned and rubbed his dark chin. "They could not mistake me. I am dark even *in* the dark."

The Moor seemed to feel a kinship with Edward, as though the man could freely speak his mind or spew his venom without fear of repercussions. The Moor, leaning on his elbows as he watched Edward eat a thick peppered stew, filled Edward in the details of his life as if they were long-parted friends catching up after a long absence. When Edward finally left, he stumbled back to his quarters, then slept till noon the next day and awoke refreshed.

A week later, a barber on Via Bartolomio answered Edward's inquiry by pointing with his razor. "Turn right two bridges up on Il Rialto. The best tailors are in that row. Leather, linen, the finest silks from China, whatever you wish. If it can be had, they will have it ready made or find a way to sew it for you."

Two days earlier, Edward had written to Burghley, answering his father-in-law's persistent cries for monetary along with his dire prediction of Edward's financial doom. Edward posted his reply after leaving the barber, on his way to Il Rialto.

> My Lord Minister,
>
> I am sorry to hear how hard my fortunes are in England. But knowing how vain a thing it is to linger a necessary issue, I appoint you to sell my land in Cornwall. To stop my creditors' exclamations - or rather, their defamations, if I may call them that -- I desire and authorize your Lordship to sell any additional portions of my lands or estates which your Lordship shall deem necessary and appropriate.
>
> Whereupon, until all such encumbrances be passed and I can better settle myself again at home, I am determined to continue my travels at whatever expense they may bear.
>
> At Your Lordship's command,
> Edward Oxford

"You *could* have these sooner," the Venetian tailor explained as he lengthened his tape across the Edward's shoulders, scribbling his measurements on a chalkboard, and then stooping to draw his tape lengthwise down Edward's spine. With the sizing complete and Edward's selections made, he asked the tailor to prepare the garments and hold them until his money arrived.

"There are those who would lend you the funds," the tailor said as he tapped a chalky finger down his checklist of measurements. "For a small remittance, of course," he said, looking up. "For an English Earl, that should be no problem. You could put up your trunks and carried wardrobe, or perhaps your boarded horse against default."

"A lender? For a fee? We have no such thing in England. 'Tis friend-to-friend unless you sell property to raise the funds."

"We Venetians are merchants and craftsmen," the tailor said. "We need a way to move our goods and services and procure our monies quickly, then let others sort out debts and collections."

"Why not lend yourself," Edward asked, "if there be a profit in it?"

The tailor drew his chin in as if offended. "I am a good Catholic. The church forbids lending for gain. The Jews serve the function as of usuries. They use money to make money. They don't believe in our God. Theirs seems to have no rule against it... I shall write down an address. If you are able to borrow enough to place down, say a quarter of what is owed, I could have these ready for you by the middle of the month."

Edward never met a Jew. None remained in England, the few that once resided there expelled by Edward I, the "Hammer of the Scots," who confiscated their properties to finance his Crusade in the Year of Our Lord 1289.

After leaving the tailor, Edward hired a gondolier to transport him along the Grand Canal to Ponte del Scalzi, his boots wet from sloshed water as he climbed out and stepped onto the landing. He walked fifty meters down an alley, then ducked his head to pass under a narrow tunnel that opened to a fortress-like square surrounded by tall buildings on three sides and blocked by a wall on the fourth. "They lock us in from dusk to dawn," the moneylender said when Edward found his shop. "The rats scurry in and out easier than we," he added, sarcasm dripping from his waist-length beard. "Only the rodents find the holes in the system... How may I assist you?"

The usurer's darkness, his beard, his clothing, his stare, haunted Edward after he signed the lender's agreement and made his way back to his apartment. The Jew, out of place in Venice except for his function, was barely tolerated within it -- a good deal like

Edward and the Moorish Captain felt in Italy. No matter how much a stranger practiced foreign customs or learned a strange language, he would always *be* a stranger. Worse than the moneylender or the Moor, Edward felt he served no practical function even in his own country.

With Elmo left behind in Verona, undoubtedly hunkered down in his wine cellar sampling for his Sunday sacraments, Edward felt alone and lonely. Emptiness truly *is* like a death, he thought.

At least his imagined characters provided him some measure of company to fill the cracks in his days. He had already thought of the Jew and the Moor as characters set in Venice much as Juliet had sprung from Verona. He thought to have his Moor in need of money to borrow from the Jew... "No," he muttered, vaguely looking up as he crossed a canal bridge. Both characters, the Jew and the Moor were strong enough to weave separate plots, each based on prejudice, one swirling around money, the other around false friendship.

To examine the plight of a moneylender would require a borrower. "Neither a borrower nor a lender be." Burghley's old admonishment would sit well here. He would create Antonio, a good Italian name as borrower, and a Shylock as lender, a man locked in a ghetto and trapped within his trade. "They all disgrace me," his Jew would grumble. "They mock me. Laugh at me. And yet they use me," Edward spoke the lines as they occurred to him. "And what is their reason?... I am a Jew. Hath not a Jew eyes? Hath not a Jew hands, organs, dimensions, senses, affections, passions? Fed with the same food, hurt with the same weapons, subject to the same diseases, healed by the same means, warmed and cooled by the same winter and summer as a Christian? If you prick us, do we not bleed? If you tickle us, do we not laugh? If you poison us, do we not die? And if you wrong us, shall we not revenge?"

Revenge, Edward thought. This shall be a play of vengeance. A story with reprisals.

"I will not excuse the villainy they teach me," the Jew spoke through Edward. "I will use it against them."

When Edward glanced up from his thoughts, his apartment stood before him.

****

Duke Duodo sent an introductory letter to his Venetian cousins who chose to display Edward like a fancy English fish they had caught in one of their canals and wished to flaunt. Edward took advantage of their favor by night. By day, he hired a gondola to ply the canals, contemplating how his emerging Venetian characters might act out their plights along those waterways. On one productive Thursday afternoon, he reached the top of his stairs, flung his cape across his bed, and scribbled a line he had carried in his head for blocks.

> Shylock: A pound of flesh. That is what I
> propose. If he cannot repay what he owes me, I
> shall demand his skin and bone.

If Christians hated the Shylock for being a Jew, why not have the Jew hate Christians for their faith? Would that not allow an audience a way to see both sides of it?

> Shylock: (to himself) I hate Antonio, for he is
> Christian.
> The Christians lend their friends their money
>   free,
> Thus bringing down the rate of usury,
> They steal from my livelihood.
> I will feed this ancient grudge I bear them.
> They hate our sacred nation, and rail
> Upon my bargains and my well-won thrift,
> Which I call interest. Cursed be their tribe.

Edward would mix pride with bigotry, favor and disfavor applied both for good and evil. His Jew would demand his contract's fulfillment -- the delivery of a pound of flesh if he was not paid. "An agreement is an agreement," as Burghley would say. If Edward finished the play and set it for the Queen, she would clearly see Burghley's part in it.

CHAPTER 38

An Uncertain Gift

"Well said, that was laid on with a trowel."
As You Like It, I, 2

Edward's imagined Shylock pointing his curved index finger toward his creator, spinning gestures in Edward's dreams and waking him to light a candle and scribble the Jew's words before morning stole them away.

Edward's emerging play -- *The Merchant of Venice* he would call it -- revealed itself in bits and pieces, many still hesitant and partly hidden. Other parts, once writ, required revision. He knew the ending. Antonio, his merchant, would lose a fortune at sea, allowing the moneylender to legally demand a pound of flesh as determined by their agreement. Yet the strictness of the law would work as much against the Jew as in his favor -- his contract calling for a pound flesh but not a drop of blood. "If he can peel the one without loosing any of the other, let him scrape it," Antonio would argue before a judge. Seeing the impossibility of that, the Jew would relent, allowing Edward to contrast the narrow, legal interpretation of the law against one of temperance and mercy.

A spider's thread of difference separated comedy from tragedy. If Edward stripped Antonio's flesh and took his life, a tragedy unfolded. If he had Antonio comically wiggle out from beneath the Shylock's blade, a farce, an insightful folly emerged.

Edward honed several plays at once, splitting his travels, his thoughts, and his energies between Verona and Venice, oft times spending a day and sometimes a night in Padua to consult its University library. Travel stimulated him. Never had so many stories swirled about in his head at once, sometimes spinning two or three before they settled down and found their separate voices.

Late one rainy afternoon, while writing at his desk in Verona and looking across the river at the Roman amphitheater, Friar Elmo rapped on the door, barging in as soon as Edward opened it and handing him Duke Duodo's copy of Da Porto's *Una Novellamente di Romeo and Giulietta*. "I brought you another," Elmo said, holding out a second red-leather volume. "More tales of Verona," he said. "A collection found in Giovanni Boccaccio's *Decameron*. We have a fair library at the cloister. Better that we read of life than partake in it. "

Elmo said he couldn't stay long, that prayers awaited. As soon he left, Edward plunked down in an armchair and skimmed Boccaccio's *Decameron,* the Italian language, from his studies at Burghley House, being far easier to read than pronounce. Bits of characters and scenes occurred to him as he read, plots and dialogue revolving around themes of misplaced loyalty and love's desperation, materializing before his eyes.

His writings over the next weeks and months required two trips to his newly acquired quill maker as he gradually filled a small chest, with drafts that drifted across his bed each night laying them aside to crawl in at night. His servants interrupted him with food trays, carrying out what he had not eaten from the last meal and carting in books and monographs that Elmo dropped off at odd intervals, sometimes on his own accord as he learned more about what Edward was writing, and at other times at Edward's request as he learned the extent of the cloister's collection.

He revised *Romeo and Juliet* several times, adding scenes and dialogue to roughly parallel De Porto's version, then fleshed out *Two Gentlemen from Verona* and outlined two scenes to the *Merchant of Venice* -- one of betrayal, the other a murder scene -- each weaving Boccaccio's local legends around Edward's accumulating knowledge of Venetian history and settings.

Edward's other world England intruded on the cloudy morning of September 27th in the Year of Our Lord 1575, when he received a letter from Lord Burghley that Anne had delivered a healthy daughter in July and that she had named her Elizabeth, after the Queen. Upon reading the news, Edward bounced from his rooms, tumbled down the stairs and out the front, seeking a hand to shake in his good fortune, then suddenly stopped to reassess. He had neither been prepared in name nor fact to bear a son by the Queen, and was not now equipped by circumstance or temperament to raise a daughter by Anne. "You are irresponsible and always shall be," his mother had gleefully pointed out. Spiteful or not, she was right. He lumbered back to his rooms, glad at least that his mother and the man who took his father's place were not there to rub his nose in the responsibilities of fatherhood.

Not withstanding his misgivings, he wrote Anne that he regretted his absence and hoped his letter found her and their child in good health. The same afternoon he received the news, he bought an Italian Bible from one of the stalls on Via Pallone and sent it along with a note, hoping that holding God's word in prayer might comfort her. He wrote her thus on the Bible's face plate:

> To Lady Anne de Vere, Countess of Oxford,
> whist her husband, Edward Vere, Earl of
> Oxford,
> is occupied in foreign travel.

Beneath these opening words, he played on his name again, as he had in other writings -- on "Vere," the Latin word for "truth," and on "E. Ver" buried in the ancient de Vere motto, "Vero Nihil Verius" meaning "Nothing truer than truth."

> Words of *truth* are fitting to a *Vere* -- lies foreign to *truth,* for only *truth* lasts, all else fleeting. Therefore, since thou, a *Vere,* art wife and mother of a *Vere*, and seeing that thou mayst with good hope look forward to being mother of an heir of *Veres,* may thy mind always glow with love of *truth,* and may thy *true* motto be *Ever Lover of the Truth.* That thou mayst the better attain this,

pray to the Author of all *Truth,* that His word may teach thee -- that His Spirit may nourish thy inner life. So that, alleviating the absent longings of thy dear husband, thou, a *Vere,* mayst be called the *true* glory of thy husband.

He also wrote to Burghley, congratulating him as grandfather, yet well understanding that the Lord Minister would be disappointed in the gender of his granddaughter. To escape his commoner's lineage, Burghley would already be scheming to marry her to a baron or an earl in hopes of sending his blood down a titled line.

He considered writing the Queen, but decided against it. She would already know of the birth. Beyond that, he and Elizabeth were apart so long, he wasn't sure how she felt in his absence. She *could* write him, but being queen, she would not. His refraining would steep her curiosity. If he continued writing plays, he would have an abundance to show in his absence to regain her good will.

CHAPTER 39

The Maze

"I am as vigilant as a cat to steal cream."
Henry IV, IV, 2

In the ballroom of the Villa dei Conti in Padua, a mere six leagues west of Venice, the Countess Louisa Cadenza curtsied to Edward, her full breasts cradled and lifted in a tightly laced bodice, their soft pink flesh exposed as she glanced up.

"Per favore, la Signora," Edward said, holding the Countess by her fingertips as she rose from her curtsy. "In England, we bow to royalty. I am hardly that."

"I hear you are close," she said as she locked his gaze.

"Sixteenth in line. 'Tis quite far down."

"And that you are close to your Queen."

"We are acquainted."

"I hear more than that."

"What exactly *do* you hear?"

"Dance with me."

She wedged her arm through his elbow and led him beneath a sparkling row of candelabras, the strum of mandolins tapping Edward's toes as he grasped the countess by her narrow waist and spun her toward the center of the room, swirling past others who cleared a path before them. It had been a long time since he had abandoned himself to a woman who danced as if she cared not what others thought -- her only concern bent to her own pleasure.

"Do you always dance so freely?" he asked when the music stopped.

"Dance *and* play," she said, panting while patting her breastbone. "What else is life for?"

"Others stare at us," he said.

"Let them. You think *these* are *their* wives?... 'Tis hot in here," she said, sliding a frilled handkerchief from her sleeve and dabbing perspiration down her neck. "Walk with me in the garden. I need to catch my breath."

"Your husband will miss you."

"I think not," she said as she slipped her moistened scarf between her cleavage and glanced up. "He is in Genoa on a diplomatic mission. A sudden calling. He won't be back this night. His diplomacy keeps him away a good deal. In his absence, he misses the beauty of our host's gardens... Come. I will show you."

Edward had forgotten the allure and excitement of a tempting, vibrant woman. He had once had it with the Queen but never with Anne, and had not laid with Anne his last months in England.

"Madam, I do not..."

"Be a gentleman, per favore." She turned and sashayed toward the veranda as though she expected him to follow. A thousand tongues in his head bid him follow and none bid him stay -- a good line to employ in *Romeo and Juliet*, lines often floating to him in the midst of living.

He hesitated, though not long. He waited until the Countess had exited to the moonlit terrace before ambling across the room, holding a discrete distance. "Vieni qui!" he heard her call as soon as he slipped outside. "This way!" She peeked around a pillar, then turned and dashed across the lawn, enticing him to follow. She looked over her shoulder and laughed, and then backed between trimmed hedges into a high evergreen labyrinth. He watched her disappear, then crossed the lawn and followed her into the maze.

"Vorresti giocare con me?" he heard her call.

He didn't answer, listening instead for her footsteps to trace her changing direction.

"Dove lei sono?" she called.

He crunched loose gravel, threading along narrow, trimmed tunnels, trying to remember his twists and turns, a task made more difficult as they grew more numerous and as he attempted to learn, as in life, by frequent error and constant correction.

"So che tu stai qui," he heard her giggle. "Have I beaten you yet?" she said in English. "Can you find me?"

At the next intersection, he turned right.

"Tu sei troppo lento! *Cosi* rallentare!... You are so slow! So *very* slow!"

Her voice rang next to him, yet beyond his reach as he encountered another dead end and turned back.

"L'inglese e perso?... Is the Englishman lost?"

He swung left and stuck another hedge wall, then reversed, scraping his shoulder on sharp needles before looping around toward the center. When he heard a shuffle in the next row, he stopped and listened. He heard footsteps and threaded toward them. Then nothing. Had she lured him into a fool's trap? The maze, a madman's foray, seemed to bend and twist in random directions, spiraling him in circles that crisscrossed, looped back over each other, and lead him down another blind alley to another dead end. He glanced up at the moon, the steady beacon shining first ahead of him, then over his left shoulder, then behind.

The tail of her dress suddenly swished across the path in front of him and disappeared. He darted toward it, laughter mocking his every step. He forked right and lost her again, his fruitless pursuit amusing her. When he heard her squeal, he turned toward the sound, then waited and listened. At the next passage, he ducked beneath a hedged-row, then straightened to realize that she had outwitted him again, that he was far better at chasing boars as a boy than pursuing a woman as a man.

"C'e un problema, Inglese?" Her voice drifted through the labyrinth. "C'e un problema? You have a problem?"

He felt this woman would not be caught unless she wished it so. When he finally reached the center, moonlight illuminated a handkerchief draped across a stone bench.

He slowly wound his way back out, avoiding previous wrong turns as best he remembered them. When he reached the entrance and peered across the lawn, she stood in candlelight in the doorway, waving a fingertip for him to follow, then quickly vanished inside, but when he crossed and entered the ballroom, she was nowhere in sight. He stood just inside the door, catching his breath and trying to appear inconspicuous when a servant eased up along the wall. "La Signora extends her apologies," he whispered. "The Countess has asked me to convey that she has taken a sudden headache and has retired for the evening… She has left you this." He handed Edward a note.

When the servant left, Edward glanced about. With no one seemed to be looking, he unfolded the note.

Ti sei trovato, Inglese?
Have your found yourself, English?

Had he *"found"* himself? What was that supposed to mean? Was she simply teasing to show her command of him?

He slipped the note in his waistcoat and meandered toward the entrance hall, briefly waylaid by a silver-haired Marquee who grabbed him by his elbow. "What is your opinion of the Church's function in the Northern Duchies?" the man asked.

"I have none… You'll pardon me. It's been a long day."

"Absolutamente."

Once outside, he signaled his steward to see to a carriage, then briefly wandered back in to thank his host, although the man seemed too well-lubricated to care, waving a drink amongst three smiling woman and thus preoccupied with their attention.

When he stepped outside again and passed through the front pillars, the hot humid night greeted him, his waiting stallions already dripping sweat down their haunches. The coachman nodded a sly grin, then faced forward as Edward opened the coach door to face a woman's bare ankle crossed over an equally bare leg. "Lei me ha trovato," the Countess said. "You found me at last. How clever of you."

"Countess. It's late. I…"

"If you are going to talk… a waste of precious time… climb in."

He thought it best to comply before someone wandered out and saw them, and reported to her husband. As soon as he climbed in, she reached across his chest and snapped the door shut as a whip cracked outside, the horses bolted, and the carriage rumbled forward.

The wine, the night, the maze, and the Countess melded as one. Well before dawn, the coach slowed in front of Edward's rooms. The door flung open and a foot booted him out of the carriage and onto the road, whereupon he clamored toward the wall, fumbled to his doorway, and crawled up the stairs.

CHAPTER 40

The Taming of Shrews

"I have had a dream, past the wit
of man to say what dream it was."
Midsummer Night's Dream, IV, 1

A throbbing headache woke Edward, his liquid brain sloshing in his skull with the slightest movement. He eased from bed, anchored his feet on wobbly floorboards, and waited for the room to steady, then straightened his arms like a bird's wings to balance toward a chair, whereupon he plunked down until the room stopped spinning. Only after he was able to sit straight enough to splash his face in the cold-water bowl his groom carried to him, did the previous night's events float back and crystallize.

He examined himself for a trace of guilt, but found none. The Queen and her chief minister had forced him to marry a passionless woman he did not love and did not miss. At twenty-five, his loins ached as much as any man's. He had been away from home fifteen mouths without the satisfaction of a woman, and had none with his wife in the months prior to leaving. The Countess had made her intentions clear -- amusement for amusements' sake. How could a gentleman refuse? How could any man? Although, in the end, he was no gentleman. He neither satisfied nor amused her.

The juice of fermented grapes and the enticement of the amply endowed countess had wet his appetite to taste, to eat, and to swallow. As the Countess' stallions rushed through the Paduan forest whipped by their driver, the Countess slid a decanter and two glasses from a chest hidden beneath the seat, sloshing wine and laughing hysterically, as together, they emptied the container and she tossed it through the curtain, smashing it into the road. When she turned back, she raised her skirt, rolled on her knees, and climbed on top of him, then slipped the ribbon from her bodice and shook her breasts free, easing them forward as he watched them sway to the rhythm of the carriage.

Neither shy nor inhibited, she seemed enchanted with her own endowments as she reached between his legs and set free his rising stiffness. "Bene, che noi ha qui?" she asked, grinning down at him. "What *have* we here?" She slapped his appendage lightly with an open hand to try to further harden it, and then lifted her dress higher, exposing the gift she offered him.

"Call me 'Cat,'" she said.

"Cat?"

"A *hungry* cat. About to devour you."

She pinned his shoulders to the seatback and spread her legs across his lap but did not find his prong stiff enough to mount. He felt her hand squeeze his softness where hardness ought to be, trying to resurrect the dead. She tried to awaken his limpness again with the slap of her hand as they both stared down and watched it jerk and shrivel further. "Zoppicamento!" she yelled. "Che e sucesso? Tuo cazzo sta floscio!"

"Perhaps in the morrow," he sighed.

"The *morrow!* There shall *be* no morrow. The *cocks* do rise in the morrow, but I think not yours."

The wine had drained what it proposed to fill. The same Countess, who an hour earlier had savored him, now chewed him up and spit him out, cursing like a shrew. She pounded the carriage wall and fisted his shoulders until they arrived at his apartment, then flung the door open and booted him out, churning obscenities as the frightened horses bolted and galloped off.

He waited the better part of the following morning for the fog to clear before he felt near himself again. In the afternoon, as evening approached, he determined to leave his rooms and walk. He meandered south beneath a row of tile overhangs, oblivious to the shops and the goods they offered. Elizabeth, on occasion and in her own fashion, showed the shrewlike habits of a woman with volatile speech and temper, though rarely employed, and never with the Countess' intensity. Perhaps all women ran that vein within their soul, although he had not detected it in Anne. Did nature offer men an impossible choice -- enjoy the heat *and* suffer the flame. He felt certain no man could tame the Countess. He sensed her husband's diplomatic missions provided as much escape for him as opportunity for her. He wondered if any man could tame Elizabeth, there being many on her list who wished to try.

He found a bench and sat, amused at the intensity and variety of human relationships. The same shrew a man would hate to have beneath his roof would amuse an audience when played upon a stage. A farce occurred to him -- the taming of a shrew who could not be tamed, with a strong willed man to test his measure against a stronger willed woman. By the time Edward returned to his quarters, he had named his hero, Petruchio, a man who could spit barbs to meet his match in Kate, a practiced shrew, who rejects his attempts to charm her into marriage and out of her dowry. Edward quickly scavenged paper and pen and sat on the edge of his bed with quill in hand. When dialogue started, he had no desire to stop it.

> Katherina onstage as Petruchio enters.
>
> Petruchio: Good morrow, Kate -- for that's your name, I hear.
>
> Katherina: Well have you heard. Are you hard of hearing?
> They call me Katharine when they talk of me.
>
> Petruchio: You lie, in faith -- for you are called plain Kate.
> And bonny Kate, and sometimes Kate the curst.
> But still, Kate, the prettiest Kate in Christendom.
> Myself am moved to woo thee for my wife.
>
> Katherina: Moved! In good time let you be removed,
> For I am neither moveable.
>
> Petruchio: Well, what's moveable?
>
> Katherina: A joint-stool.
>
> Petruchio: Thou hast hit upon it then! Come sit upon me.
>
> Katherina: Asses are made to bear, and so are you.

Petruchio: *Women* are made to bear, and so are you.
Katherina: No such jade as bear you, if me you mean.
Petruchio: Knowing thee to be but young and light.
Come to me. I have faith you anger in jest.
Katherina: If I be waspish, best beware my sting.
Petruchio: My remedy is, then, to pluck it out.

Edward was unsure of his ending, though this would clearly be a comedy. He now had the bones of a play set in Padua, along with two plots set in Verona and two in Venice. Wherever he planted himself, the seeds of a play sprouted.

CHAPTER 41

Death as End

"Speak no more."
Hamlet, III, 4

Blood spurted from Edward's mouth. He sprung up and spewed a bloody liquid on his bed linen. Good Lord! The plague had seized him. He flopped back down and lay there dying three days as shadowed figures darted in and out, dabbing his forehead with a foul smelling liniment, mopping his chest with wet rags, and wringing yellow pus that oozed from sores into a pan. "Dio's sarà fatto," someone said. "God's will be done."

At night, he alternately baked and froze, shaking violently beneath a mountain of blankets. When he finally gave into death's call, an overwhelming sense of relief enveloped him. God wrapped His loving arms around his chest, forgave him his sins and welcomed him to paradise. When the Lord's brilliance seared his eyes open, he stared into the face of God, then raised his head from his pillow and realized that he was alive. God had *not* called him home and apparently the devil had no immediate use for him. But where was he? Not London. Hedingham? Then he remembered. Padua. He was in Padua. But *where* in Padua?

A door creaked opened and an aproned woman stepped through. She glanced across the room, stiffened when she saw his eyes open, and then plunked her tray on a side table and disappeared. In an instant, he heard feet clamber up a set of stairs and watched a large-bellied man push through the door brushing crumbs from his beard. "Ahhh!... Ti sei svegliato," he cried. "Che lodi il Signore!"

"Where am I?"

"In Venice. Forgive me. English, of course. You are in Venice."

"Venice?"

"Sì, Signore. You caught the fever on your way from Padua. I am Roberto Maioli. This is my home. You do not recall any of this?… When you fell ill, as a physician, they carried you to me. My wife and I have tended to you."

"I thought I died."

"You nearly did. The plague came upon you."

"How did you know?"

"As I say, I am a physician."

"To speak English, I mean. That I am English?"

"You muttered in your delirium. Sometimes in Latin. Mostly in English."

"What day is it?"

"The day?... Thursday."

"What month?"

"August. You have been with us not quite a fortnight."

Edward lifted his legs, "I must go then," he said and then fell back.

"Signore. You must recover your strength before testing it."

"I'm imposing."

"Not at all. Our children are gone. You bring life into the house."

"You speak English quite well."

"My father managed a warehouse. He spoke the language of commerce. Whichever tongue was required."

Over the next several days, the physician's wife carried up bowls of bread soaked in clear broth, then a thicker bisque when he could tolerate it, and then bits of chopped meat and softened fruit. As time passed, her trays grew heavier. Edward insisted on compensating his caretakers for their generosity and kindness, and they reluctantly agreed, though they insisted they did not need the money.

As soon as he was able to sit up for longer periods, Signora Maiolis brought him a kitchen board to lie across his lap. He requested a quill and paper and tried to use the board to write, yet was unable to sustain a lengthy effort before nodding off. Three days beyond the third week, he felt well enough to consider his indebtedness to the Maiolises as well as his longer-term responsibilities and obligations that awaited him in England.

He had not written to Anne or inquired of their daughter in months and felt guilty. Burghley would look after Anne and the child. Still, Anne would worry for her husband even though she did not yet know of his illness. He jotted her quick a note, reassuring her that the worst of it had passed. He wished her and the baby well, and then wrote to his father-in-law.

Lord Minister,

I trust this finds you in better health and spirits than I have felt of late. I desire to thank you for discharging my duties in my absence and for your care in administering my dwindling funds. I shall send one of my servants home as soon as I am fully recovered from my present ill health with some new dispositions in these matters, wherefore I will not trouble your Lordship to continue these duties. If this sickness had not come upon me, which hath taken time from my travels, I should not have written for an extension of my leave, in supply of which I doubt not Her Majesty will deny me so small a favor as several more months.

He laid his quill down. The Queen's travel permit would expire in less than two months. In truth, he was not certain how much longer he was able to extend his stay. Not long, he thought. He owed the moneylender for his Venetian clothes and had fallen behind in rent for both his Venice and Verona lodgings. Since Burghley fretted over detail, Edward deemed it best to toss his father-in-law a few honest bones or he would find his own to chew upon. He would disapprove of Edward's borrowing, yet applaud his efforts at repayment, thus Edward added to his letter.

> By reason of unexpected charges of travel and
> sickness, I have been obliged to borrowed five
> hundred crowns, which I shall desire your
> Lordship to bring to bear so I may repay them,
> hoping by this time that money from the sale of
> my land has come in.

He reminded the Lord Minister of three land leases due to terminate and instructed him to renew those leases by selling other valuable properties.

> It is my desire that your Lordship procure these
> expiring leases back into my hands. Thus
> thanking your Lordship again for your aid and
> for your previous good news of my wife's
> delivery, I recommend myself unto your favor.
>
> Your faithful servant,
> Edward Oxford

When he was able to climb from bed and sit for longer periods in a stiff-backed chair, Signora Maioli scurried up and down the stairs with paper and food in fairly equal portion. As Edward's energy and focus increased, his Italian plots sprung to life again, many turning in new and unexpected directions, the contents of his thoughts, as usual, flicking about much like drunken monkeys. He decided to rename his Moroccan Moor, Othello, thinking it best to make him a captain. He would fashion him in the Venetian army instead of a sea captain, a prince accepted and honored for his function, yet distained and distrusted for the color of his skin. To plant the seed of discontent, Edward would have the Moor marry outside his color and then have Iago, the captain's affected friend, sew suspicion that Othello's innocent wife had executed adultery, much as Edward had executed it, or nearly so, with the Countess, and clearly so with the Queen.

Edward would call Othello's blameless wife Desdemona. But what would be her words and to whom would she speak them? He would need a character to clang her foil against. Her father, a Duke, would oppose his daughter's interracial marriage and challenge Desdemona's love and loyalty to him. Edward scribed lines as they occurred.

Act I, Scene I

The Duke: Do you perceive in all this noble
    company whom most you owe obedience?
Desdemona: My noble father.
    I do perceive divided duty.
    To you I am bound for life and education.
    Yet my life and education both do learn me.
    How do I respect you? You are the lord of
      duty.
    I am hitherto your daughter, but here be my
      husband.
    And so much duty as my mother showed
    To you, preferring you before her father,
    So much I challenge that I may profess
    Due to the Moor, my lord and husband.

A fair start. Now to Iago, the friend to Othello by day and villain by cover of night. He should outwardly profess his care and affection for Othello, yet reveal his duplicity to the audience as it unfolds and thus enjoin them as silent witnesses to his treachery. "I am not what I seem," Iago will confess in soliloquy. "And I shall prove it in the deeds that lay beneath my words."

Iago would stir suspicion to spur Othello's jealousy. Edward would have a minor character ask Iago, "What of virtue?" thus allowing the secret villain an opportunity to speak of it.

Iago: Virtue! A fig! 'Tis in ourselves that we are so.

Our bodies are our gardens,
To which our wills are gardeners.
If the balance of our lives had not one scale of
    reason,
To poise another of sensuality,
The blood and baseness of our natures
Would   conduct   us   to   most   preposterous
conclusions.
But we have reason to cool our rage emotions,
Our carnal stings, our unbitted lusts,
Whereof I take what you call love
To be a sect or scion.

Then Edward would have Iago reveal his plan.

Iago: She appeals him for her body's lust.
      By how much she strives to do him good,
      She shall undo her credit with the Moor.
      So will I turn her virtue into pitch,
      And out of her own goodness make the net
      That will enmesh them all.

Othello would disbelieve him at first, and then slowly twist to Iago's
deceitfulness.

Othello: What sense had I of her stolen hours of lust?
        I saw it not, thought it not,
        And thus, it harmed me not.
        He who is robbed, not wanting what is stolen,
        Let him not know it and he is not robbed.
        Be sure thou prove my love a whore,
        To give me proof of it,
        Only then shall I believe,
        That she is less than virtuous.

In Othello's absence from the Venetian Court, what evidence might nurture and ripen the distrust that Iago plants? What lies and innuendo, in Edward's absence from Whitehall, might his own enemies whisper in Elizabeth's ear? The truth oft be hidden in the guise of friendship. A deer's skin upon the stage, with a liar hid beneath it, doth not a true deer make.

Edward reread what he had written, crossed through lines and added others, then stood and paced until no new dialogue revealed itself. The nature of his muse oft took her pause, requiring him to stop and eat as if she herself hungered for recess, as if it knew that it could only partially live the life of others without sustaining its creator.

"You have a visitor," Signora Maioli said as soon as she knocked and entered.

"Who knows my whereabouts?"

"He says a friend. Shall I send him up or send him packing?"

"Send him up."

Friar Elmo bounced in. "The doctor tells me you are well enough to travel, so I have come to fetch you."

"I believe the good doctor is trying to dispose of me."

"I think he wants his wife returned."

Edward had lately felt that he was drawing his recovery out longer than required and suspected the Maiolis thought the same, yet he had not mentioned it and they had not complained. Their quiet care had freed him time to recuperate, think, and write.

As agreed, Elmo returned the next day to help Edward pack his writings and his few belongings. As Elmo loaded Edward's trunk into a waiting gondola, Signora Maioli slid a basket of fruit and cakes on the seat next to them. After Edward took her husband's hand and turned to thank the Signora, she embraced him, squeezing his still-weak breath away. Feeling accepted in her arms as her husband stood back and grinned, Edward realized how much he missed his father, who was quick to smile, and how little he missed his mother, who was incapable of the Signora's embrace and affection.

"How did you ever find me," Edward asked Elmo as they climbed aboard and proceeded down the waterway.

"Venice is like a small town," Elmo shrugged and said. "When you know one barber who knows another, you oft find more than you need or wish to know."

After arriving at St. Mark's Square, they transferred to a barge conveyance and headed for the mainland, and from there, boarded a carriage bound for Verona, Edward's horse tied and drawn behind, with Edward still too weak to ride.

In the days that followed his brush with death, Edward came to realize that the experience had depleted more of his energy than he initially thought. For the first time since he left England, he desired to complete his travels and return home, although he still wished to see Florence for one, and Rome in particular. He knew he would miss Elmo, yet he missed Lyly and was anxious to see his new daughter. Despite what Burghley had written, there was no telling how his father-in-law had managed or mismanaged his funds. His assets, those that remained, would require fortification to slow their downhill slide. Beyond that, Whitehall's court, as Othello's, imbued any absence with gossip, innuendo, and backstabbing. Edward's nearly two-year absence had left his own back without defense.

He resettled in his Verona apartment and rested a week, eating more than hunger urged in order to regain his weight before he determined to visit Florence, the remaining city he did not wish to miss. Florence's art and architecture, its spirit and history oozed from its cobblestones, skulked in its streets and alleyways, and then suddenly and spectacularly, flaunted its exuberance around unexpected corners in its elaborate fountains and squares. With the ancient city's immensity, Edward found neither time nor means to fully absorb its history and beauty, and barely enough to sample it.

Upon his return to Verona, with his now established habit of at least one plot from every town his shadow fell upon, Florence did not disappoint. *All's Well That End's Well,* he thought, an appropriate title and theme with his own journey about to end.

Since any plot required conflict, what Florentine characters might oppose each other to collide in drama? Perhaps a woman as lead this time, the daughter of a high-ranking Florentine, Helena by name, who loses her mother in adolescence, much as Edward lost his father. He would mirror Helena's story after his own, simply switching sexes and exchanging England for Italy. Helena would fall in love with Bertram, her wardmaster's son, as Anne, Burghley's daughter, fell in love with Edward. Bertram would not love Helena, as Edward did not love Anne, yet the King and the King's Chief Minister, a barely disguised Elizabeth and Burghley, would force marriage upon them for political reasons. Bertram, as Edward, would leave Helena to travel to foreign lands and not return until Helena was delivered of child.

Too close? All who knew them would recognize the parallels. The difference in life of life, all does *not* always end well. More often, there was no clear end. The characters in life died in the middle of their plots, their soliloquies half spoken, their entanglements still dangling, having found little satisfaction in clearing the stage for other dramas to unfold. Life found its satisfaction -- if it is to be found at all -- not in some grand final act, but as it muddled through.

CHAPTER 42

A Fond Farewell

> "To mingle friendship far
> Is mingling bloods."
> *The Winter's Tale I, 2*

Immediately upon Edward's return from his brief exploration of Florence, he called on Elmo at the cloister, where they met and talked again in the wine cellars.

"Why *did* you choose to leave England and travel here?" Elmo asked after filling two goblets and settling back.

"To learn. To experience."

"An easy answer."

"To escape, then. Truly, that was part of it."

"And what have your escaped?"

"All but myself, I think."

"And as to the learning portion, what be it?"

"That there is much yet to learn."

"Of yourself, I mean. What have you learned of that?"

"A delicate question... That changing scenes does not change character. I am as I was and always have been, yet still find no purpose to it."

"There be purpose in your writing."

"A distraction, if you wish to call *that* purpose... And what of you? Are you a writer who serves God, or God's servant who also writes? A monk at least has purpose. I am an earl who merely puts words to paper."

"Each of us serves many ends."

"Some more practical than others," Edward said as he reached for the copies of Da Porto's *Romeo and Giulietta* and Boccaccio's *Decameron* that he had carried with him to return. "I thank you for these," he said as he passed them across. "But mostly, I thank you for your friendship."

"Your travels end?"

"My license soon expires."

"Extend it. We still have much to learn together."

Edward shook his head. "I must return. But I shall hate to leave you, my friend, despite your overseer."

"The Monsignor? He will be disappointed in me. I am afraid I have not converted you."

"It's hard to set an anchor in unsettled waters. The tide shifts too easily."

"When will you leave?"

"In a fortnight."

"Where you will travel?"

"I think south to start, to avoid Milan and the Monsignor. I still wish to see Rome."

"Then, by all means, sail. 'Tis a most relaxing means. You can regain your strength and restore your pale complexion. Many vessels sail from Venice."

"I have too many trunks."

"Take only those you require for travel and send the rest ahead."

"What of my servants?

"Send them along as well, to tend to your trunks and see to your belongings."

Edward glared at Elmo. "Is sailing *your* idea or the Monsignor's?"

"He would approve. As you said yourself, you wished to see Rome."

"And I suppose arrangements could be made for an audience with the Pope? Would that be part of the Monsignor's scheme?"

"The Pope is far too busy even for an earl, I am afraid. Yet, he *is* a learning Pope. He stuffs his libraries with treatises on theology, on canon and secular law, and all manner of histories, Greek and Latin classics, myths, and philosophy. All would be available to you."

"For a man of the cloth, you practice the devil's temptation."

"One must know his ways to fight them... The Vatican also possesses a vast collection of poetry, plays, and ancient tales. After you settle in, make your way to the Basilica at St. Peter's. I will arrange for someone to meet you there."

"It would be difficult for me forget that this is the same Pope who would have my Queen's head on a platter."

"'Tis true. He is a pope of varied interests."

CHAPTER 43

Sicilian Tales

"The inaudible and noiseless foot of time."
All's Well That Ends Well, V, 3

Edward booked passage on the three-masted *Ginevra* and settled into a forward cabin as a fair wind whiffed them out of Venice, choppy waves lapping at their skirts as seagulls squawked above their heads and St. Marks' dome sunk on a receding horizon. They traced south along the Adriatic's rugged Italian boot as the captain, a thick-ribbed, burnt-faced man, held his nose to the breeze and his eyes to his sheets.

At twelve days out, they anchored at Brindisi, near the boot's heel, and then rowed ashore to stretch their legs before reboarding on an evening tide. Edward, the cook and two yeomen slept on deck after the first week out, a half-moon and pinhole stars as their canopy.

Edward spent his days leaning against the boats' ribs and writing as *Ginevra* alternately veered away from shore to catch a breeze, then drew back in to hug the coast and regain her nerve before heading out again. It had only been a generation since Magellan and Da Gama lured by the guarantee of adventure and the promise of gold, had mustered enough courage to sail beyond an endless horizon. John Cabot -- sailing under the flag of Elizabeth's grandfather, Henry VII -- had followed Columbus's trek, charting waters along the north coast of the Americas, claiming his new found land for England, and calling it *New* England. Rumor had it that Sir Francis Drake readied his *Golden Hind* to sail around the horn of Africa and then north and east beyond Da Gama's old trade route to chart a more direct course to fetch India's teas and spices, and beyond that, to return with coveted silks from China.

As a consequence of these ventures, goods overflowed on London's docks and into its scattered warehouses, and from there, into the shops along Darling Road and uphill along both sides of Albion Close and Capella Road, filtered first through London's tax office where funds were levied to line the pockets of the Lord Mayor and the new appointed City Counsel, and from what remained, to construct and supplement London's city services. As the docks prospered, so did the city's ability to cobble its streets, add new underground viaducts, and lay sewers to flush its filth farther downriver.

With fortunes pouring into the purses of London's fleet owners, merchants, tradesmen, and investors, Edward thought he might contrive a means to funnel some of that new prosperity into his own depleted coffers. Older now, and hopefully wiser from his travels, there would be much to consider and undertake upon his return to England's shores.

After rounding the heel of Italy's boot and reaching east, *Ginevra's* captain laid the ship over in Messina, on Sicily's southern tip, to rest, mend sail, replenish supplies, and replace two worn lanyards damaged in a storm. Edward procured temporary lodging in a white-painted cottage on a knoll overlooking Messina's harbor. His perch set him high enough above the beach to overlook the staggered line of pastel-hulled fishing skiffs turned upside down and layered on top of one another like multicolored fruits awaiting market. After carting up what few necessities he required, he found a corner nitch by a window from which to write and observe the harbor and its tracings of village life.

He spread his paper and laid out his quill to await his muse, not often long in coming. When he tired of writing and desired companionship, he wound his way downhill to the Red Shell Inn where he nursed a local brew as scattered fisherman eyed this odd creature who had washed up on their shores.

"What be all those papers," a squash-capped man sauntered forth and spit through his whiskers, nodding as he sat toward the stack of paper Edward had carried along to catch his muse should she return and speak to him again.

"Stories," Edward answered.

"Ahhh! Stories. We tell plenty of those. Waiting on the sea to make her mind up, there is little else to do."

"I should like to hear some," Edward said. He had crafted a play everywhere else he had traveled, why not in Sicily? After three other seamen joined them for ale and talk -- much of it bragging of famous passengers who visited their small island Edward carried two tales up the hill when he returned to his cottage -- one the fishermen called *The Governor's Daughter,* which Edward thought to rename *Much Ado About Nothing* since simple merriment seemed to touch its core. The other, *A Winter's Tale,* for the season it occurred.

He spent the next two days outlining and shaping his Sicilian inspirations in the form of plays, intending to flesh them out and rework the dialogue and detail upon his return to England, as he planned to do with all the others he had begun. There would be ample time to write and revise upon his return, since he would have little else to do.

In his considering *Much Ado,* he thought to have a local politician thwart the plans of a visiting Florentine prince who proposed marriage to his daughter. He would add a second couple, Benedict and Beatrice, to feign love that neither felt, allowing Edward to contrast the pairs and explore the nature of courtship. Unmasking truth in Sicily, in Elizabeth's Court, or elsewhere required stripping surface layers to probe beneath their surface.

In *A Winter's Tale* he would recount the legend he was told of another visitor to Sicily, of Leontes, who, like *Othello,* suspects his wife of infidelity, yet unlike Othello, Edward would have Leontes mend his marriage to explore the possibility of reconciliation, thus permitting Edward to examine his own strained relationship with Anne.

It occurred to him that writing, mulling over writing, and even brooding over writing was all that consistently engaged him. He preferred the life of his imagination to a life full of wars and battles that dawned in the dizzying midst of chaos and abruptly ended without resolution, forever spinning and unsettled. Once writ, the plots and morals in a play were set and clear. The story started when he lifted his pen and ended when he laid it to rest.

He conceded that producing plays would engender costly expense for costumes, production, and compensation to the players. Yet, with Feudalism dead and little remaining for an earl to occupy himself, why should he not write and produce what occupied his mind? What else would there be to do when his travels ended? What else when he found little else of merit in this life?

With *Ginevra* finally patched, refitted, and provisioned, Edward stowed his notes and his developing plays in the new trunk he purchased from one of the fisherman, their revision and completion awaiting unknown events at home.

CHAPTER 44

Classics

"Unpack my heart with words."
Hamlet, II, 1

Upon departing Sicily, a fair wind billowed *Ginevra* north along Italy's rocky western coast toward Naples, her final destination before *Ginevra* disgorged her cargo, reloaded and returned to Venice. After anchoring in the harbor, a boatman rowed Edward and the captain ashore.

As soon as Edward set foot upon the dock, he stepped back to avoid a rat that scurried along the edge of the pilings. By the time he reached the end of the pier and turned uphill, the pungent blend of rotting garbage and mixed animal droppings filled his nostrils, the sight before him fairing no better to the senses. The smoke of hundreds of cook fires billowed vertical streaks in the sky, forming thick clouds that rained down as black specks to pot-mark Naples homes and storefronts.

He ventured into the heart of the city only far enough to procure passage to Rome, a two day carriage ride through deep-woods that skirted a series of slippery cliffs causing the wheels to slide close enough to the edge to induce the thrill of travel and thoughts of an instant life in paradise.

Upon arriving in Rome, he secured rooms on Via San Gialloni, and then rested and changed to fresh clothes before making his way to St. Peter's. Passing through the Basilica's west portico he entered its cavernous hall, his heels clicking pat tombs of high caskets that rose beneath the depictions of saints gazing toward the heavens as if to warn him that no man -- prince, pauper, saint, or earl -- escapes death's final judgment.

"I..."

Edward jumped. "Ti sei sevgliato?," a voice whispered.

"Father?" Edward instinctively muttered, unsure if he meant his own father or the Catholic cleric.

"Sì, il signore." A frocked priest floated out into a smoky light. "I startled you."

"Indeed," Edward said, clutching his chest.

"You are here to…"

I seek an audience with…I am uncertain. I was not provided a name."

"Ah… Then you must be the Earl of Oxford. I am Father Ferinzino. We have been expecting you."

"Friar Gugliamino advises you of my coming," Edward said, grasping the man's extended hand to assure it was solid.

"No, signore. Milan's Monsignor."

"Yes, well," Edward said, dropping his shoulders. "The Monsignor seems to follow me wherever I go."

"He is well intended, I assure you. He insists we see to your safety."

"I did not realize I was in any danger."

"We are all in danger of the Lord's retribution… I am told you have an interest in our library, in our literature."

"Told?"

"Word has been passed to me."

"'Tis true. In your classics. In the ancient myths and stories."

"Nothing of Papal history? Of Catholicism?"

"Later, perhaps."

"Even limited to that, it will take you some time."

"A sampling, then, if someone could direct me."

"I will see it my duty to get you started as soon as you are ready."

"I am ready now," Edward said. "If I waste time, time wastes me,"

"So then, as to not to waste more, it might be best to begin toward the rear, in the La Stanza Rossa Room, then work forward in a logical fashion."

Edward followed the father down a black-and-white tiled hallway and into a high, arched room of circular widows, the light from the largest spilling across a round, central table. "The Lord's radiance will guide you in here," the father said, glancing toward the light. "The sun turns throughout the day yet always strikes that table as if God intended it so. The Pope himself reads here on occasion." He nodded toward a row of wooden boxes in the far corner. "All in this and the other rooms are available. We have a few written in English. Chaucer, Gower, Langland, and others. In recent times, your language has produced little of note. As for the classics, Plutarch would be among our earliest... If you have any questions..."

"I'm certain I shall."

"Then I will assign you an assistant."

"That's very gracious."

"Stay as long as you like. The Lord never sleeps."

Wishing to remain as far from God's close watch as possible, Edward chose a polished-topped table in the far left corner with ample space to spread out and study whatever he found. As he sat, he glanced around at a floor-to-ceiling treasury of poetry, history and literature, all indexed, ordered and cataloged. The Popes have spawned their fairs share of depravity and illegitimate offspring -- Martin Luther was right on that score -- yet rightly savored, preserved and protected the accumulation of human knowledge.

Edward began by lifting Plutarch's *Parallel Lives* down from a top shelf. He knew the work from Golding's tutelage -- its tales of Roman heroism and corruption depicting the parallel lives of a line of Roman emperors intermixed with the tangled saga of war and love between Antony and Cleopatra.

He perused a frayed copy of Euripides' *Titus Andronicus* he extracted from a middle shelf and discovered a similar theme of betrayal portrayed in Seneca's *Thyestes and Troades*, both writers reminding Edward of several *Metamorphoses* plots, the classics often employing universal themes that touched the core of human experience. Most, as Edward read them, seemed as fresh today as when written.

All of the Italian plots that Edward had garnered from his travels thus far -- *Merchant of Venice, Othello, Taming of the Shrew* and others -- portrayed contemporary tales -- *Romeo and Juliet* the single exception, and that only a mere two generations old. Why not revamp a two-thousand-year-old classic to suit a modern audience, bending universal joys, follies, and foibles through a contemporary lens? After all, he had just traveled from the coast to Rome and had undoubtedly passed alone the same ancient roads as Julius Caesar, Titus Andronicus, and Mark Antony. Why not strut their lives anew upon a stage?

He spent the next five days, and the morning of the sixth, hauling down volumes from scattered shelves in several rooms and spreading them out across his backroom table as he sketched characters, histories, descriptions and plot ideas, and constantly asked his assigned aid to translate uncertain passages. He reread the library's copy of Boccaccio's *Il Decameron* -- the same that Elmo had lent him -- intrigued by the ancient Roman myth of war that combined settings in Rome and Wales and praised a British warlord that Augustus Caesar called the "King of the Brits" -- an ideal theme and hero for modern Londoners who might once again be called upon to vanquish a foreign invader.

His aid carted in armloads of manuscripts and folios and laid them across two tables shoved against each other, one thin volume containing Metteo Bandello's contemporary tale of a feast that lasted near a fortnight, its pent-up exuberance finally overflowing on the twelfth night after eleven days of song, dance, merriment, and feasting. "Signore Bandello exaggerates a bit in his portrayal," Edward's aid informed him. "Yet much in it is true, if truth be known. He is still among us and will undoubtedly attend our next feast day to see if his story repeats itself."

At night, back in his rooms, Edward fashioned his own feast-day play he called *Twelfth Night,* with characters names to match their dispositions -- *Malvolio* the Latin for 'bad intentions,' *Sir Toby Belch* for a windbag who burped his words, *Feste* for his light and festive nature, and *Viola,* for her the deep voiced instrument that could switch from masculine to feminine so as to play both sides, as would Edward's character.

One well-worn folio described the recent case of a Roman judge who coerced a woman's most private favor, promising to release her condemned husband from a sentence of death upon her delivery, then letting her husband die after plucking the woman's flower. Edward could not surpass such injustice for audience compassion and empathy. *Fairness for Fairness,* he thought to call a play upon that theme, fairness being the opposite of what the judge dispensed, although Edward inked that title out and wrote in *Measure for Measure,* a more subtle turn on the same theme. An English audience would understand the fear that comes from a false promise on a larger scale -- could *Spain* be trusted to deliver her assurances of peace, or would King Philip of France promise peace and husbandry through marriage, and then rape the island when she opened herself to him?

The ancient Roman playwright Titus Maccius Plautus, in his *Prince of Tyre,* a goodly comedy of errors, added another to Edward's growing list of classic resources. He thought to combine the Plautus tale with elements of Plutarch's *Life of Timon of Athens.* He grinned at the irony. The Greek and Roman Emperors praised and rewarded their playwrights, preserving their work for posterity and electing them to the Senate *due* to their written wit and insightfulness. Centuries later, the English aristocracy refused to be seen in the company of a playwright and certainly would not sit next to one in Parliament unless, by ruse, the playwright hid his name behind the cloak of "Anonymous." Like the body's most private parts, everyone knew from whom they dangled, yet neither peeked nor acknowledged them except in innuendo. Words that revealed, in the same fashion, often required the hiding of their author.

Out in the late afternoon of the following day, Edward sat on a long, flat bench and leaned back as shadows slowly lengthened across the staggered tiles on the piazza in front of him, the sun irreversibly arching toward its evening departure, much as Edward's own life, at age twenty-six, had passed its apex and eased toward its end. He had been keenly aware of death since the age of twelve when the sudden demise of his loving father occurred precisely when a prospective earl most required a father to teach him the duties of his rank. 'Twas that death that banished him from Hedingham to fall under the heavy thumb and strict care of Cecil Burghley, now his father-in-law, whist his mother quickly remarried and thereafter had little else to do with him.

And what had his loss taught him? Certainly not enduring trust of a world in which a father could be killed only to expose him to the vicissitudes of a mother's fickle love that seemed feigned from the start. He had learned an enduring lesson from all of this -- that he was henceforth alone in this world and would have to survive on his own wit and guile.

He stood again and crossed the piazza, avoiding a puddle that had settled from a morning shower, then raised his hand high in the air with a twisted index finger simply to prove that he could follow whatever whim he chose. At twenty-six he now confessed, if only to himself, that he had neither the taste nor the desire for the duties of an earl, though he relished the privilege and accouterments that flowed from the lands and the title. With little interest in the earldom save its bounty he could do whatever he chose, as soon as he concluded what that might be. For now, the lines and plots that flowed so easily in his writing adequately filled his days. Perhaps he could make something of that upon his return.

CHAPTER 45

The Plot in the Garden

"I have in me something dangerous."
Hamlet, V, 1

Father Ferinzino sent word to the reading room requesting that Edward meet him in St. Andrews Chapel, indicating that he would delay his morning prayer until Edward arrived. "There be news for you," he said as soon as Edward entered, then led him down a winding staircase and through a caverned hall that exited into a sunlit garden of raised busts and fullbodied statues. "What you seek is down this path." The father nodded, then turned and left.

Seeing no one else in the garden, Edward ambled toward a central fountain with a raised saint lifting an open palm toward the heavens. As he passed around it, a figure darted out and startled him. "Howard?" Edward said backing away. "*Henry* Howard?... Is it truly you?"

"The very same," Howard said, stepping forward.

"I am delighted to see you. But all the way to Rome? This is quite unexpected."

"Why not Rome? Rome *is* the center of modern advance, is it not?... Come. Speak with me."

They strolled along a path of statues set in even rows among the bushes.

"I have never seen you so finely dressed," Howard said, eyeing Edward head to toe as they walked.

"'Twas always *your* dress I admired, being older than I."

"With those Italian wraps, I shall have to speak to my English tailor. The fashion conscious will stare at you and not at me."

"The father said you carry news."

"I am surprised he didn't inform you. I suppose he wished to leave that to me... I have something to show you. I take no glee in it." He led Edward back down the same path from which he came, around the fountain, up a set of steps to a terrace, and across an elevated lawn toward a chesthigh wall with the Tiber River below, its waters snaking through an ancient city shrouded in morning mist and framed by purple hills. "'Tis easy to see why the ancients set their capital here," Howard said. "'Twas once the center of the civilized world. Rome at its peak. No wonder the Lord led St. Peter to this very spot."

"It is inspiring."

"Look about you. A mere three hundred years ago all that Rome had built and inspired had fallen into ruin. The popes had fled to Avignon. What you see in front of you is all due to their return. It was they who pulled the weeds, cobbled the roads again, laid out these gardens, and bridged the Tiber to construct their new Vatican."

"Their palace."

"And why not a palace? After all, the Church *is* a State. And not simply for the popes. For *all* the faithful. You have seen the libraries. Yet, that is but a tiny part of it. There is the art. These gardens. The cathedrals. A home for the faithful."

"What is your point in this?"

"That the church had done much good."

"I grant you that."

"The Church's loss in England was a loss of beauty and learning for our people. Books were destroyed. Whole libraries."

"We had few to begin with."

"All the more important," Howard said.

"None of that was Elizabeth's doing."

"Yet she could have retained the true religion, following her sister Mary's example."

"She chose a middle course."

"To catch the slings and arrows from both sides."

"You said you had news."

"You may wish to sit for this," Howard said, nodding toward a bench.

"I'll stand."

"Very well... The Pope had wished to avoid a confrontation."

"You speak for the Pope?"

"As much as any good Catholic."

"Speak your purpose, then."

"A Papal Bull is being prepared. An excommunication edict that would declare Elizabeth persona non grata, an enemy of the Church. It would free those of faith, of which there are many, to seek their opportunity."

"Opportunity?... To what end?"

"To support their religion."

Edward stomped his boot and turned down the path, then spun around and strode back. "There are those who would use such an edict as excuse to assassinate her."

"It would embolden some, that be true."

"I will have no part in it. I support my Queen."

"Of course, you do. No one is asking any less of you."

"What then?"

"You, more than anyone, have her ear and confidence. You know both sides of it. You are close to her."

"*Was* close. That was near two years and a two hundred leagues ago."

"You are on your way home."

"Not to enter politics."

"It will enter you."

"Why did you come to Rome?" Edward asked. "Surely not to see me."

"Among others. I have friends here. As do you."

"I am less certain of my friends these days."

"You will always have your father's friends. The earls keep their loyalties."

"After Norfolk's death, you think they would have learned."

"They have learned to hold their tongues and choose their time... There is something else I wish to show you."

"The news of the Bull is not enough?"

Howard reached in this jacket and slid out a folded paper. "I bring this to you with reluctance," he said as he handed it forward. "Make of it what you will."

Edward unfolded it, four lines only, and read.

> Would God I were with you just one hour. My wits are overwrought with thoughts. Bear with me, my most dear sweet Lady. Passion overcometh me. I can write no more. Love me always as you will, as I love you.

"Tis neither addressed nor signed," Edward said as he looking up.

"I thought you might know the hand. 'Tis your rival's, Christopher Hatton's. He makes good use of your absence. She dotes on him, and he on her. Love puppies, they call them. Though I believe she tires of him. She does that, in her fashion."

"How did you come by this?" Edward asked, holding up the page.

"A friend close to the source."

CHAPTER 46

God's Glory

"Conscience doth make cowards of us all."
Hamlet, III, 1

"Cardinal Vencheza offers high mass this Sunday," Father Ferinzino said. "There will be a place reserved for you near the alter."

"I am thankful for all you've done," Edward said. "Especially for the use of the library. But, in good conscience, I cannot partake of mass. I have not since my father died."

"Mass offers absolution. I am told your father was a good Catholic."

"He practiced his faith, yet supported his king and then his king's daughter."

"In that case, I can offer you a place of quiet contemplation to consider what the church has built and still inspires."

The Father said he would instruct guards to open the Sistine Chapel for a private viewing on Sunday morning, ordinarily closed that day.

Understanding the father's intent, Edward thanked him and gracefully declined and yet, when a bright sun woke him early the following Sunday, he thought perhaps the Lord *had* nudged him awake. He dressed quickly and snapped his ducket as he breached the thick Roman air that had settled in between its hills, to make his way to St. Peter's Basilica. He wound he way along the Tiber and crossed the waterway at the Castello San Angelo Bridge, then proceeded another quarter-league and passed beneath the Basilica's huge stone pillars that appeared like God's fingers preparing to scoop him up and swoop him in should he change his mind and try to turn back. He eased up the wide marble steps, yanked a dangling chain, and waited. When an inner door cranked open, a red-uniformed guard backed inside and stood stiffly at attention, neither inviting Edward in nor blocking his path.

He skirted the guard, crossed an outer chamber, and then hesitated before a thick-fabric curtain. When he tentatively parted the barrier, he found himself swept inside a world of exploding color and intensity. As he raised his eyes toward the curved, elongated ceiling, a huge vaulted chamber shimmered before him in magentas, reds, oranges, and umbers that depicted hundreds of figures painted as if suspended in midair, miraculously hovering off the surface threatening to engulf and absorb him into the artist's work.

He stood amazed at the artist's ability to transport a viewer into the glory of heaven, the torment of hell, and the swirling turmoil of life on earth. Words could never capture what he saw before him. This painter had molded them to substance.

When he lowered his eyes and looked directly ahead, the ascended Christ drifted off the wall, his bare feet floating on a cloud, his right index finger raised, his left hand open in forgiveness toward the twisted mass of humanity beneath him. Men, woman, children, even babies, crawled and clambered beneath, atop, and around each other, each intent on seeking their own advantage as they clawed and scratched toward a higher paradise while saints and martyrs guarded heaven's gate and Jesus watched with loving indifference, leaving it to each soul to struggle along his own path.

In the midst this confusion and chaos, the Holy Mother knelt at Christ's feet, diverting her gaze from her son's wounds as puff-cheeked cherubs floated above her, pointing their horns to screech at blue-eyed devils who employed the bones of men and animals to stir their fires while awaiting those who lost their footing to stumble into hell's fires.

Edward's knees buckled. Had the Lord shown Michelangelo a true vision of eternity? Stunned and no longer able to stand, he squatted, lay on his back and stared up at a ceiling of twisted figures. In one panel, the devil's snake entwined and strangled the Tree of Knowledge, squeezing out its sap as Eve, her face contorted, dug her bloody fingernails into the serpent's skin, trying to pry the snake loose. In the scene to the left of Eve, an aging, wrinkled woman, cowered naked and spread her bony fingers to shield her dried breasts as an emaciated man flogged her with a whip of thorns, tearing crimson streaks across her shoulders and down her back.

Edward's chest sunk from the weight of such magnificence and horror. This artist had not earned this talent. No artist did. He had merely nourished what the Lord had given him. If God could lend His hand to such beauty, how could He err in His truth? How could His *church* err? Why should a king's divorce alter Devine intent? Was the Church of England God's will or Henry's?

Edward lay quietly, awaiting God's message to emerge from the artist's labor, but only silence permeated the air. Edward shivered, grappled to his feet, and stumbled out into a light.

CHAPTER 47

Treasure Trove

"And deeper than did ever plummet sound,
I have drawn my book."
The Tempest, V, 1

Leaving Rome, Edward carriaged back to Naples and sailed from there to Marseille, an eleven day journey, during which he lounged on the foredeck and inventoried his writings -- all the themes, locales, and ideas he had garnered in his travels.

FROM VERONA

Play	Detailed Location(s)	Theme(s)
Two Gentlemen of Verona	Milan and a Forest near Mantua	Male friendship, betrayal, and forgiveness
Romeo and Juliet	Verona and Mantua	Young love versus family loyalty and hatred

FROM FLORENCE

The Merchant of Venice	Venice and Belmont, a residence outside Venice	Prejudice and injustice
Othello, The Moor of Venice	Venice and Cyprus	Feigned friendship, backstabbing and betrayal
The Taming of the Shrew	Padua (betwixt Verona and Venice)	The price of ingenuous love
All's Well that Ends Well	Florence and France (Paris and Marseilles)	Strong woman and flawed male heroes

FROM SICILY

Play	Detailed Location(s)	Theme(s)
A Winter's Tale	Sicily and Bohemia	Jealousy, innocence, separation and reunion
Much Ado About Nothing	Sicily (the village of Messina)	Revenge, deception and fiery courtship
The Tempest	Italians (Neapolitans) shipwrecked on an uninhabited island	Love's confusion on a shipwrecked island

FROM ROME (Classics)

Play	Detailed Location(s)	Theme(s)
Julius Caesar	Ancient Rome and the Roman forest	Ambition, collusion and assassination
Antony and Cleopatra	Ancient Rome and Egypt	Love, ambition, revenge and war
Titus Andronicus	Ancient Rome and a forest near Rome	Lust, torture, murder and revenge
Coriolanus	Ancient Rome	Earning respect at the cost of life

He leaned back against the deck ribs, the sun warming his cheeks, pleased with his progress as he reexamined his list. Most were only fairly started -- scattered scenes, strings of dialogue, characters in sketch, plots in summary, and a few partially completed plays requiring extensive revision. All were borrowed themes, none fully his own. And yet, he wrote them well, he could make them his own in the telling. His contribution, if there be one, would lay in converting these Latin and Italian tales into English plays and devising the proper words to adequately dramatized them.

After docking in Marseille, he traveled by carriage north to Paris, a threeday journey over a well-worn road made all the rougher by a recent rain followed by a searing sun that dried the carriage tracks unevenly in the dirt. Surprisingly, as soon as he arrived in Paris, a sealed letter awaited him from Henry Howard. Edward broke the seal and read.

My Good Friend and Cousin Oxford,

Let it be known before your return that your reputation is fouled at court, being widely spoken there that your supposed daughter by Lady Anne was born in July, not earlier in March, as Lord Burghley hath reported to you and to others. Thus be it known to you, since it would soon come to you upon your arrival.

Your friend in good conscience,
Henry Howard

Edward crushed the letter in his hand, then opened and reread it. How could it be? If July be the true birth month, then the child Anne brought forth could not be his since he had not bedded her in months before leaving. If that impossible timing and spread about at court, his reputation, as Howard implied, along with his relations with the Queen, would sour further. If this offspring be not his, he felt no obligation to Anne nor the child. His already chilled feelings for his estranged wife, froze.

It seemed apparent that the Lord Minister had concocted a lie and switched the birth date to protect his own benefit and his daughter's reputation. Burghley had not written when the baby was born in order to adjust the month of impregnation to the time prior to Edward's leaving, when the Lord Minister assumed Edward and Anne were engaged in intimate relations.

Edward allowed sufficient time for his anger to cool and to consider his best course. With this bitter taste still in his mouth, he left Paris for the coast as soon as he could, then booked passage to London from Calais.

Still enraged, yet calm enough to write, he wrote Burghley a letter and sent it ahead by swifter vessel.

My Lord Minister,

For reasons which should be private and are already known to you, I have decided to address you in this fashion. I must let your Lordship understand this much: that is, until I can better satisfy myself of my discontents, I am determined not to join or touch my wife, or to accompany her farther. My reasons, because they are not to be spoken or written of, I will not deal with herein. I shall not blaze or publish my discontents until it please me. I have determined not to weary my life any more with such troubles or molestations as I have endured, nor will I, to please your Lordship, discontent myself to join your daughter.

Edward Oxford

    He had not spilled his anger, yet had at least declared his intent. Though he knew what *not* to do, he knew not what *to* do. If not return to Anne, if not to serve the Queen in ways unspecified, if not to resurrect a doomed earldom, what then? Write plays? To what end? To serve God and the Pope as Michelangelo had? Edward had neither Michelangelo's talent nor the Pope's favor. If God had given Edward his writing as a blessing, He had not yet imparted its value or utility, save for an afternoon's entertainment. And yet, without the freshness and stimulation of travel, he would now need it to fill the day's boredom all the more.

    With little sense of purpose or direction, he supervised the loading his trunks and papers, and embarked for home, wary and uncertain of his future.

CHAPTER 48

Pirates

"This blow might be the be all and end-all here."
. *Macbeth, I, 7*

Edward sailed out of Calais aboard *Misadventure,* a square-rigged merchant ship hauling casks of nutmeg and cinnamon from the Far East, transferred to her in Calais to sit among bales of woven French cloth, all to be exchanged in London for salt pork, mutton, and raw English wool for *Misadventure's* return journey across the Channel. With cabins at a premium, passengers took space as available. The captain, a sharp-voiced man with a thick braid of white hair down his back, welcomed aboard six travelers -- Edward, three wealthy merchants in tight fitting vests, and a young couple, apparently newly married and perpetually smiling. The captain frowned at the line of trunks that followed Edward up the gangplank, and would have been surprised that he had already shipped near four times that number on ahead.

Their journey would be short -- a night and the following morning with favorable winds. With *Misadventure* stuffed to her gills with cargo, passengers would sleep on deck, wrapped in woolen blankets and rocked to sleep in hammocks strung between the railings. After insuring his chests and cases were well stowed and lashed down, Edward offered the captain his remaining French coins for the privilege of resting in the captain's cabin while they cleared harbor and lay out to sea.

As *Misadventure* veered off Meir's Point, Edward stretched his legs out on the captain's bunk and closed his eyes. Protected in the ship's belly and lulled by the gentle sloshing of waves against the hull, he slept for hours.

Trepidation crept thought Edward's dreams like a poisonous snake and bolted him awake in a cold sweat, his eyes frozen wide, his backbone as tightly strung as that of an archer prepared to fling his missile at his prey.

In the dark, confused as he attempted to fathom where he was, he heard rhythmic slapping against the sides of the boat as it cut through the water. He realized that the menace lay neither in the vessel nor in his dreams. It lay on the land ahead of him -- the slithering menace of his longtime nemesis -- his former ward master, now his father-in-law. It was there, on shore, that Burghley had connived, threatened, and bribed Edward into a marriage with his daughter Anne in order to bolster his own fortunes when a grandson sprung from an Earl's seed would end Burghley's commoner bloodline.

He drew a deep breath and hung his head in the dark. He felt fouled, deceived, and abused. To add yet another sting to the snake's slow-acting venom, in Edward's absence his father-in-law had apparently ushered another into Anne's bed to assure that a seed had been planted and a child conceived as if it were his own.

Beyond the deed itself, the date of the child's birth was altered to further the deception in hopes that Edward would be fooled. That calculated falsehood, applied to the act itself, was more than Edward could abide. He clenched his fist and turned to pound his mounting anger, time after time, into the slats of the boat.

Crying in pain, he turned away, then opened and shook his bloody hand as the boat plowed on. A snake that bites, he thought, can, and will, itself be bitten.

A sudden rattle on deck caught Edward's attention then soon thereafter the sound of a man screaming. Unable to make out the words, he rose and opened the hatch. At first, all he heard was the splash of the sea and all he saw was an empty horizon. Then, as he stepped up the ladder, he caught a flash astern and a sail giving chase.

"Haul in!" he heard the captain shout. As Edward rushed on deck, he saw a seaman heave *Misadventure's* single cannon across her planks and heave the barrel through an open breach.

"We shant stop'm," the captain shouted, suddenly at Edward's side. "Slow'm if we're lucky."

"Pirates?"

"She ain't the Queen's navy. They'll have our stores and our hides."

"Can we outrun them?"

"Not for long. They carry half our load with twice our sail."

"If they are out to slay us anyway, why not try and best them?"

The captain glared at Edward.

"If we are going to die," Edward said. "Let us die as men."

The Captain nodded. "Full sail, then!" he turned and yelled. "Bend to the wind!"

The crew rushed about tightening sheets and hauling in lanyards that slowly plodded *Misadventure* forward, her canvas puffed and strained, her shrouds stretched to capacity.

Edward leaned over the rail and watched their pursuer quickly gain as *Misadventure* chopped waves and spit spray back on deck. At a quarter-league off, the pirate ship angled closer in, her gun ports open, her cannons aimed.

The captain looked to his gunner, cupped his hands, and hollered, "Stand ready!" He turned his gaze to the sea and waited, and then glanced back yelled, "Fire!"

Misadventure shot low. Her ball missed and splashed in empty sea.

"Aim for her bow." Edward said. "Maybe that'll blow her off."

From two hundred meters distance, a pirate gun fired, its ball striking close off *Misadventure's* starboard, forcing her to turn and cross her own wake. A second raider cannon belched, its projectile whistling through the air and landing close enough to shake *Misadventure's* tackle and send a whiff of gunpowder through her shrouds.

"Their guns reach longer," the captain cried. "We'll haul to."

"Swords, then. We'll make our stand aboard," Edward said and turned, grabbed a broadsword from a rack with his injured hand,

and climbed up a shroud as best he could to better view the approaching pirate's foredeck.

"Brace!" the captain hollered. The pirate ship, looming large, smashed *Misadventure* broadside, crackling wood as two pirates swung onboard from ropes, their weapons drawn and cutting air, their eyes flicking about for targets. As Edward dropped down on deck, his weapon raised in front of him, a tangle-haired pirate with a pointed beard twirled the tip of his broadsword in the air, grinning at Edward as he lunged toward him.

Edward parried and jumped back, drawing in his stomach to barely miss the blade. He ducked beneath the next swing and spun around as the pirate raised his sword again and swept its tip down in a curve that stuck the ships rail and chipping off splinters that flew toward Edward, stinging his cheek just below his eye. As Edward raised his hand and shifted right he could no longer hold on to his sword, and the pirate lunged, licking his lips as if about to savor the moment of truth. As Edward stepped back to firm his stance and clear his vision, a sudden blow to the back of his head dropped him face-first to the deck. The last he saw, the pointed tips of well-worn boots stood before him as the bearded pirate stared down at him.

Within minutes, the pirates opened the first of Edward's trunks and tossed shirts and papers aside, bellowing disappointment at finding nothing of value.

~~ *BETRAYAL* ~~

"How cams't thou in this pickle?"

The Tempest V, 1

CHAPTER 49

Home

> "I am tied to the stake,
> And I must stand the course."
> *King Lear, 3, 7*

After his brush with pirates, Edward's mood further soured as England's shores rose up on the horizon. Travel had given him purpose he could measure in time and distance. Ahead lay a fickle wife who had produced a daughter not his own and a Queen whose affections had reportedly shifted in new directions. Many of his most expensive Continental purchases -- those he had carried with him, along with near all his writing -- fed the fish in the Channel, tossed overboard by pirates. At age twenty-seven, with many dead at forty, he had seen no military service, save his brief Scotland skirmish, and the Queen, for reasons of her own, had offered him no administrative post. He had bartered half his estates to pay his debts and would have to sell yet another to prevent his remaining creditors from scraping their pound of flesh. And what had he to show for his accumulating misturns and misadventures? Nothing solid he could count with his fingers. Nothing to bequeath, and no son to bequeath it to if he had. He had accomplished little of what his father and the fifteen earls that proceeded had.

A lull in the wind stalled *Misadventure* near the mouth of the Thames, drifting her in place until the afternoon tide buoyed her upriver to be met by two longboats to haul her the final half league to port where Edward spotted Lyly bounding on the dock, waving his cap, while to Edward's relief, he saw no sign of Anne or Burghley.

"Ahhhh!" Lyly called as soon as Edward stepped ashore. "Our man from the Continent!... And those clothes!" he said, looking him over.

"The Italian influence," Edward said, grasping his friend and hugging him, then stepping back and dusting the first London soot from his sleeves.

"'Tis good to see you, dressed in any fashion."

"You should have seen what I lost."

"Lost?"

"Pirates. Dutch, I believe. They took our cargo but left us our lives."

"Drinks on me, then. We celebrate the luck of the living."

After seeing to the unloading of what little remained of his scattered belongings, he and Lyly crossed Fleet Street and ducked into the first inn for an English ale.

"How has my reputation withstood my absence?" Edward asked as he sipped his first froth. "Tell me what they say of me?"

"They say little."

"I count on you for truth. There are few I can rely on these days for that commodity."

"They *do* say a little."

"A little oft says a lot."

"There are rumors."

"I know a few. That Anne's daughter is not mine."

"*Is* she?"

"Unless nature's changed her rules, she cannot be."

"What then will you do with this?"

"I know not. I have gotten used to living alone. I need time for now to think things through. I shall take rooms."

"Tell me of your travels then. I wish to know all. What you have seen and learned."

They leaned back and twice had their tankards filled as Edward spoke of Parisian banquets, Tuscan towns and villas, a city floating on stilts, horse fountains spitting water from their nostrils, stories sung as operas, and images of Heaven and Hell painted on walls and ceilings.

"And what of your writing?" Lyly asked. "What have you done?"

Edward tapped the table and grinned. "So, you think I may have written some?"

"Did you eat? Did you breathe?"

"The pirates threw them overboard."

"Good Lord!"

"They left a few I was able to retrieve. The rest, I carry here." He touched his forehead. "I know them all well. I plan to reshape Italian tales, their legends, their classics, and a few contemporaries into plays."

"Why not our English legends? Why not our own?"

"Robin Hood? King Arthur? They've all been told. Not well, I grant you. I wish to write something new that an English audience hath never seen. Besides, I know the Italian settings. I have walked them. *Felt* them enough to bring them back here... But enough of me. How are matters at court?"

"Hatton, your nemeses, has moved to center stage. The Queen dotes on him."

"And he on her, I have heard."

"You never took her seriously, then."

"She is the Queen."

"He flatters *her*. He may be a lap dog, yet of the sort a woman likes to pet."

"What then beyond Hatton?"

"Well," Lyly said, quietly sitting his mug down, "there's always the Spanish threat. Phillip makes headway in the Netherlands. We, of course, support the French against him. Not that we trust the French. 'Tis the devil or his handmaiden, a sword through our side or through our belly."

"The French did treat me well."

"They would. 'Tis nothing personal. They simply wish to devour us. To change us back to Catholic."

"How does Burghley stand on matters?"

"You *have* been away. Walsingham has been recalled from abroad. The Queen has appointed him foreign minister. Burghley handles only internal matters, Walsingham all else."

"I know him not."

"Be assured, he knows you. His ears hear all. That's what she calls him. 'My Ears.' Burghley would accommodate the Catholics. Appease them even, much as the Queen. Walsingham would sheer their legs and cut their throats as they crawled away. He favors eradication. Your northern Catholic friends are on his list."

"They mean the Queen no harm."

"When next you see your uncle Henry Howard, advise him keep his neck protected lest he…" Lyly looked away and hesitated.

"Speak your mind."

Lyly leaned across the table. "So long as the Queen of Scots is still alive, even as captive, the Catholics foster hope. They may hide like rats, yet they still scurry about and plot. If Elizabeth were to fall ill, or die, for whatever reason…"

"They would never go that far. 'Tis mere talk."

"Such talk is dangerous in these times."

"The Queen could still marry. An heir would put an end to it."

"She is getting on in age. And even if she were to marry, there is still the question, could she…"

"Conceive."

"Bear a *legitimate* son."

"How am I to take your meaning?" Edward asked.

"Take it directly. A son recognized by all."

"That would require a husband."

CHAPTER 50

The Queen's Request

> "Never say I was false of heart."
> *Sonnet 98*

Upon settling into to his new quarters, Edward had no intention of breaking his silence with the Queen. When she finally summoned him, word arrived in midmorning. He told the messenger to inform Her Majesty that he was not properly dressed and that he would come by presently.

He waited until late afternoon, and then slowly walked the long, welltrod lane he knew well, entering Whitehall through the same Bishop's Gate that first opened to him after his father died and his mother shipped him off to Burghley House.

After informing the Queen's secretary of his presence, he was ushered to a bench in an anteroom. He had made her wait, and as in their ongoing chess match, she would return the favor. After the better part of an hour, a lady-in-waiting peeked through the door and informed Edward that the Queen would see him. As the door opened, Edward stood, straightened his backbone, lifted his head, and entered.

The Queen sat hunched over a table at the far end of the room, scratching notes as though she had forgotten she had asked him to her presence. As he approached, she glanced up and laid her quill down. "Edward," she said. "You're home… And I see you have found suitable clothes." She eyed him closely. "Italian, it seems."

"Many went overboard when we encountered pirates."

"So I've been informed. Have you forgotten how to bow to your Queen?"

He half bowed.

"'Tis not surprising. They have no monarchs in Italy. Dukes and duchies only. Save the Pope, of course, who thinks himself as such."

A silence fell between them.

"May I sit?" Edward finally asked.

"Of course... Bring a chair."

He pulled a chair next to her table and sat across from her.

"Much has happened in your absence," she said. "But tell me of the foreign courts. I shall never see them myself. Their ambassadors inflate their grandeur to make me jealous."

"Many *are* quite grand. I rich ed il bello."

"You've mastered their language."

"'Tis Latin based." He hesitated. "How is our..."

"Wriothesley?... He is fine. Three now and well raised. When he is older, I shall see to his education, much as I did yours after your father passed."

"'Twas that not Burghley?"

"At my command and at your father's behest. The Lord Minister doth provide the best."

Edward grunted.

The Queen reached across the table and touched his hand. "Neither you nor I could give him..."

"Parents," he blurted.

"Neither of us had our own. Not fully."

"Why did you summon me?" he asked.

"We are close. We can part but never fully separate."

He glared at her.

"In truth?" she asked. "You always were one for the truth... I missed your company. I am glad of your return. If I had not summoned you, would you have come?"

"Why did you not write me?"

"Neither did you write your queen," she said, her voice softened. "I must be careful what I mark. They see meaning in everything. If I have snails for lunch and write of it, they find a code for conspiracy in the number of shells I leave... *Would* you have come if I had *not* commanded?"

"A queen's command, or a woman's request?"

"Either or both."

"I would have obeyed, either way."

"Shall we stop sparring now?"

"But we do it so well."

"'Tis not all we do. I need you now more than ever. There are few I can trust."

"Madam," he said, feeling a sudden empathy for Elizabeth's isolation as it reminded him of his own. He lifted her hand and kissed it, feeling the distance fall away from them.

"Thank you," she said. "For your loyalty. Your companionship. They mean a great deal to me."

"How may I serve?"

"I tiptoe a razor's edge. If I lose my balance and topple, they will cut me to pieces. Yet, I am not concerned for my own safety. 'Tis England's that concerns me. 'Tis this crown that holds the land together. Without that to unify us, I fear we shall break apart. While my subjects fight each other at home, those abroad, seeing the least crack in our resolve, would use it as a wedge to split us further."

"All see your strength. Your crown shall hold us together."

"My crown is temporary to hold and keep for the next to wear. Yet, 'tis all I have. I hide my weakness."

"As do we all, but I don't see how…"

"'Tis the people who support me, not the nobles. My strength is in them."

"Their love for you is genuine."

"Yet few ever see me. I dare not stray too far or too often from Whitehall. Even my summer progresses hold risk. That's where you can help, if you will."

"I see not how."

"Your writing. Your plays."

"How did you know I still write?"

"Lord Minister Burghley informs me. He has friends in Italy."

"Spies. Not friends. Even if I write plays, I don't see…"

"The stage," she interrupted, "has come into its own since you've gone. My father understood the power of the mistrals, banishing them when they supported the Pope. Yet, what works against a cause could well work for one. I wish to see you use your plays to our advantage."

"Unless things have truly changed, many would oppose. Certainly the Puritans."

"Let them oppose. I *am* Queen… Few see me, yet many see dramas. And many more could, if there were more to see."

"You wish me to write on behalf of the Church of England?"

"Not religion. That would merely stir the fires. I wish to bind us."

"You've put some thought to this."

"I anticipated your return. You are needed here… Religion divides us, yet we have ourselves in common. We fall or flourish together on this tiny island. I wish to nourish our roots, our history, and our sense of common purpose. I can go to few places safely. Plays go everywhere."

"I have been writing a few, but with no thoughts of presenting. I thought to leave that to others."

"Why not write *and* present? 'Tis a natural joining and you could present the way you wish without interference."

"Most of what I've started are Italian tales taken from my travels. I have one earlier from England, though I've marked it from Denmark to hold it at a distance from those who would see it as too close."

"Write your Italian plays. But write them for an English audience. And write our histories to play and present among them. I don't command this. I ask it."

"As my Queen, or as a woman?"

"As both. But most as an Englishman."

"Then I accept."

CHAPTER 51

Edward's Boys

"The play's the thing."
Hamlet, II, 2

Edward sat on a stool and rested his elbows on his knees as he waited for his players to stop jostling each other on the Blackfriars stage and settle down on the floor of the stage in front of him. The Dominican Blackfriars had located their priory on a hill above the Thames where they could view God's bounty barged downriver and enjoy an occasional sample of the Lord's harvest it as spilled at their feet when a vessel swung too sharply around a flowing curve and shook loose a bit of ripened grain. God must have intended the friars to have it. Why else would He have delivered it so easily fetched? Now, five hundred years later, as Edward ambled along those same banks he could still stoop and scoop up a fist full of grain intended for London from the villages of Weston, or Welford, or Stratford-Upon-Avon.

Richard Farrant, a dramatist who once produced plays for the Queen's pleasure at court and for exclusive audiences at the guilds, had converted the abandoned priory into a playhouse for his own theater company he called The Blackfriar Boys. "'Tis simply wasted space," Farrant had convinced the Queen. "As a playhouse, the crown could draw a modest rent and the players, mine and others, could rehearse and polish their performances before presenting at Court. If the Crown *owned* the playhouse, a play's content could be more easily controlled."

When Edward showed Farrant an early play that Edward had begun before his travels -- a drama close to the events of his own life -- Farrant leaned back in his chair and rubbed his hands together, knowing the Queen would gleefully favor its presentation at court and offered the priory as available for rehearsals.

"We stage *Hamlet,*" Edward announced to the players. "A misunderstood hero who hesitates, who weighs his actions so much, he takes none." Edward had distributed fair copies to his boys, uncertain how many had actually read them as he nodded to Bert Farthingay, a fair-skinned lad whose yellow hair flowed down to cover his eyebrows. "You shall be the lead in it," he said.

"Play Hamlet?"

"Can you carry it?"

William Eagan, a scrawny lad next to the meaty Bert, tightened his brow. "'Tis *my* turn to lead," he said. Bert had the lead in *Merry Wives.*"

"We do not *take* turns," Edward said. "We each play the part that suits."

Adam Jaggers, a strappy lad with the pliable limbs of an acrobat and a voice to match, would act the part of Horatio, Hamlet's younger cousin and closest friend, much as Horace, Edward's own younger cousin, was fast becoming his closest confidant.

Thomas Naper, whose crow's voice could crack the starched lips from the stiffest audience, would appear as the Queen, Hamlet's mother. "You must *make* her regal," Edward instructed. "Yet set her vulnerable. That will be your greater test."

Odem Williams, with a deep barrel-chested voice that oft matched villainy, would, this time, float onstage as the ghost of Hamlet's father, much as Edward's father had once haunted him.

"A *ghost?*" Odem said as he flipped through the opening pages. "I speak but few lines."

"Read farther. You enter early on, and then return in the middle. 'Tis a crucial part. 'Tis the ghost that drives the story."

Odem grinned.

Edward assigned his other boys their characters, some to play more than one. With only six actors to draw upon, he had to tend to logistics to insure that no one found himself onstage with two parts to play at once. He clustered the boys around him. "We open at Blackfriars in three days," he told them. "If all goes well, we perform for the Queen in a fortnight."

Jeggers raised his hand, his body bobbing.

"Jeggers?"

"My bladder overflows."

"Hurry up about it, then. And don't fill it again from your jug."

Jeggers bolted up and darted out.

"Inject subtlety to your characters," Edward told the rest. He had learned, with these boys, to forgo too much reading and let them prance about the stage with their parts still fresh. "We omit a prologue," he said. "We tell the audience what they need to know from the mouths of two guards, Francisco and Bernardo, as Horatio greets them. Jeggers... Speak your part to open."

Jeggers stood and read.

> Horatio: Harbingers precede the fates
> And prolong the omen
> As heaven and earth demonstrates
> Upon calamites and countrymen.

Edward raised his hand and halted Jeggers, the boy's voice as flat as the English countryside. "Think Horatio's thoughts *before* you speak them. Give your *thoughts* sparkle, *then* yield your words and gestures to their meaning."

Bert and Odem rolled their eyes. They had heard all this before. Edward frowned and ploughed on. "Sprout *wings* when wings are called for, but do not bat the air."

When Edward glanced about, he realized he had lost his audience and that he sounded suspiciously like Polonius, his Burghley parody in the play.

As the boys read, the story revealed itself. Hamlet's ghostly father, the recently murdered king, admonishes his son to avenge the crime. The ghost informs Hamlet that Hamlet's own mother, the Queen, participated in the killing in order to marry her husband's brother, Hamlet's uncle. The Queen marries in haste just as Edward's mother had upon the death of his father under mysterious circumstance. Pretending madness to ferret out the truth, Hamlet, in his despair and grief, questions his own sanity. Twice he retreats from an opportunity to slay the new King and avenge his father, then bemoans his lack of action.

> Hamlet: 'Tis it nobler in the mind to suffer
> Slings and arrows of outrageous fortune?
> Or to take up arms against a sea of troubles,
> To make us rather bear those ills we have,
> Or fly to others that we know not of?
> Conscience doth make cowards of us all,
> And thus the hue of resolution
> Is paled in a cast of doubt.
> Enterprises of great pith and moment,
> Their currents turned away,
> Lose the name of action.

Polonius -- the Chief Minster and advisor to the old and new king, just as Burghley was the Chief Minster to Elizabeth -- tries to wed Hamlet to his youngest daughter, Ophelia, just as Burghley married Anne to Edward, although, as with Anne and Edward, Hamlet does not love her and thinks of her as sister.

Odem, playing Burghley in the guise of Polonius, bids his son Laertes off on a journey while Ophelia listens.

> Polonius: The wind sits in the shoulder of your sail,
> And you are stayed for it. My blessing go
> with thee!
> Add these few precepts in thy memory.
> See thou to character. Give thy thoughts no
> tongue,
> Nor any unproportioned thought his act.
> Be thou familiar, but by no means vulgar.
> The friends thou hast, and their adoption
> tried,
> Grapple them to thy soul with hoops of steel,

But do not dull thy palm with entertainment
Of each new-hatched, unfledged comrade.
Beware of entrance to a quarrel, but being in
one,
Bear it, that thee opposed may beware of
thee.
Give every man thine ear, but few thy voice.
Take each man's censure, but reserve thy
judgment.
Costly thy habit as thy purse can buy,
Be not expressed in fancy, rich, not gaudy.
For apparel oft proclaims the man.
Neither a borrower nor a lender be,
For loan oft loses both itself and friend.
And borrowing dulls the edge of husbandry.
And this above all, to thine own self be true.
Then it must follow, as night to day,
Thou canst not then be false to any man.
Farewell my son. And blessed season this in
thee.
Laertes: Most humbly do I take my leave, my Lord.
Polonius: The time invites you. Go. Your servants
tend.
Laertes, turning to Ophelia: Farewell, my sister.
And remember well what I have said to you.
Love itself is oft forlorn.
Ophelia: 'Tis sadly in my memory locked.

Edward knew these words well, as anyone with the fortune and misfortune of living with Cecil Burghley would know them.

CHAPTER 52

Love in the Reeds

"Set the heart on fire."
Venus and Adonis, Stanza 65

Henry Howard invited Edward and a dozen others for a late afternoon feast of herring, a thick leek and potato soup and roasted meats laid out on narrow tables set up along the Thames' bank at Westminster. All present, having well-eaten toward sunset, climbed aboard barges and floated out on the river for the Queen's fireworks display in celebration of her ascension day. As Howard's canopied vessel shoved from the dock, a crimson setting-sun sparkled off the flowing water, inducing all to ease back, relax, and drift at their leisure, several hands dipping in the water, leaving a swirling trail behind.

"What are you thinking?" Howard asked Edward, seated next side him.

"For a change," Edward said, "I think of nothing."

"It does you good to get out of your apartments and take the air. Too much writing in the dark breeds ill health. You should take the sun more often. You seem pale of late."

"There be much danger *in* the air these days. Coming *out* could do you harm."

"Not this evening," Howard said, lifting a jug from beneath his feet and refilling the half-empty goblet that Edward had carried onboard. "We are safe in the Queen's presence, she also floats downriver."

When another vessel nudged their barge, Howard leaned over the rail to tether the line and keep the two from drifting apart. "Well," Howard said in a bright voice, rising to greet his new arrival as she lifted her skirt above her right knee with one hand and offered her other to Howard as she stepped onboard. "I wasn't sure you'd come," Howard said as his guest planted both feet on deck.

"I would never miss fireworks," Nan Vavasor said, glancing down at Edward.

"Edward," Howard said. "You remember Nan."

"I should *hope* he remembers," Vavasor laughed.

"How could I forget such beauty?" Edward said, standing awkwardly, already dizzy from the afternoon's drink.

"No. Please. Sit. I will join you." She squeezed into the narrow space between him and the barge ribs. "I'm flattered you remembered, although we've never formally been introduced. We saw each other at a joust. You were the day's champion. We met, but only eye to eye."

"Indeed, we did."

"I missed you at the masque that evening. I was hoping I might meet you there, hand to hand as eye to eye," she grinned. "I hear from Henry you have traveled since. He say's you've matured."

"Grown older, 'tis true."

"I am certain that is only part of it. Henry speaks quite highly of you."

"He exaggerates… What does he say?"

"That you are the foremost earl in the land."

"By birth. I've done nothing to earn it."

"He says you write."

"For a select few… Mostly for myself."

"I should like to read some of it."

"That's most kind of you. 'Tis mostly plays to be watched."

"I would still be interested."

When Edward glanced away, he realized that Howard had wandered upfront to attend his other guests.

"He's leaves us to our own vices," Nan smiled and moved closer. "I suppose we shall have to manage on our own."

They nibbled pears and honeyed apples as the sun slowly disappeared and a servant lit candles fore and aft. Their barge bobbed and sparkled among others as the first fireball shot from a hill and burst overhead.

"Weeeeee!" Nan stiffened and called out. "It's started!"

Lutes strummed from a nearby floating platform, filling the spaces between the lights and crackles from the fireworks. "Dance with me," Nan said when the show subsided, replaced by the lilt of tambourines and lutes.

"Dance?... *Here?*"

"Why not?" She stood, looked down, and offered him her hand.

When he rose to join her, they entwined fingers and circled slowly in the confined space, easily anticipating each other's shifts and turns.

"You dance skillfully," she said.

"It takes two."

She spun unexpectedly, falling back against the rail and sliding down, giggling at her awkwardness. "Come. Help me up."

When he grabbed her hand, as much to steady himself as to lift her, she tugged him down beside her. "What's it like?" she leaned against his shoulder and asked.

"Hot."

"Not the night... Your title. Being an earl."

"I have never known otherwise. That burden was passed to me as a child."

"Why do you call it such?"

"Duties. Responsibilities. I am not made for any of it."

"What *are* you made for?"

"That, I have yet to determine."

"Such things should come naturally, should they not?"

"As does villainy, which makes it neither good nor useful."

She shrugged, then reached for the jug that Howard had left and topped his goblet and her own. "Out on the river like this?" she said, leaning back again and sipping. "It seems we are worlds away from all else. Perhaps, like watching one of your plays and being carried away, losing yourself within it."

"Plays are enjoyed, yet not always well received. They are not an approved sport of Earls, I'm afraid."

"I find that sad."

"How so?"

"You should be rewarded for your efforts."

"In a just world, that would be the case."

"Do you recall when we first we saw each other?" she asked. "'Twas Henry who rushed me off that day. I'm not sure why. I did so wish to meet and dance with you at the masque. I knew so the moment I saw you from the viewing stand." She twisted around and raised her eyes to his. "Yet, now we *have* met. And here we are. Would you join me on my boat?"

"I…"

"If you will."

She rose, then turned and glanced over her shoulder before climbing over the rail and onto her barge, lifting a canopy and disappearing beneath. He slurped the rest of his drink, stood and gripped the rail, then raised his leg and followed. Pulling her canopied curtain back revealed shelves aglow with candles, and pillows and blankets scattered about a raised platform. When the barge jarred, he lost his balance and fell upon her.

"Slow down," she said. "We have plenty of time."

He felt suddenly adrift, as if someone had cut their tie-line and set them afloat on an incoming tide that buoyed them upriver and away from the others. After the last firecracker launched, the sound of Nan's breathing melded with the song of a loon and the trickle of water gently lapping against their hull.

CHAPTER 53

Court Praise

> "The time is out of joint that
> I was ever born to set it right."
> *Hamlet, I, 5*

Edward's boys gathered in the afternoon at a slightly later time than usual, their presentation at court to proceed at the Queen's pleasure. His actors knew their parts -- their Hamlet, their Ophelia, their Polonius -- having been performed twice before an enthusiastic audience at Blackfriars Hall. Edward had modified several of Laertes and Hamlet's speeches for the production and had coached his boys on the nuances of their entrances and exits. As ready as they could be, he herded them down a Whitehall tunnel with their heads bobbing like frightened lambs shunted toward the slaughter yard on feast day. "Whatever turn it takes," he reassured them as they gathered at the end of the hall, "the audience will not eat you... *Skewer* you, perhaps," he grinned. "Yet no more than the playwright."

He draped their capes around their shoulders and adjusted costumes in a tiny, outer chamber, Odem complaining of the length of his robe, afraid he might trip on it, and Jaggers, in his exuberance, stuffing his arm too quickly through a sleeve and ripping the hem as Edward hummed a madrigal to sooth nerves, his own included. He knew the audience would await the Queen's opinion before expressing their own. Swaying the Queen swayed all. They played to one.

When he heard commotion in the adjoining room, he peeked through a crack in the curtain as Elizabeth entered dragging a velvet trace behind her gown, her bodice sparkling with polished shells and silver striping. Those present turned and bowed to Her Majesty as two ladies-in-waiting entered behind her, both adorned in slightly less elegant, front-laced gowns. "I am well aware of costume," the Queen had once confessed to Edward. "They wish a show and I give them one."

Edward motioned his boys to their places and whispered his final instructions. "Play to the parts, not to the audience."

When the Queen sat and all had settled, she nodded. Edward opened the curtain and strode to the center. He bowed to Elizabeth and acknowledged her guests with a sweep of his palm. "We present a humble tale," he began. "And yet, as we play it, we make it seem as real as it may be. Our modest fantasy, written on insubstantial parchment," he lifted a fair copy and held it out, "shall trace memories as flimsy as dreams. It will show on stage, as in life, that we are all of insubstantial matter, and all have ghosts that haunt us."

He bowed again and exited as the two boys playing the castle guards entered from opposite sides, looking about as though searching in the dark.

> Francisco: Bernardo?... Be that you? Who goes there?
> Bernardo: 'Tis me. *'Tis* Bernardo.
> Francisco: You come most carefully upon your hour.
> Bernardo: 'Tis now struck twelve. Get thee to bed, Francisco. If you meet Horatio and Marcellus, the rivals of my watch, bid them make haste.
> Francisco: I think I hear them. Stand, ho! Who is there?

> Horatio and Marcellus enter.

> Horatio: Be there friends to this ground?
> Marcellus: Has this thing appeared again tonight?
> Bernardo: I have seen nothing.
> Marcellus: Horatio says 'tis but a vision,
> And will not let belief take hold of him,

Touching this dreaded sight, twice seen by us.
Therefore I have entreated him along
To watch the minutes of this night,
That, if again this apparition come,
He may speak to it.
Horatio: Tush, tush. T'will not appear.
Bernardo: Sit down awhile.
Let us once again assail your ears,
That are so fortified against our story,
What we two nights have seen.
Horatio: We shall sit,
And let us hear Bernardo speak of this.
Bernardo: Last night of all,
When yon same star that's westward from the
pole
Had made his course t'illume that part of heaven
Where now it burns, Marcellus and myself,
The bell then beating one.
Marcellus: Peace, break thee off. Look. It comes
again!

The Ghost enters.

Bernardo : Tis the same figure, like our king that's
dead!

Midway through the performance, Edward sneaked a peek
from behind the curtain, the Queen seemed pleased as she leaned
forward in her chair, the audience intent more upon the stage than on
her -- a good sign. Burghley, who rarely attended a theatrical
performance, stood stiffly in the back. Upon seeing himself
lampooned as Polonius, he spun and slithered out, much as Hamlet's
King would leave on seeing himself parodied in Edward's play
within the play.

In *Act I, Scene V,* the Ghost, played by Odem, appeared and glared accusingly at Hamlet.

> Hamlet: Where wilt thou lead me?
>   Speak or I shall go no farther.
> Ghost: Mark me well.
> Hamlet: I will.
> Ghost: My hour is almost come,
>   When I to fire and tormenting flames
>   I must render up myself.
> Hamlet: Alas, poor ghost!
> Ghost: Pity me not, but lend thy hearing
>   To what I have foretold.
> Hamlet: Speak. I am bound to listen.
> Ghost: So art thou bound to revenge.
>   I am thy father's spirit,
>   Doomed for a certain term to walk the night,
>   And for the day confined to fast in fires,
>   Till the foul crimes done in my days of nature
>   Are burnt and purged away. But that I am forbid
>   To tell the secrets of my prison-house,
>   I could a tale unfold, whose lightest word
>   Would harrow up thy soul and freeze thy young blood
>   And make thy two eyes, like stars, start from their
>   spheres.
>   Thy knotted and combined locks to part,
>   And each particular hair to stand on end,
>   Like quills upon the fretful porcupine.
>   But this eternal blazon must not be
>   To ears of flesh and blood.
>   Listen, listen, O, listen!
>   If thou didst ever hold thy dear father dear.
> Hamlet: O God!
> Ghost: Revenge this foul and most unnatural murder.

> Hamlet: Murder!
> Ghost: Murder most foul, as in the best it is.
> But this most foul, strange and unnatural.
> Hamlet: Haste me to know it, that I, with wings as swift
> As meditation or the thoughts of love,
> May sweep to my revenge.
> Ghost: I find thee apt.
> And duller shouldst thou be than fat weed
> That roots itself in ease.
> Wouldst thou not stir in this?
> Now, Hamlet, hear.
> 'Tis given out that, sleeping in my orchard,
> A serpent stung me, so the whole ear of Denmark
> Is by a forged process of my death
> Rankly abused. But know, thou noble youth,
> The serpent that did sting thy father's life
> Now wears his crown.
> Hamlet: O God!
> Ghost: And you alone can set it right.

As Edward watched, the audience held a collective breath, their emotions laid upon the stage as real as in any night dream. Bert as Hamlet, alone in soliloquy, faced Elizabeth as if staring straight through her, as though *his* world were real and hers not. "To be or not to be," he began, and then paused, as though thinking his thoughts as he spoke them.

> Hamlet: Whether 'tis nobler in the mind to suffer
> The slings and arrows of outrageous fortune,
> Or to take arms against a sea of troubles,
> And by opposing end them, to die, to sleep
> No more, and by sleep, to say we end
> The heartache and the thousand natural shocks
> That flesh is heir to, 'Tis a consummation

Devoutly to be wished. To die, to sleep,
Perchance to dream. Aye, there's the rub.
For in that sleep of death what dreams may come,
When we have shuffled off this mortal coil.

Knowing from whence his words came, Edward felt the slings and arrows of his own father's ghost, having undone all that his father and his father's fathers had built and accomplished.

In the final act, as death crept onstage to take its satisfaction, Hamlet, looking into Horatio eyes, spoke his final lines.

Hamlet: Heaven make me free!
I am dead, Horatio.
Wretched queen, adieu!
You that look so pale and tremble at this chance,
Thou are but mutes, an audience to this act.
Had I but time, I could tell you
But this foul sergeant, Death,
Is strict in his arrest.
O, Horatio, I am dead.
Thou livest. Report me and my cause aright
To those unsatisfied.
Horatio: You shall live.
Here comes some liquor left.
Hamlet: Nye. As thou art a man, I die.
O, good Horatio, what a wounded name is mine.
Things standing thus unknown, shall live beyond me.
If thou did'st ever hold me in thy heart,
And in this harsh world draw thy breath in pain,
As potent poison over-crows my spirit.
And silence creeps upon me.
Tell my story true.
Hamlet dies.
Horatio (sitting and cradling Hamlet's head in his lap):

Good night, Sweet Prince... Fair thee well.

The audience sat stunned in silence as Edward's boys held their positions, frozen in their parts. First Odem, then Faraday, raised their eyes and chanced a glance. Elizabeth, her body trembling, rose and brought her hands together in a steady rhythm, nodding toward Edward, then toward the boys as the guests around the Queen stood and swelled the hall with applause.

"Well accomplished," the Queen said to Edward as her guests mingled and chatted. *"Exceeding* well."

"I am proud of them."

"As I am of you, the author of their words."

"I am glad they met your favor."

"But then again, the story sounds familiar. Drawn from the life, it would seem."

"Past is prologue, even for a playwright."

The Queen laughed. "Did you observe Burghley?"

"I watched him skulk out."

"You did not disguise him well... Did I see others in the court shadowed in your characters?"

"If truth be struck, it should stick many."

"Some more shapely than others."

"As many as want to see themselves."

"You touch us all. Your gift is our joy."

"I wish I could serve better."

"You have and you shall."

CHAPTER 54

The Tower

"Lord, what fools these mortals be."
Midsummer Night's Dream, III, 2

Nan Vavasor remained in London at Henry's apartments, entertaining friends while Howard returned north to see to his position. Since the night of the fireworks, Nan filled Edward's thoughts, squeezing out his appetite and any hope of writing. He languished in her absence and longed for her presence. He saw her when she made herself available, although often she did not, either not at her apartments or not answering when he came by. And yet, when she did open her door, she opened it wide and gave her all, drowning him in ecstasy.

"She is using you," Lyly warned Edward his second month of seeing her and speaking of nothing else. "You sleep through the mornings, you stare at the walls, you walk about half crazed. Your friends hardly see you any more."

"If she uses me, she uses me *well,*" Edward grinned.

"To your undoing. 'Tis Howard's idea. He wishes to separate you from the Queen's good graces, using Nan as bait."

"The Queen is not as favorable to me as she once was. Other matters occupy her."

Vavasor's pregnancy by Edward well concealed itself its first two months and, as nature would have it, eventually made itself apparent even in the fullest frock. What the Queen did not herself observe, Walsingham and Burghley saw and reported to her. "Whore!" the Queen was said to have shouted, stomping her foot when Walsingham reported the delivery of a healthy boy. "Toss all three in the Tower. The baby as well."

A third child now carried Edward's name -- Liz Beth by his wife Anne yet not his own, Henry Wriothesley, now seven, by the Queen, and now an illegitimate son by Vavasor, whom he heard she named Edward to flaunt Edward's mark as the boy's father to further taunt him.

Three guards awakened Edward before breakfast, the captain barely allowing Edward time to stuff a trunk before escorting him out and barging him downriver to the same Tower that he and Lyly had floated past the day they escaped Gray's Inn to see *The Temper of the Moon* at the Red Lion, which Edward rewrote and renamed *A Midsummer Night's Dream*.

"Lord Oxford," the Captain of Tower's Guard smirked as Edward stepped onto the landing. "Your accommodations have been prepared. Not quite what you are used to. Still," his grin widened, "we have entertained those of higher rank. For an earl, we shall do what we can."

He led his prisoner up a winding stone staircase that opened to a bare room with a single door opposite and a halfmoon shaped porthole dug through the wall. As Edward entered, a shiver suddenly shook him. "Can we have a fire?" he asked.

"We could set the floor on fire, if that would help warm you," the Captain said. "There are blankets in back." He nodded toward a door as Nan Vavasor opened it and stepped through, a scowl on her face, a baby in her arms with its head flung back. "I would have thought an earl would be better cared for," she flatly stated, dangling the baby like a sack of grain.

"Enjoy your stay," the Captain said, mocking a bow and backing out.

"And what am I to do with *this?*" Nan said, holding the child up. "My nipples ache. They were not made for tugging and stretching. They were made for play."

"Play has its consequence," Edward said, avoiding her glare as he ambled toward the window. While he was confined to the Tower, this single hole in the wall would be his only view outside -- fortunately a favorable one. The London Bridge below drew more life and commerce across its span than most English towns. It reminded Edward of the Rialto in Venice.

"Look at me," Vavasor demanded.

He turned and smirked.

"You find this amusing?"

"I find it sad," he said. "Nauseating, even."

"Nauseating? Do you refer to me?"

He thought perhaps he did, yet held his tongue. He recalled Lyly's warning that Howard had encouraged this relationship to separate him from the Queen's affection, and well understood the Queen's intent in confining them together. Passion that burned brightly in the open air often suffocated in restricted quarters.

Late one afternoon, Nan asked, "Is that *all* you do? Sit there? Write? Do nothing?"

He had managed to persuade the magistrate, who appreciated the value of good coin, to provide paper, ink, and quill.

"Writing *is* something," he said without glancing up.

"And what am *I* supposed to do?"

"Be patient. She won't hold us forever."

"I need my stockings."

"I as well."

She glared down at his work. "What *is* that?"

"A scene."

"Scribbles," she said. "They warned me you wasted your fortune and fritter your time away. Why should *anyone* wish to marry you? You *are* married." She ran a finger down the page, smearing the ink. "Try to be of some use. Apply your influence with the Queen. Get us out of here."

He laid his quill aside and corked his bottle. "'Twas my influence that got us *in* here."

"You are less than a man. And too short for one."

"Then you should have bedded someone taller."

"I have. Many times. And shall again."

"What is it you want of me?"

"Why, everything, my Lord. All you've got." She eyed the baby, asleep in his cradle. "Certainly not *that.*"

"Then I shall raise him."

She snickered. "I think not. What do you know of children?"

"What do *you* know?"

"I know their value. If I raise him, you shall pay. Why do you suppose I named him Edward?... To remind you from whence he came and what is owed."

"Others will know the name and recognize the badge you wear."

"Let them. I take pride I plucked an Earl."

Without prior notice, a Queen's order suddenly released them after two-and-a-half month's confinement, whereupon Nan grabbed the child and hurried down the staircase without glancing back as Edward gathered his clothes and papers.

CHAPTER 55

Blood by the River

"Suit the action to the sword."
Hamlet, III, 2

A man's baby-making joint his "will or "willy" as the
commoners called it - was more a follower than a leader. It oft
skipped reason and acted on a will or desire of its own, ensnaring a
man whether he willed it or not -- and as often as not, *against* his
will. A man's "will," -- both his conscious will and his physical
"willy" -- follow the temptress, the man attached simply dragged
behind.

Edward continued to visit Nan when she would have him
and when she was not with other company. He found pleasure in her
presence and otherwise ignored what he did not wish to see or know.
She had both his will *and* his willy.

To ease his anguish, he set his torment to sonnets, plying
words to extract the sting. Language forced a measured reason,
sometimes soothing what it could not cure. He had no intent to show
her what he wrote. She would use it to her favor. Nonetheless, wrote
as *if* to show her.

Whoever hath her wish, thou hast thy "Will,"
And "Will" to boot, and "Will" in overplus --
More than enough am I that vex thee still,
To thy sweet 'will' making addition thus.
'Wilt' thou, whose 'will' is large and spacious,
Not once vouchsafe to hide my 'will' in thine?
Shall 'will' in others seem right gracious,
And in my 'will' no fair acceptance shine?
The sea all water, yet receives rain still
And in abundance addeth to his store.
So thou, being rich in "Will," add to thy "Will"

> One 'will' of mine, to make thy large 'Will' more.
> Let no unkind, no fair beseechers kill.
> Think all but one, and me in that one "Will."

Some women, by their beauty and their tempting nature, drew men to them. The best used their draw to please, the worst to twist and tease. Nan's affections slid around the chessboard, attaching to a power piece as she found one, then discarding that and moving to the next, either to a bishop or a pawn, or to whatever man of whatever rank she found of use at the moment.

On one Saturday afternoon in early May, as Edward basked in Nan's company -- ostensibly to see their son -- a man, half-naked and yawning, wandered into the sitting room. Nan stood and introduced the two, inviting them to sit face-to-face and exchange conversation whilst she served warm cider.

Edward, upon escaping, poured his obsession and self-loathing into his writing. When he called Nan "Love," as he once had, he named her such, recalling times he woke in bed beside her, thankful for God's great gift and his good fortune.

> The little Love-god lying once asleep
> Laid aside his heart-flamed brand,
> Which legions hearts had warmed.
> For men diseased -- but I, myself enthralled,
> Came there for cure, and this by that I prove,
> Love's fire heats what water cools.

Yet, once dashed and cooled, a lover's fire turned to stone, and then from stone to hate.

> From what power hast thou this powerful might
> With insufficiency my heart to sway?
> The more I hear and see just cause of hate?
> If thy unworthiness raised love in me,
> More worthy I to be beloved of thee.

Honest writing wrung understanding from confession. After all, *he* had cheated on Anne, disavowing his marital oath. He had sworn faithfulness and devotion, and meant it so, and *still* meant it in his imagination with Nan when he did not take the full accounting of her.

Returning home late one evening from the bliss of Nan's bed, a shadow stepped forward, blocking his path on narrow steps that led up from the riverbank. "Who goes there?" Edward asked, squinting at a face shadowed beneath a hood.

"No friend of yours, my Lord," the man said as he lifted his hood to reveal himself.

Edward knew him. Thomas Knyvet. Nan's uncle. "I have no quarrel with you," Edward said, flattening his back against the wall to allow Knyvet past, hoping he would slip by without incident.

"Yet, *I* have one with you. My niece's honor."

Edward wished to say, she has none, but thought the better of it as the threat inched toward him. Just as Knyvet passed close in, he suddenly swirled and kneed Edward's groin, bending him over in pain.

"That be the part that gets thee in trouble," Knyvet said, stepping down to the riverbank and backing onto the rocks.

Edward sucked in air and straightened.

"Perhaps we'll remove that offender," Knyvet said, drawing his dagger and passing it hand-to-hand.

"I take your meaning and have no wish to fight you," Edward said, but as he turned to climb the stairs again, heels clicked above him and two men leaned over the rail.

"Your wish is of little concern," Knyvet said.

"Not daggers then," Edward said, turning to face Knyvet, not wanting to maim or be maimed.

"Fists?… I think not. Something sharper."

"You have a right grievance," Edward admitted. "Can we resolve this in the morrow, in the good light of day?"

"I shall breakfast on my satisfaction in the morrow. Draw your weapon or I'll lop your hands before you're able." Knyvet resheathed his knife and drew his rapier.

"I have no weapon."

Someone tossed a sword from above, clanging it onto the rocks. Knyvet nodded toward it.

"Men can talk."

"I know your cleverness with words. Put them to task." Knyvet raised the tip of his weapon and circled it in the air. "We shall test your manhood beyond your willy."

"I am guilty," Edward said. "I have no argument against it."

"None that will suffice. You have cuckolded my niece, brought her to child, and left them."

"She would not have me."

"She *could* not. You are married, my friend." Knyvet lunged. "Take up your sword or perish without it."

Edward reluctantly stooped to lift the sword, then eased back, widening the gap between them. "I do not desire this."

Knyvet sprung. "'Tis beyond your desire. 'Tis my pleasure."

Knyvet teased his index finger across the face of his quillon to exact better control, the practiced sign of an expert familiar with the blade. When Knyvet stepped forward in an even line, Edward struck first to hold his opponent back but stubbed his toe and grimaced. Seizing the opportunity, Knyvet cut an angled delivery. Edward parried and deflected. Knyvet sprung from his shoulder, advancing one step at a time, driving Edward to the water's edge. Edward swished downward, then up, fending off a salvo. Knyvet feigned right, slicing the air. Edward countered, beating the space between them. Swords clanged. Knyvet advanced, rhythmically sticking the ground with his leading foot.

Edward ducked beneath a swish and barely slipped from under. He straightened and met his attacker blow for blow, yet always weaker of the two. Edward knew the sport, yet Knyvet taught it and practiced daily. He outmatched and outmaneuvered Edward. "You show a good defense," Knyvet grinned. "Yet only a fair delivery." He sideswiped, nicking Edward's elbow, drawing first blood. "When you sully my niece, you sully me." He looped, driving Edward back to the wall and pinning him there until Edward mustered enough strength to shove him away with his elbows, then pivot and scamper out of reach.

"If you swing your dangle as poorly as your sword," Knyvet said, nodding toward Edward's crotch. "'Tis a wonder what she saw in you."

"Coin," Edward said, confessing what he knew to be the truth.

Knyvet thrust forward, swept down, then side-to-side. Edward jabbed. Knyvet catapulted. As Knyvet's blade sliced down, Edward twisted left. Too late. The blade caught Edward's calf as he backed away. Its point cut deep and ripped upward. He lost focus. He wobbled. His sword dropped. He plunged to his knees and flopped on his face. Blood gushed across the rocks as Knyvet moved in for the kill.

"Halt!" a voice yelled. "Leave him!"

CHAPTER 56

Loving Care

"I am in blood, steeped in."
Macbeth, III, 4

They carried Edward to Anne, knowing she would nurse him whether he deserved it or not. When the Queen heard of Edward's injuries, she dispatched the royal physician, who shook his head and called for lard to grease the wound and plug the bleeding. "'Tis cut to bone," he muttered. "The loss of blood will kill him."

Anne bandaged Edward's wound to stop the bleeding and changed his linen. She propped him up and plied him with a stinging warm broth, dabbing what dribbled down his chin. She laid cold, damp rags on his forehead to lower his fever and leaned over the physician's shoulder when he came by to examine his patient. When a clandestine priest rapped on the door to offer confession and last rights, Anne booted him out and slammed the door.

Fever roasted him at night, mixed with chills that sporadically shivered him. His torn calf shook uncontrollably, a good sign, the physician said, that the muscle was still partially intact and that it might heal should his patient survive. Edward kicked his blankets and spit forth a string of curses in English, French, and Latin and in some strange language Anne did not know. In lulls, she placed a stiff-backed chair next to his bed and dozed while he slept, tightening a scarf around her shoulders to hold back the drafts and jolting awake whenever he winced.

Day visitors knocked, full of concern and false cheer. Lyly sat for hours, and then went out to fetch whatever Anne required. Men and boys came by she had never met -- theater people and gamblers she thought. None stayed long.

After a week and a half, Edward remained awake long enough to ask for what he wanted, yet more often than not, fell asleep before it arrived. Slowly, he sat up and swallowed porridge that Anne boiled longer to soften, although his cheeks remained sunken and void of color.

Word arrived with news that Knyvet had suffered superficial cuts even though Edward, when he was able to speak, said he could not remember inflicting any. When Anne, with Lyly's help, finally eased Edward out of bed on a cane, he hobbled a few feet, grunting and contorting in an odd shuffle before he flopped back in bed.

"Will I ever walk again?" he asked.

"Of course, you will," Anne reassured him.

"Walk right, I mean."

"Of course, you'll walk."

He slept unevenly at night, his waking moments altering between alertness and confusion. As time passed and his fog cleared in spurts, he requested quill and paper, more to cling to something familiar than to write. As he ate more and stayed awake longer, he scribbled a sentence or two, then a page before he napped. Once when he woke, he caught Anne sitting next to him reading a sonnet. "I don't truly understand it," she said when she saw his eyes open.

"Neither do I much of the time," he confessed, his voice still weak. "At times, I read it later to see what I meant."

"I just want you to get well," she said, looking down at him with soft eyes.

"I know you do. And I thank you for caring and tending me. I ill deserve it."

Anne looked older through the eyes of sickness, a signpost of Edward's own long downhill journey. He asked her to remove the only looking glass in the room, not wanting to see the harbinger of death mocking him.

He thought of Anne's daughter, who bore his name yet not his blood. Late one evening, he awoke to find Anne sitting in her chair, staring at him.

"What is it?" he asked.

"You are my husband," she said, a tear in her eye.

He had little left to offer Anne, save himself. He had all but depleted his funds and properties and had alienated the Queen by tying his eros to a wasp that stung. A near cripple now at thirty-one, he felt none the wiser for it. His writing, his plays, his only real productions, cost him more than they earned. It seemed the more he lived, the more forgiveness he required and the less he felt he deserved.

To better aim his thoughts and avoid biting Anne with the fullness of truth, he wrote her a letter and asked her to read it and respond as she chose.

> My Dear Anne,
>
> I am a little better of health now thanks to your good care, yet in a hopeless state of my endeavors. I have little to offer should you desire my full return. I am your husband, separated from you these five years. Your father doth think ill of me and for good reason. Yet, I do desire to amend my faults if it be not too late and if that still be allowed in your heart.
>
> Your unworthy husband,
> Edward

Late on the same afternoon of receiving Edward's note, a boy delivered Anne's reply while she was out.

> My good Lord,
>
> I most heartily thank you for your letter and am most sorry to perceive how unquieted you are, whereof I am not without some taste myself. If God so permit that it might be good for you, I would take the greater part of your adverse fortune and make it my own. As for my father, I do assure you,

whatsoever hath been reported of him, I
know of no man who can wish better for you
than he doth, although others at court, I fear,
seek the contrary.

I beseech you in the name of God, who
knoweth my true thoughts and love towards
you, let me know the truth of your feeling
towards me and what you would have me do
to recover your favor so as your Lordship
may not be led to detain me in an uncertain
state of mind and happiness.

Your loving wife,
Anne

He was not entirely certain why he wished to mend his
marriage. His emotions were mixed and he was uncertain what
hidden reason lay beneath them. Desperation? Guilt? Convenience?
Despite Anne's infidelity -- which she never admitted -- he knew she
loved him in her gentle way. His obsession with Vavasor had seared,
scared, and wounded him, and now he feared, left his leg as crippled
as his heart. Yet Anne's slow embers might warm their home and
hearth, and perhaps, in time, his feelings.

According to Lyly, the Lord Minister had reportedly said to
others, "My son-in-law lives in daily fantasy and neglects his
ordinary house." Yet Burghley, a prudent man, desired a grandson
beyond Anne's daughter, whom he knew was not Edward's. The old
fox had always hoped for a male heir to send his blood down the
Oxford line. "Beyond progeny," the Lord Minister admitted to
Edward when he heard of Edward's intentions to return to Anne.
"Consider that your reputation at court reflects on mine. All know of
your dalliance and your estrangement from your husbandly duties.
Accepting your responsibilities would assuage a few. That be to the
good. Should you hold to your word, gossip would soon leech to
better prospects."

In revising *Merry Wives of Windsor,* Edward wrote in the guise of Slender: "I will marry her, Sir, at your request. But if there be no great love, let heaven increase it upon better acquaintance." He hoped such would ensue between he and Anne.

As soon as he regained strength, he had his furniture and belongings moved out of his Savoy apartments. Anne bid farewell to her father, with whom she had been living, and moved with her husband into the last house on the north side of Fliesh Row with only six servants between them -- three stewards, two maids and a cook. A year after reuniting, Anne bore Edward a son who died in infancy and, a year later, a healthy daughter, Bridget, and then again, a year and a half beyond that, his youngest daughter, Susan. And yet -- as Edward, Anne, the Lord Minister, and all else knew -- without a son and heir, the Oxford line would not survive.

CHAPTER 57

A Reluctant Confession

"The web of life is a mingled yarn,
Good and ill together."
All's Well That Ends Well, IV, 3

With the growing presence of regularly scheduled plays at the playhouses in London, Edward agreed to take over the Chichester boys and add them to his own troop, The Oxford Boys, when the Earl of Chichester died of consumption leaving his acting company at loose ends. Edward would take on another lad or two as one left as required by the season or by the plays they performed in the towns and villages on their yearly rounds, the farther from London, the more freedom he felt to write and perform without the close scrutiny and watchful eyes of censorship so prevalent in London and across the river in Southwark.

As Edward toured the circuit, he revised and polished his Italian plays and added English histories as the Queen had urged, trying them out in the courtyards of local inns or, when available, at the Blackfriars Hall in London, to perform them better honed and practiced for court when the Queen was of mind to see one.

Elizabeth had forgiven Edward his Vavasor fling and told him she was rightly glad to see him back with Anne. The passion between Edward and the Queen had proportionally cooled as their understanding and friendship increased. They saw each other less, although neither time nor distance diminished their mutual fondness and affection. When they spoke, they spoke freely -- life being too short for anything less. Edward's brush with death with Knyvet left him with a painful limp and a gnawing sense of age and life's fragility.

The Queen herself had aged. At fifty-two, with no prospects bearing a child, her bargaining chip, a continental alliance through marriage and pregnancy, was no longer possible. With a wedding ring no longer the target of the Continent's princes, they aimed to ring her neck. The Queen of Scots, now forty-six, still sat idly knitting in the Queen's captivity, still itching to replace Elizabeth on the English throne as a new generation of Catholic enemies plotted to help her achieve that end. To bolster her defenses, Elizabeth had strengthened her ability to call men to arms and had slowly assembled a navy, yet her forces remained untried, unpaid or underpaid, and of questionable loyalty. Beyond the issue of defense, other more personal matters weighed heavy on her thoughts. "I once had high hopes for our son," she told Edward when she summoned him late one spring afternoon. "He is, unfortunately, an irresponsible lad. A follower, not a leader. And, I am afraid, not too bright. Yet, I wish you to speak with him. Then advise me of your consideration."

"I have played no part of his life. I have no right."

"Right is sometimes the least consideration."

Edward waited a fortnight before seeing Wriothesley, and even then, felt uncertain what to say. He needn't have worried. His son, now twelve, curly haired and straply limbed, cut to the chase.

"Is it true what they say?"

"I know not what they say."

"That you are my father?"

Edward hesitated. "If so, I am a poor one."

The boy's appearance reminded Edward of himself, only twelve when his own father died, the same age that Wriothesley, for the first time, confronted his.

"And that *she* is my mother?"

Edward put his fingers to his lips. "We don't speak of that. 'Tis treasonous."

"'Tis not unknown. There are rumors."

"Rumors fuel politics. Your... The Queen herself starts a few and sharpens others to her purpose."

"If it be true, am I to be the future king?"

"Do you wish it?"

"All I've known are toy knights and soldiers. Would I have to fight?"

"A king might."

"Then I do not wish to be one."

"Then hold your silence. That would serve us all well."

The ghost of Edward's own father had stalked him since Wriothesley's age, unwittingly inserting his advice in *Hamlet* in the guise of Hamlet's ghostly father and playing on Edward's conscience whenever opportunity arose. Edward had three daughters by Anne -- Liz, whom Edward knew not to be his own -- along with Brigitte, and Susan, his youngest. To those, and out of wedlock, he conceived a son, now four, by Vavasor, yet raised him not. Wriothesley, his son by the Queen lived a comfortable life -- catered to, educated at court and given a lesser earl's title. Still, peril swirled around his very existence. Elizabeth's foes, desiring a champion to wrap their cause around, would exploit the boy to their own ends if then knew. If convincing Wriothesley to their side proved futile, they might just as easy slit his throat to bleed away the danger of his heritage. Still, if Wriothesley settled down and fostered any practical or serious bent, the Queen might yet spring him as her heir. In the meantime, she would hold that card up her sleeve. "You mother will watch after you," Edward reassured his son.

"Which mother? The one of issue and the one who raised me."

"The two who care for you... When I was twelve..." Edward choked

"What is it, father?"

"Nothing. 'Tis nothing."

CHAPTER 58

Retribution

"Ambitions' debt is paid."
Julius Caesar, II, 1

The tale of Mary Queen of Scots, should Edward ever scribe it, would enact a tragedy of comic proportion, the ill-fated queen erring at every turn. If favor lay to her right, she instinctively veered left. If the devil sat to her left and grinned at her, she turned in his direction and nestled in his lap.

"I wish you to serve on her tribunal," the Queen told Edward.

"I prefer not."

"*All* prefer not," the Queen said, irritated. "Yet, some must."

After twenty years of confinement, Walsingham and Burghley had finally trapped the Queen of Scots with enough evidence to irrefutably charge her. They had intercepted incriminating messages from the Scottish Queen to her Catholic supporters passed back-and-forth in false-bottom beer barrels, the brewer being on Walsingham's secret payroll.

At the Queen of Scot's trial, Edward and a dozen others arrayed themselves staunchly and resolutely along both walls in the great hall of Fotheringhay Castle, six to the right, facing six others to the left on the opposite side. Another six spread out along a head table, Lord Bromley, as trial magistrate, sitting in the largest chair in the middle, with Lord Burghley to Bromley's left. A canopied throne stood high on a platform above and behind the assemblage to remind all present of Elizabeth's authority in her absence.

When the Sergeant at Arms stomped his mace and called the prisoner forth, Mary entered in a plain black dress that covered her feet and allowed her to glide as effortlessly as Jesus walking on water. Her back stiff, her chin raised, she floated into the dock with both hands at her sides and stood expressionless as the Sergeant-at-Arms read the indictment.

"Mary Stuart, Queen of Scots, you stand here summoned and accused of high treason and conspiracy to overthrow the rightful Queen of England, Her Gracious Majesty, Queen Elizabeth, and place yourself upon her throne. How say you to these charges?"

Mary shook her head and cleared her throat. "May I speak plainly?" She looked toward the Lord Magistrate and asked.

"'Tis your privilege," the Magistrate nodded and answered.

"Then I say to you this. I am myself a Queen, the daughter of a King and as true a monarch as the Queen of England. I came to England on my cousin's promise to assist me against my rebellious subjects and was at once imprisoned. As an absolute queen, I cannot submit to any foreign sovereign, nor to any laws of this or any other land without injury to myself or to my son James, now King of Scotland in my long absence. For myself, I do not recognize the laws of England nor do I know or understand them. I am alone without counsel or with anyone to speak on my behalf. My papers and notes have been taken from me, so that I am destitute of all aid, and thus, taken to disadvantage."

The accused's strength, steadfastness, and forthrightness impressed Edward, particularly as the accumulating evidence fanned out against her, some substantiated, some rumored, some collected to strengthen the case against her. Instead of defending against it, she challenged an English tribunal's authority to try her. Edward might have taken that same stance were he in her position. He was certain Elizabeth would have if similarly charged in Scotland.

She admitted participating in an effort to gain her freedom, yet not to any intent to take her cousin's place. "I came in this kingdom under promise of aid and assistance," she testified. "Instead of aid, I have been detained and imprisoned. I do not deny that I have earnestly wished my liberty and have done my utmost to procure it. In this, I acted from a natural wish. Can I be responsible for the criminal acts of the few who planned conspiracy without my knowledge, participation or consent?"

When confronted with the written statements of witnesses who substantiated her willing compliance to overthrow Elizabeth, she questioned their motives, intent, and honesty.

"I do not wish to accuse those who have been loyal to me," she said. "But I plainly see that they have spoken in fear of torture and death. In order to save themselves, they have faulted themselves at my expense, fancying that I could thereby more easily save myself, not suspecting the manner in which I have been treated. If they were in my presence now, they would clear me on the spot of all blame and would put me out of danger."

The trial lasted four days, the predictable verdict pronounced by the Sergeant-at-Arms late in the afternoon of the fifth. "Guilty of treason as charged."

When asked if she had any final words, Mary stood, looked about, cleared her throat, and spoke in a strong, unwavering voice. "Good Lords and gentlemen of England. There is not one among you, let he be the cleverest and most capable, able to defend himself were he in my place. My lords and gentlemen, I place my cause in God's hands and ask him to mercifully keep me from ever having to see any of you again."

Edward did not attend her execution, although, weeks later, he read the official account as recorded by Robert Wynkfielde, the tribunal's appointed scribe.

"Mary Queen of Scots knelt in prey," Wynkfielde wrote in a neat, flowing hand as though taking the account of cargo loaded on the docks. "The executioners," Wynkfielde scribed, "after requesting the Queen of Scots to forgive them for her death, she did answer, 'I forgive you with all my heart, for I hope you shall make a quick end of all my troubles.' Then they, with her two women helping her, began to disrobe her. That done, and after laying her crucifix upon a stool, one of the executioners took from her hand the *Agnus Dei Prayer Book,* which she, looking over and laying her hand upon it, gave it to one of her women.

"She then suffered her two women to take her pomander beads and all other of her remaining apparel, and then, with joy rather than sorrow, asked them to help her make ready, pulling off her remaining sleeves.

"All the time they were disrobing her, she never changed her countenance, but with smiling cheer uttered the words that she never had such grooms to make her this prepared for what be forthcoming.

"Then she, being stripped of all save her petticoat and kirtle, her two women made great lamentation, crying and crossing themselves and praying in Latin.

"Being thus accomplished, one of the women holding a *Corpus Christi* cloth, kissed it, then put it on the Queen of Scots' head and pinned it fast. Thus now stooping on her knees and groping for the block, she did lay her head down upon it, put her chin in its notch and reached both hands aside to hold herself steady. Then lying most quietly, she did cry *'In manus tuas, Domine'* three times.

"Thereupon, she endured two strokes of the executioner's axe, making a quiet moan with each stoke yet not stirring any part of the rest of her. And thus the executioner did cut off her head, save one little gristle for the rendering of his final stroke. He then lifted her by her hair and displayed her head for all to view, the assemblage crying *'God save the Queen of Scots.'*

Then her wig, attached to the little remained of her own hair, did fall off and she appeared as gray as threescore and ten years beyond her age, her face at that moment being so much altered from its living form that few would recognize her. To all those assembled, thus amazed, her lips stirred for a quarter of an hour beyond her death as though she still continued to apply her lips to her defense.

"Whereupon when the executioner's aid pulled off her garters, he did spy a little dog which had been kept in secret beneath her slip, and which would afterward not depart from its master's dead corpse, but did came and laid its head upon her severed neck, thus being imbrued with the blood from her severed head before being pulled away and carried off to wash it clean, as all said, 'God save the Queen of Scots.'"

"And God save us all," Edward muttered as laid the report down.

CHAPTER 59

A Woman Beneath the Crown

"Could I find out the woman's part in me?"
Cymbeline, II, 5

Was not a queen a woman? And did not a queen have a woman's needs, a woman's inclinations, a woman's natural desires?

Elizabeth awoke lost in a fog of images and feelings from an erotic dream that she wished to hold close to her breast lest it leave too soon.

The panel in her bedchamber door creaked open and her chambermaid peaked inside to determine if her queen was awake and to see to empting the chamber pot and alerting the Ladies to part the thick tapestries and prepare the queen's wardrobe for the day.

Elizabeth remained perfectly still feigning sleep, her eyes tightly closed until the opening eased shut again. A frown knotted her brow. Her dream had cowered in a dark recess of her mind where it lingered, mocking her, until a sheepish grin curled her lips as the apparition reemerged in her mind's eye.

Still warm beneath the layers of spreads and covers that held the castle drafts at bay, she sensed the ghostly apparition grinning back, as this particular spirit was always wont to do. Perhaps it was his youth, his stature, his eyes that studied her and rendered her vulnerable to his desires. She slipped away the protective warmth of her covers and leaned back against the pillows and the carved-oak headboard that supported her canopy.

The door creaked open once more and the chambermaid's head poked through again. "Not now" she said, with more irritation in her voice than she intended. She was simply not prepared to be disturbed by her duties and responsibilities. She preferred to dwell in sweet dreams and reverie a bit longer, an indulgence too often interrupted by lingering nightmares of tower guards imprisoning her as a young girl, preparing her for death as her sister Mary pondered her fate. She shook her head and stiffened her backbone to banish those thoughts, as she loosened her gown and gathered it up around her.

"Edward," she quietly whispered, as she summoned back the apparition of the lover she knew and on whom she had come to rely -- her lover with the impish, devilish grin that well suited his nature. She trusted this man despite his relative youth -- this man who spoke and wrote with the accuracy and sharpness of a skilled lancer, this man who aimed for the heart of truth without regard to consequence. Whist others took the measure of their words, Edward sliced to the core with an incisive beauty and authenticity.

Yet it was precisely Edward's innate disregard for authority and playfulness that drew her to him in a way she found disturbing and dangerous, yet irresistible. It touched on the spirit of freedom and innocence she once felt growing up at Hampton Court exempt from the burdens and responsibilities of a queen -- a time when she ran barefoot in the fields in late afternoons, cooled her toes in the brook and rolled in tall grasses with her six spaniels. It was a time when no one, least of all herself, thought of her as the future monarch, and she was free.

She secretly admitted to herself, though never to Edward, that his youthful spirit revived her own, a confession that would offer him more power over her than she wished him to possess. He was, in truth, her grownup playmate. And how does a healthy woman's natural inclinations command mature playmates spend their time? Was it not a romp in a farmer's haystack, or in a queen's bed, or the ultimate act itself whereby nature enticed their bodies to act with the intent of procreation and future issue?

She was married to England, her crown her wedding ring, yet was her body not her own to enjoy? If political circumstance negated legal marriage, must she forgo the pleasures of the marital bed? Edward stimulated her mind and pampered her secret desires. He pleased her, and she indulged him. Like children, they played when they could, even though his sentiments and loyalty shifted with the seasons, blowing hot with passion when in her bed, then tinged with anger when he felt snubbed, and aloof and cold when offended.

She grinned recalling an occasion in which they had fought and he stomped out arguing with himself, then returned and burst into her chamber, poking forth a huge erection in one hand and brandishing a mock sword in the other, inquiring through his grin, "Do you wish to play or fight? I shall lay down one if you take hold of the other."

Utterly relaxed in her bed, still not wishing her queen's duties to begin, she reached between her legs and slowly fondled her moist parts, gradually increasing her rhythm and pressure until familiar waves of delight spasmed through her body, flinging her head back against the headboard.

She collapsed and rolled to her side, laughing and rubbing her head, then lay quiet until her breathing settled and she felt she could speak with a queen's calm deliberation. Then reaching above her head, she yanked the dangling summoning cord and rang for her day to begin.

CHAPTER 60

Test of Faith

"Wouldst thou be a breeder of sinners?"
Hamlet, III, 2

A black-robed father, a fisher of men and anointer of kings, stood on an ankle-high platform above six others who knelt before him -- Charles Arundel, Francis Southwell, and two of Southwell's neighbors, along with Henry Howard, Edward's uncle, and finally, Edward de Vere, the Seventeenth Earl of Oxford. All, save Edward, were northern Lords and gentleman who had escaped the noose after the northern rebellion.

The death of Mary Queen of Scots had neither dulled their scheming nor softened their resolve to replace Protestant Elizabeth with a Catholic monarch. If a successor would no longer rise from the grave in the guise of the now dead Mary Queen of Scots, perhaps a savior could be induced to sail across the Channel from France or Spain. Philip had long injected clandestine priests onto England's shores to soften resistance and test support for a Spanish invasion, one of them, the Catholic father who now stood above them.

On his knees, his head bowed as Edward had knelt so many times next to his natural father he felt guilty and repentant. He recalled when he and Father Elmo knelt in Duodo's chapel, and then again, alone in the Sistine Chapel, cowering beneath Michelangelo's awesome representation of God's power and magnificence. His travels had merely churned his doubts concerning Henry's religious conversion for political reasons. His Uncle Henry Howard was right. The original Church had rested on the solid rock of Peter, as Howard had rightfully claimed, and not on the wheelings and dealings of whom a King could or could not marry. Rome's Church had christened, married, blessed, counseled, consoled, and buried sixteen prior Oxford earls, including Edward's father, all of whom practiced their faith. Yet, his father had kept his faith and still faithfully served his monarch. Why could not Edward split his allegiance in the same fashion? Elizabeth did not demand a religious oath, or even total obedience as her sister Mary had. She merely required a veiled practice and a loyalty to a unified England. As she often said, "I cannot govern men's hearts and do not care to try."

The priest lifted a silver cross dangling on his necklace, kissed it, and turned his back on the praying men and knelt before an improvised altar. "In nomine Patris," he chanted in Latin, and then crossed his head and heart in a sign of faith. "Filii et Spiritus Sancti... Amen."

As he stood and turned back, a boy in a white robe sauntered forth balancing a silver tray.

"Introibo ad altare Dei," the priest intoned.

"Ad deum qui laetificat," the boy followed in a high-pitched voice.

"Judica me Deus," the priest sang. "Et discerne causam meam, de gente non sancta."

Henry's Protestant zealots, and the sickly son who briefly followed Henry, had stripped the church's of it tradition, along with its color and ritual, storming into Catholic cathedrals, churches and monasteries, breaking centuries old stained glass, ripping portraits of saints from the walls, tossing alters across pews and down aisles, and resurfacing frescos with a dull Protestant gray and then, even more devastating in Edward's view, expunging Latin from the liturgy, squeezing God's mystery from the language and replacing it with an ordinary English everyone knew but whose deeper understanding slipped from their grasp. Henry's Church, to those used to the richness of the old, had sunk in a barren void without its saints, its shrines, its robes, its language, and its familiar ritual. The newly sterilized church inspired neither feeling nor commitment.

"Quia tu es Deus fortitudo mea," the priest monotoned, flattening his palm and passing it across his chest. "Quare me repulisti... Et quare tristis incedo... Dum affligit me inimicus?"

Edward knew the words -- *God, give me strength. Why hast thou cast me off whilst my enemy afflicteth me?* Yet, it was its rhythm, its steadiness, and familiarity that reassured him.

"Qui pridie quam pateretur... Accepit panem in sanctas ac venerabiles manus suas."

The priest lifted a thin wafer from the silver tray the boy held up and then, one at a time, as each of those kneeling before him raised his head, closed his eyes, and opened his mouth, the priest laid a sliver upon an outstretched tongue. "Hoc est corpus meum... Quod pro vobis datur touto esti to soma mou to uper umon didomenon... This is my body which is given for you," he chanted his first English with a Spanish accent. "This do in remembrance of me."

He raised a silver chalice the boy passed to him, wiped its rim with a folded white cloth, and touched the lip of the cup down the row extended lips, repeating to each as he passed. "This is my blood, shed for the remission of sins. Do this in remembrance of me," then moving on to the next.

The priest sat the chalice down on a table next to him, lifted a small bell, sounded it, and then sat the bell down and raised his eyes toward the heavens. "Lord, we pray for these Englishmen, thy loyal followers of the true Christ. We ask for their commission of faith in preservation of the Holy Roman Church and of the Pope as thy anointed representative. Amen."

He stepped down the row again, stopping at each man and waiting for each to repeat, "Amen" before moving to the next, until he reached Edward. "Do you accept the Lord, my son?" he asked.

"I do."

"Do you confess your sins?"

"I do, Father."

"Do you accept the Pope?"

When Edward said nothing, the priest gently laid his right hand on Edward's head.

"I do," Edward whispered.

The priest stepped back, bowed his head, clasped his hands in prayer, and closed his eyes. "Lord, we pray for these, thy loyal servants, that they shall rise in abeyance to thy will. In nomine Patris, et Filii, et Spiritus Sancti. In the name of the Father, the Son and the Holy Ghost. Amen."

When the priest turned and spoke quietly to the alter boy, and Arundel and the others rose and chatted among themselves and Henry Howard motioned for Edward to join him outside.

"What we just accomplished in there may be sacrilege," Edward said, feeling much like a spiritual feather tossed about in a savage wind.

"And what about that forbids us our faith?" Henry asked as they ambled down between a row of graves and monuments.

"Elizabeth does not forbid it," Edward countered. "She simply bans open display."

"Open display is *part* of our religion. 'Tis the Lord's commandment." Henry stopped and glared at him. "Edward. Be aware. More danger lurks here than you know."

"If you are considering further insurrection, the rebellion is over. Norfolk is dead."

"Hope lives eternal."

"Hope all you like. I want no part of it."

"And what of your profession of faith?"

"'Tis a private matter, as it was with my father."

"All we ask is this. If it comes to choosing, choose well. The fate of England is in store."

"I shall keep the faith. That's all I can say."

"*Which* faith?"

"My own."

"Come then," Henry ginned and lightened his tone. "Join me for drink in the company of friends. What say you?"

Ale at the Horsehead -- food and a hardy brew mixed with rowdy cheer and laughter -- loosened moods along with tongues as the group gathered around a thick oak table.

"The Queen shall *never* marry," Arundel said, an issue that always arose in any discussion of the Queen.

"She has had many suitors in her time," Southwell jibbed. "Simply none that suited her."

"And what of you, Edward?" Arundel asked. "You accompany her enough. Have you had this lady?"

"Had her?... She is my queen."

"Queen, yes. Yet she sings and plays, and I am told, has varied other interests."

"I hear she dances," Southwell laughed.

"Far better than she sings," Edward admitted as he looked across the room and raised a finger for the innkeeper to carry over a pitcher to refill their mugs. "Her voice doth crow, that is true," he said, turning back. "Yet not so well as the cock in the morning."

They drank and made merry until Edward's head floated unevenly on his shoulders. He bid Howard and the others adieu and stayed the night upstairs at the Horsehead Inn, awaking in the morning with the feeling that his horse had thrown him and kicked him in his skull. At Edward's request, the innkeeper carried up a tray of boiled eggs and smoked pigsrind, along with a mug a foul green liquid which he drank in one gulp after first tasting what he could not swallow in dribbles.

He slept again until late afternoon, when his stomach finally settled, his thoughts partly cleared, and he better recalled the events of the previous evening -- the clandestine mass and his conversation with Henry Howard in the graveyard. He dressed and found the innkeeper in his storage room, frowning and bent over his accounts. "The priest," Edward demanded. "Where is he? Where can I find him?"

"Priest?... We have no priest."

"The *Spanish* priest." Edward grabbed the man by his collar and lifted him off his stool. "Where is he?"

"I know no such. If you mean the man in black, look to the cottage by the graves."

Edward retraced his steps of the previous night and banged on the cottage door at the rear of the graveyard until a hefty-aproned woman squeaked it half opened.

"I wish to see him."

"I am alone."

"Tell him I have come to..."

"Let him enter," a man's voice called from inside, his accent Spanish.

Edward pushed through the door and stepped into a darkened room where the wide-shouldered man slumped at a table in the center, dunking a fistful of bread in what appeared to be a thick soup. "Join me," the man said without glancing up. "I thought you might come. I rather hoped you would."

Edward crossed the room and stood above the man. "Howard and the others. What are they scheming? What are their plans?"

"Nothing of consequence. A profession of faith."

"Why have you come here?"

"To bring solace to the faithful."

"Do you spy for the Spanish crown?"

The man laid his bread down, slid his bowl away and looked up, his eyes sunk well back in his head, shadowed beneath thick eyebrows. "It is not Spain that has broken the faith. If I spy, I spy for the Lord. There is no sin in that."

"This is *not* Spain."

"Faith knows no boarders."

"You risk your life and that of the others."

"Did our savior not sacrifice his life to save us all? Mine is of little consequence."

"Is rebellion planned?"

"Are you for us or against us?"

"I am for what is right."

"Let me show you something," the man said. He nodded toward the woman. "Bring him forth."

The woman hesitated.

"Bring him forth."

When she opened a door to a back room where a shadow swayed on a bench.

"Come here," the priest said. "Let him see. He needs to know."

The shadow slowly rose and hobbled into the room, rags wrapped around his elbows the length of his wrists.

"Show him."

"No."

When the priest glared, the man stuck out what remained of his arms -- two stumps where his hands should be.

"This is the work of your Queen," the priest said. "His only crime was writing of his faith and passing it on. *You* are a writer. This one writes no more."

Edward shuddered.

"There is much else I could show and tell you," the priest said. "This much I *will* say. If Spain *should* come to power on this island, no harm would come to those who remained faithful. The Pope would bless them."

"And what of our Queen?"

"She would have her opportunity to repent. Our Lord is forgiving."

As soon as Edward left, he quickly returned to the Horsehead Inn and gathered his belongings. Repent indeed, he thought, as he mounted his horse and galloped toward London. The Spanish would offer the Queen forgiveness just before a Spanish ax fell upon her neck to speed her journey to her maker.

CHAPTER 61

Lies and Innuendo

> "Fair is foul and foul is fair."
> *Macbeth, I, 1*

A shifting tide never rests. Whichever way it runs, in time, it turns and tugs the other way. Edward might never settle the conflicting currents of his religion. He had never written a play with God as a character, as had the ancient Greeks, with their pantheon of gods to draw upon, trotting out a different deity to suit their varied purpose. Christians embraced a single, all-purpose God, yet could not agree on precisely what He allowed or demanded nor how He preferred to be worshiped, nor precisely which holy scriptures carried His divine word, nor how the candles should be set upon His alter or how to paint or decorate the walls in His place of worship. The Christian God either did not speak clearly or those who proposed to speak in His behalf misheard, misspoke, misused, or misunderstood His intentions.

Despite his previous injury from the sword fight with Vavasor's uncle and the chronic pain that ensued, at least it did not incapacitate his ability to ride as he galloped south at full stead, exchanging exhausted horses at every livery until well after dark had fallen. When he breached Whitehall's gates, he set his mount free, startling the guards awake as he clambered down the corridors and burst into the Queen's outer chamber, swords drawn ahead of him, others rushing up. "Wake your captain," Edward demanded.

In less than a minute, a uniformed officer sauntered forth, yawning.

"Inform the Queen I must see her."

"Her Majesty has long retired."

"I suggest you tell her that I am here. That her life is in danger."

The captain groaned. "Wait here."

Edward paced, clasping his hands behind his back to contain his energy. When an inner door opened, a lady-in-waiting leaned out. "The Queen has consented to see him," she told the Captain.

As Edward entered, Elizabeth sat at the far end of the room, a thick, purple robe wrapped around her shoulders, her wig set too high and too far back on her head, exposing a creeping baldness. "My *life* in danger?" she said, glancing up as Edward crossed. "There is nothing new in that."

"Madame." Edward rushed to her, knelt, and kissed her hand.

"Edward. Such deference… This is not like you… Rise. Tell me, what is it?"

"They plot against you."

"Of course, they do. Sit beside me. They have as long as I can remember."

"Howard and the others."

"What in particular?"

"They draw up plans."

"You know this for certain?"

"Not in detail."

She jutted her chin out and nodded. "The Spanish Papists," she said.

"There *was* a Spanish priest."

"Walsingham has warned me. What else do you know of this?"

"Only that they…," he hesitated.

"Wish me dead?" she finished his sentence.

"Their blinders show them no other way."

"I take your warning, then. Go home and wait. I shall see to this and send for you when I learn more of it."

Drained from his ride, from the gravity of what he had learned, and from Howard's direct involvement, he retrieved his horse and slowly trotted back to his Fliesh Row apartments. Three days hence, a contingent of guards banged on his door and arrested him in the name of the Queen, carrying him off to court, and from there, immediately escorting him into the Queen's privy chamber,

Her Majesty elevated on a working throne, Henry Howard and Charles Arundel grinning from a table beneath and to the Queen's left. When she nodded for Edward to come forth and sit at an empty table across from the others, Howard and Arundel eyed Edward as he passed.

"We have conflicting accusations here," the Queen began. "I have decided to pursue both sides and see which fits the truth." She glanced at Edward and then turned to the others. "The Earl of Oxford," she began, "has charged Lord's Howard and Arundel with sedition and has seen to warn me of their impending plot." She faced Edward. "In their defense, Lord's Howard and Arundel have signed a petition denying these allegations and laying out charges of their own, to which they have writ the following." She lifted a scroll and read.

> To record the full vices of this monstrous Earl of Oxford would be a labor without end. They be so numerous, vile, and scandalous that it would be a sin to write them all, and a loss of time to repeat his impertinent and senseless lies. He hath perjured himself a hundred times and damned himself to the pit of hell. He is a most notorious drunkard, very seldom sober, and in his drunken fits he has spared neither man, be he ever so honorable, nor woman, be she ever so virtuous.

The Queen glanced up. "If I am to believe the one," she tapped the scroll, "I cannot believe the other." She eyed Edward. "I have read and heard Lords Howard and Arundel in their defense and their accusations. What say you in your behalf, my Lord Oxford?"

Edward stood.

"You may sit."

"I prefer to stand above these two... I say this. That those who create lies know full well how to tell them. 'Tis those with little virtue who speak the most of it, who spit fancy words where deeds are lacking. As far as drunkenness, while we were together, the pitcher did seem to swing full around the table, often empty, to my chagrin, by the time it reached me."

"There is one other charge," the Queen said, looking down and reading again. "It be here attested and agreed upon that the Lord Oxford, having railed against his Queen, did say, 'she does not sing, but crows. Her voice be not so well as a cock in the morning.'"

Edward tried to hold his grin and thought himself successful. "Madam," he said. "I do confess to being drunk and saying something of that order. Yet, in full awareness now, I still confess my judgment may be true. I believe I added that Your Majesty's crowing did not make you the poorer Queen."

"That poor? As *poor* as a cock?"

Edward shrugged.

"Your honesty, even disguised as charm, does not fit the point of this inquiry."

"Nor is it intended."

The Queen lowered her head, stared at her knees, and shook her head as though tired of this burden. "My judgment is this then," she finally looked up and said. "All three of you confined to the Tower until I sort it out."

As the guards escorted Edward out, he thought her decision wise. With all locked up, whatever the danger lie, the Tower would confine the body of it.

He spent two nights twisting uneasily on the most uncomfortable rope bed of his life and then, when he opened his eyes on the third morning, he found the door open and no one there to impede his departure. On his way through the west Tower Gate, the Sergeant of the Guards handed him a single stemmed rose without a note of explanation as he glanced up at Howard, who stared down through a hole in his tower confinement. Edward sniffed the Tudor rose. She knows, he thought.

Three weeks hence, Walsingham, after passing Edward in front of Crumpet & Worthings Tailors on Gilford Row, slowed as he passed and then spun around and strolled back. "Lord Oxford… A word?"

"Mr. Secretary."

"It is good to see you out in the sunshine."

"The sun doth shine even in the Tower, if that be your implication. I had a room with a view."

"Perhaps they'll glass those windows in someday. 'Tis the latest fashion, you know. We already have a modern means of drawing and quartering. Have your heard?"

"What makes you think I have an interest?"

"Perhaps for use in one of your plays. 'Twould make a rather graphic scene, would it not? Drawing and quartering would grip an audience. All that pain and blood. They would imagine *themselves* torn apart."

"I have my own imagination to draw upon."

"Yes, that is what it takes. Imagination. Someone to think of how to do it."

"You?"

"Our new method?… I do not recall who conceived it. There is so much on my mind these days. So much sedition in the air. Yet, I am well acquainted with the manner of it. A man, a known and proven traitor, is laid naked on his back in the middle of a village square. His wrists and ankles tied separately, each tethered to a different horse to pull in four directions. That, of course, after disgorging his intestines and laying them on his chest. He's still alive with that. 'Tis quite amazing. The horses are the delicate part. That requires precision, a team effort. They must pull evenly so the arms and legs rip off in one full splatter. Those villagers in front get the better view, yet are obliged to wash their shirts. That is the point, is it not? The view? The lesson? That it could easily happen to them? To anyone really, no matter their station. That *their* body parts could paint their neighbor's shirts?… If accomplished well, we end up with five pieces, counting the trunk as the largest. And then, if the head be severed, that allows a sixth. Each can be staked in a different village and then moved about from time to time to spread the message. Her

Majesty's subjects are unfortunately illiterate. Like your plays, they understand what they see."

"Why tell me this?"

"No particular reason... If you are concerned that we might use such methods on a priest, we *could* not. That would go against the Queen's directive. She tolerates them. Spies are a different matter. Spanish Catholics who pretend to be priests, who offer mass to traitors as part of their conspiracy. Genuine priests are not allowed in this county. Therefore, none here *are* genuine. Do you see my reasoning? If we happen to catch a pretender and put him to the rack and stretch him far enough he will admit to anything, deny Jesus even. Drawing and quartering would be the natural result of his own confession... Have a pleasant day," Walsingham said as he turned his back on Edward and ambled off.

CHAPTER 62

Hope and Devastation

"Praising what is lost."
All's Well That Ends Well, IV, 3

London's merchants, its businessman, its crafters, its tailors, its haberdashers, its importers and all manner of movers, shifters, and shakers extracted or skimmed a profit or else collected taxes, tariffs, or handling fees for unloading, storing, hauling, or passing on a myriad of imported, furnishings, clothing, spices and any number of sundry goods that Edward and others required or desired. Commodities and their associated proceeds poured onto London's docks from the realm's increased seafaring and trading ventures, the city even profiting from pirate plunder of French and Spanish merchant vessels, the pirates sailing freely up the Thames with impunity to sell their pilfered wares.

Yet none of England's newfound wealth filtered into Edward's purse. He was more adept at outflow. Of the forty-two estates, lands, keeps, castles and apartments that Edward had inherited, now, at the age of thirty-eight, only seven remained, the three largest of these being de Vere House in Savoy, Bilton Swan on the Avon, and Hedingham, his ancestral birthplace.

The levy that Burghley had withdrawn for Edward's lengthy wardship, along with the indebtedness of his two-years' travel expense had piled atop the continuing cost of his player's companies, the upkeep of his remaining properties, and the regular allowance paid to Vavasor to raise their son. That, of course, was added to his yearly tailoring and wardrobe outlay and the general cost of living in a style befitting his station. Beyond those expenses, he had lately added the additional outlay from a newly acquired card-playing habit where coin changed hands for fun and profit, a pastime that acquainted him among friends when he tired of writing and desired company in the evenings. He learnt well, the more experienced gamblers teaching him the most costly lessons.

"There be a key to unlock the wealth of it," Martin Frobisher told Edward as they walked outside the busy Mercantile Exchange on a sunny afternoon in early August.

"A key you know of?" Edward asked.

"I believe I do. Get there first and return the quickest." Frobisher nodded across the road toward the masts lining the docks. "Already, a quarter of these ships you see there transport commodities and spices from India, and silks farther around from China. Should a faster way be found to get there..." He raised his eyebrows.

"You *know* such a way?"

"Not south. *West.* South requires sailing around the Horn. West, if straight, would get there and back far quicker."

"Through the Americas?"

"There be bays and inlets everywhere. I have sailed past more than I can count. One of them *must* outlet to the west to China. Riches would flow to those who find it first."

"*If* one be found."

"Judge for yourself." He spotted a barrel across the road, led Edward to it, and there upon unfurled a chart and flattened it with the side of his hand. "With all this land," he said, running a curved finger along the partially charted coast of North America. "Sailing *through*..." He scratched a fingernail across uncharted territory. "Saving all that distance, saves time. Less time means more money. By the time others learn our route, our profit is secure. We shall be rich men. I have a Queen's permit and have her blessing to established a company and seek investors. She would profit, as well. All those involved would."

"And the Queen pointed you to me?"

"I thought of you myself."

Edward had lost his wealth slowly, frittering it away. With Frobisher's scheme, he stood to lose a bit more or regain a great deal. Frobisher said he would send around a copy of the Queen's grant and did so in the morning.

GRANT GIVEN AT THE QUEEN'S
CONVENIENCE
TO M. FROBISHER AND HIS COMPANY OF
CATHAY

TO SAIL AND MAKE DISCOVERY of new lands and passages in the Americas, and thereupon seize and explore by all means, seas, lands, lakes and countries northwest and as farther west as passage allows, and there within to plant the flag of England where no Christian county has hitherto claimed and bring back such bounty and riches as might thereby profit and benefit the realm and the investors in the Cathay Company.

Upon this Seal of the Queen,
Elizabeth R

Edward sold another estate to invest in Forbisher's first expedition. When Frobisher returned with further hope and promise, yet in need of additional funds to pursue them, Edward considered the matter. Failure would cut his financial legs at the knees. Success would stand him tall again. It would allow him to restore his good name and reacquire most of his lands. His father's ghost could rest.

He calculated what further funds he could garner from an additional sale of lands, and then wrote to William Pelham, Cathay's Commissioner, and Thomas Randolph, Forbisher's appointed treasurer.

William Pelham and Thomas Randolph
In bond of M. Forbisher

Very Good Sirs:

After considering and understanding the wise proceedings and orderly dealings for continuance of the voyage for the discovery of a Northwest Passage by the Company of Cathay, to which Martin Frobisher hath already been honorably charged and is now intoned to be employed for the better achieving thereof, I offer an additional sum as included here and request your answer to certify my submission.

Edward Oxford

Six months after leaving port on his third and final expedition, Frobisher limped back at dusk, his holds empty, and sneaked ashore at night. To those investors who discovered him half drunk on Fleet Street, he simply said, "You can chase the wind as long as you want but never catch it. There be no passage."

CHAPTER 63

The Warning

"Nature teaches beasts to know their friends."
Coriolanus, II, 1

Edward quilled a title on a blank sheet. *The Life and Death of Richard the Third,* and below that wrote, "About 1483," and then dipped his pen and listed his characters.

> Richard, Duke of Gloucester, afterwards King Richard III, brother to the ruling king.
> Henry, Earl of Richmond, rightful king who becomes Henry VII, first Tudor and Elizabeth's grandfather.
> Edward, Prince of Wales, afterwards son to the ruling King.
> Richard, Duke of York, second son to the ruling king.

He inked in the words, "various others," then thought a second, grinned, and wrote, "The Fourteenth Earl Of Oxford." Why not include an Oxford in a play written by an Oxford? After all, Edward's great-grandfather *had* stood at Henry VII's side, supporting the Tudors against the usurper, Richard, thus assuring the Tudor reign. Edward's own father, John, the Sixteenth Earl, had supported Henry VIII and then his daughter, Elizabeth. The Oxford earls had championed the English crown since the first earl stood by William the Conqueror in 1066. Thus, Edward would give an Oxford a walkon line here and there, just enough to allow his friends a nod of recognition and his adversaries a reluctant groan of acknowledgement.

He stared vaguely out the window, waiting for words or an image to emerge, then dipped his quill and wrote.

The Old King (near dying):
When Oxford found me down,
He rescued me, and said, "Live, dear brother, live,
    and be the king.
T'was Lord Oxford who told me,
When we both lay in the field
Frozen near to death, how he did love me
Even of his own garments, he gave himself,
All thin and naked, to numb's cold night.

Then later, as the Fourteenth Earl of Oxford, Edward's great-grandfather, examined his scruples, Edward wrote his Oxford line.

Oxford: Every man's conscience is a thousand
    swords,
To fight against this bloody homicide.

Elizabeth and those in her court would see Edward's theme in present politics, where current conscience forced a choice between old and new, between traditional Catholic and Henry's new Protestant church.

In the final act of *Richard,* Edward would have his Oxford great-grandfather wield his sword for Henry VII. "And thus I seal my oath," that Oxford would say before he bid a fond adieu, thus emphasizing Edward's continued loyalty to the current Tudor.

He scribbled a passage, then scratched it out and thought instead to write a second play exclusively about Henry VII and plant an Oxford in that to keep the family shadow ever present. He wasn't certain if he dangled his name for vanity or simply to reassure the Queen of the Oxford's continued allegiance, yet maybe both, with life too complicated to effect a single truth.

Where to begin *Richard?* He would start where he oft began. He would strut a character engaged deep in thought upon the stage and fill his engage his speech by his character strengths and weaknesses.

ACT I, SCENE I, a London street.
Enter RICHARD alone, a soliloquy

Richard: Now is the winter of our discontent
Made glorious summer by this son of York.
And all the clouds that low'red upon our house
In the deep bosom of the ocean buried.

Richard would be a cunning complainer willing to use his discontents to serve his own selfish ends. If Edward struck the chord right, Elizabeth would see a seething parallel with the malcontents within her own court.

Edward wrote steadily three weeks running -- sleeping little and leaving more on his plate than he took to his mouth as he teased and tested lines, scenes, and speeches to suit his shifting inspiration and his character's demands. Fair writing, he had learned, was in the vision and the sound of the words, in replacing a "gong" with a "tinkle," or a "wink" with a "blink" when a speech or soliloquy required a softer nuance. He informed the Queen of his progress, telling her the outline of it.

"Why set Richard as a hero and name your effort after him," she glared at him and asked. "Be he not a villain?"

"I have him neither, simply as a man taking his affliction out on others, to which an audience would have some sympathy."

"Why thus?"

"We each have our villainous side. Many think of Richard as a villain. I show him more complicated, as a hero gone awry and thus a Tutor enemy in the course of being human."

Her frown deepened.

"Those who support Your Majesty need no convincing of your cause. 'Tis those who seek change, as Richard sought against your grandfather, who need convincing. 'Tis they who need to understand the flaw in Richard's reasoning."

"But Richard?"

"'Tis a tale our history has told, and recently, so all will know of it. I simply show him in his true light. Broken in body *and* spirit, but nonetheless clever and cunning and able to persuade others by promising to share his ill-gotten power, much as Your Majesty's adversaries have pledged. I have a line for Richard, near the end, in which he says, 'My conscience hath a thousand tongues,' and then have him add as after-thought, 'Each to bring a tale to condemn me as a villain.' Your enemies and those uncertain will reexamine their conscience in this."

Edward added and subtracted lines from *Richard*, reshaping speeches and gestures as they rehearsed, molding his script closer to his intent before trying it out with Burbage and then presenting it to the Queen. Upon gaining Her Majesty's approval, they would circulate *Richard* throughout the countryside to spread its patriotic message of support the Tudor reign and to ready her subjects for England's defense, should one be required.

With the Queen's approval, Edward practiced and presented at Blackfriars. As Edward chided his players to return their costumes to the bay -- they had developed a habit of pilfering caps and leggings -- Lyly walked backstage with a tall, slender, slightly older woman in tow. "Marvelous!" Lyly said. *"Exceedingly* well accomplished! I could not have done better myself. I *have* not... Oh," he added. "My usual impoliteness." He turned toward the woman who accompanied him. "May I present Beth Trentham? She enjoyed your play so much she wished to meet its author. May I present Edward de Vere, Earl of Oxford."

"I so admire your work," she said. "If we had more like you, I do believe England shall be the envy of the Continent. May I ask you a question?"

"Of course."

"On the playbills. Your name... Posted as Anonymous...'"

"Lyly hath not told you?"

"Told me what?"

"Simply that the theater is not approved for a man of peerage, for an earl. My name upon a play is as my name upon a cockfight and worse. 'Tis considered a disgrace."

"How so?"

"My connection with the court. Playwriting is supposedly meant for commoners, though it breaks my heart to see my labors attributed to another, even though nameless."

After a silence, Trentham looked down and then glanced up again and said, "Nonetheless, I enjoyed your work, be it by Anonymous or by Edward de Vere."

Edward thanked her, but said he doubted English plays would ever outdo the Italian operas or the French playwrights, and certainly not the classics. They spoke a few minutes before she excused herself, saying her carriage waited, and she hoped they would have an opportunity to speak again.

Burbage held *Richard* over two weeks on good attendance, playing to a full house with some attending twice or more. "What *others* do you have?" Burbage asked at the end of the week. "A cart that quickly empties needs refilling."

When the Queen heard stirrings from those attending the production who suspected Edward's intent and seeing contemporary parallels, she ordered an immediate performance at Whitehall, commanding friend and foe to attend to gauge their reaction. She set her own playbill thus:

KING RICHARD III
A Tragedy in Five Acts
Addressing the Start of the Tudors
Author: Known Yet Nameless

In Act V, in front of Her Majesty and an audience of fifty, Richard, newly crowned, addressed his army on the field, about to face the army of Henry, Elizabeth's grandfather.

Richard:

    Our arms be our conscience, our swords be our law.

    Let us whip these stragglers over seas again,

    Lash hence these foreign rags,

    These famished beggars, weary of their lives.

    If we be conquered, let men conquer us,

    And not these bastards, whom our fathers

    Have in their own land beaten, robbed and thumped,

    And in record, left them the heirs of shame.

    Shall they enjoy our lands?

    Lie comfort our wives?

    Ravish our daughters?

Drums far off.

    Hark! I hear them come.

    Fight, gentlemen of England! Fight, bold yeomen!

    Draw, archers, draw your arrows to the head!

    Spur your proud horses and ride in blood.

    Amaze the leachmen with your staves!

None in the audience whispered or moved when Richard, mortally wounded, staggered across the stage, his bitter enemy, the future Henry VII in pursuit as Richard raised his hands toward the heavens and pleaded to the gods. "A horse! A horse! My kingdom for a horse!" As Richard staggered forward, Henry caught him from behind, whacked his feet from under him and slayed him, thus assuring Henry's Tudor reign.

"Splendid! Splendid!" the Queen raved after a long silence. "Do you think they'll take your meaning?" she later asked Edward.

"A story is never just a story."

"Clearly not when *you* write it. If war with Spain should come," she said. "If anything holds us together, it shall be our history and our common spirit." She shook her head. "Then we shall *all* know the final act."

~~ *SHAKESPEARE* ~~

"A fair house built on another man's ground"

Merry Wives of Windsor, II, 2

CHAPTER 64

A Hidden Asset

"What's past and what's to come."
Troilus and Cressida, IV, 1

Sedition seeped through the countryside like an underground poison that seeped through the country's wells, lakes, and streams, and trickled into its shires and villages. The farther the distance from London, the more Catholic subversion increased and Protestant loyalty diluted, the Northern Earls employing that to their advantage. Yet, as much as religion still divided, England increasingly nourished its deeper roots in its heritage, in its legends and myths, in its rediscovered *Robin Hood, Excalibur, King Arthur and his Knights of the Round Table* and increasingly in Edward's growing list of recent England's histories -- in *King Henry IV, Henry V* and *VI, King John, Richard II* and III, and even *The Merry Wives of Windsor,* a contemporary comedy of English manners.

Lyly took pride in his and Edward's endeavors. "We invent a language to suit our ourselves as we resurrect our birthright," he bragged. "We build our future upon our past."

As Edward's boys sprouted beards and grew to men, he replaced them with younger actors, holding the troop's name to The Oxford Boys, although still not assigning his name to his plays as he and Lyly toured the land, drawing a wide circumference around London through Cheshire and Derbyshire, and south through Staffordshire. In Stratford-Upon-Avon, as they edged toward a longer stay in Oxford, they enacted *Merry Wives* three days running to a lukewarm audience unaccustomed to the subtleties of a female character played by a male presenting the feminine perspective. With attendance poor and enthusiasm lackluster, Edward canceled Friday's performance in order to rest in a tent he had set up for his actors to relax, and refresh, and bathe in the Avon River. As afternoon approached, Lyly asked a nearby innkeeper to send his daughter with a tray of sustenance whist Lyly proceeded to nap and Edward amended some of Fallstaff's lines.

"Sit it anywhere," Edward said, bent over his script as his tent flap opened and a presence entered.

"I brought a mug, as well," a male voice said.

Edward raised his eyes to a partly balding, lightly bearded man in his early to mid-twenties. "Sit it anywhere," he said again and glanced back down.

"I asked to bring it myself," the man said, sliding the tray on a barrel and straightening it.

"That was good of you."

"If there is anything else I can do. I see plays whenever I can."

"We need patrons."

"I have even thought of coming to London. Perhaps to work in the theater. I hear there are opportunities."

Edward laid his quill down and looked up, realizing he would have to deal with this fellow in order to get rid of him. "Do you have experience?" he asked.

"Not as yet. My father is a grain merchant and a glove maker. I help him with the grain, loading the barges. I'd be willing to do most anything."

"There are often odd jobs about. Look me up if you get there."

"I shall. I shall. And thank you… How will you know me?"

"What is your name?" Edward asked.

"Shakspere. Pronounced like 'shack.' William Shakspere."

Edward wrote the name "Shakspere," when the man left, then scribbled…

Shack
Shakek
Spear
Spear Shaker

Shaker-of-Spears
ShakeSpeare

Edward liked the ring of it and determine to leave the hyphen and capitalize both *Shake* and *Spear* to hold the two parts separate. The hyphen played on the ancient Oxford crest, which depicted a lion shaking a broken spear. Beyond that, he had once been referred to as a goodly "shaker of spears" for his prowess in the jousts, and many would remember him as such. If he ever needed a name attached to his plays -- certainly not Edward de Vere, the Seventeenth Earl of Oxford -- but *ShakeSpear,* a shaker of spears, might well do. It hinted his identity enough for those who knew him and refuted enough when denial was required.

CHAPTER 65

Battle at Sea

"Courage mounteth with occasion."
King John, II, 1

By 1558, King Phillip of Spain had finally grown tired of Elizabeth's perpetual promise of marriage to one of his sons, having finally seen through the Queen's marital ruse. Long hungry to possess the island kingdom, he ordered his Spanish fleet, his Armada, to sail up the coast and assemble for attack and invasion at Corunna on the northwest tip of Spain, just a hundred leagues from Falmouth on England's exposed southwestern coast.

In times of impending disaster, assets are of little import. With little left to scrape from his near empty coffers, Edward sold his two remaining estates, including Hedingham, the family's ancestral castle, in order to purchase, man, and provision the retrofit *Bonaventure,* a five-hundred-ton merchant vessel rebuilt by the Bristol Shipworks and commissioned as one of the smaller, fighting vessels England had christened in recent years.

The threat of a Spanish invasion squelched all interest in the plays, or the theater, and all manner frivolous entertainment. All able-bodied men busied themselves cutting and storing half-ripened grain, or sharpening their knives and battle axes, restringing their longbows, and constantly eyeing the horizon for Spanish sails while maids and maidens laid away stores for an impending siege as they tucked their children into their beds or hid them in the folds of their aprons.

Spain conceived a simple plan -- gather in Corunna and sail up the Channel in mass, plow though any English navel resistance with larger sail and heavier cannons, and then load Parma's army, waiting in the Netherlands, and ferry them across for a land invasion.

Any opposition the invading army encountered would stain the island red with English blood. If the Spanish plans bore fruit, any Englishman still alive when Philip's army marched across the island and reached the Irish Sea would wave his rosaries and shout, "Buenos días, Conquistadores."

Medina Sidonia, the Armada's Commander, proudly led the Spanish fleet of one-hundred-eighty war ships. Francis Drake, Elizabeth's Admiral, commanded a mere thirty-four first-line ships, *Bonaventure* among them -- most recently built, refitted and unproven.

Edward readied *Bonaventure* as best he could, stowing aboard bags of dried beans and rice, kegs of water and rum, and barrels of salt to preserve carp or mackerel should *Bonaventure* be chased and forced to run for days. He stocked away crusted biscuits, waxed cheese rounds, and mixed crates of dried pears and berries that he scavenged from what remained from Plymouth's country villages. He hauled onboard cannonballs, gunpowder and fuse, along with additional lanterns, candles, ropes, hemp, and extra water buckets to douse fires. He stored away spare lanyards, bolts, tackle, cable and shrouds, all hauled aboard from ferried lines of longboats that rowed out and around Plymouth harbor like overbloated ducks fortifying their nests for an approaching storm.

At night, while most hunkered down to await news that the Spanish had gathered and set sail, Edward supervised the storing of his gear and tackle into every crack and crevice available before he fell asleep on deck and woke early to oversee the preparation of *Bonaventure*'s weapons, checking fuses and aim and rolling cannon balls down gun gullets to ensure they rolled freely, the Spanish noted for grappling on boarding before a gunner could load and fire.

"No one expects us to win," Edward informed his men, candidly repeating what Drake had told his the captains. "If that be so," he added on his own, "we shall send a few to the bottom before they sink us."

Late on a Wednesday afternoon, after week of mulling on fear and apprehension, George Fleming sailed in with news that the

Spanish had been spotted nor' east of the Scilly Isles, making favorable speed toward the coast. Edward passed Fleming's report on to Lee Meriwether, the experienced captain he had hired to sail *Bonaventure*. Drake, the only English commander with Spanish experience, sent word that they still had time, that they would slip out after sunset and surprise the enemy at sunrise. "Besides," Drake added. "That will give me time to finish my card game," a flippancy he knew would embolden his sailors.

As evening approached, those on shore lit a string of fires that burned along England's southern coast, sending the attack warning from village to village, then north along the main road all the way to London. By first light of day, after slipping out of Plymouth, Edward stood on *Bonaventure's* foredeck, a stiff breeze blowing through his hair, Captain Meriwether at his side, and one-hundred-forty-three sailors at their posts, all silent as the sea held steady in an uneasy calm.

And then slowly, almost imperceptibly as Edward leaned across the rail and squinted, black specks appeared on the horizon -- two or three at first, then half a dozen, then more than he could count, all bobbing and jiggling in the morning haze as if tiptoeing across hot coals. As the specks grew larger, those in front seemed to sprout white-puffed wings that spread like bloated dragonflies, hunched forward and flying toward them, frenzied at the sight of prey.

As the Armada emerged full-sail and charged the tiny English fleet, *Bonaventure* and the other vessels huddled close together with two dreadful options. To beat to the wind would devour them. To haul to port would trap them in the harbor with Spanish canon blasting forward door.

Edward leaned away from the same wind that blew the Spanish fleet toward him, his brow furrowed, his stomach soured. It was one thing to cheer the Queen and shake his fist for England, quite another to face cannons aimed directly at his belly. Death skimmed across the water and grinned from the decks of the Spanish fleet.

Captain Meriwether, sniffing the breeze, his nostrils flared, ordered his mainsail full-hauled, spun his wheel starboard, and headed straight into hell.

At a half league distant, the Spanish formed their battle crescent, their swiftest, their sharpest teeth, leading the wedge and chopping waves.

Bonaventure slowly gathered sail. She cut through water, her sails billowing along both sides of her hull as the Spaniards fluttered green and yellow streamers from their mizzens, their polished rails glistening in the sun, their gun turrets rhythmically rising and sinking to the motion of the waves.

An unexpected gust puffed *Bonaventure's* sails, jolting her forward in fits and starts. Meriwether shaded his eyes and looked aft to judge his angle as *Bonaventure* reached closer to heel and gathered speed as a Spaniard fired, the first shot splashing short, a warning more intent stoking fear than striking.

With little room to maneuver, Meriwether ordered *Bonaventure* heaved to, hoping to slip back into shallower shoals, the heavier Spanish drafts requiring deeper sailing waters. Two other vessels *Merchant* and *Revenge* followed *Bonaventure's* lead, their guns aimed at the Spanish starboard flank.

"Windward!" Meriwether shouted, stabbing his finger in the air. "Hold'er steady!"

Two Spaniard galleons peeled off, tightened sail and veered in *Bonaventure's* direction as the English trio clustered and ran close at heal, neither gaining nor losing. They held an even pace for the better part of an hour, *Bonaventure's* crew gaping over their shoulders as they hauled in halyards and staggered downwind close to shore, their pursuers compelled to retain enough distance to keep from scrapping bottom.

When an unexpected cove forced *Bonaventure* to venture outside the shallows, the largest Spaniard -- *San Sebastian,* her gold-plated name gleaming in the sun -- quickly closed the gap and raised its rack of starboard cannons. She blasted. Her first shot fell leeward. Her second hit closer, its reverberation shaking

Bonaventure's shrouds. Meriwether answered. His forward gun blasted and bolted back across middeck, scorching gunners' hands as two crewmen quickly rolled the weapon forward again, lit its fuse, and sent a two-hundred-pounder screeching toward the enemy.

"A bite on their snout might slow'm," Meriwether said, clutching Edward's shoulder with one hand as he cupped his mouth toward Edward's ear. "Get up to the helmsman. Tell'm we'll swing full to port on my signal. We'll try'n cross their wake and swing up channel before they see our intent and follow. If luck be with us, we'll slide by'm."

Edward staggered forward, his old leg wound burning his calf. "Haul close in on captain's signal," he hollered, the helmsman nodding back understanding. When Meriwether raised and lowered his hand, his sailors complied as he spun his wheel and slowly whirled *Bonaventure* about, her sails flapping in the breeze, and then catching the wind on the other side. *Revenge*, seeing *Bonaventure* turn, followed course. *Merchant,* furthest behind and slower to swing about, still managed to follow. Sailing close together, the three angled windward and crossed the Spanish track, slowly easing toward open sea.

San Sebastian, with more sail, severed the line that separated *Merchant* from the other English vessels, then turned in and bore down broadside upon her. *Merchant* fired. She missed. *San Sebastian*, three times *Merchant's* tonnage, aimed for *Merchant's* underbelly, intent on ramming her. As Edward watched in horror, *Merchant's* sailors scattered like ants with a boot above their heads about to stomp.

San Sebastian struck *Merchant* broadside, ripping into her inners and scattering wood and disgorging bodies from her deck, the cries of men soon fading in a cold sea, their arms flailing, their heads bobbing, the wave of a hand the last to be seen of them.

After plowing into *Merchant, San Sebastian* swung about and eyed its two remaining targets. *Bonaventure* lumbered as close to the safety of the shoals as she was able, taking slight advantage of a changing current. *Revenge* tucked her tail in and followed, the two vessels holding close throughout the afternoon and early evening.

San Sebastian, forced to run in deeper waters, found herself too far a distance to fire and too heavy in weight to venture closer in. As night mercifully fell on a quarter-moon, *Revenge* escaped into the blackness of sea.

Uncertain of his bearings in the shoals, Meriwether hugged the shore and skimmed shallow water until just before light when he dropped anchor, perched on his foredeck, cupped his ears and listened. With no telltale sounds the first hour, Edward ordered rum all around, hoping to ease nerves, encourage rest, and bolster resolve for a renewed attack in light of the morning. Exhausted and drained himself, a second portion of rum easing his own nerves, he stumbled to his cabin and succumbed to sleep. The next he knew, a boot kicked his door open and a bright morning sun seared his eyes open. "We've drifted out!" Meriwether yelled. "They're upon us!"

Edward bolted up on deck as men scampered about, pulled up anchor and sails and rolled cannons across the deck and poking their noses into open turrets as *San Sebastian* barreled in from a blazing sky, her bow dipped low and cutting water as *Bonaventure's* gunners loaded, lit and fired.

San Sebastian answered, her first ball toppling *Bonaventure's* forward mast, crunching limbs beneath its weight. The galleon aimed directly at *Bonaventure's* middeck, loomed large and growing amidst the blaze of cannons. She angled starboard at the last minute and scraped *Bonaventure's* hull, two of her fighters swinging onboard from ropes as two others crossed on a ladder. As Edward glanced aft, a grappling hook caught *Bonaventure's* stern and hauled the ships together, their transoms scrapping and bouncing off, banging in a rhythmic hug.

Meriwether shouted orders that Edward couldn't understand. As one of *Bonaventure's* seaman severed *San Sebastian's* tether, two others tilted the Spanish ladder back into the sea as *San Sebastian's* sails caught an unanticipated gust and pulled away. As the galleon disappeared in haze and mist, *Bonaventure* found herself alone in the water, hugging the shore and heading in the opposite direction.

CHAPTER 66

The Power of Words

"Why, then the world's mine oyster,
Which I with sword will open."
Merry Wives of Windsor, II, 2

Meriwether's crew tossed *Bonaventure's* broken ribs and rigging into the water and lashed her wounds enough to limp back to Plymouth, whose citizens, after surveying *Bonaventure's* damage, doused their cooking fires and boarded their shutters in fear the Spanish were not far behind.

Lyly rowed out in the first longboat and hollered up to Edward, standing on deck. "You're to come at once!"

"Where?"

"To Whitehall. A horse awaits."

Bonaventure had avoided disaster. England would not. Spain's main force, Edward later heard, had cleared Eastbourne and slipped northwest toward Dover. Once through the Straights and into the wider North Sea, Spain's maneuvering ability would expand and allow for tactic the narrower Channel would not condoned. The English fleet, being smaller and lighter, ran swifter. They couldn't inflict damage, but like a slippery flies on the wall, they couldn't easily be taken either. Rumor had it that Sidonia was more intent on reaching the Netherlands to ferry Parma's troops across for a land invasion than chasing an uncatchable English enemy.

Drake gave chase, realizing, even if he managed to catch and engage Sidonia's superior force, he would lose in any all-out battle. The Armada would flick the English off like pesky gnats, then sail on to load Parma's waiting army and deliver Spanish to shore where they would slash English throats.

As soon as Edward stepped ashore, he mounted the steed that Lyly had held for him and galloped east, resting only as his mount required and reaching Whitehall well after dark.

"I'm to bring you to her at once," the Captain of Guard said as soon as Edward's feet hit the ground.

"Is she asleep?"

"Awake *or* asleep, she will see you," the captain said, escorting him down a long hall and into an anteroom.

When the door swung open, he entered a darkened chamber where an old woman wrapped in a faded crimson robe sat at a small table, candlelight flickering on her sagging skin. As Edward approached, the woman shook and raised her eyes.

"Your Majesty?" Edward bowed and said.

"Edward?" She smiled weakly. "It's been a while since you've called me Majesty. We have called each many things in our time, have we not?"

"Some better left unspoken, at least for my part. I shall call you my Queen and say it with pride."

"We *have* loved each other, in our way, have we not?"

"In many ways."

"How goes the battle?" she asked. "How did you fare?"

"Bonaventure took some damage. Six men were lost."

She tightened her brow. "We shan't win at sea, which means we shan't win."

"Your Majesty…"

She tapped her thin knuckles on the table. "We can do no more than peck at Philip's ships," she said. "Parma has fifteen thousand trained troops waiting in the Netherlands with ten thousand horseman to back them. Beyond those, Sidonia carries six thousand onboard from Spain. We have thirty thousand troops in London. Most who meet twice a week to drink and drill, who shake in their boots at the thought of a good fight. By the time Parma's army reaches Aldgate he will have slaughtered more Englishmen than survive. The rest will cower beneath their beds and have their woman throw their slop pots out the window. As my last defense, I have five thousand troops in reserve in with Leicester in command."

"Leicester!" Edward muttered, more venom in his voice than he intended.

"Robbie is my best general. My most experienced."

"At losing. And best at what else?"

"My, my. Jealous after all these years. You flatter me."

"Twas not my intent."

"Robbie will die for me. As to his men, I am less certain. They are paid little and oft not at all. Many are split in their allegiance."

"Then I wish to refit my ship," Edward said, "and do what I can."

"There is no time for that. And no resources. I need you here."

"Then my sword."

"'Tis not your sword I need... Come closer. I wish to show you something."

As he sat, she opened a small chest beneath her table and lifted out a folded letter.

"Read this."

He leaned toward the candle and read.

> With humbleness in my heart, I crave to speak with your Highness. I would be so bold as to make the truth clear. As for that traitor Thomas Wyatt, he might have writin me a letter, but in all faith I received none from him. As far as the letter they say I sent to the King of French, I pray God confound me, I sent no such letter. I humbly ask to lay the truth before thee. Let conscience move your Highness to see the better side of me. I humbly beg but one chance to answer for myself.
>
> Your Highness's most faithful subject as I have been from the beginning and will be to my end.

Elizabeth

When Edward finished reading, he glanced up. "What is this?"

"'Tis a letter pleading for a life. My own. A letter I wrote to my predecessor, Mary, my half sister. She had accused me of plotting with the King of France and others against her. I had wished to plead my case in person, but she would not allow it."

Edward held the letter up. "Then she never read this?"

"I was told she had, yet she gave no reply. Burghley, a young man then kept it. He thought perhaps it might prove useful someday. He returned it to me many years later."

"Why do you show me this now?"

"Because I have no shame." She ran her fingers in what remained of her orange hair and yanked her wig off. "*This* is what I truly am. An old woman. Half bald from smallpox that once near killed me."

"Majesty. Do not do this. We all grow old. It makes not the lesser of us." He stood, walked behind her, placed her wig back on her head and centered it. "I myself am limp from life's misfortunes, from a fight that still pains me. Do not humble yourself."

"*Life* has humbled me... They brought the French Ambassador to me when I was twelve. He and three others to look me over to see if I was suitable for marriage. They looked me over well. I was sent naked to a bare room with no chairs or furniture. Only sunlight through a window and me. I was told to slowly turn and show all sides. When I refused, they said father ordered it."

"Good Lord!"

"It was the first of many insults, yet not near the least... After I wrote that letter," she nodded toward it. "My sister confined me to the Tower while she sought further evidence of my association with Thomas Wyatt. There *was* a plot to overthrow her on behalf of the King of France, but no proof of my involvement though my name was clearly used. To Wyatt's credit, even as they stretched and bled him, he denied my participation to his death. After his execution, they brought me his bloody hands in a bucket. I took their threat and made my peace with God. When they came to fetch me, I wore a plain, black dress for my execution, yet my sister merely wished to speak with me. I think she thought I took the lesson. For some reason, the Lord spared me."

"Perhaps to lead."

"Or die among my subjects… But enough of this. We must see to the present. The Spanish have more men, more training, and more reason to fight. They believe themselves on a mission for the God and the Pope. We have no Pope, and I cannot ask my subjects to fight for God. They quibble over *which* God."

"They will fight for *you.*"

"Some will. Others would as soon see my crown rest in Madrid. That is why I sent for you."

"They will certainly not fight for *me,*" Edward said.

"Not for you, but they might for an idea. One well thought and well spoken…. Do you recall your speech before your attack on the Scottish rebels? Word of it spread on your return."

"Those men feared for their lives."

"Yet your words charged their spirit. You were outnumbered, as I recall."

"I spoke as I felt… *I* was afraid."

"Your plays rouse those who see them."

"As entertainment."

"I am to ride to Tilbury to rally Leicester's troops. Yet, I know not what to say. Shall I speak honestly? Tell them 'tis their duty to die for England? Say that they will lose, that their cause is futile? Shall I say that I am just a woman, never meant to lead an army or be queen?"

Edward jumped up. "No… You *shall* speak honestly. I cannot give you the words. They must be your own. Yet, I can tell you what would touch them. You *are* a woman. Take that as your advantage, as you always have. Yet, you are more than that. You are English, as is everyone among them. Tell them that you *will* lead.

And that, if it comes to it, you will die an Englishman, no more nor less than they."

At dawn on August 19th in the Year of Our Lord 1588, after a light breakfast in her tent at Tilbury, the Queen, dressed in crimson and cream -- her Tudor colors -- mounted a pure white mare and strode out to ride among her troops. She trotted slowly, nodding and smiling, and sitting tall in her saddle. After dismounting, she climbed an improvised platform and there turned to face her troops with nothing between her and them. In a clear, strong, resonant voice, she spoke words she had committed to memory. "My loving people," she began. "We have been persuaded by some to take heed how we commit ourselves to these armed multitudes in fear of treachery at home. I assure you, I do not desire to live to distrust my faithful and loving people. Let the tyrants fear. I have placed my strength and safeguard in the loyal hearts and good will of my subjects."

She looked about, all eyes upon her. "I come amongst you, as you see me, just as I am. In the heat of battle, I will live or die among you. I will lay down my life for my God, my honor, and my country. I know I have the body of a weak and feeble woman. I, above all, know that. But I have the heart and stomach of a king, and of a king of England, too. Think foul scorn that Parma, or Spain, or any prince of Europe would *dare* invade the borders of our realm. By your valor in this field, together we *shall* defeat them."

A roar erupted. Elizabeth peered down at Edward, standing in the shadows to the left of the platform, nodding encouragement, knowing the last of those lines were his, well writ, yet better spoken. After extended shouting and cheers, the Queen reviewed her troops again, the circling and returning to Leicester who helped her from her saddle. "Robbie," she said. "Wait for me. I wish to speak to Edward."

Leicester turned and marched off.

"Edward," she said. "You are good for England and for me. I shall never forget all we've done together and all you've meant to me."

"I have made many mistakes."

"As have I. As we have together. Yet, I am told they have no kings or queens in heaven or in hell, that all are equal. And I believe it. If we float in one or roast in the other, we shall meet again, you and I."

CHAPTER 67

Celebration

"They have in England a coin that bears
The figure of an angel."
Merchant of Venice, II, 7

In the embers of defeat, on a lucky day, an unforeseen spark sometimes ignites a glorious triumph. In the wake of the Queen's unexpected victory, six black stallions pulled the Queen's open carriage through the streets of London as a frenzied crowd shoved and jostled for a glimpse of the monarch they now called "Glorianna," the ruler who had rallied them to victory in the face of certain defeat. She had routed the invincible Spanish Armanda and thrust England in commanded of the seas.

Despite Drake's harassment, Sidonia's ships had put safely into Calais harbor, bent on waiting there for Parma to amassed his troops for loading and invasion. Lying outside the harbor, Drake well understood that the enemy could easily ram or blast their way out anytime they chose. He thus devised a secret plan. Instead of waiting for Sidonia to bring hell-fire to him, he would bring it to Sidonia.

At three hours past midnight, as the Spanish fleet slept, Drake set nine longboats adrift on an incoming tide, each stuffed with rope and hemp soaked in lamp oil and set afire. When the first boat bumped an anchored frigate, the initial glow illuminated the vessel's underbelly as if teasing it closer before sinking in its fiery teeth. As the first flames flashed, a second fireboat struck a larger galleon closer to the center. That blaze erupted, seemed to hesitate, then suddenly burned a running fire line across the vessel's wooden planks before curving its fiery fingers skyward, reaching the upper deck and catching canvas lashed across the yardarms.

Cries erupted as a third longboat slipped between two ships and nudged a galleon's hull, the careened off and struck the ship next to it. With several Spanish vessels now aglow, their masts lit vertical fire-lines that reached for the sky as flames spread from them in several directions, whipped by an incoming breeze. Flames jumped from ship to ship like fire dancers lighting everything their toes touched as men scurried on deck, some on fire themselves. Within minutes, the first gunpowder exploded, ripping through a hull, blasting wood and stores into the air and sending flames farther across the harbor to breach other vessels.

"¡La vela!" a Spaniard shouted. "¡Levante la vela!"

An anchor cranked. A sail half rose. A lopsided galleon fouled its lines and plowed into its neighbor as two vessels broke free and scrambled to sea, Drake firing as they lumbered past.

Flames and cannon belched throughout the night, lighting a smokefilled sky that soon gave way to a dull morning gray that revealed the scorched silhouettes of ghost ships, some sunk, most blackened and smoldering in a graveyard harbor.

Drake sent word to Elizabeth that the Spanish devils would not return to face the English dog that bit them. Those which escaped to stagger northward, fighting storms and savage winds the long way around Scotland, would soon turn south to face the worst of a seaman's foes -- the Irish squalls that tore through the hearts of men as their insubstantial vessels were thrown on the rocky shores of Ireland. Sidonia would be lucky if half his number survived to see Madrid again. Parma's army, stranded in the bogs of the Netherlands, would starve awaiting transport that would never arrive.

Drake and his sailors, soon after returning home, led a victory parade from Whitehall to the gates of London, followed in turn by the Queen's ribbon-draped coach, the carriages of ambassadors, dignitaries and other of the Queen's guests, and lastly, by Leicester's army who, through luck and the wily ways of Drake, never saw battle. Carriages clattered along cobblestones as the mass of proud English citizens ran alongside dogs yelping at their heels as maids hugged each other or lifted fragile old men and squeezed the breath from them.

No one had ever seen or heard anything like it.

At Ludgate, the only barrier that lay between the city and Whitehall, London's Lord Mayor symbolically unlocked the gate and joined the pageant, angling his coach behind the French Ambassador's, with Edward riding next in line on a coal-black mount, his hat topped with a yellow-feather plume, his shoulders draped in his finest purple cape that flowed down his back and across the haunches of his steed.

They circled around to the north of the city before parading back through Ludgate marching to the steps of Westminster, the spiritual heart of the country, where all halted, awaiting the Captain of Her Majesty's Guard to open the Queen's carriage door and the Queen to step forth.

Elizabeth, clad in pure white, stepped out, helped by Edward, who held her hand and escorted her to a shoulder-lugged portage box, which carried her to the foot of Westminster Abbey where she stepped out and lowered her eyes before her father's Church of England. She knelt in solemn prayer as all others behind fell to their knees in a human wave that swept across the square as somber silence fell upon the city, all present quietly thanking God for sparing them, and the Queen for delivering them.

CHAPTER 68

An Unrequited Loss

"My grief lies all within."
Richard II, IV, 1

Anne, Edward's wife of seventeen years, though estranged from him for five in the midst of those, died of consumption one year after the death of their only infant son, Bulbecke.

Anne -- six years Edward's junior, half his age when he moved to Burghley House -- was a child then and remained so, always beneath him, always looking up, always giggling as she played and frolicked in the same household. Yet she grew into a budding young woman with a young woman's charms and assets, and he became of an age to notice that increase and grow before it.

Anne – even with her child-like compliance -- had little else to offer, and their marriage bred boredom and soon contempt. She spent her days determining what clothes to wear and was of little help in picking his -- she preferring plain attire whilst he favored frills, puffs, and brighter shades.

Her enthusiasm for his plays matched her enthusiasm for boiled soup that quickly cooled her taste. She could always be bedded, but lay there deathly still and let him bring it to her, then quickly fall asleep. She was his wife in name, but he found himself with dwindling interest. A line occurred to him, perhaps to use in a play: "A young man married is young man marred." And yet a certain affection, if not love, dwelled in him and he had never wished to hurt her.

The court physician, dispatched by the Queen, had bled Anne to drain the poison, yet that merely seemed to further weaken her. Maids had massaged a pepper-paste into her temples after lifting her head and forcing pig bile down her throat until her coughing turned to a deep guttural growl -- a bad sign, the physician had said -

- that the devil had entered her and taken root. Upon hearing that dire pronouncement, the Chief Minister procured the finest, fist-size, imported leeches to suck the devil's venom from his daughter's breasts, but the leeches shriveled up and died soon after attaching.

Late into the evening of the sixth day taking no food and little water, Anne called Edward to lean forth and whispered in his ear that she was very tired, then sunk back and closed her eyes. Her breathing eased -- no stirring, no straining, no wheezing. Drained himself, Edward slumped in a chair next to her bed, held her hand, and drifted off.

When he awakened, and bolted up, and laid his hand upon her forehead, her skin felt cold and hard, the little life left within her having slipped away.

He took her hand and sat beside her a long while, their three daughters asleep in the rooms above, all of whom, save one, would not exist if the Queen, urged on by Burghley, had not encouraged Edward's marriage. Life oft bent on unexpected forces delivered along to a path headed somewhere else.

Burghley's fury, long simmering, bubbled over on the loss of his daughter. "She had earned more and deserved better," he rightly said. "*I* shall raise the girls myself. You make as poor a father as a husband."

The Angel of Death hovered over Edward's father-in-law, quickly striking again. The Lord Minister's own wife, Mildred, died a mere six weeks after Anne and was buried in Stamford, north of London, where the Lord Minister planned his own internment. Frances, Burghley's third and youngest granddaughter, had died in infancy less than a year before Anne, almost as if Frances could not stand to be in heaven alone and called her mother home.

Some months later, the Lord Minister commissioned an immense monument for his daughter in Westminster's North Portal, facing it with imported alabaster-carved effigies of his three surviving granddaughters -- Liz Beth, Bridget and Susan -- perpetually kneeling in prayer, the Lord Minister hoping they might comfort Anne in death with their constant presence. His memorialized words, etched in stone, said little of Anne, describing instead, her progeny, while barely disguising the Lord Minister's disgust with Edward, much in what he scribed, as what he left unsaid.

> Liz Beth Vere, daughter of Edward, Earl of Oxford, and his wife Anne, the daughter of Lord Burghley, born on the 2nd July 1575. Liz Beth is fourteen and grieves bitterly and not without cause for the loss of her grandmother and mother but feels happier because her most gracious Majesty has taken her into service as a Maid of Honor.

> Bridget, born on the 6th April 1584, the second daughter of the Earl of Oxford and Anne, was four years old when she placed her mother in this grave, yet it was not without tears that she recognized her mother had been taken from her, and shortly afterwards her grandmother. It is not true to say that she was left an orphan, seeing that her father is living and her most affectionate grandfather acts as her painstaking guardian.

> Susan, the third daughter, born on the 26th May 1587, is just thirteen months old. On account of her age, she was unable to recognize either her living mother or her grandmother. She is just beginning to recognize her most loving grandfather, who has the care of all these children so that they may not be deprived either of a pious education or a suitable upbringing.

Unwelcome at Anne's service, Edward bid his adieu to Anne in private. Though unfaithful once, she had been his wife and a far better mother than he a father. His father-in-law would raise the girls, knowing Edward would not protest. As Edward knelt before Anne's monument, staring straight at his daughters' tiny effigies, tears welled up. He prayed, if God be just, that in His mercy He provide and care for his three daughters and afford their mother a better life in heaven than her husband had provided her on earth. He stood and turned and slowly walked away, silence surrounding him.

CHAPTER 69

Coupling

"Her voice was ever soft.
An excellent thing in a woman."
King Lear, V, 3

Beth Trentham, unmarried and childless at forty-three, had given up on men and matrimony to manage the Staffordshire lands that she had inherited as the eldest daughter in a family with no sons. Edward had met her years earlier at his performance of *Richard III* at Burbage's Theater. He remembered she had asked to see him backstage and spoke well of his production. Whereupon, a month after Anne's death, she wrote Edward a note expressing her sympathy. He thought that kind of her, since they barely knew each other. He wrote back and thanked her, and then didn't see or hear from her in months until he thought he saw her strolling on the Strand and limped to catch up.

"Beth?... Is that you?" he called.

She turned. "Edward?"

"I'm not as fast or as young as I used to be. Not with this leg."

"None of us are," she smiled. "How have you been? It must be difficult... Without Anne, I mean... Well, I guess I *don't* know. I've never married."

"That must be lonely," Edward said.

"I am used to it. But *you*. How be you?"

"Managing."

"And how are the girls?"

"How do you know of them?"

"From Lyly... Remember? 'Twas he who brought me backstage to see you that day."

"The girls are with their grandfather. And well cared for. They miss their mother, of course."

"Are you still writing?"

"A little."

"I am glad to hear that. I so enjoyed your *Richard.* Lyly tells me you have written others. Well received, he says, yet after all these years, I still don't hear them speak your name."

"Nothing has changed. I ghostwrite for myself."

"Your collar is ajar... Would you mind if I straightened it?"

"I ah... No." When he leaned forward, she reached beneath his chin and made adjustments.

"There," she said, stepping back and examining her work. "I'm not used to caring for a man."

"Thank you for your note."

"I was sorry to hear of your loss."

"In truth, it was not the best of marriages."

"I fear marriage is not easy. I have given up myself."

"Why so? You are an attractive, hardy woman."

"Hardy you say?... You mean for my age?"

"Many marry at your age."

"Widows with children... I shall never..."

"Perhaps it's not too late, but you would have to hurry if you..."

"Are you offering your services?" she lowered her eyes and grinned.

He felt his face flush, surprised he could still be embarrassed.

"Where are you off to?" she asked.

"Nowhere."

"May I accompany you?"

Thoughts of Beth lingered after they parted. He found himself wandering back to the same block on the Strand two days running in hopes of seeing her again, though he did not. Did *he* wish to remarry? Anne had not been dead two years. Was it Anne he missed, or simply someone to straighten his collar, or perhaps provide a little noise about the house beyond the mice scurrying in the walls? Someone to talk to, perhaps? Certainly not passion. Not Anne's. Maybe he feared growing old and dying alone.

And if he married, *whom* to marry? In truth, he enjoyed different sides of different women -- Anne's caring, Vavasor's eroticism, the Queen's intelligence, even Beth Trentham's teasing as she grinned and adjusted his collar. Anne had bore him three daughters, one of them in name only, and a son and daughter who died. Vavasor birthed him an illegitimate son whom she held and raised for ransom. Elizabeth delivered him a son he could not claim in fear of retribution. At forty-one, without a legitimate male heir, the Oxford title and earldom would end with him. He could hear his father's ghostly reprimand, Edward as a playwright, having set forth his father's complaint in the mouth of the ghost of Hamlet's father.

> Ghost: I am thy father's spirit,
>> Doomed a certain term to walk these nights,
>> Until my heirs have done their due
>> And passed upon my name and rights.

"'Tis too late for me," he argued with the Ghost. "Marriage is a young man's folly, led by nature's blindness, hoping for progeny."

Edward found himself distracted and unable to think or write. After telling his head he would not, his feet carried him back to the Strand to catch a glimpse of Beth three days running, yet found her not. When next they tapped mugs, he asked Lyly if he thought he *should* remarry.

"In general or in particular?"

"In general."

"Marriage never seemed to suit you. Get a dog."

For a dreamer and a writer, life's reality was always less than what he imagined. The castles he built in his mind had no cracks in their foundations unless he chose to place one there for dramatic purpose. His characters flaunted perfect flaws to match their foils against, yet his imagination, even with its heated passion, did not warm him on a frigid winter night nor keep him company when the air was still with the heat of August. Marriage, as with any road taken, left the dust on a backward horizon safely gazed upon in hindsight's vision, yet never trod for truth. Was reality worth an honest test against the fantasy drawn by a writer-dreamer? Perhaps men and women were meant to nightly bed together, both to hold close and push away.

Not finding Beth on the Strand in his fourth attempt, he ambled to her apartments to ask if he might see her. She said that would please her, but only if he agreed to read her some of what he had written. When he came by again, they strolled through Covent Gardens on a warm summer day, sitting on a bench at the edge of the lake, feeding the ducks and languishing in the sweet smell of lilacs that drifted from the gardens. He read her a sonnet he had purposely chosen to suit the day.

> Shall I compare thee to a summer's day?
> Thou art more lovely and more temperate.
> Rough winds do shake the darling buds of May,
> And summer's lease hath all too short a date,
> Sometime too hot the eye of heaven shines,
> And often is its gold complexion dimmed,
> And every fair from fair sometime declines,
> By chance, or nature's changing course untrimmed:
> But thy eternal summer shall not fade,
> Nor lose possession of that fair thou owest,
> Nor shall death brag thou wander'st in his shade,
> When in eternal lines to time thou growest,
> So long as men can breathe or eyes can see,
> So long lives this and this gives life to thee.

"That is *so* beautiful," Beth said, a tear in her eye.

"'Twas not meant to make you cry."

"Such beauty overwhelms."

"I'm a cripple," he told her when they walked again, his leg dragging more than usual.

"Then I suppose I shall just have to find someone a little more perfect," she grinned.

After seeing Beth and no one else for six months, he informed Lyly that he had decided against a dog, that he would ask Beth to marry him.

"She is far better than a dog," Lyly said. "I would have made that choice myself."

On August 14th in the Year of Our Lord 1591, just after Hackney's church bells struck three in the afternoon, Edward de Vere, the Seventeenth Earl of Oxford, married Beth Trentham in a brief ceremony in Hackney's Rowe Chapel. The Right Reverend Philip Newington, before inviting the party out on the south lawn into a bright sunlight, felt obliged to offer a few words on the advantages of late marriages. "More settled. Less fervor," was his parting advice, although Edward hoped for an equal portion of each.

Beth wished to start their married life in a new home and thus the couple moved into King's Place on a ridge overlooking the village of Hackney, the manor house and fourteen hector garden a short carriage ride from the village church in which they married. After establishing their household, Edward wrested his daughters away from Burghley to live with them -- Susan, his youngest, the only one allowed to nestle in his lap while he wrote. Pregnancy followed in less than a year and Beth delivered Henry, the future Eighteenth Earl, who peeked his head out tentatively, glanced about, and then screamed his way into this world much like his father had. What, Edward wondered, would this new life bring? Better than his own, he hoped.

CHAPTER 70

What's In a Name?

> "False face must hide
> What false heart doth know."
> *Macbeth, I, 7*

The old ghosts and demons that sprouted from Edward's father's untimely demise, his mother's immediate remarriage, and his banishment from Hedingham, sprung forth again and strutted on stage as Edward wrote Hamlet, whose characters portrayed his own festering anger, confusion and guilt.

The ghost of Hamlet's dead father wore the robes of Edward's own father, both found dead under mysterious circumstances. Polonius -- the king's advisor in Hamlet -- stomped about with advice for Laertes using the same words Burghley used to instruct Edward and the other wards. Ophelia, Polonius' daughter in the play, edged to the brink of madness over Hamlet's shifting affections for her, much as Burghley's daughter, Anne, wallowed in her own confusion over Edward's ambiguous feelings for her.

As a playwright writing of his own life, Edward penned a play within a play to ferret out the truth of Hamlet's father's death and assuage Hamlet's guilt as well as his own for actions never taken. Hamlet took no action to avenge his father's death. Edward, with those villains in his life now dead, found there was no action to take. Did writing of a bloodletting reopen and purge the poison from old wounds, or did it further infect and deepen them?

A familiar uncertainly gripped him and bent him over. Perhaps, he thought as the pain eased and he straightened again, watching the characters he had written play their parts over and over again, would finally end his grief and put his ghosts to rest.

Edward's reverie was gratefully broken as Lyly rushed into the room without warning, breaking off Edward's depressed mood.

"Burbage wants a name for his playbills," Lyly said. "Your plays are drawing well. He thinks a name would spur a following on the name alone."

"He never required a name before," Edward said, picking up and laying out a flat-cuffed shirt on his bed next to a puff-sleeved garment to compare their measure. "Which?" he asked.

"Which what?" Lyly asked. "The name or the shirt?"

"The shirt. This or that?"

"I like the puffed. Anonymous could be anyone."

"I think the flat-cuffed," Edward said, lifting it, laying it across his shoulders, and facing his looking glass. *"A Midsummer Night's Dream* by Edward de Vere," Edward muttered. "Give him that, then."

"Why not simply dedicate them all to the Queen and have done with it? Perhaps the Queen might even play a part in one. The mother or you common..."

"Enough!"

Lyly, when he wasn't writing, served as Edward's secretary and negotiator. Seventeen years earlier, soon after Edward's return from his European travels, London's alderman enacted their Puritan Stage Code, requiring all plays in London, both new and previously performed, be reviewed for salacious, rebellious, and ungodly content. Burghley and his emissaries having already censored most on behalf of the crown.

With his imagination filled with plots and characters fresh from the continent, Edward had spoken to Burbage regarding the censor code. The Red Lion's owner said it little affected him one way or the other, and may aid his cause for the same prudish aldermen who imposed their ban London trotted across the bridge to buy tickets beyond their jurisdiction in Southwark to partake in exactly what they disallowed on their side of the river.

"What others do you have?" Burbage asked in those early days, raising his eyebrows and his interest after the success of the first two of Edward's early efforts.

"I have a few Italian tales. Comedies. Tragedies. And several English histories I am working on."

"For exclusive rights as we play them?" Burbage asked. "What percentage might you require?"

"Half."

"*Minus* expenses," Burbage countered. "Which is the greater part of it... You *have* no expenses. Ink and paper. I pay for the building, upkeep, playbills, and various sundries. Which leaves little left to divide."

"Then we split the little. Show me your list of sundries."

"How many have you writ that are ready?"

"A dozen in progress. With more coming" Edward said, without revealing that most were tentatively formed and in constant revision. No matter. Burbage could only present one at a time.

"How do we know your others will draw as well as those we've played?" Burbage asked.

"I plan to try them out in the villages on the circuit and revise as needed."

"That is the city across the way," Burbage said, nodding over his shoulder. "Not the villages. I have added another tier to my courtyard playhouse to hold a bigger London draw. Well attended, I could squeeze in maybe two hundred, or perhaps two-fifty with the standers. The bear pits hold better than that. They are round. Wooden 'O's. If I could build a bigger bear pit, it might hold... I don't know. Five hundred? Perhaps more? At a pence a piece for the groundlings, two for the decks... Let's see. That would be... Well, certainly worth the building of it. *If* I could procure a steady stream of plays to fill my playbook... Can you provide enough?"

"Not alone, but with others. Kyd. Marlow. Lyly. If there be an audience for more, there would be plays to fill the need. If there was a regular schedule, a few might even draw a modest living from it."

"Modest, for sure."

Two of Edward's early offerings -- *All's Well That Ends Well* and *Cymbeline* -- packed Burbage's theater their first weeks running. When Burbage called for more, Edward quickly revised and polished one of his Italian dramas, *The Merchant of Venice,* an offering he had performed for the Queen years earlier. Credit for the work at court referred to no one in particular or else to "Anonymous," although everyone knew the playwright to be Edward. All others knew enough to keep their lips tight and their tongues tied, since the plays often parodied the court and court personages.

With speculation ripe as to the meaning and implication of the plays and their author's connection with the Queen and whatever intimacies might have ensued, Francis Meres, a frequent court attendee, after seeing *All's Well* at Whitehall, praised Edward openly as "the best at comedy," in Meres' *Wits Treasury: A Comparative Discourse of our English Poets and Writers,* but without specifying a particular play in fear of reprimand or reprisal by the crown.

"I think Burbage may be on to something," Lyly said. "A name *would* draw a better audience. Yet not de Vere, which would better draw the hangman's noose."

Edward tossed his flat-cuffed shirt aside and selected the puff-sleeved. Perhaps Lyly was right about the shirt and the name, Edward thought. The Queen, even without Burghley's wailing, would never approve Edward's name on plays no matter how much she thought his histories forged a bond among her subjects. The parallels with the court already hinted as close as she dared allow. *Hamlet's* Polonius parodied Burghley word-for-word, whisker-for-whisker. Edward *was* Hamlet. Ophelia *was* Anne. Horatio *was* Edward's cousin Horace. And that was just a single play.

"What name might satisfy Burbage?" Edward asked, sitting on the edge of his bed and tossing both shirts aside.

"I don't think he cares, so long as it be a steady maker he can trade on. Something he could stamp on his playbills that all would recognize."

"We'll use your name then," Edward said. *"Hamlet,* by John Lyly."

"I think not. Your plays are far better than mine, and more in number. I make my stand on poetry. I shall stick with that."

"Very well, then… Silver Sylvester."

"That would suit your comedies."

A steady name might benefit and increase profit, Edward thought. Beth, after marrying him, expressed her surprise at the sorry state of his finances, having thought an earl would have prospered better. Upon Beth's chiding, Edward had already reworked his earlier poem, *Venus and Adonis,* as a new creation he was intent to print and sell for profit.

"*Venus* be a tale of love, sex, and a goddess chasing a mortal man," Lyly had remarked when Edward told him of his plan. If you keep to the theme, that should sell well. But by an Earl?"

"I plan to dedicate it to Wriothesley," Edward said.

"To Wriothesley openly?"

"His name openly, not mine. The boy is old enough, whoever they think the author be, they'll take him as the patron of the author, not the son. I have given him little. If the poem does well, *he* might be known for it, though its author never will. I shall take my satisfaction from the compensation, which I sorely need."

With a name for *Venus* not determined, Lyly said he would put some though to the matter and brought it up again when Burbage pushed, once again, for a name on the plays. "We need think no more," had informed Edward. "You have a name that would fit your poem and well suit Burbage."

"That is unbeknownst to me."

"Remember when we toured the counties? A man wished employment in the theater. You spoke to him. You thought, if you ever required a pseudonym... We spoke of it. Do you recall?"

"Shakspere. That surly little fellow from Stratford."

"He is in London now. He has been here several months. He's been trying to see you."

"Is that so?"

"They sent him to me. I could see no use in it, yet now I do. They say that he's in debt, that he has moved from Cheapside for ill payment of rent. The sheriff is after him. I suspect he could use a few coins in his purse."

When Edward instructed Lyly to ask of the man, Lyly said he found it most easy. "When you talk to one or two from a small village" he said, "you learn all you need to know and more. Shakspere had a licensed to marry an Anne Whately. Yet, on the date the license set, he married another, an Anne Hathaway, eight years his senior. She bore him a child six months hence. Apparently, he intended to wed the one and was forced by circumstance to wed the other, who was already showing of child. They had more children, twins, before he escaped to London, leaving his family in Stratford."

"Will he be of fair use?" Edward asked.

"He is enamored with the theater. To have his name on plays? On anything? To take credit for *something?* He would delight in it. Especially with payment in hand and no effort on his part. I do believe we have a hungry pigeon here and the seed to feed it. And even better..." Lyly added.

"Yes?"

"Like most from the county, or from the city for that matter, the man is *unable* to write. He is near illiterate. He cannot steady his hand enough sign his name. They say his parents are unable to write, nor will his children learn, there being no school in the village. If he is to be our author, there is no chance they will match his script to yours. He has none."

"Speak with him, then" Edward said. "See what he'll agree to."

Venus and Adonis dedicated to Henry Wriothesley and, for the first time, printed under the hyphenated pseudonym "William ShakeSpeare" sold briskly, the heart of it taken from Edward and Golding's English translation of Ovid's *Metamorphoses.*

"Congratulations," Lyly said, rushing in and holding up a copy of *Venus* fresh from the printer. "You are no longer no-name, nor our most famous author, 'Anonymous.' You are now anonymous *with* a name."

"It has its advantage," Edward said. "If a work be poor, they can hurl their barbs at Mr. Shakspere. Yet my spirit is pained. My life's work laid on the foundation of another."

"They may come to know you yet," Lyly said. "That foundation only lightly veiled."

"How shall we pay the man?"

"I have already paid him in coin for *Venus* and spoken to Burbage on payment for the plays. We *shan't* pay him for those. We'll offer him a small stock in Burbage's new theater for Burbage to deliver. Not much. Five percent. After Burbage makes his withdrawals for expenses, it won't amount to much. Yet, with the promise of more as plays come out, it will be enough to keep him quiet."

"William Shake-Speare," Edward muttered, getting used to a name he knew he would hear a long time.

CHAPTER 71

A Trial and an Offering

"Use every man after his desert
And who should 'scape the whipping?"
Hamlet, II, 2

"I wish to see the prisoner alone," Edward said to Robert
Cecil after storming into Cecil's privy counsel chamber.

Robert Cecil, Burghley's son being groomed for his father's
replacement as the Queen's Chief Minister, lengthened his neck and
drew in his chin. "It is most irregular for a member of the jury to
interview the accused alone."

"My relationship with the accused *is* most irregular."

"That is irrelevant to this matter."

"I *wish* to see him," Edward repeated, banging his fist on
Cecil's desk to challenge the new and untested minister.

Cecil shrugged and stood. He ushered Edward into a
single-windowed anteroom with a bare table and two benches. "Wait
here," he said.

When the door opened again, Wriothesley, short in stature
and thin-boned like his father, entered. Before the boy spoke,
Edward touched his lips and pointed for him to sit. When the door
clicked shut, Edward flicked a glance toward it, and then leaned
across the table. "What is your part in this?" he asked in a quiet
voice, almost a whisper.

"I have no good answer."

"Your best, then."

"Foolhardiness."

"That does not explain it."

"Guilty as charged. There is nothing to explain."

"Son…"

Wriothesley stiffened. "You have no *right* to call me that."

Edward leaned back. "You're right. I do not." He waited for Wriothesley to settle and his shoulders to drop. "I claim no privilege," Edward said. "Yet, in this situation, I wish to help."

"You are my judge. Perhaps you can make *that* right."

"I did not seek the task."

"My Queen?... My mother?"

Edward shook his head.

"Whatever she be," Wriothesley said, "she sends my father to judge me."

"You put the Queen's life in jeopardy along with your own."

Wriothesley lowered his eyes.

"She and I *could* not marry, though there was love between us." Edward said. "It was her availability that kept us from war all those years. Her enemies courted her instead of attacking her. If she had married an Englishman, England would not have survived. Others would have taken us."

After a silence, Wriothesley said, "I cannot say I was led astray in the matter. Yet, I did not know its gravity."

"The Queen had high hopes for you."

Wriothesley raised his eyes and glared across the table. "My birth or its circumstance was not of my choice," he said. "Perhaps the Queen's hopes did not fit what *I* wished. I never desired anything beyond what they named me, Henry Wriothesley, the future Third Earl of Southampton. 'Twas quite enough station in life. And the Wriothesleys did raise me, though I suspect they were well paid to do so."

"Is *that* why you followed Essex?... Revenge?... Bitterness?... Anger at me? At your mother?"

"It had little to do with you *or* her. Essex was my friend. He *is* my friend. He accepts me as I am. Nothing more. I thought his cause just."

"Which cause? His *Irish* cause? Where Essex took actions upon himself without the Queen's approval? When you followed Essex across the Irish Sea into Essex's debacled campaign to quell the Irish? And upon his returned to London, out of favor for his handling of the matter, when gathered three hundred men, you among them, to march on Whitehall with a predictable result. The Queen's guards and the London militia blocked your passage, surrounded, and arrested the both of you."

"I did not know his intent with the Queen," Wriothesley said. "I truly did not."

"You know he marched."

"To gain her attention."

"That, he well accomplished."

"She would not see him."

"He disobeyed her, as did you."

"Of your play," he said, looking down. "I truly *am* sorry for that. I had no part in it."

The day before Essex's march, a few of Essex's followers performed *Richard III* -- a play Edward had once writ in Elizabeth's defense to rouse citizens to their favor. Now, with the Queen at sixty-seven, the theme of an aging monarch played against her. The theme -- replace the old with the new -- hinted that her time had come and passed.

"The Queen has forgiven you in the past," Edward said. "You will not get off so easily this time. Others watch. She cannot afford it."

"What will they do with me?"

"Her Majesty has placed me on the jury as a gesture. Those who know your birth will take that into account."

The trial lasted three days, both Wriothesley and Essex taking the stand in their own defense. Essex - young, arrogant, and misunderstanding the forgone outcome - defended his motives, ill-realizing that logic ruled not -- the Queen's pleasure ruled. After less than a day's deliberation, the tribunal reached its decision and ordered the Sergeant-at-Arms to recall the prisoners to the high chamber. When all sat, the Sergeant-at-Arms banged his mallet and commanded the prisoners to rise. Robert Cecil, as Lord Chief Judge, nodded for the clerk to read the verdict.

"Earl of Essex, you have pleaded not guilty to a charge of high treason. Your peers, who have heard the evidence and your defense, have found you guilty. What say you why we should not put you to death?"

Essex pleaded misunderstanding and misinterpretation, and then fell back in his chair.

The Clerk turned to Wriothesley. "Henry Wriothesley, the jury saith, as to whether the future Third Earl of Southampton be guilty of high treason... Guilty... What say you as to why you should not be put to death?"

When Wriothesley stood and glanced in Edward's direction, Edward nodded. "My Lords," Wriothesley began. "I say for my part as I have said before, that since the ignorance of the law hath made me incur its danger, I humbly submit myself to Her Majesty's mercy. And therefore my Lords, I beseech you, seeing you are witnesses, I am condemned by the letter of the law. It would yet please me to let the Queen know that I meant her no harm. I know I have offended her, yet if it please her to show mercy unto me that I may live, and by my future service, deserve my life, I shall be most grateful." With nothing more to offer, he eased down.

On the 25th of February in the Year of Our Lord 1601 a hooded executioner fitted a noose snugly about the neck of the Earl of Essex, adjusted it, and tightened the loop. At the executioner's nod, a trapdoor sprung, dropping Essex's body through the opening where he dangled until his feet stopped twitching.

Henry Wriothesley, after pondering his fate a fortnight, received news in the Tower that his sentence had been commuted by the Queen to a Tower confinement of undetermined length, to be released as it might later please Her Majesty.

When Edward heard of the commutation, it occurred to him that Elizabeth, at her age, would not be pleased on many more occasions. His own body ached at fifty-one. He traveled less, and on some days, especially when his leg pained him, remained at home by the fire and traveled not at all. He still wrote and revised daily, although his eyes strained in candlelight and he found it easier to work from a shaded bench in King's Place garden in the mornings or in front of a sunny window after the noon meal.

Six weeks after Wriothesley's conviction, Burghley, himself aged at seventy-nine, wrote to Edward requesting his presence on a matter he said was of some import. "First," the Lord Minister began as soon as Edward arrived, the Chief Minister's shoulders bent, no longer able to straighten, his voice a squeak of its former self, "the Queen wishes to thank you for your participation in the trial."

"Why does she not thank me herself?"

"She has, if you will listen."

"We have sparred and parried so long, you and I," Edward admitted, "it has become a habit."

"Life has thrown our fortunes together. Yet, we are all reaching the end of that."

"What is the urgency of which you called me?"

"Understand this, that I do not speak for myself, but on behalf of the Queen."

Edward waited.

"She wishes to take you under her employ."

"At my age?... What could I do?"

"Not much, I agree. Yet, it be her wish."

"I shall listen."

"That's most forbearing of you. Her Majesty wishes to grant you an annual annuity of one thousand crowns for the remainder of your years."

"An annuity?"

"Derived from her personal funds and paid to you twice annually with no accounting by the Lord Treasurer. No one is to know her reason, other than you and Her Majesty."

"And you, of course," Edward said.

"Only as it please her."

"And what *is* her reason?"

"One, I believe you will agree, that will not be distasteful to you. The Queen believes your plays have had some measure of value. She desires you to continue revising and presenting them in public."

"Is *that* it?"

"Not quite... There is a stipulation that you yourself initiated. Your plays may or may not have value. That is a matter of opinion. Your name on them, however, is a concern of State. I personally wish Her Majesty to end her reign with her reputation intact and the throne unimpaired by usurpers."

"Usurpers, as...?"

"*Any* usurper... Your name cannot be allowed. I am told you use another. 'William Shake-Spear.'"

"As usual, you are told everything."

"I have many ears and use them all to protect my queen, which has always been my burden and my duty. Thus, I have taken the precaution of gathering all writings in your own hand that have circulated about. None, of course, that you yourself possess. See to it that those are protected and kept at close quarters. Continue to present your plays as someone else, as the Queen desires. Having instructed you thus, I wish to die in peace and have little else to do with you."

"Your honesty has always done you favor," Edward said, knowing how Burghley truly felt, always sharp in his criticism, and yet in equal measure, keeping his sharpest knives sheathed.

Edward had been a constant sore in Burghley's side ever since he entered Burghley House as a ward and soon digging up one of Burghley's prized roses, then later killing a cook, and then, with near devastating consequence, ingratiating himself with the Queen and producing a child with her, and beyond that, having the gall and impudence to write and present scandalous plays that intimately connected him with the Court. His marriage to Burghley's daughter Anne had caused the Chief Minister great disappointment. He was long tired of his son-in-law and Edward could not blame him.

"I have served," Burghley said. "'Tis all I care about."

CHAPTER 72

The Tides of Time

"I have lived long enough."
Macbeth, V, 3

Elizabeth stood alone in the great hall of Hampton Court that her father Henry had built to honor Jane Seymour, his third wife, the only woman he truly loved. The Queen craned her neck and stared up at gargoyles perched high on protruding outcroppings, their eyes squinting, their ghoulish glares staring down, their bodies crouched as if prepared to leap and pounce on anything below of which they disapproved.

Elizabeth felt certain that Henry had intended intimidation, especially as he grew older and weaker and overwhelmed the court with the trappings of a king and his expanding bulk. She felt small in this immense hall, dedicated more to huge banquets and elaborate masked balls than to the presence of any single individual, especially a woman who lacked her father's girth and booming voice. Increasingly, as she approached him in age, she bore the ravages of time that her father despised and she herself hated.

She considered aging an insult, an affront to God's dignity, the withering of a grape on the vine until it puckered, shriveled, and dropped to the ground, of little further use save serve as fermentation for the next crop. If God, in His infinite wisdom, as the church contended, chose a king or queen as His emissary on earth, why did He allow his chosen ones to grow old, no differently than the serf who toiled in the fields? The Lord seemed to smile no more, nor less, on her than anyone else.

Alone in this massive empty chamber -- feeling small, weak, and frail -- Elizabeth shivered, sensing the Angel of Death hovering above her, patiently waiting as Heaven's light shimmered through stained glass and spread its colored streaks across the floor, bright and dancing when at first they struck, then slowly fading and dying in dark corners.

Rows of stag heads and antelope antlers lined the walls as a tribute to Henry's ultimate power over life and death. His propensity for trophies and severed heads extended well beyond the annual Hampton Court stag hunt to encompass a dizzying array of wives and enemies, none of whose heads were stuffed for display, save those flaunted on bloody stakes on the bridge as gristly warnings to those who might oppose the crown and its Protestant reformation.

Elizabeth disfavored such gruesome flamboyance, yet overlooked it on Burghley's insistence that such warnings were both necessary and effective. She often wondered if she would be held culpable in God's eyes for acts required of a monarch and yet, when she knelt in prayer seeking answers, her knees ached on cold stone while God held his silence.

The head of Anne Boleyn, Elizabeth's own mother, once lay separated from her body as her flesh slowly rotted on the executioner's platform a fortnight for all to see and smell before her two portions were dumped into an empty arrow chest. Elizabeth herself had barely escaped death by cowering before her sister Mary when as a young Princess she refused to recant her father's Protestant faith. Only Burghley's intervention saved her from the tower's final retribution.

She had narrowly dodged an assassin's blade when a watchful guard, at the glint of the knife, adroitly diverted its aim. The would-be assassin soon found his own neck separated from his body. Nonetheless, at her advanced age, despite past escapes, the increasing sting of pain and stiffness reminded her that time marched on and that death lay on the horizon.

As she reached the far end of Hampton's great hall, she turned to face the empty throne that her father's bulk had easily overtaken. Standing in the shadow of her dead father, she oft felt like a child in the pretense of a Queen. Many a moonless night she suddenly woke with clouded memory, forgetting that it was herself who now sat on the throne.

She sighed as she eased her back against the wall and allowed herself to slide to the floor, feeling neither more nor less significant than a castle rat who scurried along these walls at night, so driven by hunger that it might easily turn and devour its own, much as Henry's hunger for the bosom of his next queen led to the swift beheading of Elizabeth's mother.

Had Elizabeth, in turn, also destroyed and devoured? Had Burghley been her implicit instrument whist she glanced the other way? She had had her lovers, yet they had all kept their heads. Most had come and gone, in and out of favor, in love and in anger, hither and yon. Yet two, in the end, endured as friends when passion waned. Robby, the Earl of Leister, whom she had known as a child and who had served her well as lover, friend, and soldier. And, of course Edward, whom she had first met at Hedingham when she still was a young queen and he as brash and impulsive as ever.

She had not intended Edward as her lover, and certainly not as sire of their clandestine child, a progeny whose very existence edged England toward the precipice of invasion by France or Spain, both nations coveting her as the "virgin queen" with whom to join their crowns and bear a future king. The existence of an heir to England's throne would have negated those future hopes. With no acknowledged son, she had held herself as virgin material, open to negotiation.

She leaned away from the wall to stretch away a sudden pain that stuck her calf. When she glanced up again, golden, red, and amber stained-glass beams shimmered through waves of dust. She recalled brighter days when she and Edward danced in this hall and how he had openly flirted with her to taunt other suitors who dared not try.

In their time, she and Edward had danced, frolicked, and loved. They had shouted in anger, agreed and disagreed, and ultimately agreed to disagree. They had stomped away in the heat of argument and disgust, yet always, as tempers waned, slowly regained their respect, affection and lust for each other to join together again. And all the while, through it all, as the seasons came and went, Edward scribed and pampered his plays -- his true children, the loves of his life – now cruelly attributed to another to distance Edward and his name from the court and their child born of love.

She recalled listening hour upon hour -- the two of them blissfully alone in her chamber -- to words he penned that delved beneath life's surface to capture its essence and beauty, and yes, pain. "Upon such sacrifice," he once wrote, "The gods themselves throw incense."

Death, she thought, as she struggled with great effort to stand, would be a welcome relief from the sacrifice and loss these times required. "Sleep that knits the raveled sleeve of care," he wrote and read to her ''Tis the death of each day's life." And now, as day added upon day, sooner than later, the long sleep of death would reach for her with outstretched arms.

CHAPTER 73

Death's Rumination

> "Sans teeth, san eyes, sans taste,
> Sans everything."
> *As You Like It, II, 7*

Lord Cecil Burghley -- the Queen's Chief Minister, counselor and protector, and Edward's former wardmaster, father-in-law, paymaster, nemesis, conscience, baiter, debater, and arbitrator -- died before sunrise after a restless Friday night, August 4th in the Year of Our Lord 1598, undoubtedly still fretting over matters of the Crown. On the death of the Chief Minister's daughter Anne twelve years earlier, he had financed an elaborate Westminster tomb for her internment, although the Lord Minister had planned his own final rest under a smaller monument in the tiny church of St. Martin's in the village of Stamford, forty leagues north of London, far from the politics that had swirled about him all his life, some of which he created.

Burghley's demise further depleted the Queen's sagging energy and spirit. Barely able to straighten her backbone any longer, she increasingly found less reason to try. The affairs of State, as always and without lessening, still weighed heavily on her aging shoulders. Phillip's Spanish Armada, severely reduced and battered in its defeat, had not been totally destroyed. Phillip commissioned faster, sleeker vessels, his humiliating loss merely whetting his appetite for revenge. He may have lost the battle but still occupied the Netherlands and had not conceded the war.

Neither had Elizabeth's burden lessened in her domestic realm. Her subjects had demonstrated their loyalty during the immediate threat of foreign invasion, although many still harbored

Catholic hopes and lent an ear to those who conspired to restore that legacy. The old aristocracy -- the Lords, the Earls, the landowners -- quite naturally wished to retain as much wealth and power as possible, while the growing majority, particularly the newly emboldened tradesmen, merchants and craftsmen, wished to shake loose some of that power and coin to trickle down into their purses.

Parliament, split into a House of Lords and Commons, found collective agreement in their desire to wrestle control from an aging and vulnerable queen. Since she had no independent source of monies of her own, Parliamentarians, whose power had gradually grown since Parliament's inception as "Advice Council" under William the Conqueror in 1066, increasingly used their tax authority and financial control of the crown as leverage to gain concessions. Younger parliamentarians simply wrung their hands and waited for the old Queen to die, sharpening their political daggers and speeches to use against the next monarch, although whomever that be would not be loved, respected, or revered as the Glorianna who had ruled for a tremulous thirty years before.

Beyond the dealings and connivings of politics, Elizabeth's long reign had spurred corruption in the daily administration of her government. Midlevel bureaucrats, those who greased the wheels of state, doled out jobs as personal favors or sold them directly to line their purses. In the countryside, after two disastrous harvests, many had abandoned their homes to sleep in London's alleys and doorways, many resorting to crime for sustenance.

The Queen's health, always teetering on a thin thread, deteriorated further as age dug its claws in deeper. She well understood, with the slightest slip, her enemies would kick her throne out from under her and she could never climb back again. With Burghley, her shield, and Leicester, her lifelong companion, both dead, the question hung in the air, how much longer could Elizabeth last, all eyes fixed on any sign of weakness.

Edward, in his time, had loved his Queen, defended her, mocked her, performed for her, fought for her, made love to her, fathered a child with her, and now, toward the end of her life, admired and respected the woman who became England's head, heart and soul. He had not seen her in months, knowing she hated aging and found the face in her mirror repulsive even when painted pure white -- the face of an angel to some, of an aging clown to others.

"The Jester of Age doth sting with his cruel joke," Edward wrote as he thought of her, the Jester stinging its cruel joke in him as well. Edward's old leg wound, a daily reminder of Nan Vavasor's sting, intensified his dislike of aging as the years further withered his calf muscle. With little left to occupy him, he poured his discomfort, his disappointments, and his anguish into his writing.

To Henry Wriothesley, his misnamed son, deprived of his father's name and his mother's crown, Edward hoped his fond wishes might soften his son's loss. Wriothesley's true worth hid in the shadows, his name lamed, like his father's leg, by fortune's spite.

Sonnet 37

As a decrepit father takes delight
To see his active child do deeds of youth,
So I, made lame by fortune's dearest spite,
Take all my comfort of thy worth and truth.
For whether beauty, birth, or wealth, or wit,
Or any of these all, or all, or more,
Entitled in thy parts do crowned sit,
I make my love engrafted to this store,
So then I am not lame, poor, nor despised,
Whilst that this shadow doth such substance give
That I in thy abundance am sufficed
And by a part of all thy glory live.
Look, what is best, that best I wish for thee.
This wish I have -- then ten times happier than me.

Edward thought his own life wasted, full of tired words, more tongue than truth that would soon perish in his own brief time. He wrote a Sonnet for his Queen, meant for her eyes only, assuring her that her name, if not her blood, would survive through her accomplishments. Her blood, without her name, would ever flow through Wriothesley and through Wriothesley's offspring and even, perhaps, through Edward's verse, should there be those who saw the truth in it.

Sonnet 17

Who will believe my verse in time to come,
If it were filled with high deserts?
Though yet, heaven knows, it is but as a tomb.
So should my papers yellowed with their age
Be scorned like old men of less truth than tongue,
And your true rights be termed a poet's rage
And stretched meter of an antique song.
But were some child of yours alive that time,
You should live twice -- in it and in my rhyme.

CHAPTER 74

Nothing Truer Than Truth

"A old man, broken with the storms."
Henry VIII, IV, 2

Life inevitably plodded forward, never back. What might be was never fully settled until its time had passed. Yet the past always set the path lived in the present. Edward had begun his life as a frivolous youth setting fire to his father's stage and tying to skirt responsibly for it, then scandalously poked fun at the new queen in a play she herself witnessed. To add to that he played tricks on Cecil Burghley by exchanging weeds for his prize roses, and then flaunted Gray's Inn's rules by sneaking across the river to view plays at theaters that were banned by the law. In the foolhardiness of his youth and young adulthood, he had squandered the family fortune on travels, clothes, furnishings, and producing plays, and then, to outdo even that, he had arrogantly regarded the Queen as his equal and together produced with her produced an illegitimate child whose very existence threatened the stability of the realm.

T'was only now he understood -- too late, as with many lessons in life – that t'was not what birth had handed him -- neither the Earldom, nor its accompanying status and privilege, nor even his love of writing that made for a honorable and good life. T'was how he used or squandered those advantages. What truly mattered as his bones decayed in eternal darkness was what became from his stewardship, talent, and accomplishments.

Unlike Rome's crumbing ruins that Edward had seen as a young man, his last wife Beth, near the end of his own life, provided a the solid presence he needed. She stirred neither Vavasor's erotic excitement, nor the childish devotion that Burghley had foisted upon him in Anne, whom he had come to reluctantly accept until her death. Nor did Beth provoke the Queen's churning hot and cold love, anger, and inconsistent devotion.

Beth patiently listened as he ruminated over the past, trying to piece it together and make sense of it as best he could. Of great appreciation, she accepted him at his advanced age with all his frailties and imperfections. She tolerated him more than he deserved and more than tolerated himself. A warmth enveloped him in her presence that he had not found in the cool aloofness of a solitary life. As always, of course, the characters in his plays were his constant friends who spoke to and even chided him. But Beth was real. She was no ghost. She was there. She was a friend by his side as he passed the long days polishing the plays he knew could never be staged or presented under his own name.

In the end, what does life signify? What did anyone's life signify? 'Tis the fool who thinks himself wise, yet, in the end, the wise man knows himself to be a fool.

Near death, the Queen refused to sit. Despite her weakened condition, she stood three hours, clutching the back of a chair and occasionally asking for help to hold her balance, but refusing to sit or lay, as though she knew that would be her end. When she finally succumbed and let loose, they carried her to her bed where she spent the afternoon, barely opening her eyes. When Robert Cecil leaned across to ask her whom she would have as next monarch, her lips locked. No matter. Cecil had his candidate. Within an hour of the Queen's death, he sent a message to James, son of Mary Queen of Scots, to ride south at once.

An unusually warm sun brightened Elizabeth's funeral procession as if God lit her path on her final journey. Bowed heads and tears intermingled with the clomp of prancing horses and the gleaming sight of polished armor as six black mares pulled her black-draped coffin from Whitehall to Westminster. Edward, too weak and ill to attend, grieved at Hackney, the Queen's loss another reminder of his own loosening grip on life.

In less than a year after the Queen's demise and James I's ascension, the first brown spots appeared down the center of

Edward's back and then in lines along the underside of his forearms, burrowing deep beneath his skin and then reaching upward to eat him from the inside out.

The plague had struck the land before, killing thousands in its last invasion, closing the theaters, the inns, and all other places of public gathering and even bolting the church doors. In the mornings, then as now, when London's maids tentatively opened their shutters, they found stricken cats and dogs wallowing in the gutters on their sides, blood dripping from their trembling paws having clawed their legs down to bone in an attempt to dig the plague away. The dogs died first, then the cats, foaming at the mouth, followed by the rats slinking out from beneath piles of garbage or from holes in the walls, their wet fur pasted to their skin as they jerked, spasmed, and nipped at anything that moved, trying to rid themselves of the scourge by passing it on.

The plague infected men and woman two or three weeks after the first animals had succumbed. It had even struck Edward once before in Italy, but he had survived the mild case. But this time it more than struck. It bludgeoned. The first brown spots soon swelled to red pot-marked boils that spouted others across his shoulders as they worked their away down along the back of his neck, and from there, crept down and around his back, across his abdomen and down his legs until they covered his entire body, burning trails behind that scratching farther inflamed, leaving a putrid stench that hovered over every inch of him. Death reeked in his nostrils and he sensed that others smelled it on his breath and in his sweat.

He developed an intolerance for light and an acid taste on his tongue that he could neither swallow nor spit out. His testicles burned, then turned purple, then swelled the size and shape of partridge eggs, and then hardened to the size and color of small green apples that festered until they grew so large and tender that he could no longer lie on his stomach. When he began to flail in bed, they stretched his arms and lashed his wrists to the bedposts to keep him from stripping his skin.

When he refused a vinegary liquid, they wedged a funnel down his gullet and poured it in. "He looks a bit better this morning," he heard someone lie. A woman's familiar face hovered over him. Buy who could it be? Susan? His daughter. His youngest? Or was it Anne standing above him, glaring down in reproach? No. Not Anne, unless returned from the grave. Why would her ghost appear to him now? Perhaps to lay guilt upon an already thick pile.

If not Anne, it must be Susan looking down, her gentle face reminding him of her mother. What watchful cares do impose themselves betwixt these gentle eyes, he thought. He tried to tell her he was sorry, that he should have done more, that he should have been a better father, that he loved her more than she knew, but all that ushered forth were garbled words.

Whatever fate's intent or folly, Susan had grown to be his only constant, the only shining star in his now dull and fading life, and the only of his children who seemed to care more for him than for themselves. She had been the only one able to engage him enough to draw him away from this writing.

He remembered building a toy village for Susan when she was seven, a replica of Colne, the village at the foot of Hedingham. They played on the floor and laughed as if they both were children. Now his fingers refused to bend. He could no longer pick up a toy soldier or move a knight. He could not sit up and hold a quill in his hand to write. It occurred to him that he would never compose a sonnet, or a play, or build a toy village again.

He thought he saw Lyly, a *young* Lyly, weaving in and out of his awareness wearing an old man's mask. *Age doth bare life's creeping insult.*

In delirium, or perhaps in clarity, familiar characters pranced about and gestured as though refusing to take their final bows and relinquish the stage. Lord Melun, wounded in battle and dying in *King John,* repeated his forlorn speech.

Have I not hideous death within my view?
Retaining but a quantity of life,

Which bleeds away, even as a form of wax?
Whose black contagious breath
Smokes about my burning chest?

Then Hamlet sauntered onstage again and said, "Death is strict in its arrest," then turned his back and ambled off as Macbeth replaced him, mocking Edward with his own words.

Life is but a walking shadow
A poor player,
That struts and frets his hour upon the stage,
And then is heard no more.
It is a tale, told by an idiot,
Full of sound and fury,
Signifying nothing.

Were Edward's words right in their reproach? Was life's sound and fury all for naught? Were we *all* idiots? Is *that* what it had come to? Under his own name he could take full credit for his disgrace, for the loss of the lands and castles and the family fortune. He had placed the nation in dire jeopardy with his youthful dalliance with the Queen and the issue they brought forth. He had raised none of his children, leaving that burden and responsibility to Burghley and their mothers. Vavasor, the only woman he ever truly loved, had used him for her own ends and neither deserved nor returned his affection. He had inherited the Oxford title at a time when its value was diminished and then sullied, besmirched, and frittered away the little that was left.

It was true that he had written plays that seemed to entertain and yet, even in that small measure, he took no claim beyond the few who knew, who themselves would soon depart life's stage, their shadows buried beneath the dirt and weeds their boots once trod.

Mortimer, an old Mortimer, in Edward's *Henry IV, Part I* sauntered out, playing Death and speaking lines Edward could no longer say.

Deprived of honor and inheritance.
Now the arbitrator of despairs,
Just death, umpire of men's miseries,
With sweet enlargement doth dismiss you hence.

"I love you father," he heard his youngest daughter movement, then felt a gentle kiss on his forehead. He tried to shoo her off in fear she might catch his scourge, but couldn't lift his fingers.

On his seventh night in bed, the first of his sores burst, squeezing out pus. His fever boiled and the skin on his face burned at the slightest whisper of the air around him. Was this how life ended? The ancient de Vere motto, *Vero nihil verius,* 'nothing truer than truth' vaguely floated to his mind. He reached for a quill. His fingers twitched. His hand flopped open.

CHAPTER 75

A Devil's Trade

"Our remedies oft in ourselves do lie."
All's Well That Ends Well, I, 1

How could death end memory? How could it erase time or bury the past? Susan de Vere, Edward's youngest daughter, now Susan Herbert, the Countess of Montgomery, sat on a sun drenched porch at King's Place, her father's last home, looking downhill toward the village of Hackney, a sight that reminded her of Colne at the foot of Hedingham and of the miniature village her father had build for her there as a child. Much had changed since then. More had changed since her father's death. An England, once strengthened under Elizabeth, had floundered under James, who, as his primary accomplishment thus far, had commissioned a new translation of the Bible to be called *The King James Bible,* thus assuring he would be remember beyond his meager achievements.

After Susan's father died, Beth Trentham, Susan's stepmother, posted directives in her will that the family honored upon Beth's death eleven years after her husband.

> I commit my body to the earth from whence it came, desiring to be buried in the Church of Hackney as near unto the body of my said dear and noble Lord Oxford as may be, and that to be done as privately and with as little pomp and ceremony as possible.

Hamlet's words whispered to her, as they often did.

> Good Hamlet, cast thy nighted color off,
> And let thine eye look upon a friend.

Do not forever with thy veiled lids
Seek thy noble father in the dust.
Thou know'st 'tis common,
All who live must die,
Passing through nature to eternity.

Susan's eyes welled up. She had watched her father labor over *Hamlet* in his final days at King's Place, changing a single word, a phrase, or a sentence a dozen times, oft switching it back or adding another to merely cross that one out. Ink -- which he had oft called "the blood of my life," -- had surged throughout his creative life. When he wrote, he lost and found himself in his characters and fantasy. Thus swept away, he both forgot his problems and his chronic leg pain. Near the end, his fingers twitched in his sleep as if they couldn't stop, as if they were constantly prepared to write to follow a scene or line he dreamt.

His plays, with a life of their own, continued beyond their creator, parceled out from Beth to Burbage, then to Burbage's sons when they built their new Globe. Lyly negotiated fees for Beth, as he had for Edward, with a small sum set aside for Susan. "Your father would have wanted you to share in it," Beth had assured hr. "You were his favorite, you know."

King James, inept at politics, cowered under his predecessor's long shadow and well understood that any son of the well-loved former queen, particularly one fathered by England's premier Earl, would tempt James' Catholic enemies to weigh their options, especially those who considered James a Scottish import and not worthy of an English crown.

As one of James' first act on assuming the throne, he visited Wriothesley, still confined to the Tower after the Queen's death. Shortly after that encounter, James released Wriothesley, then a man of twenty-nine, and moved him into Whitehall where the new king could keep an eye on him. James had given Wriothesley, Susan's unacknowledged half-brother, a choice -- one requiring little thought.

A short walk from the Tower to the gallows or a long and comfortable life working on James's behalf.

Susan recalled the King's line from her father's *Henry IV.* "Uneasy lies the head that wears a crown." Wriothesley was immersed in the crowns dangers and intrigues since childhood. "I have been around the Queen all my life," Wriothesley would undoubtedly have told James. "'Tis fraught with danger. Too much resting on thy shoulders and too easy to lose thy neck." Wriothesley agreed to hold his tongue in exchange for a comfortable life at court and a lifetime living allowance.

After a long and successful run, Edward's earthly footprints, his plays, faded with time and indifference. New dramatists took the stage to explore fresh plots and themes -- John Webster's revenge plays, Francis Beaumont's satirizations of the *nouveau riche,* and Ben Jonson's *Volpone* and *Alchemist* poking fun at greed and corruption. By 1623, nineteen years after Edward's death and seven after William Shakspere's, the "Shakespeare" plays were no longer being performed. Yet Susan, remembering how much they meant to her father, could not bring herself to let them fade into obscurity, and thus sought an audience with James, whose continuing censorship laws were still enforced to stifle sedition.

Susan balanced her own dilemma, one far more nuanced than her half-brother's -- lose the plays to time, decay, and disinterest, or preserve them, at least for the present, under the pseudonym her father had chosen. If she gained James' permission, she *would* publish under that false name, yet quietly imprint her father's identity for those who looked close enough to see it. Having determined her course, and after obtaining a royal audience, she began the negotiations with James with her second request. "As the leading Earl of the realm," she reasoned aloud, "my father rightly deserves a burial in Westminster, in the Vere crypt, along with our uncle Francis and other distinguished Veres."

"*Re*burial." James corrected her. "Agreed," he said after a pause. "Yet with this, there shall be no record of a Westminster internment. Let others think he lies quietly in Hackney."

Susan knew that James would favor distancing himself from the troublesome plays and their playwright who fathered a son still alive and still a threat to James' legitimate right to the throne. She knew that the new king would delight in adding additional evidence that the plays characters and contents had nothing to do with Elizabeth or her court, that they were written by an uneducated, country bumpkin with no royal connections.

"And as to the plays," James said, "and the name that he applied."

"Shakespeare," Susan said, glad but not surprised that James broached the subject himself. "William Shakespeare."

"The man be dead of late?"

"Seven years."

"And buried at...?"

"Stratford. In the village where he lived and died. He rests in the church, just beneath the altar."

"At whose expense?"

"His own. He came into some money."

James glanced down and thought. "This then," he said when he looked up. "Publish them, but with this. Construct a monument above his grave at your expense. If he is to play the part a dead playwright, let him look like one."

After gaining James' consent to print a full collection of her father's thirty-six plays, Susan carried her father's handwritten originals down to Blount and Faggard Printers on Printer's Row, and there instructed Isaac Faggard to set, block, and bind five-hundred copies.

After four months of setting type and running a large expense, Susan was informed that the project was complete and advised to retrieve the bound folios. She had determined to keep a hundred copies for herself and her own needs, and cart the remainder down to Crane and Weavers Booksellers on the north side of St. Paul's churchyard. Profits, if there be any, to be divided equally between bookseller and Susan.

Burbage and his sons had previously registered half the plays – eighteen -- as they played them. Phillip, Susan's husband, along with the Earl of Pembroke, Susan's brother-in-law, paid for the folio printing. The dedication, as customary, acknowledged them as investors.

To the most notable and
Incomparable pair of brothers.
Phillip, Earl of Pembroke and
William, Earl of Montgomery,
Both Knights of the Order of the Garter
and singular good Lords.

"One other consideration," James had insisted. "Put a face to the name. A face that no one knows." To fulfill that requirement, Susan contracted Martin Droeshout, a respected Flemish engraver. She had the engraver float a Flemish head above a torso to look as though the head *was* floating above the body to hint that the playwright's true identity lay within the plays themselves. Susan further instructed Blount and Faggard to print a disclaimer on the page following the bogus likeness:

To the Reader:
The figure that thou serest here put,
Was for gentle Shakespeare cut.
But gentle reader,
Look not on the picture,
But to the book.

Susan thought that hint subtle enough to slip past James' censors, yet strong enough to add another clue to her father's identity.

James further insisted on an introduction by Ben Jonson, a task that earned Jonson, near broke at the time, the post of England's first Poet Laureate, along with an annual stipend. Jonson began his introduction:

> Draw no envy on the name,
> And thus apply it to book and fame.

James had ordered a bust above the Stratford-Upon-Avon grave, but had unwittingly not specified its nature. Stratford's sculptors, knowing their former villager -- dead only seven years -- to be grain merchant, thus fashioned his bust as such, with his hands resting on a sack of grain.

Susan felt a partial vindication, a cup half-full. She had not insured survival of her father's name as the playwright, but had preserved his work and pointed a shadowed finger to his name as author.

James continued Edward's annuity as long as Edward lived, leaving Elizabeth's stipulation in force -- a Shakespeare pseudonym to front the plays and deflect suspicion. Lyly had delivered regular payments to William Shakspere on Beth Trentham's behalf as dramas previously presented at court under "Anonymous" surfaced one at a time for public presentation under the hyphenated name "William ShakesSpeare," soon shortened to "William Shakespeare."

William Shakspere prospered in early retirement. After an initial, lump-sum payment, he retreated to out-of-the-way Stratford and immediately purchased the second best house in the village, rarely visiting London, the center of the theater, once his name appeared on scripts and playbills. He kept to his agreement, avoiding scrutiny and questions to assure a continuing livelihood.

When Beth died, her executors followed the instructions in her will to "bear regular payments" to "that dumb man" "dumb" meaning "illiterate" as well as "deaf-and-dumb" - "as long as he shall live." When William Shakspere died, the payments to "that dumb man" stopped.

Fittingly, no one praised or eulogized Shakspere upon his death. Stratford quietly buried their unremarkable son beneath the simple floor stone he had paid for in Holy Trinity Church. The engraving on the footstone read:

Good friend, for Jesus' sake forbear
To dig the dust enclosed here.
Blessed be the man that spares these stones,
And cursed be he that moves my bones.

Simple doggerel. Bad rhyme and bad poetry. Impish words that no one could possibly believe were written as the final eulogy by the same playwright who penned *Hamlet, Othello* and *Macbeth*, and hardly anything Susan's father would have written for any reason, let alone to mark his final testament.

Percival Golding, Edward's cousin and the son of Edward's former tutor, Arthur Golding, recorded Edward's secret reburial in Westminster Abbey on page 51 of his *Matches and Issues of the Ancient and Illustrious Family of Vere,* a family history intended for the family only. He knew Edward's body had been quietly moved from the Hackney Churchyard and had takin its proper place in the de Vere family crypt. Percival wrote...

> Edward de Vere, only son of John, born the Twelfth day of April, 1550, an Earl of whom I will only speak what all men's voices confirm. He was a man in mind and body absolutely accomplished with honorable endowments. He died at his house at Hackney in the month of June of the Lord's year 1604 and lieth buried in Westminster Abbey.

As Susan de Vere sat on a bench on the front portico of King's Place, she felt disappointed she could do no more, yet knew she had planted the seeds of doubt as to the authorship. When her husband Philip, after strolling through the gardens, ambled back around, Susan stood and smiled quietly. She recalled the ancient de Vere motto -- "nothing truer than truth" -- and hoped that truth would one day prevail as she tucked her arm beneath his elbow, nestled close to his side, and walked though King's Place gate without looking back.

CHAPTER 76

Death and Revival

"If this were played upon the stage
I should condemn it as improbable fiction."
Twelfth Night, I, 4

One-hundred-fifty years hence
March 17, 1768

David Garrick -- five-feet-one-and-a-half in his boots -- looked up to most men, though none stood above him in acting. His voice, even his whisper, filled a room and raised the hairs on the necks of even the furthest theater row. Garrick's portrayal of *Richard III* had resurrected a long-forgotten play and its playwright from his hundred-fifty-year-old grave and restored them both to full life again.

Garrick had previously played the leads in Cibber's *Love Makes a Man,* Otway's *The Orphan* and a dozen other plays, all with modest success, yet it was Garrick's discovery, or rather *re*discovery, of an outdated and out-of-fashion playwright that catapulted him to instant fame. *Richard* seemed made for Garrick. He had the voice. He understood the character. The moment he strutted onstage, he *was* Richard.

After performing *The Orphan* to a less than half-full house in Dublin's Drury Theater, Garrick had, years earlier, stumbled upon a dust-encrusted trunk in a closet in Drury's prop room. Without fully understanding why, on instinct perhaps, he pried the trunk open and rummaged through a pile of old plays and manuscripts, lifting out a bound folio near the bottom and studying its title and faceplate.

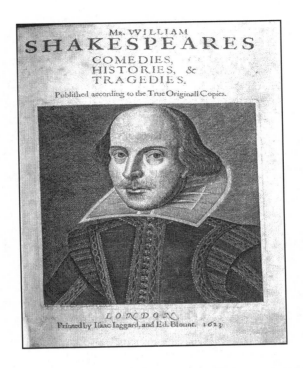

Mr. WILLIAM
SHAKESPEARES
COMEDIES,
HISTORIES, &
TRAGEDIES.
Publifhed according to the True Originall Copies.

LONDON
Printed by Ifaac Iaggard, and Ed. Blount. 1623

Garrick pulled up a chair and perused what appeared to be a collection of thirty-six little known plays, none of which, at least to Garrick's knowledge, had been performed on any stage in well over a hundred years, perhaps longer. Resurrecting antiquated plays held its risk, yet this collection, as Garrick studied them more closely, seemed to spin universal themes and had the advantage of a long-dead author who would not haggle over the nuance of interpretation nor demand a playwright's fee.

After strutting about and speaking several lines to gain their feel and temper, it occurred to Garrick that old *is* new to those who hadn't heard it. He understood, just as 16th Century audiences had once grown tired of their contemporary dramas, current theater patrons had likewise gown weary of the stilted plays that present-day English playwrights copied from the French. Modern audiences desired less morality and more character. They wanted emotion that tugged a tear, or drew a laugh, or satisfied the taste for revenge or justice. They wanted a language, even archaic, that supported a more natural delivery.

Fancying himself a performer, a showman, *and* a businessman, after successfully playing *Richard* to rave reviews and enthusiastic applause in Dublin, Garrick hoped to build on his initial success by performing others in the *Shakespeare* folio. But how to accomplish that and draw a better living from it, he pondered as he traveled to the village of Stratford-Upon-Avon, where he had performed before and where he recalled the bust of *Richard's* author hung above the playwrights' grave in Stratford's Holy Trinity Church.

Garrick was well aware that little money could be had from playing the yearly theater circuit around the country. Building a large theater in the right location was where the real money could be made. At fifty-two, with fewer parts left to fit his age, Garrick's future concerned him as his carriage bumped across the Avon Bridge. Yet he carried a plan in the back of his mind -- a *Richard*-like scheme -- as he procured his usual second-floor lodging at Stratford's Ram's Head Inn, then nibbled a thick lamb and potato stew in the dining room before retiring.

After discovering the Shakespeare folio, a notion had occurred to him on his last visit to Stratford. His production then -- *The Lies of Love,* a farce he wrote himself -- had drawn little attention and less audience. "Stratford is not the town it once was," the mayor confessed over a cold mug. "There is little money for plays these day. For anything, really. The Avon has silted up. We are no longer able to barge our wheat to market. The town itself is drying up."

Garrick had considered eliminating Stratford from his yearly rounds, yet he knew the town had a hidden asset and he had an idea how to play upon it. Stratford had a native son whose play *Richard III,* Garrick had tested. Stratford had the physical body of the man who wrote *Richard* and Garrick had the body of the playwright's work. The question was, how to fuse the two? The town was too small and too distant from London, or from any town of sufficient population, to support a playhouse, let along a theater company.

"Of course we know him," the Mayor explained when Garrick met with the Mayor and village council. "He is buried in our church. His bust is on the wall. He must have had a bit of money."

"From what source?" Garrick asked the mayor, seated next to him, and the rest of council spread out around the table.

"From grain," the Mayor shrugged. "Our chief commodity. At least it was then, that long ago. On his bust, his hands rest upon a grain sack."

"For what I have in mind, a sack of grain might require alteration," Garrick said. "Rework the grain sack to a scroll," he suggested. "And place a feathered quill in his hand befitting a playwright." He glanced around at confused counsel faces, pausing dramatically and smiling at each. "Gentlemen," he began in his deepest stage voice. "You have an asset here that could give something back to Stratford. William Shakespeare was *not* a grain merchant, at least not simply so. He wrote plays. I know them. I *have* fair copies. At least as far as I can ascertain, they were well received in London in their day, though I doubt they fetched much money. They *could,* however. Produced properly, under effective management, this town could thrive again."

The councilmen glared at each other. "What precisely do you propose?" a bearded councilman leaned foreword and asked.

"Nothing less than raising the dead," Garrick said. "A revival of Shakespeare *and* Stratford. I propose placing both on the map again… What say you?… Worth considering?"

The first Shakespeare Jubilee sparkled, stomped, and rollicked through the long weekend of September 14, 1776, a full century and a half after the playwright's death, despite a light sprinkle in the morning that soaked caps and temporarily dampened spirits. The lynchpin, Garrick realized, was promotion that would draw an audience from afar. That, he determined, would require more than a play or even several plays. It would require a well-promoted extravaganza, a full day's entertainment advertised in London and Oxford on poles and posters in the inns, by paid street hawkers and whatever other means could be employed to rouse an audience. He arranged a line of free, round-trip coaches to Stratford from Oxford and London to transport as many bodies as the coaches allowed.

"We get them here at our expense," Garrick had told the council, "then shake their purses loose when they arrive."

The initial Shakespeare Jubilee -- two plays, a horse race, pony rides, spinning carts and greased slides for the children, a masked ball, an allday smoked pigs and skewered mutton roasts, and all manner of foods anyone could eat -- lasted three days. That success seeded a second Jubilee the following year. After three profitable seasons -- skipping a fourth to expand and extend lodgings to increase overnight accommodations -- a permanent theater rose on the banks of the Avon for year-round performances.

The town, capitalizing on their little-known son, constructed a one-room schoolhouse in a style they thought to exist in Shakespeare's day, although no records were found that any school existed during Shakespeare's life. Considering what *must* have happened, the counsel assumed, if Shakespeare wrote the plays, there must have been a school to teach at least the rudiments of writing. Beyond that assumption, and for more practical reasons, constructing a one-room schoolhouse to traipse visitors through not only added to the background of Stratford's obscure local son, but also better filled the village coffers by charging a fee for a Shakespeare tour.

In similar fashion and for similar reasons, the town's elders purchased a central house on Henley Street and designated it as "Shakespeare's birthplace," filling it with period furniture and explaining to increasingly interested tourists that the bed they placed in a second floor room was "Shakespeare's birth bed," quietly adding that "at least a bed of that sort must have been here."

While expanding the physical structure and filling in the probable life of a sixteenth century man that the eighteenth century villagers knew nothing of, the town council, under the advise of its newly appointed Stratford Visitor Commission, bought Anne Hathaway's old house, the only structure that did have documentary evidence associating it with William Shakespeare. The town's archival register recorded the marriage a "William Shakspere" to an

Anne Hathaway on November 27, 1582, although the sir name on the marriage record was spelled differently from the "William Shakespeare" printed on the front page of the plays. Close enough. Hathaway house had been owned by Richard Hathaway, a farmer and Anne Hathaway's father, although there was no recorded to indicate that either Anne or her husband William Shakspere ever lived in that house after their marriage. Nonetheless, the structure was added to an expanding Shakespeare tour that ended with the bust and grave in Holy Trinity Church, although no name -- either with the spelling "Shakespeare" or "Shakspere" -- was chiseled on the floor stone above the body it supposedly protected.

"We don't sell plays," Garrick had explained to the Stratford Council. *"Shakespeare* is our commodity. The *man.* The plays merely make him so."

Garrick's inspiration resurrected a largely forgotten dramatist and launched Stratford-on-Avon as a thriving Shakespeare tourist center. When Garrick died in 1779, a mere three years after starting his Jubilee and while the first Stratford Shakespeare Theater was still under construction, King George III, citing "significant contributions to the British theater," authorized the actor/producer's internment at Westminster Abbey, one aisle down and around the corner from a newly erected Shakespeare bust. Garrick's self-written memorial read:

> To paint fair nature by divine command,
> Her magic pencil in her glowing hand,
> A Shakespeare rose: then, to expand his fame,
> Wide o'er this breathing world, a Garrick came.
>
> Though sunk in death the forms the Poet drew,
> The actor's genius bade them breath anew,
> Though, like the bard himself, in night they lay,
> Immortal Garrick called them back to day.
>
> And till Eternity with power sublime

Shall mark the moral hour of hoary Time,
 Shakespeare and Garrick like twin-stars shall
    shine,
And earth irradiate with a beam divine.

Epilogue

Frank Gibbons' 10th Grade English Class
Madison High School
Vienna, Virginia

Frank Gibbons peered across his desk at his high school class of thirty-seven adolescents -- two of them chewing gum, one poking his neighbor in the ribs, a few with their eyes in their laps texting, most slouching in their chairs, bored and anticipating their next period, lunch.

Mr. Gibbons cleared his throat to gain attention with little notable effect. He often wondered if the local mall Cinema Eight actually projected their one o'clock afternoon matinee if no one bought a ticket and slid into a seat. At least at the mall, audience enthusiasm determined future presentations. The Virginia Board of Education *required* teaching at least one Shakespeare play in high school, with or without student satisfaction.

Gibbons would lecture Shakespeare in the playwright's appointed hour. The Board of Education paid him to do so and many of Madison's parents expected Gibbons to stir a sizable interest in the same four-hundred-year-old playwright who had bored most of them when they were in tenth grade.

"We always think of Shakespeare as a dead man," Gibbons began, hoping to see at least one face brighten. "Yet he was, in his time, quite alive and *lively,* and quite popular."

Gibbons looked around the room but found no eyes set in his direction. "We don't know much about the author," he plowed on. "He was born in Stratford, England in an out of the way country village, and probably went to school there. Not high school, though. They didn't have high school in those days. Unfortunately, there are no records of his having gone to school. He may have traveled though. We don't know. There are no records there either."

"Mr. Gibbons?"

"Yes, Billy?

"I feel sick. May I go to the…"

"Yes. Go… Now. One thing we *do* know. The man was a genius. With little education and little experience of the world, he overcame those huge hurdles to compose the greatest, most literate plays ever written in any language, *Hamlet* being the most telling and profound among them."

"Mr. Gibbons?"

"Yes, Joey?"

"Who *was* Hamlet? I mean, did Shakespeare know him? Don't writers usually write about themselves and their experiences?"

"That *was* his genius. The plays had nothing to do with him. He made it all up."

APPENDIX

Young De Vere

Older De Vere

De Vere with Sword of State,
Queen with Tudor Roses

Ancient De Vere Crest
Lion Shaking a
Broken Speare

FIRST FOLIO DEDICATION PAGE

TO THE MOST NOBLE
AND
INCOMPARABLE PAIRE
OF BRETHREN.

WILLIAM
Earle of Pembroke, &c. Lord Chamberlaine to the
Kings most Excellent Maiesty.

AND

PHILIP
Earle of Montgomery, &c. Gentleman of his Maiesties
Bed-Chamber. Both Knights of the most Noble Order
of the Garter, and our singular good
LORDS.

Dedicated to

The Earl of Pembroke
Susan de Vere's Brother-In-Law
The Earl of Montgomery
Susan de Vere's Husband

A HUNDRETH SUNDRIE FLOWERS DISCLAIMER

Edward de Vere played on his own name in the form of *"E.* Ver," *"Ever"* Vere and "N. Vere" in his *Sonnets,* starting with Sonnet 76, and *not* in *A Hundreth Sundrie Flowers* as depicted here in Chapter 32. Sonnet 76 reads, in part:

Why write I still all one, *ever* the same,
And keep invention in a noted weed,
That *every* word doth almost tell my name,
Showing their birth, and where they did proceed?

A NOTE ON JAMES BURBAGE AND ELIZABETHAN THEATERS

Loves Labor Lost generally follows the historical facts and time sequences as best they are known. An exception is the development of the Elizabethan theaters, particularly the Rose, the Swan, and the Globe, all three of which were built later in de Vere's life than depicted in this book. The actual theater sequence was changed here for dramatic purpose in order to describe the events and atmosphere of Southwark, across the Thames from London, with its bearbating, its gambling and its prostitution.

The first English plays by any playwright were performed by roaming players plying their trade on the roads in front of the inns and taverns where they laid their caps on the ground in hopes of inducing generosity from the passing audience. The roving players later teamed up with the innkeepers who, to the benefit of both, could close a courtyard off and charge a shared admission. During this same period, plays were performed for a selected audience in London's exclusive guildhalls or for invitationonly performances at court.

Gray's Inn -- where Edward de Vere studied law and wrote his first plays as a student writer/performer -- formally opened its theater doors for invited performances in 1576, nine years after de Vere wrote and performed there for his classmates.

The earliest "Shakespeare" plays that were openly performed for a general audience were presented in 1576 in the first round amphitheater built by James Burbage in Finsbury Fields, north of London, just beyond the city's gates and jurisdiction. Burbage called his playhouse a "Theater," named after a Roman amphitheater, and built it on land he leased from Giles Allen, a staunch Puritan. When Giles refused to renew the Theatre's lease twentyone years later, James Burbage's sons, Richard and Cuthbert, dismantled their Theater boardbyboard and rebuilt it as their new Globe Theater on Bankside, Southwark, directly across the Thames from London in 1597. Many of the "Shakespeare" plays -- well known from previous runs in Burbage's original playhouse -- were carried over and frequently performed at the Globe.

The Rose (1587), the Swan (1595), and the Hope (1613) theaters were soon constructed close to the Globe to form London's new Southwark theatre district which flourished until it was shut down by the Puritans in 1642 when the Puritan dominated Parliament issued an ordinance suppressing all theaters stage performances. It was not until eighteen years later, in 1660, under the crown of Charles II, that the theater was allowed again, flourishing this time in the city itself.

ELIZABETHAN THEATERS

Amphitheaters

Opened	Name	Location
1576	The Theatre	Finsbury Fields, Shoreditch, London (Burbage)
1576	Newington Butts	Southwark, Surrey
1577	The Curtain	Finsbury Fields, Shoreditch, London
1587	The Rose	Bankside, Surrey (Southwark)
1595	The Swan,	Paris Garden, Surrey (Southwark)
1599	The Globe	Bankside, Surrey (Southwark) (Burbage sons)
1600	The Fortune	Golding Lane, Clerkenwell
1600	The Boar's Head	Whitechapel, London

Playhouses

1573	Middle Temple Inn	London
1576	Paul's	London, St. Paul's Cathedral Precinct
1576	The Blackfriars	Blackfriars, London (the first)
1576	Whitehall Theatre	London
1576	Gray's Inn Theatre	London
1596	The Blackfriars	London, (the second)

London's Inn-yards

1576	The Bull Inn,	London
1576	The Bell Savage	London
1576	The Cross Keys	London
1576	The Bell	London
1576	The White Hart	London
1576	The George Inn	London

Author's Bio:

Dr. Hutchison is Ph.D. clinical psychologist, former Maryland forensic evaluator and expert witness for Maryland's District Count. He had taught in the Graduate Psychology Program at the Washington College and has presented national and international workshops in psychology and on the topic of the Shakespeare authorship controversy. He has followed the trail of Shakespeare and of Edward de Vere from the castles and catacombs of England to hidden graveyards and secret papers buried in basements. Based on Dr. Hutchison's forensic experience and the evidence he has uncovered, he is convinced that the authorship cover-up is a genuine story of

intrigue and conspiracy at the highest levels. It is a sad but exciting adventure of the most famous writer who ever lived – a man no one ever heard of. Loves Labor Lost tells that story. Bruce lives in Santa Fe, NM and Annapolis, MD with his wife, Nancy, who assisted in the research for this book.